Glendalough Fair
A Novel of Viking Age Ireland

Book Four of The Norsemen Saga

James L. Nelson

Fore Topsail Press
64 Ash Point Road
Harpswell, Maine, 04079

ISBN: 0692585451
ISBN-13: 9780692585450

To my beloved Abigail, my little Viking, my beautiful daughter, with a father's pride and love.

Glendalough - (pronounced Glen-da-lock) means Valley of Two Lakes. Located in the Wicklow Mountains, Glendalough was founded as a hermitage by St. Kevin in the latter sixth century and soon developed into one of Ireland's most important medieval monastic cities.

(For other terms see Glossary, page 328)

Prologue

The Saga of Thorgrim Ulfsson

There was a man named Thorgrim Ulfsson who owned a large farm in East Agder in Vik in the country of Norway. The farm had rich fields and every year they yielded an abundant harvest. Thorgrim also had a substantial herd of cattle as well as many servants and slaves.

Because Thorgrim was frugal and clever and worked as hard as any man, and harder than most, the farm prospered. Thorgrim was liked and respected by his neighbors and by the people in his household, and his opinion was often sought. Sometimes, however, as the night came on, he would fall into a dark mood, and then none would dare approach him. It was thought by some that Thorgrim was a shape shifter and because of that he earned the nickname of Night Wolf.

Years before, when Thorgrim had first grown to manhood, he had gone a-viking with the jarl who ruled in East Agder, a man named Ornolf Hrafnsson who was known as Ornolf the Restless. The two men became close during their many voyages and when they returned home Ornolf offered his daughter Hallbera to Thorgrim in marriage. It was a good match and Thorgrim and Hallbera were happy with their lives on the farm. Hallbera bore Thorgrim four children, two sons named Odd and Harald and a daughter named Hild and another named Hallbera, who was named after her mother.

Thorgrim's wife was past her thirtieth year and no longer a young woman when this last child was born, and she died giving birth. This broke Thorgrim's heart and when Ornolf asked Thorgrim to once again go a-viking (for Ornolf was never content to remain at home with his shrewish wife) Thorgrim agreed to go.

Thorgrim's oldest son, Odd, was married by then and had children of his own, and a farm which Thorgrim had given him. Thorgrim did not think it was right for Odd to leave his family then, so he did not ask Odd to accompany them. But his second son, Harald, was only fifteen and was eager for voyaging, and so Thorgrim brought him along. Though Harald was young, he was stronger than many grown men and had spent much of his youth training for battle, sometimes in secret, and so he proved to be a good warrior and a well-liked and respected member of the crew. As he grew older his strength increased and soon he earned the nickname Broadarm.

Ornolf sailed his ship *Red Dragon* to Ireland. For some time the Northmen had been going to that country to plunder and had even set up longphorts at Dubh-linn and other places. The raiding was still good then, despite others having gone before, and Ornolf and Thorgrim and their men, around sixty in number, earned much plunder for themselves. Things in Ireland were very unsettled, for the Irish were not only fighting the Northmen but fighting each other as well. Ornolf and Thorgrim and Harald found themselves entangled in a great intrigue that revolved around Tara, the seat of the Irish king of Brega, and it was only through hard fighting and the help of the gods that they were able to get away with their lives and with considerable treasure.

During that fight Thorgrim was wounded, and once he had recovered from his wounds he took a crew aboard his ship and left Dubh-linn, determined to return to his home in East Agder and go a-viking no more. But the gods, who delight in playing tricks on men, damaged his ship during a storm and he and his crew were forced to sail into the longphort of Vík-ló. There, the lord of the longphort, a man named Grimarr Giant, took a liking to Thorgrim, but soon turned against him and wished him dead. This led to considerable trouble for Thorgrim and his men, but in the end Grimarr was defeated and Thorgrim was made lord of Vík-ló. This was the year following the time that Olaf the White sailed with a great fleet from Norway to reclaim Dubh-linn from the Danes. By the Christian calendar it was the year 853, and Thorgrim and his men had then been in Ireland for more than a year.

It remained Thorgrim's only desire to return to his farm, but he could see that whenever he tried to do so, the gods prevented it. Thorgrim had a good friend named Starri Deathless who was a berserker. Thorgrim did not often ask advice of Starri, because he knew that the best advice was not to be had from berserkers, but in this matter he thought Starri might have some knowledge.

Thorgrim said, "Whenever I have tried to leave Ireland the gods have thrown me back. Now I have been made the Lord of Vík-ló. Do you think that if I determined to remain in Ireland the gods would allow me to leave?"

Starri spent some time thinking about that, and then he said, "Thorgrim Night Wolf, you are blessed by the gods, but for men like us, who reside in Midgard, sometimes their blessings are hard to understand. I cannot say what the gods are thinking any more than another man, but what you say makes sense to me, and the trouble the gods have sent your way seems to prove your words right. I think you should indeed remain in Ireland and see if the gods will favor you enough to let you leave."

Thorgrim considered Starri's answer and in the end took Starri's advice and decided to remain in Vík-ló in hopes that the gods would then allow him to return home.

Here is what happened.

Chapter One

Varonn, the time of spring work, had come to the longphort of
Vík-ló after the long, dark months of winter. For the
Northmen it was like waking from a deep slumber, and their
fancy turned to thoughts of mayhem, bloody and violent.

Starri Deathless heard it first, as he so often did. They were
sitting in Thorgrim's hall, the biggest building in Vík-ló, with a main
room that approached thirty feet on each side and rose to a peak
twenty feet above their heads. It was raining hard that afternoon, the
steady downfall forming a curtain of sound like surf, the note rising
and falling as the wind gusted and drove sheets of water against the
clay and wattle walls. The fire in the hearth crackled and popped.

Thorgrim and some of his men were gaming, and the click of the
game pieces and their low murmured conversation were nearly lost in
the steady drone of the rain. Thorgrim's son, Harald, sixteen years
old, lay snoring on a pile of furs on a raised platform against the far
wall.

Starri sat in a corner, sharpening weapons that were already as
sharp as anyone could hope for, and the scrape of his stone added
another layer to the sounds of the day. When it came to sitting, which
Starri did not often do, he preferred to be high above everyone,
perched at the mast head of a ship, for instance, or in the rafters of a
hall. Or, barring that, he chose to be down low. The middle that most
men occupied held no attraction to Starri Deathless.

Thorgrim was losing at the game he played, but he was only
vaguely aware of it. He rattled the dice in a leather cup, spilled them
on the table, moved his pieces in a mechanical and thoughtless way.
His mind was far from the game table. He was thinking of the ships

down by the river, one already in the water, the other two needing only the proper ceremony and sacrifices before they could follow the first in. The smaller of the remaining two was even now sitting on its rollers.

It had been an extraordinary effort, but they had done it, had built the three longships from the keel up. And they were good ships. They were well built and Thorgrim knew they would take the seas the way a good ship was meant to do.

He was less sure about the men. They were coming apart, the ropes that bound them as a single unit rotting and falling away. It was a race now to see if they could get to sea, to begin raiding, to find some outlet for their frustrations before the internal divisions, which he had struggled through the winter to hold together, finally tore them all apart.

"Night Wolf…"

Thorgrim looked over at Starri, who was staring up toward the roof, his ear cocked. "Yes?"

"Trouble, I think," Starri said. "Fighting." Starri was a berserker, in some ways completely mad, and one of the things that set him apart from normal men was his extraordinary hearing.

Thorgrim stood fast enough to knock his seat over, and some part of him was pleased to have something to do other than waste his time on a pointless game. "Harald! Wake up! Turn out the guard!" he called, but Harald was already half way to his feet. When Harald slept he slept like a bear in hibernation, but a call to arms always roused him in an instant.

The others at the table stood as well. Starri, whose movements were somewhere between those of a cat and a squirrel, seemed to gain his feet with no effort, as if the wind had lifted him. Godi, big as a tree, and Agnarr leapt up from their places by the fire. More men appeared from one of the rooms at the far end of the hall. These were the household guard, so designated by Thorgrim when he had assumed his place as lord of Vík-ló. His son, Harald Broadarm, he had put at the head of them.

"Come, follow me," Thorgrim said and turned for the door, but Starri spoke again.

"Thorgrim, I hear steel…"

Thorgrim paused. There had been fighting often enough during the winter months, but those brawls had never involved weapons beyond the occasional sheath knife.

"Swords?" Thorgrim asked. Starri nodded.

"Very well, you men grab your shields. No time for mail."

The household guard scattered and grabbed up their shields. They were wearing swords already – the Northmen would no more go about unarmed than they would go about naked – but they had not bothered to take up shields. None of them had thought this altercation would warrant it. But if swords were out then they knew this could be something more than a drunken free-for-all.

Thorgrim threw open the door and stepped out into the rain, a manic downpour. The wind lifted his long hair and whipped it off to leeward, it tugged at his beard, and before he was half way across the plank road he was soaked down to the skin. He was, however, quite accustomed to this, having been more than a year in that country, and so he did not pause as he crossed over to the hall that stood opposite his on the other side of the road. He pounded on the door and shouted, "Bersi! Turn out! Turn out your guard! Trouble!"

He did not wait for a response, but waved for his men to follow and headed off at a jog for the river. He could hear the fight now, the shouting and the clanging of weapons, and he knew it was coming from that direction. He had no doubt Bersi would be right behind with his own contingent of men.

Bersi Jorundarson had been second to Grimarr Giant, the former lord of Vík-ló. When Grimarr had been killed, Bersi might well have claimed the mantle for himself. But Bersi was not the sort who relished leadership, or so Thorgrim had come to understand. Instead, Bersi had convinced the others that it was Thorgrim who should command there, and so Thorgrim did.

But Bersi still had his following, particularly among the men who had once followed Grimarr, and Thorgrim was careful to include the man in his council and let him give voice to any concerns he might have. What's more, Thorgrim had come to like Bersi.

He hurried on, wiping the water from his eyes, the footfalls of the men behind him inaudible in the driving rain. Down the plank road, past the small houses and workshops, so familiar to him now after all these months gone by. It was all dismal to look at. Color seemed to have been banished from the land. Everything - the houses, the ground, the sky, the road, the distant sea - was brown or gray or black, and it matched Thorgrim's mood exactly.

The shouting could be more clearly heard now, and the familiar ring of weapons striking weapons, but Thorgrim could not see the combatants yet. The rise and fall of angry voices, muted by the rain, sounded like big surf on a shingle beach.

Anger, rage, frustration had all been building within the walls of the longphort for months now, dormant but growing and strengthening in its subterranean place. There were near three hundred men in Vík-ló, warriors accustomed to the release of battle or the mellowing effects of women, but they had neither.

The winter rain had been nearly constant, the wind vicious and cold. It had kept them shut indoors when they were not working, and when they were it made that work a misery. In all of the longphort there were only two dozen women, and half were married or old or both. There was, however, an ample supply of wine and mead and ale. In the same way that rot will grow in the dark, wet places in a ship's hull, so the fury of the Northmen found a perfect environment to flourish that winter in Vík-ló.

Thorgrim Night Wolf had done everything he could think to do to stop it, but it felt to him like trying to claw a ship off a lee shore; he could use all his skill and all his knowledge, but he knew the wreck would happen anyway, and there was little he could do beyond delaying the moment when it came.

The tricks that Thorgrim had used to stave off disaster were varied, and for a while, effective. Hard work was at the heart of it, because he knew that there was nothing better for keeping passions in check.

The previous summer's fighting had left them with only a single longship named *Fox* which could carry no more than thirty warriors, so building ships became the chief priority They had built three during those long months, crafting the fine vessels that Thorgrim envisioned with ax and adz, chisel and drill. Other men were sent into the woods miles from the safety of the longphort to fell timber for the ships, doing battle with the wolves and the bandits as they dropped logs of oak and pine into the River Lietrim and floated them down to the longphort at the river's mouth.

Still others were set to repairing the earthen wall that encircled Vík-ló, which in better days had formed a substantial barrier, but now consisted of a crumbling earthwork and rotting palisade. That was miserable, filthy, exhausting labor, and when the short hours of daylight were over, the men had little energy for anything other than eating, drinking, and then falling asleep. That was how Thorgrim preferred it.

He tried to be fair to all the men under his command, Norwegians and Danes. No one was kept at any one task for long. Each man took his turn in the shipyard, at the woodcutting and at the wall building. Save for those with special skills, such as Mar the blacksmith or Aghen the master shipwright, each man worked equally at each job. It was as just as Thorgrim could make it. And the men growled and complained about it all, with the same unremitting constancy as the rain.

Work, Thorgrim knew, was the best means for preventing discontent, much like salt poured in a ship's bilge would stave off rot, but he knew as well that work alone would not do the trick. He could not make women appear, but he did make certain there was food enough and plenty of feasts that included all the men of the longphort.

On the proper night in midwinter he staged the *blót*, one of three such celebrations held by the Northmen each year. The midwinter blót was aimed at convincing the gods to make the soil fertile when the planting season came. It was a raucous affair, as such things were wont to be. Cattle were slaughtered and, as the meat cooked over a roaring fire, Thorgrim, as lord of the place, splattered the animals' blood on the walls and floor of his hall, which served as their temple. Horns of mead were lifted in celebration, and for that night at least the men forgot the winter's misery. But then the blót ended, the wild bacchanal over, the new day began and the work started all over again.

The weeks passed, and as they did the days grew longer and the cold loosened its grip. Thorgrim hoped that as the weather eased and the work began to near completion that the mood would lighten as well. He hoped that for the men of Vík-ló the shorter nights and the occasional glimpse of sun would bring a new, more hopeful view of the world.

But they did not, at least not in any meaningful way that Thorgrim could see. In those long, cold, wet months, attitudes had hardened more than even Thorgrim realized. Factions had been formed, animosities compounded, and the easing of labor that came with the spring weather just gave the men more time to ponder their grievances.

Minor irritations turned into fully fledged hatreds. Fistfights flared into brawls, leaving in their wake broken furniture and broken bones. But none of that seething anger, and none of the violence, had ever ended in drawn swords or dead men.

Until now.

Chapter Two

Goddess of golden rain,
who gives me great joy,
may boldly hear report
of her friend's brave stand.

Gisli Sursson's Saga

Thorgrim approached the rise in the ground that stood between him and the river and blocked his view of the fight. His hand rested on the grip of his sword, Iron-tooth, and the rain continued with not the least respite. He heard footsteps behind him and he turned to see Bersi Jorundarson come running up and fall in at his side.

"Thorgrim," Bersi said. "What's the trouble?"

"I don't know yet," Thorgrim said. "But whatever it might be, I can well image who's behind it."

"Kjartan?"

"That's what I would imagine."

Thorgrim had never doubted that the men of Vík-ló would sift themselves out into this or that group, and that some hostility would arise between them. It's what men did. His chief concern was that they would divide themselves up into Norwegians against Danes. But in the end it did not go that way. Instead the men had divided up by those whom they would follow, the chief men, the men who would be masters of the ships.

Thorgrim's crew mostly remained loyal to him, but some, those who had joined him in Dubh-linn just six months before, had become friends with the Danes and had gravitated to other camps.

Most of the men who had followed Grimarr Giant remained loyal to Bersi, and so in turn were willing to show some loyalty toward Thorgrim. Skidi Oddson, known as Skidi Battleax, was another who had gained great stature among the men after the slaughter he had inflicted on the Irish and the death of so many of Grimarr's chiefs. Skidi had his own following, and they were not so pleased by Thorgrim's having been made Lord of Vík-ló. But neither were they so opposed to the arrangement that they were willing to start trouble, and they could be counted on if not pushed too hard.

But some of the men, a ship's crew, fifty or sixty, came under the sway of Kjartan Thorolfson, who was called Longtooth. Kjartan was loyal to none but Kjartan, and it was that very spirit of defiance that his men admired in him, and emulated.

Kjartan had spent the winter undermining Thorgrim in a hundred subtle ways, never pushing so hard as to provoke a response that involved edged weapons. But that was coming – Thorgrim could feel that the careful balance would soon be upset – and when it did he would kill Kjartan and see what Kjartan's men would make of that.

Maybe the time has come at last, Thorgrim thought. He took the last steps up the rise, stopped and wiped the rain from his eyes. Spread out before him on the open ground near the river, the place where the wood for the ships' construction had once been stored, was perhaps the oddest sight he had ever seen.

There were a hundred men at least, too many to consider what they were doing a fight or a brawl. It was more akin to a battle, with swords flailing and men lying motionless on the ground and others shouting and struggling over the field.

For a moment Thorgrim stood dumbfounded. The action of the men seemed slowed down in the driving rain which flooded Thorgrim's eyes and made it difficult to get a clear view. The ground was soft and the fighting had churned it into a quagmire. Some of the men were streaked with mud where the rain had not washed it away, and others were thoroughly coated with the stuff.

Maybe half the men were still standing. The others were thrashing and rolling in the muck, fighting with one another, fighting to regain their feet, fighting for breath. They slipped and staggered and seemed to struggle as hard to remain upright as they were struggling with one another. Swords and axes gleamed dull in the muted light, and Thorgrim could see blood on faces and arms, red and diluted by the downpour.

He spent ten seconds, no more, looking down on the scene. Long enough to see that half the men at least were those who followed Kjartan Longtooth, and that Kjartan was himself in the thick of the fight. The rest were rallying to a man named Gudrun, one of Skidi's men, though Skidi himself was nowhere to be seen. Sleeping off the previous night's indulgence, no doubt. What could have started this all, Thorgrim could not imagine.

"Come on, follow me!" Thorgrim shouted to the men behind him. "Break them up, and do it without killing or wounding any if you can!" He stepped forward, shield on his arm, Iron-tooth above his head. He shouted as he charged down the slope, a battle cry, a quivering wolf-howl that he hoped would get the attention of the combatants.

Thorgrim hit the edge of the fight, charged into the closest group of brawling men. Came in with shield swinging. None of those in this melee had shields, Thorgrim saw, which meant they had not come to fight, and it gave him and his house guard a great advantage.

He stepped in and the man to his left slashed with his sword, but Thorgrim caught it on the shield, the steel of the blade ringing on the iron boss. The man staggered from the impact and Thorgrim swung his shield the other way, catching the man to his right with the shield's edge and sending him sprawling in the mud.

"Put up your sword! Stop this foolishness!" Thorgrim shouted and the man, drenched and exhausted, nodded dumbly as Thorgrim plunged farther into the fight.

A battle ax came swinging through the press, appearing as if by magic, and Thorgrim managed to get his shield up in time to stop it. He felt the blade dig into the wood and he twisted the shield hard. The motion jerked the ax from its owner's hand and Thorgrim smacked the man hard with the flat of his blade, and as he swung he felt his feet coming out from under him.

With a curse he went down, bracing for the jarring impact with the ground, but it felt rather like dropping onto a pile of furs. He felt the mud grabbing at him but his eyes were up and he saw a sword coming down. He lifted his shield in time to take the blow, half sat up and swung his blade at the man's legs. Again he hit with the flat of the blade and that was enough on that slick field to trip his assailant up.

Thorgrim stood as the man fell, using his shield as a prop to help him to his feet. Another warrior was ranging up in front of him and Thorgrim, now aware of what an ally the mud could be, pushed the man and watched him fall backwards.

This is madness, Thorgrim thought. There was no animosity in the men he was fighting, none that he could see. No reason for the fight. They were just worked up into a rage, all the frustrations and anger of the winter pent in the longphort coming out on this field of battle. It was like a brawl in a mead hall writ large. He had seen sharks frenzied in the same way.

Someone was charging up on his side and he turned his head in time to see Godi grab the man and lift him bodily, one massive hand on his neck, the other grabbing his crotch. He hefted the shouting, flailing warrior over his head and flung him into a knot of fighting men and they all went down in a heap.

Farther to his right Thorgrim could see Starri Deathless hurling himself into the fight and knew there was trouble there. Thorgrim wanted the fight stopped, not escalated. That called for restraint, and restraint was not something Starri was good at.

He turned to his right, certain that Harald would be standing there, and he was. As he opened his mouth to speak Harald slammed his shield into the two men to his left who were struggling, arms around one another. The blow knocked them both to the ground where they released one another and struggled through the thick mud to regain their feet.

Harald had sheathed his sword and now as one of Skidi's men made a lurching attack he reached out and grabbed a fist-full of the man's hair, right on the top of his head, and slammed it down on his upraised knee. The man seemed to bounce off the knee, his face now a smear of blood as he toppled back, bringing two more down with him as he fell.

"Harald!" Thorgrim shouted. "Go fight with Starri! See he doesn't hurt anyone any more than he has to!"

Harald nodded, turned, slipped and went down with a curse, just as Thorgrim had. Thorgrim held his shield above both of them and offered the boy a hand. He pulled Harald to his feet, and only a wide stance and good luck prevented them both from going down again.

Harald pushed off through the crowd and Thorgrim drove his shield into the men in front of him and sent them reeling, and in the moment of peace that bought him he looked around.

His men, fresh and bearing shields, were making progress in getting the fighting men apart. Some who had been in the midst of the brawl were now abandoning the fight, some upright, some sprawled out, maybe wounded, maybe dead. Some had staggered off to collapse in the places that still sported grass. But many were still flailing at one another with swords and axes and fists.

Thorgrim looked to his left. One of Kjartan's men, a big son of a bitch named Gest, second in command of *Dragon*, came bursting from the press, battle ax raised, his mouth, framed by a massive beard, wide in a scream of fury. The ax came down at Thorgrim with an execution blow and Thorgrim just managed to get his shield up in time to stop it before it cleaved his head in two.

The ax lodged in the wood of the shield and Thorgrim felt his feet going out from under him in the slick mud. But before he could fall Gest jerked his ax free, pulling Thorgrim back on balance, allowing him to keep his feet and Thorgrim thought, *Thank you.*

Gest took another awkward swing and Thorgrim was able to sidestep it, but before he could counterstrike he saw another of Kjartan's men come from the crowd, sword in hand and lunging for his guts.

Thorgrim swung Iron-tooth at the coming blade. He pushed his right foot down until the mud had hold of it. He pressed the shield against his shoulder and shoved it into Gest who was just then bringing his ax back over his head. Gest stumbled and his feet went out from under him on the slick ground and he fell back with arms splayed and a roar of outrage.

In the space opened by Gest's fall Kjartan Thorolfson stood, sword in one hand, ax in the other. He was breathing hard and coated with mud, his hair and beard soaked through, his eyes locked on Thorgrim. He stepped quick around the struggling Gest and came at Thorgrim with weapons on the move.

You should be trying to stop this, you whore's son, Thorgrim thought even as he fended off Kjartan's attack and lunged in counterpoint. Subversive as he might be, Kjartan was one of the leading men of Vík-ló. He should be stopping the men there from killing one another, not trying to cut down the lord of the longphort.

14

Thorgrim saw a motion to his right and parried with his blade, quick enough to stop a death thrust, not quick enough to stop the blade from piercing his tunic and running along his side, opening up a wound, sharp and warm.

"Bastard!" Thorgrim shouted and brought Iron-tooth up and drove it into the man's stomach, all thought of restraint gone in the fighting madness. He turned back toward Kjartan with a whirling motion, leading with his shield, knocking Kjartan's weapons aside and lunging for his chest. He felt the familiar sensation of his blade scraping off chainmail, then he swung back in the other direction as yet another of Kjartan's men joined the fight.

Mail... Thorgrim thought. *Mail...* Some warning was ringing in his head, but with the rain and the shouting and searing wound in his side he could not understand it. He batted the new attack away, slashed at the attacker, missed his face by inches as the man leapt back.

Again Thorgrim felt his feet going out from under him, but he managed to step back before he went down and met a new attack from Kjartan.

Mail! The man's wearing mail! No one else in this fight was wearing mail, but Kjartan was. As if he had been anticipating this all along. Planning it.

Thorgrim met Kjartan's sword with Iron-tooth's blade, caught Kjartan's ax with his shield. He stepped in and gave Kjartan a kick in the stomach which sent him reeling but he did not go down.

"Is this what your fight is all about?" Thorgrim shouted. "All this to kill me?"

Kjartan made a sound somewhere between a growl and a shout. He pushed himself off, leading with his sword, ax raised. Thorgrim dropped his shield to his side and waited, Iron-tooth ready to move. Two steps and Kjartan was on him, but Iron-tooth stayed where it was. Thorgrim brought his shield up fast and slammed it into the oncoming man, stopping him dead, hurling him back. Kjartan stumbled, arms wide, eyes wide. His feet came up and he shouted as he fell and came to a stop flat on his back, half sunk in the grabbing mud.

Thorgrim leapt forward. There was a ringing in his ear that seemed to blot out the liquid noise of the rain and the shouting and the odd voice calling, "Lord Thorgrim! Lord Thorgrim!"

The voice seemed to come like a dream and then hands grabbed his arms and shoulders and stopped him as he was stepping up to Kjartan to drive his sword through the man's chest. It was only after he heard the words repeated again that he realized someone was actually calling for him.

"Lord Thorgrim!"

Thorgrim lowered his sword and shield and his body relaxed, and those holding his arms and shoulders let them go and stepped aside. Thorgrim turned to see a young man running up to him, one of Skidi's men who had been posted as a sentry on the newly rebuilt wall.

"What?" Thorgrim asked. His eyes were back on Kjartan.

"Skidi bid me tell you there are riders. Riders coming. Irishmen."

Thorgrim let those words swirl around in his mind. *Riders. Irishmen.* That could be anything. Important. Mundane. But the one thing it could not be was ignored.

Thorgrim looked at the blade of his sword. The rain had washed it clean. He thrust the weapon back into his scabbard. He looked down at Kjartan, still supine in the mud. "I'm called away by other concerns," he said. "We'll see to finishing this later." He turned his back on Kjartan and walked away. He did not wait for a reply.

Chapter Three

The country west of Vík-ló, the land that the Irish called Cill Mhantáin, rose quickly as it left the sea, climbing up into a series of high, rounded mountains that marched away inland. These were not the ragged and inhospitable cliffs of the Irish coast or those of the Northmen's homeland, but altogether more gentle and welcoming hills. And in those days of early spring the high country did indeed seem to welcome the traveler and tempt him to weave his way through the lush valleys.

Twelve miles into those mountains, nestled in a valley where two lakes where held like water cupped in God's hands, was the monastic city of Glendalough.

Christianity had come to Glendalough two hundred years before with the arrival of St. Kevin, who sought only solitude there. The valley of the two lakes was well chosen. Anyone standing by the placid water and looking out at the green rolling land above could see there was something eternal and mystical there. For two centuries since pilgrims had flocked to that holy place.

Glendalough had boasted no more than a simple clay and wattle church in the beginning, but it had become home to one of the great monasteries of Ireland, one of the strongholds of faith and learning that had preserved the cumulative knowledge of civilization when the unifying power of Rome had crumbled into warring chaos. Glendalough, rich in the monastic spirit, was now fat with wealth from the herds of cattle that grazed the surrounding fields and the gold and silver and the jewel-encrusted reliquaries that adorned the massive stone cathedral.

The church was Glendalough's physical and spiritual center. As solid as a granite outcropping, it rose fifty feet above the trampled ground and stretched for one hundred feet on a line running east to west. The lesser buildings that supported the monastery, monastic cells and guest houses, a cloister made of heavy oak beams roofed with thatch, a library of sorts, the abbot's house, gathered around the great church like courtiers around a king. The whole was enclosed by a *vallum*, a low wall meant not for defense but rather to mark the boundary of the sanctuary offered by the monastic community.

A second low stone wall, two hundred feet from the vallum, encircled the rest of the land that made up the monastery. Within its confines stood the more secular and prosaic of the monastic buildings: the bakery, the kitchen, the creamery, the stables. This outer wall was higher and more substantial than the vallum, but in terms of defense it was only marginally more impressive.

Beyond the outer wall and huddled up against it was the town that had grown in the shadow of the monastery at Glendalough, a town at least by Irish standards. A few dirt streets – mud now in the incessant rain – ran off like spokes and were crossed here and there by others that met them at various odd angles. Scattered along the streets were sundry small homes with their workshops attached, the blacksmiths and glass workers and butchers and leatherworkers and weavers, all the commerce that clung to the monastery and flourished like moss on a boulder.

Just as the church was the heart of the monastic site, so the town square formed the center of the outlying community. One hundred perches on each side, the square was filled with people and stalls on market day, and even more so on feast days and fairs. The wealthy merchants and landowners who chose to live in Glendalough enjoyed homes that looked out over the square. The best of those bordered the monastery's outer wall which put them closer to the church and the sanctuary to be found there.

It was in one of those homes, the finest of them all, the biggest in Glendalough, that Louis de Roumois found himself. It was wattle and daub built, the construction no different than the miserable homes of the craftsmen, but it was well made with a high, steep-pitched thatch roof. It boasted a stone hearth and kitchen walled off from the main room and bed chambers in a loft overhead that took up half the length of the building. It had two small windows, high up, with glass in them. The front door opened onto the town square. A door in the back opened onto an alley that ran along the monastery wall and offered a fine view of the church on the far side.

Louis was a young man, twenty-two, and unlike most men in Glendalough he did not think the house particularly impressive.

This would be a fine place, he thought, *if it were a sheep herd's hut or some peasant farmer's hovel.* But it was, in fact, the finest home in all that miserable town, and to Louis that was laughable. Still he continued to go there, and frequently, a thing he was strongly motivated to do.

The streets of Glendalough were crowded and busy that morning, and growing more so despite the rain that fell like a plague from God. Temporary stalls were going up around the perimeter of the town square and running in rows down its center, and stages were building in the open areas. Flocks of animals driven in from the countryside were herded into makeshift pens; merchants from all over the south of Ireland arrived in their carts or with their bundles on their backs, and sought out one of the few taverns with beds and ale or set up their own shelters in the fields. There was an air of anticipation that hung like smoke over the town.

The monastery at Glendalough and the town that rose up around it were nothing when compared to the great Norse longphorts of Dubh-linn and Wexford and others, but in a country made up of farmers and landowners and minor kings flung like barley seed across the land, Glendalough was an important point of trade. As such, Glendalough hosted market days and festivals through all the months when it was possible for the people to leave their homes and their farms and ringforts and gather in the town.

And of all of those, none was as important, as popular or as lucrative as the one for which the town was now readying itself: the yearly *Oénach*, the Glendalough Fair.

It was a springtime event, the first real chance for the people to emerge from the misery of winter and to indulge in something beyond mere survival. The fair would not begin for another three weeks, but already preparations were full underway.

In truth, people had been anticipating it for months, and it was not just the local craftsmen. Merchants from as far away as Frankia and Frisia sent their wares to the Glendalough Fair. At Fair time, pilgrims of a different sort - actors and jugglers and animal trainers and cutpurses and whores - made their way to the monastery town in hopes of grabbing up some of the silver that flowed through the streets during the week-long celebration.

The preparations were in full swing now, but the sound of the hammering and chopping, the shouts of the working men, the groan of the wagons and the lowing of oxen were barely audible to Louis, drowned out as they were by the driving rain and the gasping and moaning of the young Irishwoman who was at that moment writhing beneath him.

Her name was Failend and Louis guessed she was probably around twenty, not much beyond that, certainly. As beautiful a woman as any he had been with, and he had been with many. Her skin was white and smooth as butter, her hair long and black and at that moment spread out in a wild profusion over the fur on which she lay.

Louis began to move faster and Failend dug her heels into the small of his back and continued clawing his shoulders with her nails, a gesture that at first he had found arousing but now found simply painful. She gasped and shouted out something Louis did not understand. He had been in Ireland for less than a year, having arrived speaking nothing but his native Frankish. He could now speak the local tongue tolerably well, but he could not understand Failend's words, spoken through clenched teeth as she bucked and twisted under him.

He didn't think the words mattered. In his considerable experience, women under those conditions all said pretty much the same things, regardless of the language. He moved faster still and Failend wrapped her arms around him and pulled him down on top of her and pushed hard against him. They were both gasping for breath now as they worked themselves up to that final moment and then pushed one another over the edge.

For a long moment they just lay there, sunk deep in the thick furs that were spread out over the raised seating platform in the outer room. When he had first come by her house that morning, knocking lightly on the door and glancing around the square to make certain no one was looking in his direction, he had envisioned grappling in the bed chamber above as they had on past occasions. But they never made it that far.

Failend had opened the door, pulled him in from the rain, pulled him into her arms. She pressed her lips against his and he wrapped his arms around her thin body and soon they were pulling at one another's clothes and grabbing handfuls of hair and pressing their mouths hard together. They fell onto the pile of furs by the hearth and abandoned themselves to it. They did not make it ten feet from the door.

Now Louis let his breathing return to normal and wondered about the servants who usually were bustling about. *She must have sent them away*, he thought. The girl planned ahead. He liked that.

Then he heard the voice behind him, calm, measured and cold. "Done now, are we?"

Failend gasped and Louis rolled over, the warm, luxuriant feeling entirely gone. Standing by the door that led from the kitchen, having apparently come in through the back, was Colman mac Breandan, owner of the house, likely the wealthiest man in Glendalough, and, largely because of that fact, Failend's husband.

Colman was not a pretty man. He was twice Failend's age at least, of middling height and stout, his hair thinning and mousy where it had not turned gray. His fine clothes could not hide the general lumpiness of his physique. But Louis's attention was drawn not to his appearance but to the long, straight sword he held in his hand. Louis was not so transfixed by the weapon, however, that he failed to wonder just how long Colman had been standing there watching.

Maybe he likes that, Louis thought. *Maybe I do him a service.*

But like it or no, Colman did not appear to be in a grateful mood. He took a step in their direction and Failend gasped again and Louis's eyes darted off to the side, looking for his own weapon.

And then he remembered that he did not have one.

"You don't have a sword," Colman said in the same instant that Louis realized that fact. Colman took another step forward. Louis sat more upright.

"Do you recall *why* you don't have a sword?" Colman asked. Louis did, but he remained silent.

"It's because you're a man of God," Colman said. "Have you forgotten?"

Chapter Four

Many a sweet maid when one knows her mind
is fickle found towards men...
Hávamál

L ouis rolled over and onto his feet, landing in a semi-crouch, a fighting stance. It was a nice, athletic move, and Louis would have been impressed with his own easy grace if he had not been so acutely aware of his nakedness and vulnerability.

He saw Failend snatch up the fur and cover herself but he had no such cover to grab. There was nothing he could say to Colman other than to beg the man for his life, and he was not about to do that, so he said nothing. Instead he backed away, glancing left and right, looking for something he might use as a weapon.

Then Colman stopped advancing and lowered his sword. "You can stop running, you cowardly shit," he said. "I'm not going to kill you for rutting with my slut wife. If I did that I'd have killed half of Leinster by now. Just get out."

Louis remained silent. He took a step sideways, his eyes on Colman, his arm outstretched as he reached for his clothing, which consisted of a monk's robe and belt, nothing more. Colman's sword came up again.

"Leave it," he said. "I'll keep that as a trophy. Or maybe my wife can wear it when I send her to the convent. Now go."

Louis stepped back again, making for the front door, unwilling to turn his back on the man with the sword, regardless of the safe conduct he had been offered. He pictured himself stepping naked into the rain-drenched square. When he arrived the place had been crowded with people. He wondered how he would get back to his cell unseen, or how he would explain the loss of his only robe to the abbot.

"Stop," Colman said. He stepped sideways and pointed with his sword to the back of the house. "Out the back door, you Frankish turd."

Louis was happy to acquiesce to that demand. He moved cautiously in the direction the sword pointed, making a wide arc around Colman and the wicked blade. It seemed incredible that Colman was willing to spare him the humiliation of being tossed naked from the house. And then he understood. Colman was in fact sparing himself the humiliation of being so publicly shown off as a cuckold.

He moved around Colman, who stepped back to make way, and then he was lost in the gloom of the dark kitchen. The back door was still ajar, the dull light of the deep overcast sky framing the oak boards. Louis pushed it opened and stepped out into the rain. His bare feet sank half an inch into the mud, or what he hoped was mud. It was cold, but that at least kept at bay the flies and the fetid stench of the household waste heaped in the narrow alleyway.

The instant he stepped from the house he was soaked, his shoulder-length hair plastered on his neck and forehead, rain running down his naked flesh. He shivered and hugged himself. Over the monastery's low outer wall, which was no higher than Louis' chest, he could see the church standing like one of those rocky outcroppings one saw where the land met the sea. Just beyond it he could see the corner of the small, ugly building in which his cell was situated, that tiny room with its straw-filled mattress, single chair, and the desk at which he was expected to make painstaking copies of scripture and other ancient texts. It was not more than five hundred feet away, but with the open ground he had to cover it might as well have been five hundred miles.

From where he crouched behind the stone wall he could see men in black robes moving back and forth along the trampled church yard or under the roof of the cloister, and, worse still, sisters from the nearby convent. He had no notion of how he would ever reach his cell and its blessed if illusionary privacy. The irony of using the monastery wall as a sanctuary to hide his nakedness and sin was not lost on him. Reflexively he crouched lower still and looked around, but there was no one else in that alley between the rich houses and the wall.

A gust of wind buffeted him. He shivered again and his teeth began to chatter. He hugged himself tighter, and with the misery of the cold and the wet came a wave of despair and self-pity.

How, by the grace of God, do I find myself thus? he wondered.

Failend looked up at her husband who in turn was looking back through the kitchen to be certain that the Frankish novitiate Louis de Roumois had indeed left. Apparently satisfied that he had, Colman slid his sword back into its scabbard.

Colman was a Lord of Superior Testimony and had command of the defenses at Glendalough. But that was more of an honorary title bestowed by the local *rí túaithe* to whom Colman gave allegiance, a sinecure that allowed him to indirectly shift wealth from the lower castes of Glendalough to himself. Colman may have been a warrior once, but those days were past, and his physique had been lost to the good living only a man of his means could afford.

Failend could not help but reflect on the difference between her husband's appearance and that of the lean, well-muscled Louis de Roumois. Had Louis been armed, and had they crossed swords, Failend guessed that the young Frank would have killed her fat whore monger husband, though she was not certain.

And it seemed she would never find out. Colman had let Louis go. It was as much as saying that she was not worth the trouble that a charge of murder would bring, or the price of a wergild.

She wondered if Louis de Roumois would have been willing to kill Colman if given the chance, if he would risk his life or freedom for her honor.

Maybe if Colman had arrived before he finished humping me, she thought, *but probably not after he was done.* Failend was not a woman given to romantic notions.

Colman swiveled around as he sheathed his sword and their eyes met and Failend felt an ugly brew of emotions swirling around in her head: disgust, contempt, hatred, anger. Regret was not among them, nor was sorrow or humility.

"Don't think I'm ignorant of how long this has been going on," Colman said, his voice a menacing calm. "Don't think I don't know how often you've fornicated with that little bastard."

Failend glared at him. "If you were man enough, maybe I wouldn't have to look to other men for satisfaction," she spat, but she knew she had missed the mark. Colman was too wealthy, too powerful and too old to be much bothered by attacks on his brusque efforts in bed.

She had been a virgin when they wed, of course, four years past. Her father was not a poor man. He was one of the more prosperous merchants in Glendalough, one of the *aire déso,* a Lord of Vassalry, an important man, but nowhere near Colman's standing. He saw the marriage of his daughter to Colman mac Breandan as a way of greatly elevating his family's position, not just in the monastery town but in all of that part of Ireland and beyond.

Colman had hundreds of head of cattle and received a hundred and fifty more each year from the clients over whom he was lord. He owned forges and breweries and half a dozen ships that carried his goods to England and beyond. He made generous contributions to the church. He was respected and powerful. He was an ideal husband, his age, appearance and occasional mendacity notwithstanding.

Failend, young and knowing nothing of the world, had not been opposed to the marriage, and any revulsion she might have felt at the thought of laying with Colman she dismissed as a natural fear of losing her maidenhead. Her wedding night was as painful and unpleasant as she imagined it would be, but she told herself it would get better as time went on. And it did, though not by much.

The first year passed and Failend, maturity thrust upon her, found herself growing restless and increasingly curious about the wider world. Through the judicious use of shouting and the withholding of favors she convinced her husband to take her with him as he made a tour of his holdings beyond Glendalough. For weeks they traveled the country around. Failend enjoyed nearly every moment of it, but it did not sate her restlessness. Quite the opposite. Her curiosity grew, and with it a craving for something she could not quite define.

More years passed and Failend decided that the missing thing she was looking for might be a lover, one with more patience and skill, with less hair on his body and more on his head than her husband possessed. So she found one, and then another. Then Louis de Roumois, best of the lot. And that satisfied her. Somewhat. But she knew it was not all she was looking for.

The thrill she had experienced with this current ugliness, her husband and Louis, the brandished weapons, was closer to the mark. It took her thoughts back to the time when she and Colman had been set on by bandits during one of their journeys through the countryside. It had not been any great affair. In the life of a real man-at-arms she imagined it would hardly have warranted mention. But to her, innocent of such things, it might as well have been a great clash of armies.

They had spent the night at an inn at a crossroads, the sort of place where the shadows and the smoke were welcome because they hid whatever else was lurking in the dark corners. They left at first light, riding on horseback. Colman never traveled with less than a dozen men in his guard, but that morning five of them had been delayed over some matter, Failend could not recall what. Sent to collect some overdue rent, she thought. With those men left behind their party consisted of only eight riders alone on the road, and one of them clearly a woman. It was probably those small numbers that had given the robbers the courage to fall on them when they did.

They came out of a stand of trees set back from the road. They came running, with clubs and axes and one man with a sword raised high, ten of them she thought, though she had been far too panicked to count. The guards drew their swords and Colman drew his sword. Failend reigned her horse to a stop, and before any of them could do more than that the brigands were on them.

The captain of Colman's guards spurred his horse and charged the robbers, slashing with his sword, and he was pulled from his saddle. He went down with a shout, sword flailing as the robbers' crude weapons finished him. Failend heard the stomach-turning sound of bone being crushed and the man was silent, and the others spurred forward into the press of outlaws. Another man was pulled from the saddle and the outlaw with the sword killed him as he hit the ground.

It was madness. Screaming men and panicked horses, steel hitting wood and flesh and mail, horses and armed men whirling around. Colman plunged into the fight, sword raised. Failend was happy to see that, because up until then she had only heard stories of his courage and prowess in battle, and those from Colman himself. Now he roared like a proper fighting man and slashed with his blade and jerked the reins of his horse left and right. Failend saw his sword come down on one of the brigands' head, saw the long spray of blood, the man's eyes wide as death came even before he fell.

The fight did not last long. When Failend thought about it sometime later she guessed it had all been over in about five minutes, if that. The rest of Colman's guard had been riding to catch up, and when they heard the shouting they came at a gallop. Seeing their approach, the robbers who could still run did so. Those who could not run and had not had the good sense to die in the fight were killed where they lay. The little bits of silver and whatever else of worth they possessed were divided up among Colman's men.

Two men of Colman's guard had died. Their bodies were wrapped in blankets and strapped to their horses to be given a Christian burial at the next village church the riders reached. The bodies of the brigands were left to the ravens and crows, which were already taking tentative stabs at the still-warm flesh as Colman, Failend and the guard rode away.

It was no epic battle, just a sharp fight between a gang of robbers on the road and men-at-arms protecting their rich employer. The sort of encounter that happened a dozen times a week in Ireland. But in the year since it had taken place, not a day had gone by that Failend had not seen it all again in her mind. She knew that the memory should have filled her with horror and revulsion, but it did not. She knew she should tell her confessor about the perverse pleasure she took in recalling the event, but when the time came to do so it always slipped her mind.

Colman took a step in her direction. "Get up," he said. Failend pulled the fur further over her and glared up at him. "I said get up," Colman repeated, the menace thick in his voice.

It was pointless to resist him. Failend knew that. She was five feet two inches tall and weighed not much more than seven stone. Colman might have been old and fat, but he was not weak.

She threw the fur aside, got to her feet and stood facing him, not trying in any way to hide her nakedness. She could not stop him from doing what he would. The best she could do was to make her contempt and defiance clear, to show no fear. So she stood and held his eyes and did not move at all as his fist swung around in a wide arc and slammed into the side of her head.

Failend fell sideways, sprawled out on the rush-covered floor, landing just inches from the fire in the hearth. But she would not know that until she regained consciousness forty minutes later.

Chapter Five

Greetings, my host! A guest has come.
Where shall he be seated?
He must be sharp, seated by the fire,
And demonstrate his wit.

Hávamál

The riders were still half a mile away, dark moving shapes against the dull green of the spring grass. A dozen perhaps, no more. From that distance, through the pouring rain, it would have been difficult to say they were riders at all if Thorgrim was not so accustomed to the sight of men on horseback seen from some ways off.

"They have not changed the direction they were riding?" Thorgrim asked Sutare Thorvaldsson who had command of the guard on top of the wall.

"No, lord," Sutare said. "Not since we saw them. They were making right for the longphort and have not changed course at all."

Thorgrim grunted in acknowledgement. They had to be Irish. Northmen, if they rode across country at all, would not do so in so small a number. In fact, Thorgrim was fairly certain he knew who this was, but he kept his own council because he might also be wrong, and it never did a leader's reputation any good to be wrong, even in small matters.

He turned to Sutare. "I'm getting out of this cursed rain. When they reach the gate send word to me. If they choose to attack I'll trust you can hold them off."

Sutare grinned. "I'll call for help, lord, if there's a danger of them overrunning us."

Thorgrim climbed down from the wall and crossed the plank road to his hall. He could feel the effects of the fight in his arms, in various bruises, in the laceration in his side which had not been attended to. No one seemed to think the brawl had been more than an outbreak of the spontaneous violence to which bored, half drunk, frustrated men, men who lived lives of violence, were prone. But Thorgrim could not shake the image of Kjartan making his bold attack, sword and ax in hand, mail gleaming dull in the rain, his chief men surrounding him.

The fire inside the hall was roaring and the relief was immediate as he pushed through the heavy oak door. He reached up to undo the cloak which he had somewhat pointlessly donned, but his slave, a young Irishman named Segan, was there in an instant. Segan had been wounded and left behind in the Irish attack on Vík-ló the previous year. He was not the smartest lad, which was why he had not yet contrived to escape, a thing that should have been fairly easy to do, but he served Thorgrim tolerably well.

Segan took Thorgrim's cloak and set it aside, then took the sword and belt that Thorgrim handed him. Thorgrim did not bother to tell Segan to dry and oil Iron-tooth because Segan knew to do so without being told. Segan had gained considerable experience in dealing with rain-soaked gear. He met Thorgrim's eyes and gestured to a dry tunic and leggings that were laid out on a bench near the fire.

They had no language in common, which made things awkward at first. When necessary Harald, who had all but mastered the Irish tongue, translated Thorgrim's commands. But now that was rarely needed. Segan had learned to anticipate Thorgrim's orders, had come to understand his habits. Thorgrim in turn treated Segan decently, did not beat him or starve him as some did their slaves, and allowed him to sleep on straw in a corner of the hall.

With Segan's help Thorgrim stripped off his wet clothing, as wet as if he had leapt into the sea. Segan sucked in his breath as he saw the bloody wound on Thorgrim's side, the sound a bit more dramatic than was called for, Thorgrim felt.

"Agnarr," Thorgrim called, "would you please bind this up," he said, pointing to his side. "I would wish to have it secured before our Irish friends arrive."

Agnarr stood, took a cursory look at the wound, and then found some bandages and bound them around Thorgrim's side. He did the work quickly and skillfully and Thorgrim was grateful for that. If the newcomers were the men he thought they were, he did not wish them to know the Norsemen had come close to the point of killing one another.

Wound bandaged, Thorgrim dried himself and pulled the new clothes on, which were blessedly warm. It was a luxury to have a shift of clothes, a luxury that Thorgrim had not known since leaving his farm in East Agder. The new garments had belonged to Fasti Magnisson, one of the former leaders of Vík-ló who had been killed by the Irish before Thorgrim arrived at the longphort. It was Fasti's hall which Bersi now occupied, but Thorgrim had laid claim to the clothes, which fit him admirably.

Most of the house guard were back and seated in the same places they had been before they turned out for the disturbance by the river. The windows were shuttered against the storm and the only light in the hall came from the great fire in the hearth, which made for brilliant illumination within a dozen feet of the blaze and increasing dark and shadow in the farther reaches of the big room. Gusts of wind and rain hammered the building and blew smoke back through the smoke holes in the roof until it swirled around above the men's heads.

As Thorgrim shifted clothing Harald stood a few feet away, looking for an opportunity to be helpful. "Did you see the riders, father?" he asked, taking the wet clothes from Segan. "Are they many?"

"A dozen perhaps. If I don't miss my guess, it's Kevin...mic..."

"Kevin mac Lugaed," Harald offered. Thorgrim struggled with the odd Irish names but Harald seemed able pronounce them like a native, if Thorgrim was any judge. Which of course he was not.

"Yes, Kevin mac Lugaed," Thorgrim repeated, mangling the pronunciation once again. "Him and his guard."

Thorgrim was not worried about the possibility of being wrong in front of Harald. They were father and son, and after more than two years of raiding and voyaging in each other's company there was nothing Harald did not know about him, the good and the bad, the strength and the weakness. And still Harald seemed to view him at times as some character from the old stories of the gods, some denizen of the Asgardian realm. Thorgrim was content to leave that impression intact, and he knew that the occasional mistake on his part would not shake it. If it did, then it would have been shaken long before.

Starri looked up from where he was sitting on the floor, leaning against the wall and nearly lost in shadow. "That Irishman, you say?" Starri asked. "The one who came before?" Starri did not even try to pronounce his name.

"Yes, I think it is," Thorgrim said. "He rides with that banner, the green one with the raven. It seemed to me I could see one of them carrying a banner aloft, though it was too far to see what emblem it bore."

"I wonder what he wants now," Starri said.

"Not sure," Thorgrim said. "Whatever it is, I'll wager it's interesting."

"Huh," Starri said. "We sit on our asses for four months, and then everything of interest takes place on a single day."

Everything of interest, Thorgrim thought. He wondered if the three men Starri had knocked to insensibility felt the day had been interesting. At least Harald had managed to stop Starri from killing anyone in his berserker frenzy.

But still Thorgrim was intrigued at the possibility of Kevin mac Lugaed's arrival, of what he might bring. Perhaps he would bring the very distraction that the men of Vík-ló so desperately needed.

The door opened and Sutare Thorvaldsson stepped in, and with some effort he shut the door behind him. Water was running off his tunic and dripping from the end of his scabbard. "Lord, the Irishmen are at the gate. It's that fellow, been here before. Kevin…."

"Yes, let them in. Bring him and half his men here. Send the other half to Bersi's hall, let them drink *his* ale."

"Yes, lord," Sutare said. He opened the door and a gust of wind carried the rain in with such force that Thorgrim felt it on his face where he stood by the fire. Sutare ducked out and again closed the door behind him.

"Godi," Thorgrim turned to the big man who was standing by the hearth, hands held out as if trying to fend off the flames. "Go and tell Bersi that the Irishman is here. Ask him to come join me so we may talk with him. Find Skidi Oddson and tell him the same."

"Yes, lord," Godi said. He grabbed up his cloak and swung it around his shoulders, giving Thorgrim a few seconds more to make a decision. By all rights Kjartan should be included in this council. He was one of the lead men of Vík-ló and had taken part in every other.

But then he had just staged a bloody fight for the express purpose of luring Thorgrim in and killing him.

Or had he? Thorgrim had not yet had time to discover the cause of the fight, and the more he considered his suspicions, the more lunatic they seemed. He did not want the men of Vík-ló rent by further division, and he did not want Kevin mac Lugaed to see any weakness there.

"Godi," Thorgrim said as the big man reached for the door. "Get Kjartan as well."

"Yes, lord," Godi said, and good man that he was he did not question that decision.

Let Kjartan come, Thorgrim thought. *We'll discover the truth of his loyalty soon enough.*

Godi opened the door and once again the rain blew in. Thorgrim felt a twinge of regret at sending the man, who had nearly dried himself, out into the deluge once again.

Ah, you grow old and soft, Night Wolf... he thought to himself. In his younger days the comfort of his men would not even have crossed his mind. He was not certain which was the better man, Thorgrim then or now.

Chapter Six

Gauls, Aquitanians, Burgundians and Spaniards,
Alemanians and Bavarians thought themselves distinguished
if they deserved to go by the name of servants to the Franks.
Notker

I n truth, Louis de Roumois knew exactly how he had come to be
standing in the mud, naked and shivering in an alley in some
monastery town at the very ragged edge of civilization. It was an
unhappy story, if not a particularly unusual one. If he could take
comfort in only one thing, it was the fact that this fate was not his
fault. At least, not entirely.

Louis was from the region of Roumois in Frankia, from the city
of Rouen on the banks of the Seine, forty miles from where that
wide, twisting river emptied into the sea. It was a beautiful county of
low, rolling hills and fertile fields, where the weather was mostly good
and it did not constantly rain as if God was trying to put an end to
His creation.

The rich soil and the tolerable climate made for a general
prosperity among the people of Roumois, or so it always seemed to
Louis, who did not in truth have much interaction with the class of
men who worked the land. He tended to see them only on those
times when he and his warriors rode up to the beaten yard of some
pathetic hut and demanded that the terrified farmer or his wife or
children find water for their horses. He knew better than to ask for
food or ale. Even if the people had it, it would not be anything Louis
de Roumois would consider putting in his mouth.

If the farmer and his family did as they were told, and did it
promptly, Louis might reward them with a silver coin and then order
his men to remount. They would ride off and leave the people in

peace, which was the reward they wanted most of all, though Louis never understood that.

Louis' father was Hincmar, the count of Roumois, son of Eberhard, count of Roumois. After the death of Louis the Pious, Hincmar had stood by Charles the Bald, fourth son of the late king, in the subsequent civil war that broke out between him and his two brothers. He stood by Charles during the worst of the fighting, during his struggles with Aquitaine, remained loyal and kept up the fight even when Charles's army could boast of nothing beside their tattered clothes, weapons and horses.

Following the Treaty of Verdun, Charles the Bald gained the kingship of West Frankia, which he had in effect been ruling for the five years previous to that. Hincmar's loyalty, steadfast through the worst of times, was not forgotten by the new king. Hincmar found himself in a very good position indeed: his land, tenants and titles much increased, his position and influence in the court of Charles the Bald unassailable.

All of this the young Louis de Roumois knew in a general way. For a good part of his childhood his father had been absent, either fighting or intriguing at court. Louis spent his days pursuing those things that interested him. He became skilled at horseback riding and hunting, falconing, wrestling, fencing, archery, swimming and avoiding his tutors.

Though he had been too young to participate in the war, Louis was drawn to the notion of fighting. Unlike his father, however, he had no interest in nor aptitude for politics, intrigue or statecraft. But Louis did not have to worry about affairs of state because he was not the eldest son.

His brother, named Eberhard after their paternal grandfather, would inherit the title of count. The governing of the Roumois was his problem. Louis had only to enjoy the great bounty of the region, and the benefits of being born into the *regnum*, the ruling class, while remaining free of the responsibility of actually ruling.

Like any young man of his standing, Louis had trained with weapons from a young age, and unlike many he had a natural gift for the use of them, and loved all things military. At fifteen he begged his father to give him some role in the defense of Roumois. His father considered his son too frivolous and immature to take on such a responsibility, and he made no secret of the fact. But Louis persisted, and managed to make such a nuisance of himself that his father relented, as much to shut the young man up as anything.

Domestic tranquility was not Hincmar's only motive, however. Charles the Bald had secured peace with his brothers, but now there was a new threat to Roumois, carried on the very river that ran like life's blood through the region. Norsemen. Danes, mostly. The brutal raiders from the north were coming upriver in their swift longships and plundering the countryside. Their appearance was a profound terror but it was no surprise. The riches to be found in Frankia, the churches bursting with silver, the wealthy estates at the water's edge, could not go unnoticed forever.

Roumois had warriors enough to counter the threat but Hincmar needed the right man to lead them, someone he could trust completely, someone who would maintain the prestige of his family and not see this as a chance to gain power for himself. Louis was impetuous and sometimes foolish, but he had proven his courage and his skill, and Hincmar did not doubt his loyalty. He appointed Louis to lead a division of two hundred horsemen and set him the task of defending Roumois against the Northmen when next they appeared.

To act as counterweight to Louis' rash tendencies, Hincmar also appointed as second in command a man named Ranulf, an old campaigner with whom he had fought during the war for West Frankia. Hincmar made his wishes perfectly clear; Louis was in command, but when it came to fighting Ranulf would make the decisions. Someday, Hincmar told his son, with enough years and experience behind him, and if he learned what Ranulf had to teach, he might lead the men in something other than name only. But not yet.

Louis understood what his father told him. Then, a month later, when word came that the Northmen were on the Seine, he promptly ignored it all.

The mounted men-at-arms had been training under Louis's ostensible leadership when the first of a stream of messengers arrived, this one from Fontenelle, twenty miles downstream from Roumois. The Danes had come.

Not a moment was wasted. The men-at-arms slipped on mail, belted on swords, strapped helmets in place and rode off west. Plumes of smoke rising up over the rolling green hills marked those places where the Danes had come ashore and done their work, moving faster than even mounted troops could travel, and Louis led the men in that direction.

"Lord," Ranulf said, his horse keeping pace with Louis's as they rode. "Where the smoke is, the heathens have already been. If we want to catch them, which we do, we should send scouts down to the river, east of where that village is burning."

Louis understood the point that Ranulf was making and he ignored it the same way he was ignoring his father's instructions. He did not care to be told what to do. As the son of the count he was not accustomed to it.

"I want to see what's become of this village," he said, hoping to justify the mistake he had already made. "I want to see if there's any help we can bring."

They reached the place an hour later, realizing as they drew nearer that it was a village by the name of Jumièges, home to an abbey established there two hundred years before. They rode slowly past burning huts of wattle and thatch, the dead laying strewn in the dirt yards, blood dark on their worn and filthy clothing, the living staring blankly at them as they passed. A man lay propped to a tree, eyes open, mouth wide, an arrow jutting from his forehead and pinning him in place. At his side was a pathetic ax with which he had apparently been defending himself. An old woman lay hacked nearly in two, her hand still clutching a basket, its contents gone.

Louis swallowed hard. He would not let himself vomit in front of Ranulf and the men.

They came at last to the abbey. Most of the smaller buildings that surrounded it were burning, many already collapsed into piles of smoldering debris. But the church at the heart of the community was a stone and slate affair and would not be easily burned. From a distance it seemed unharmed, but as they closed with it they could see the big oak door at the western end had been hacked apart, the splintered remnants still hanging from the black iron hinges.

"Nothing we can do here, Lord," Ranulf said, a note of urgency in his voice, which Louis dismissed as he had dismissed everything else the man had said. He climbed down from his horse and stepped cautiously through the doors of the church. Nothing moved in the twilight interior; there was not a sound to be heard save for Louis's footfalls. It was more like a tomb than a church now. The body of a priest lay sprawled out on the floor. The blood from the sword blow that had killed him was barely visible against the dark fabric of his robe, but beneath him it spread out in a wide pool on the slate floor. Another priest, nearly decapitated, lay ten feet away.

At the far end of the nave the ornate tabernacle door had been wrenched off and taken, and manuscripts lay strewn around the alter where they had been tossed after their covers, trimmed with gold and jewels, had been torn away. Gold monstrances, reliquaries, the sacred vessels, all the things that Louis had seen during the many times he had celebrated mass in that church, they were all gone.

Louis heard more footfalls and turned to see Ranulf approaching down the nave. He did not so much as glance at the dead men on the floor.

"Savages," Louis said. "Damned, damned savages."

"Yes, Lord. And we have time yet to catch them."

"Where are the sisters?" Louis asked, still too stunned by the horror he was seeing to respond to Ronulf's none too subtle suggestion. "Are they hiding, do you think?"

"No, Lord. They're gone, I have no doubt."

"Gone?"

"Taken. Off to the slave markets in Frisia. Or…." He stopped. Louis looked up at him and nearly insisted that he finish the thought. But he didn't, because he knew what Ranulf was going to say and he did not want to hear it.

"Do you think they've gone? The Northmen? Are they going west, back to the sea?"

"They've had good plundering so far," Ranulf said, "and no one trying to stop them. I don't think they'll want to give it over just yet."

"Let us ride, then. East. Let us fight these sons of whores before they do any more of this."

They mounted and they rode off east, Louis leading the way. His horror had turned to rage and he wanted only to be at the Danes, to cut them down. For all his fencing and archery and wrestling and such, Louis de Roumois had never actually been in combat, had never drawn blood in anger. But he was not afraid to do so. Indeed, he was eager for it now, ready not just to draw blood but to spill it.

As they rode they met more people fleeing the Northmen, the folk from the villages who had nothing beyond their poor hovels for defense, streaming away from the demons that had been loosed on them. They had with them what few sorry possessions they could carry and they led cows and sheep and goats behind, and Louis had to wonder if the Danes would have even bothered taking such pitiful things as these people owned.

The men-at-arms continued on, riding toward the place from which the others were fleeing. "There." Louis pointed to the west where the first trail of black smoke was rising up above a stand of trees. "There they are, the bastards, they're burning the village. We'll ride hard, go right at them, cut the sons of bitches down."

"Lord," Ranulf said, "there's better ways. They're ready for an attack now, expecting one I should think, and we do not know how many they are. Nothing we can do for the poor bastards in that village. Let the Danes return to their ships, let them pull for the next. We'll send riders to watch them and keep us informed, and we'll stay clear. When they land, that's when they are vulnerable. When they beach their ships but are still sorting themselves out. We fall on them then, and we'll do a great slaughter, that I promise."

Louis looked at Ranulf as if the man had blasphemed during the consecration. He wondered if perhaps the old warhorse was getting a bit backward in his courage, comfortable as he was at Rouen. "Nonsense," he said. "We attack them directly, like men. No skulking around."

And they did, because for all his father's instructions that Louis was to listen to Ranulf, the simple fact was that Louis was the commander and he was the son of the count and his word carried that authority. It was Louis, or more precisely Louis's father, that the men feared most. They were not privy to any restrictions that the count might have privately imposed.

They rode hard for the village, pounding down the dirt road made dry by an unusually long stretch of fine weather. The hooves of their mounts raised a great cloud of dust, a cloud that must have betrayed their approach half an hour before they arrived, or so Louis would later realize as he reviewed over and over the many stupid things he had done that day.

Chapter Seven

Childerich, who had the name of king [of the Franks]
Was shorn of his locks and sent into a monastery.

Annals of Lorsch Abbey

The village was already burning as they approached. The Northmen were there, but just a few that Louis could see, and they did not seem overly prepared to fight, staggering along with armloads of loot. As the mounted Frankish warriors charged down on them they dropped their loads and fled into the cluster of squat thatch and wattle buildings that comprised the village, now nearly lost in the smoke and flames.

Louis led his men on at full gallop as they chased after the fleeing Danes. They pounded down the village's single road, swords draw. They rode straight into the smoke, then the heat of the flames, and then a lethal swarm of arrows from archers who were arrayed on either side of the road and hidden from view.

It all fell apart before Louis even knew what was happening. He saw one of his men knocked from the saddle as if he had been punched, an arrow jutting from his mail-clad chest. Another horse stumbled and its rider went over its head and landed in a heap on the ground, two arrows thumping into his back even before his body had come to rest. Then Louis' horse reared up and shrieked. Louis saw the arrow jutting from its neck and he felt himself going down.

"Damn you! Damn you! Damn you!" In the noise and the confusion and panic it was all Louis could think to say. An arrow glanced off his helmet and the ringing and the vibration stunned him. He saw one of the Northmen leave the line of archers and race toward him, pulling a battle ax from his belt and screaming as he came. He had red hair tied in two long braids and Louis was transfixed by them. He watched the ropes of hair bouncing and swaying like serpents and seemed unable to move as the man ran at him.

Then a horse was between him and the Northman and, though he did not see what happened, he heard an ugly, guttural scream and saw a spray of blood from where the Northman's head must have been. He looked up. Ranulf was on the horse, sword in hand, a bright stream of blood running down the blade.

Louis pulled himself to his feet, and without a word Ranulf reached down and grabbed him by the mail shirt and hefted him up, an extraordinary display of strength Louis would later realize. Without ceremony he draped Louis over the saddle as if he was going to spank him, and then kicked his horse forward and shouted to the others.

Louis could not understand the words. He did not know where they were going. He could only twist his neck and watch the country pass by, doubled over Ranulf's saddle. They were already beyond the village by the time he realized they were retreating.

The Northmen had won a fine victory: five of Louis's men killed outright, seven wounded, three of whom were unlikely to live. Eight were captured, and no one liked to think on what their fate might be. But for all that, the sight of so many mounted warriors apparently convinced the raiders that their luck and the easy takings were over, at least in Roumois, at least for the time being. They loaded their loot, their prisoners, their plundered stores onto the longships and pulled for the open sea.

Louis went to his father on his knees, which was not his wont. Usually he would deny his transgressions, craft excuses, attempt to ward off blame that was rightfully his, but not this time. He was no stranger to sin and error, and he never gave them much thought. But neither had he ever committed any that were so grave, so unforgivable as those he had that day. He confessed it all to his father. He stated plainly that Ranulf had been right all along, that he had ignored the man's advice. Had it not been for Ranulf, Louis admitted, he would be dead and his body picked clean by ravens.

And his father, not always a forgiving man, forgave him. He was impressed by Louis's sincerity, which was not something he had often seen in the boy. He not only forgave him, but he offered to allow him to continue in his soldierly pursuit if Louis in turn would promise to listen to Ranulf in the future and learn from him. And Louis did.

Impetuous, headstrong and arrogant though he might have been, Louis de Roumois was no fool, and some lessons he did not have to learn twice. When next the Northmen came to plunder along the Seine Louis listened to everything that Ranulf had to say, and soon the Danes were fleeing back to their ships, leaving their many dead and wounded in their wake. Now it was the Frankish warriors who set the traps and watched as the Northmen fell into them and died. It was, in Louis's eyes, a beautiful thing.

A friendship was sparked between Louis and Ranulf, and eventually a mutual respect, as Louis began to master the art of war-craft, and to lead the men against their enemies in ways that were every bit as well considered and successful as those of Ranulf, and sometimes more so. Louis showed a fearlessness in battle that served as an inspiration to his men, a fearlessness born of youth and a natural skill that left him feeling invulnerable to his enemies.

For four years Louis and Ranulf and their men fought off the Danish incursions. Their mounted warriors were known in the northern countries and feared. Louis de Roumois had found his calling.

He loved the life of a soldier. Riding, fighting, drinking, whoring, he loved it all. He loved his men and they loved him, and they would have happily followed him through the fiery gates of hell without so much as pausing for a sip of water. The heathens' vision of paradise, their heaven, Louis knew, consisted of a life of fighting and feasting, and though he would never say as much out loud, at least not sober, he understood why.

Four years, the happiest four year of his life, and then it came to an end. Louis was adept at seeing dangers on the battlefield but he was not so quick to see them in his own home.

He had become, in those four years, a man to whom others looked for leadership. The warriors of Rouen loved him and obeyed him. If he needed more soldiers he had only to send word and the men-at-arms of all the neighboring regions would rally to his banner.

The people of that province loved him as well. They saw him as their protector, the handsome young man on the black steed who rode in to fight the heathen raiders and kept their homes safe.

It would have been no great trick for Louis to set himself up to succeed his father as count of Roumois. Such a title usually went to the eldest son, but in Frankia that was not always the case. Louis, however, was enamored of the life he led and had no interest in rule. The very thought that he might use the power and status he had amassed to take his father's office never occurred to him. But it did occur to his brother, Eberhard.

On a cold February day in the year 853, with the wind blowing desultory flakes of snow around the great house at Rouen, their father died. He had been ill for some time with a wet cough and a fever. The doctors treated him with various herbs, examined his urine with learned and serious expressions and bled him copiously, but he died all the same. It was only then that Louis realized the effort to which Eberhard had gone to prepare for that very moment.

The late Count Hincmar was still lying covered on his deathbed when Eberhard ordered the arrest of Ranulf and the captains of the men-at-arms who served under Louis. The rest were stripped of their weapons, mail, and horses and put under the guard of troops loyal to Eberhard, house warriors he had organized in secret. Louis could do nothing to stop any of it. He could only look on in horror and rage and wait for the ax to come down on his neck or the knife to slip between his ribs.

But that final stroke never came. Louis was allowed a liberty of sorts as his brother solidified his rule over Roumois. He was allowed free movement in the house and on the grounds, always under the watch of at least one armed guard he could see and, he guessed, several whom he could not. He was not allowed a horse and he was not allowed to leave.

Five days after their father's death, on the day his body was laid to rest in a marble sarcophagus in the church at Rouen, Louis was summoned to his brother's chamber, the great room from which their father had once ruled. Eberhard had begun making use of it even before Hincmar's death, even as the old man lay coughing out his life. Louis stepped through those familiar doors, half expecting to see his father sitting there, unhappy to see his brother instead, comfortable in Hincmar's chair.

"Brother," Eberhard began, "our late father, you know, was always concerned for your education, and for the state of your soul. He never thought this soldiering was any means of gaining heaven."

"Our late father was happy to see me keep the Danes from burning Roumois to the ground," Louis said. "If you are going to kill me, you had better have another who can do that office."

"Kill you?" Eberhard said with a tone that sounded like genuine surprise. "I would not kill you, brother. What a thing to say. No, quite the opposite. I want you to have life, eternal life. Like father, I fear for your soul. I think it's time you abjured the way of the soldier and its inherent sinfulness. Tell me, have you ever heard of the monastery at Glendalough? In Ireland?"

And that was it. Eberhard did not dare kill him because he was too popular with the men-at-arms and with the people, or so Louis came to realize. Second sons were generally given over to be warriors or churchmen. Louis had picked the first and now his brother was forcing the second choice upon him. It was not unprecedented, not at all. Louis the Pious had bundled two of his troublesome half-brothers off to the monastery. But they, at least, had remained in Frankia. Eberhard was making certain Louis was much farther removed.

Two weeks later Louis was sent to Glendalough to study with the monks and to copy out manuscripts and to eventually take his priestly vows. He took to monastic life the way a fish takes to a hook, fighting and struggling and gasping for breath. Of all the novitiates, he was not the abbot's favorite. In truth he and his bad attitude and his subtle insubordination were barely tolerated. On those few occasions when he prayed, he prayed to be cast out of Glendalough and sent packing back to Roumois. But that never happened, and Louis guessed it was because his brother sent heaps of silver to the monastery to make sure they continued to suffer Louis's presence.

The path that had led him to where he was now, naked in the driving rain, as completely alone and miserable as a man could be, was long and twisting. And as he stood there, a new thought occurred to him. In his haste to get past Colman's sword he had left Failend to the fate of her furious husband. When it came to bedding her he had been eager and unhesitant, but when she stood in need of defense he had slinked away like the coward he was.

By God, I am despicable, a slave, a ruined man, he thought. He guessed that tears were rolling down his cheeks, though in the rain he could not tell for certain. He started walking along the wall toward the gate that led to the monastery grounds, no longer concerned about who might see him in his nakedness. He was ready to just drop to the ground and let the rain and the mud cover him up.

He staggered as he walked, the mud grabbing his feet, so lost in his despair that he was unaware of anything outside his sphere of agony. And so he was startled enough that he jumped when a voice called out, "Brother Louis?"

He turned toward the sound. On the other side of the wall stood Father Finnian, one of the priests of the monastery. He had a half smile on his face, a look of vague amusement as he reached up and unclasped the broach that held the cape over his shoulders and said, "Here, Brother, you look as if you are in need of this."

Chapter Eight

In thy home be joyous and generous to guests
discreet shalt thou be in thy bearing,
mindful and talkative, wouldst thou gain wisdom…
Hávamál

No sooner had Godi closed the door then Sutare opened it again. He stepped in and held it open. Out of the wind and driving rain came a hooded figure in a long robe which, when dry, might have been any color, but soaked through as it was looked coal black. The figure stepped farther in, and behind him came a man bearing a long pole from which hung the raven banner, wet and dark and dripping on the floor, and behind him another half-dozen well-armed men.

The man with the hood reached up and pulled back the soaked cloth to reveal the full face and short, neatly trimmed beard of Kevin mac Lugaed. Despite his small stature and unassuming appearance he seemed to wield considerable authority in that country that the Irish called Cill Mhantáin, part of the region known as Leinster.

Thorgrim crossed over to Kevin as the last of his men entered and the door was pushed closed against the wind. "Welcome," he said and extended a hand, which Kevin took. The Irishman replied, something in his native tongue, some acknowledgement of the greeting. Harald was there, but he did not bother to translate.

Segan approached, showing more supplication to Kevin than he ever showed Thorgrim, and took Kevin's cloak. The clothes underneath were no more dry than the outer garment but that did not hide their quality, the best suit of clothes Thorgrim had yet seen on Kevin, and he guessed that silver was flowing from various directions into the man's purse.

He took the Irishman by the elbow and led him over to the fire. Segan reappeared with a horn of mead for him and one for Thorgrim. Such hospitality was expected of a host, and Thorgrim genuinely wished to make his guest comfortable. But not too comfortable. If negotiations were to follow it would be to Thorgrim's advantage to be warm and dry while the Irishman remained soaked and miserable.

Kevin stood in front of the fire for a moment, silent, looking into the flames, shuffling as close as he could without singeing himself. He took a deep drink of mead then turned to Thorgrim and spoke. Harald, standing at Thorgrim's side, translated.

"He says, 'What think you of our Irish weather, now spring has come?'" Kevin wore the hint of a smile as he waited for the answer.

"Tell him the weather is what I would expect of a country so clearly and so deservedly cursed by the gods."

Harald translated. Kevin smiled broader and spoke again.

"He says, 'There is only one God, and he has indeed cursed this land,'" Harald said.

Thorgrim smiled and lifted his horn and Kevin did the same and they touched them together. This was perhaps the third or fourth time the men had met, and each of their meetings had been more beneficial than the last.

The first had taken place just a month and a half after the Irish army under Lorcan mac Fáeláin had attacked Vík-ló and had been crushed by the Norse defenders. Lorcan had been killed, and dozens of others with him, including most of his chief men who had been in the forefront of the fighting. Grimarr Giant, lord of Vík-ló, had been killed as well. In the course of thirty bloody minutes, the entire structure of power and rule in that part of Ireland had been tossed in the air and blown away like chaff.

After the fight the Northmen had seen nothing of the Irish until the day Kevin rode up to the walls of Vík-ló. He had approached the earthworks with caution, forty armed men behind him. Thorgrim had been summoned to the wall as soon as it was clear the riders were making for the longphort. He brought Harald and Bersi with him. He did not know why the Irishmen had come, though he had some idea which he kept to himself. And that was a good thing, because his idea was entirely wrong.

The Irish delegation was just beyond a comfortable arrow shot when they stopped and Kevin called out in a voice calculated to sound commanding.

"He says he is Kevin mac Lugaed and he is the lord of this area," Harald translated, "and he would ask safe conduct to speak with the lord of Vík-ló."

The shouted negotiations continued on for a few minutes more, but once it was clear to Thorgrim the Irish did not have men enough to pose a threat to Vík-ló, and once Kevin felt confident he would not be killed or bundled off to the slave markets in Frisia, the gates were open and the riders came through.

Kevin missed nothing: the rebuilt walls and palisades, the stacks of logs and cut wood down by the water, the smoke rising from the two halls and the blacksmith shop and the various homes. Thorgrim could practically see him calculating the power and the wealth of the longphort. He wondered if spying was the real reason for the visit. He assumed the Irishman had come to try to dislodge the Northmen from Vík-ló, to either tell them to leave or bribe them to leave, depending on the strength of Irish arms.

Kevin mac Lugaed, it turned out, had not come to threaten or bribe. He had come to trade. The men of Vík-ló, he figured, would be in need of food and drink, particularly with winter coming on. He suspected that the Northmen had a considerable amount of silver and gold, a thing that he needed to bolster his status and to keep his men happy and loyal. Surely, he thought, a deal could be reached.

"Perhaps," Thorgrim said, speaking through his son. "Perhaps not. I don't know if you are even in a position to make such deals. Who are you, exactly?"

Kevin mac Lugaed was not offended by the question, and Thorgrim was starting to understand that he was not the sort of man who would ever take offense when there was money on the table.

"I am the rí túaithe of the lands around here, including Cill Mhantáin, which you Northmen apparently call Vík-ló," Kevin answered.

This was translated and Thorgrim and Bersi nodded. Kevin continued on. "Before, I was of the *aire forgill*, the Lords of Superior Testimony, not the rí túaithe, you see…." Harald translated. Kevin saw the looks of confusion on the Northmen's faces. He waved his hand.

"It doesn't matter," he said. "The point is, Lorcan was killed and most of his men were killed, and as it happens I am the man of highest rank still left alive, and so I am now lord of these lands. And that is why I have the authority to bargain with you. And I wish to bargain with you, because it is in my interest to do so. And I think it will be in your interest to bargain with me."

And it was. Kevin's arrival had been timely, because Thorgrim, as newly-minted lord of Vík-ló, was just starting to worry about the very problem of keeping his men fed and sufficiently inebriated throughout the long winter months. At the time of Kevin's arrival they were still able to make the voyage to Dubh-linn in the diminutive *Fox* and bring supplies back to Vík-ló, but soon the winter weather would close that down. Thorgrim did not know how they would supply themselves after that. And here the answer came riding in from the hills like a gift from the gods.

Thorgrim did not trust Kevin, of course, or at least he was wary of him, as he was of all Irish. But Kevin proved as good as his word. Wagons loaded with sacks of flour made from barley and rye, barrels of ale, smoked meat, dried fish and wine soon rolled up to the gate in Vík-ló's earthen wall. The quality was as good as Thorgrim had dared hope, which was not very good, but it beat starving by a league. Thorgrim had paid Kevin in silver for the foodstuff, a bit more silver than it was worth, and Kevin had gone away greatly satisfied.

The next time Kevin arrived Thorgrim could not help but notice that his clothes were a bit finer than the last, his men better fitted out. He wore a gold chain around his neck. He and Thorgrim, along with Bersi, Skidi and Kjartan, ate and drank and discussed expanding their trade, and soon Kevin was selling the Northmen cloth and grindstones and coils of rope along with the meat and fish and ale.

The next time he came he brought women. Just a few, and not slaves, but Irish women who were looking for men, for husbands. Thorgrim imagined that after all the carnage of the past summer there were not Irishmen enough left for all the young women and new-made widows.

Thorgrim almost turned them away, knowing that a few women among all those men could be more of a problem than none at all. But by the time he and Kevin had even begun discussing it, word had raced through the longphort and there would be no way to send the women away without starting an ugly war.

The commerce between Vík-ló and whatever passed for the kingdom of Kevin mac Lugaed continued to grow and prove beneficial to all concerned. Thorgrim and Kevin developed a friendship, of sorts. Thorgrim was not so sentimental or soft in the head as to think Kevin actually liked him, or was pleased by the presence of the Northmen on Irish soil. Their friendship was more superficial and self-serving than that.

And so, as the rain lashed his hall and the fire in the hearth popped and hissed and flared, Thorgrim Night Wolf found himself wondering once more what Kevin mac Lugaed was bringing to him, what new bargain, what intrigue he had concocted during the long winter nights.

They stood at the edge of the flames and continued to speak by way of Harald, each man asking the other how things fared for him and the men and women under their authority, both probing none too subtly for information, for some advantage. The door opened, bringing with it a blast of cold and wet and Bersi stepped in, wrapped like a farm wife in a wool blanket. A few minutes after that Skidi Oddson joined them

Segan brought drinking horns for the newly arrived men and refilled Kevin's as quick as the Irishman could drain it, as Thorgrim had instructed. He hoped it might make Kevin a bit less crafty, a bit more open in his speech, though in truth he had never seen the man in the least affected by drink that he could tell.

At last, their legs growing tired, Thorgrim ordered a table and chairs brought close to the fire and the four men and Harald sat. No introductions were needed. Bersi and Skidi had both been part of the earlier bargaining. Kjartan as well. Thorgrim knew it was better to make his chief men part of such things rather than let suspicions grow into distrust and anger.

Segan put a platter of roasted beef, cheese and brown bread on the table. Thorgrim said, "All right, Kevin, you have drank enough of my mead, what new thing brings you to Vík-ló?"

Harald was halfway through the translation when the door opened again and Kjartan came into the hall. He wore no mail this time, just a hood and cloak which draped over the sword hanging at his side. His eyes darted around the space, a quick assessment of potential threats. He did not know what he was stepping into and he was wary.

"Night Wolf, you sent word of a meeting," Kjartan said.

Thorgrim said nothing at first, letting his emotions settle before he replied. He wanted nothing more than to drag Kjartan back out into the rain and finish what they had begun, but this was not the moment. Not with Kevin watching their every move, gauging any weakness, even if he could not understand the words they spoke.

"Yes," Thorgrim said at last, spitting the words like they were sour in his mouth. "Kevin mac Lugaed has come to speak with us. You have the right to join this council."

And then I will kill you, he thought.

Kjartan pulled up a stool and sat. Thorgrim looked at Kevin, who was understandably confused by the Norse jabber, the sudden and obvious tension in the room. He looked at the other men, but their expressions were unreadable. He turned to Kevin once more and said, "You were telling us what business it is that brings you here?" he said.

Kevin leaned back and took a long pull of his mead as Harald rendered Thorgrim's words into Gaelic. His eyes moved around the table, taking each man in turn, gauging him, getting the sum of him. Then he spoke. Harald translated.

"Kevin says, 'Have you men ever heard of a monastery called Glendalough'?"

Chapter Nine

God's house is threefold. Some pray in it, some fight in it, some work in it.
Aldalbero, Bishop of Laon

Louis de Roumois trudged along in Father Finnian's wake, cloak wrapped tight around him, head down, lost in his physical and spiritual misery. He paid little attention to where they were going, expecting, without really thinking about it, that they would head for the small building which housed the monks' cells, Louis home for the past year or more. And so he was surprised to find himself in the stable, sheltered from the rain by the thatched roof, embraced by the familiar smell of leather and straw and the horses in the stalls that lined the north side.

"Wait here," Finnian said and disappeared back into the rain. Louis found a dim corner of the building and sat on a heap of straw and listened to the rain coming down. The stables were deserted, no one was much interested in being on horseback on such a day, and Louis was glad for the solitude and the chance to further indulge his despair.

But soon Finnian was back and he carried a robe with him, which he handed to Louis. Louis did not ask where he had found it, and he was grateful that Finnian did not ask how he had come to lose his old one. He took off the cape and handed it back to Finnian and then slipped the robe over his head. It was rough and penitential, as such things generally were, but dry and warm, and it felt marvelous.

Finnian handed Louis the cord belt and Louis tied it around his waist. He heard the sound of footsteps, soft on the straw-covered floor, and turned toward the front part of the stable to see who was coming. Finnian did not look. Whoever the newcomer was, Finnian was apparently expecting him.

It was Brother Lochlánn, a fellow novitiate, a few years younger than Louis but one who had been at the monastery at Glendalough much longer. Louis knew little about the boy and cared even less. He was a surly sort, always grumbling about his superiors and lording it over the younger and weaker boys. Louis had never given Lochlánn much thought, but he understood that the young man came from wealth and had been sent to the monastery against his will, no doubt by parents eager to be rid of him, which Louis could understand.

Surprising as it was to see Brother Lochlánn there, it was more surprising still to see that he held two swords in his hand, each sheathed in its own scabbard. He held them awkwardly, as if he felt he was doing something he knew he should not be doing.

"Ah, Brother Lochlánn, there you are!" Finnian said. He stepped over and took the swords from the boy's hands. "Brother Louis, Brother Lochlánn here thinks he is more fit to be a man-at-arms than a priest, isn't that right, Brother Lochlánn?"

The young novitiate shrugged and did not say anything. His expression, however, strongly suggested that he thought Finnian a fool and Louis a fool and likely the rest of the known world a fool.

"Brother Lochlánn," Finnian continued, "has been telling some of the other novitiates who will listen that monks and priests and such are weaklings and cowards. He has proved his own manhood by thrashing some of the younger boys."

Finnian handed one of the swords to Louis, who took it with some reluctance.

"Brother Lochlánn is very brave with those younger than him," Finnian continued, "and since he fancies himself a bold warrior I thought perhaps you might let him take a few passes at you. To show his prowess against one closer in age and size to himself."

Louis drew the sword from the scabbard. He gave no thought to doing so, his arm seemed to move of its own accord, and there was the long straight blade gleaming dull in the twilight of the stable. It was not the finest weapon Louis had held, not by far, but it was decent, and he relished the sensation of holding the sword, at once so familiar and yet so long denied. He felt a thrill run through him, like the first time he ran his hand over Failend's smooth skin.

"Will you?" Finnian said, interrupting the reverie. "Will you let Brother Lochlánn take a pass or two at you?"

Louis looked up at Finnian. "Why do you think I know the use of such a weapon?" he asked.

Finnian shrugged. "I had a notion you might." He handed the other sword to Lochlánn, who took it less willingly that Louis had. "Go ahead," Finnian said, "draw the blade."

Brother Lochlánn glared at Finnian and then glared at Louis. "If I wound him or kill him I'll be brought before the law," he said grudgingly.

"What," Finnian said, "are you afraid of the law? Or…are you afraid of Brother Louis?"

"Afraid of…" Lochlánn spluttered. "No, I am not afraid of that…" His voice trailed off.

"That what?" Louis asked, but Lochlánn just glared at him with an expression equal parts contempt and anger.

"Very well," Louis said, stepping away from Finnian and swinging his sword idly left and right to warm the muscles of his arm. "I give you my word as a gentleman you will not be brought before the law for any grievous injury you do me."

He understood now exactly what Father Finnian was after and he knew very well how to deliver it. He had doled out such lessons many times before, to arrogant young bucks all puffed up with themselves who had come to join his men-at-arms.

"Go on," Finnian said, looking at Lochlánn and gesturing toward Louis, who now had fighting room around him. Lochlánn pulled his sword and tossed the scabbard aside. He held the sword in a way that told Louis quite a bit. The young man was not entirely unfamiliar with weapons – he had had some training – but neither was he very well practiced in swordplay.

A little knowledge, dangerous, dangerous, Louis thought, and as he did Lochlánn took a wild lunge. It was too awkward to warrant much of a response, so Louis flicked his blade sideways and knocked the attack out of line and then stepped aside so the stumbling Lochlánn did not fall into him. As the young man staggered past, Louis gave him a firm whack on the backside with the flat of his sword.

Lochlánn straightened and turned and his face was red with anger.

"Don't get angry," Louis said. "You'll lose every time."

Lochlánn made a growling sound and advanced, more cautiously this time. Louis extended his sword and Lochlánn began to parry it, but then made a quick circle around Louis's blade, a move he no doubt thought was very clever, and lunged again. Once again Louis carelessly knocked the blade aside, stepped in and hit Lochlánn even harder on the backside, stepping clear as Lochlánn tried to counterstroke.

"You Frankish whore's son," Lochlánn growled and Louis shook his head.

"What did I tell you?" Louis said. "Don't get mad." The boy was hopeless. Louis lowered his sword so the point was resting on the ground and gave Lochlánn his most arrogant smirk, one that was certain to send the young man into paroxysms of fury, which it did.

He came at Louis one more time. Subtlety had not worked with the last pass, so this time he tried brute strength, swinging hard with the sword. Louis held his own blade up and let the steel take the force of Lochlánn's blow. He felt the impact in his hand – Lochlánn was not a small boy, nor was he weak – but he managed to check the blow as if Lochlánn's sword had struck a wall.

They held one another's blades, just for an instant, than Louis twisted his wrist and brought the flat of his sword down hard on Lochlánn's hand. Lochlánn shouted in pain and dropped his sword. Louis stepped in once again and once again hit the young man hard on the rump, then grabbed his arm, spun him around and kicked him in that same place which sent him sprawling to the ground.

"Hmmm," Finnian said, looking down at Lochlánn, who had turned over and was glaring up at the two of them. "I am happy you did not harm Brother Louis. Now run along and please think twice before you treat any of the other boys like they're your slaves to be beaten and ordered about."

Lochlánn scowled at Finnian and then at Louis. He looked as if he was going to say something but thought better of it, scrambled to his feet and made his way from the stable as quickly as his last bit of dignity would allow.

"Thank you, Brother," Finnian said to Louis. He bent over and retrieved Lochlánn's sword. "I fear young Brother Lochlánn will not learn all he should from that lesson, but it's a start."

"He might," Louis said. "He might not. I've seen plenty of his sort. Some turn out well. No doubt he'll be one." He tried and failed to put some conviction in his voice.

"We must pray for him," Finnian said with considerable more sincerity on his tone.

More prayer, Louis thought. *Compline, vespers, mass, all we do is pray, I haven't the energy for one more.*

"Are you still in need of me?" Louis asked, and by that he meant, *have I not paid off my debt to you for saving me?*

"Yes, there is more we need to discuss," Finnian said in a tone that suggested this nonsense with Brother Lochlánn was but a prelude, that the real business was about to begin.

Finnian gathered the swords, sheathed them and tucked them under his arm. "Please, Brother Louis," he said, "come with me." He made his way out of the stable with Louis following dutifully behind.

This day has not been dull, Louis thought, *and that at least is something.*

Chapter Ten

I love not the gloomy waters
Which flow past my dwelling
Annals of Ulster, 846

Louis was reluctant to leave the stable and subject his dry robe to the driving rain, but he followed Finnian without question. The distance they walked was blessedly short, short enough to avoid another soaking, and ten minutes later Louis found himself and Finnian seated in the abbot's house, in the abbot's room, in fact, the one in which he conducted his private business.

They were alone; the abbot was not there. What right Finnian had to make use of the abbot's chamber Louis did not know, but the priest had led him there and offered him a seat as if it was the most natural thing in the world, as if he were inviting Louis into his own home.

Father Finnian was a mystery to Louis, and this incident in the stable with Brother Lochlánn made him even more so. He and Finnian were no more than passing acquaintances; how had Finnian know he would be able to handle Lochlánn as he had? If Lochlánn had bested him it would have sent the wrong message entirely, but Finnian did not seem to have been concerned about that possibility.

Most of the monks and priests with whom Louis lived in Glendalough seemed of a sort, the sort he was accustomed to when it came to priests and monks. More humble and less worldly than those he knew in Frankia, but still of a sort. They went to vigil and lauds, sext, vespers and compline, they tended their fields and brewed their ale and baked their coarse bread. They lived the life that Louis imagined a monk or priest would live. But not Father Finnian.

Sometimes Finnian was at Glendalough and sometimes he was not. Sometimes he was gone for a day or two and sometimes for weeks. He was open and friendly and gregarious, and for that reason it took Louis some time to realize that the man never revealed a thing about himself. It was intriguing, but Louis knew better than to ask. It would be hopelessly rude to do so, and pointless as well.

"Better?" Finnian asked. He had added peat to the embers burning in the abbot's small hearth and now the fire was blazing once again. The heat was delicious, almost painful, and that put Louis in mind of Failend's nails digging into his shoulders, and he felt himself flush with embarrassment.

I am becoming a monk, I swear to the Lord I am, he thought. There was a time when he would have shown off those lacerations to his fellow horse soldiers with pride, as if they had been had on the field of battle.

"Yes, that is very nice, *merci beaucoups,*" Louis said.

"*Vous êtes les bienvenus,*" Finnian replied. He stepped over to a small table against the wall, took two glasses of surprisingly nice crystal and poured wine from the abbot's bottle. He handed a glass to Louis, took the other, and sat in the straight-backed chair facing him.

Louis took a sip of the wine. Like the crystal, it was surprisingly good. He glanced around the room. It was part of a small stone-built structure with a beamed ceiling supporting a roof of thatch. The floor was covered in muddy rushes. The muted late afternoon light and the rain made the thick glass in the windows look as if it was painted gray on the outside. This was the private home of the abbot of one of the most important monasteries in Ireland. Louis smiled to himself.

Upon learning of his exile, and resigning himself to the fact that he could not avoid it but could only hope to make it as short as possible, Louis had found comfort in knowing that he was going to Glendalough, a place he had heard of often, a seat of learning and a hub of Christian civilization in Ireland. He had imagined a soaring cathedral there, a sprawling town that surrounded it, and the many pleasing things that he would find that would help ease the misery of his condition.

He had been surprised when he finally set eyes on the place, and not pleasantly so.

Ireland, he found, was not Frankia. Louis de Roumois's life had been lived in the great halls and castles and magnificent cathedrals that dotted his home like some natural part of the landscape. He was accustomed to high domed ceilings and intricately inlaid mosaic floors and stained glass windows that shone with the glory of God.

He was used to the homes of counts and dukes that sprawled over acres of cleared land and towns that boasted of taverns and shops and all manner of civilization.

He had found none of that on his arrival in Ireland, stepping off the wide-beamed trading ship on which he had taken passage and onto the dubious wharf of the sorry fishing village where they had made landfall.

But this is not Glendalough, he thought, looking around in disgust. *Glendalough will be something much finer than this.* And it was. Glendalough was certainly a finer place than the fishing village. But it was not Paris or Rouen. Indeed, compared to those great cities of Frankia it might as well have been the fishing village. Riding down the muddy main road of Glendalough for the first time, he wanted to either laugh or cry. At first he had laughed. That morning, standing naked in the alley, he had finally been driven to tears.

"You like the wine?" Finnian asked, a polite means of pulling Louis from his reverie.

"Ah, yes, thank you," Louis said, taking another sip. "Surprisingly good," he added, realizing as the words left his mouth that they might be taken as an insult. He glanced at Finnian, but as usual the man showed no reaction.

How is it you get to dole out the abbot's wine? he thought. Perhaps if he could get enough of it into his stomach it would give him the courage to ask.

"It is not as fine as what you have in Roumois, I think," Finnian said.

"Few things here are," Louis said. His words sounded more bitter than he had intended, but again Finnian did not react, only looked into the flames and took another sip of wine.

"Father..." Louis began and then stopped as he realized he had no idea what he was going to say.

"Yes, Brother Louis?"

"Are you...do you wonder...at how you found me?" Finnian still had not mentioned Louis's having been walking stark naked toward the abbey in the driving rain. Now the priest just shrugged as if it was a matter of indifference to him.

"Do you..." Louis stammered on, "are you hoping to hear my confession?"

"Hoping?" Finnian asked and Louis saw the flicker of a smile. "Do you wish to make a confession?"

"No," Louis said.

"Then my answer would be no as well. But let me say if you do wish to make a confession...and it might be worth considering... then I would be happy to hear it."

Louis nodded. He had, of course, made many, many confessions in his life, though it was some years since he had been willing to articulate all his sins. He had made confessions since coming to Glendalough, but grudgingly. Now he realized that if he were to voluntarily make a confession, he would want to make it to Finnian. Something about the man invited honesty.

But he did not want to make a confession.

"Thank you, Father," Louis said. "And I will seek you out when I feel the need for reconciliation." He paused again for another sip and then added, "And thank you for rescuing me as you did."

"You're welcome," Finnian said. He paused a moment before continuing. "But now...and here's my confession...it was not entirely for your own benefit that I gave you my cloak this morning. I have been looking for the chance to speak with you. And what better time than when you feel you are obligated to me?"

Louis straightened a bit and looked more directly at Finnian, wary and intrigued all at once. He realized at that moment, with an insight that startled him, that it was not the smallness of Glendalough or the dreariness of the countryside or the labor of monastic life that so ground him down. It was the sameness of the days, the invariable routine that was driving him to madness.

But here, possibly, was some new thing, and he perked up like a dog being offered a bone.

"You are aware, I am sure, of the threat the heathens pose to all of Ireland," Finnian continued. "They have plundered our coasts for a generation now. And they strike farther and farther inland."

"I am aware," Louis said. "The heathens are not strangers to Frankia, either. But here...in your country...the Northmen build towns and the Irish suffered them to remain. The Irish trade with them. The...rí túaithe and the rí ruirech use them to fight one another. They use the heathens to help them in sacking Christian monasteries. Which the Irish seem to do as much as the *fin gall*."

Louis had been observing these things and pondering them for months now, and the words spilled from his mouth.

Finnian nodded. "Yes, you're right. In Frankia you have your several kings and you have your great wars. Here we have many kings and many little wars. I wish it was not so, but it is. However, those are the concerns of men far greater than me. Will you hear my own petty worries?"

"Please, Father, speak," Louis said. "I didn't mean to distract with my pointless observations."

"I travel around quite a bit, as you know," Finnian said, "on the abbot's business. I hear things. And what I have heard is that the Northmen are intending to raid Glendalough. They did so before, years ago, and frankly I'm surprised they have not come back before now. But I hear…from people I trust…they will return soon, and it will be as if hell has opened up."

Louis de Roumois met Father Finnian's gaze. The young novitiate showed no expression because he had learned from Ranulf, and learned well, that it was always better to keep one's real thoughts hidden. The Northmen had never seemed like much of a threat to Glendalough. He had never really considered their coming there. But with Finnian's words he felt the thrill of pending danger like a muscle he had not exercised in some time, like some delicacy, the taste of which he had nearly forgotten.

"It will be like hell," Louis said. "Worse. We can use prayer to defend us from hell, but they will have little effect on the Northmen, I think."

"You don't think God will be our sword and shield?" Finnian asked.

"We must pray he will. And we should also pray for the use of more earthly swords and shields. But why do you tell me of these things? I have no sword, no shield. I am now just a simple and peaceful man of God."

At that Finnian actually smiled. "Yes, you are. But you have not always been, have you? Before you came here, it was you who led your father's men against the heathens who came to Roumois, was it not?"

"It was," Louis agreed. "But how do you know such things?"

"We like to know something of our novitiates here. It helps us to shepherd them onto the right path."

Louis knew he would get nothing beyond that enigmatic answer, and Father Finnian spoke again before he could even try.

"The Northmen are a grave threat to Glendalough, Brother," he said. "I've seen what they can do. You have as well. We need someone who can lead our men against them. Someone who knows this business. You."

Louis looked into the fire and did not speak. He did not allow Father Finnian to see his spirit soaring, to sense the joy pumping like blood through his veins.

He looked up, and when he spoke there was no emotion in his voice. "You wish me to lead the men? What men?"

"I think you know very well what men we have," Finnian said, and he was right. Louis had taken note of the few times the pathetic rabble had been gathered to drill with arms. It had been the most amusing thing he had seen since coming to Glendalough, but of course then it had been none of his concern.

"Yes, I do," Louis agreed. "Farmers and butchers and blacksmiths and the like. They are not men-at-arms. The Northmen will kill them all, and they will not even be out of breath when they are finished."

"Then you must teach them," Finnian said, and before Louis could protest he added, "but there are other men to be had. The rí túaithe will send their house guards, trained men. I have the trust of Ruarc mac Brain who rules at Líamhain. From him I'm sure I can get two hundred men, good men. Warriors. Ruarc will consider the defense of Glendalough to be important enough for that. Would that do?"

Louis considered that. Two hundred experienced warriors along with the handful already at Glendalough and the farmers and butchers to fill out the ranks.

"Yes," he said. "With those men I can fight the Northmen, as long as their numbers are not too great."

"Good," Finnian said. "Then I will speak with the abbot and make the arrangements. And I'll be off to speak with Ruarc mac Brain. We'll call up your farmers and butchers and you can begin to train them in earnest."

"It will be my pleasure," Louis said and he meant it. In the past few hours he had gone from deepest misery to the greatest happiness he had felt since arriving at Glendalough.

"Oh, one other thing," Finnian said. His attempt to make his words sound like an afterthought fell short, and Louis felt himself stiffen, waiting for what might come.

"The thing of it is," Finnian said, "neither I nor the abbot have the authority to actually put you in command. We can and will insist that you be given leave to direct the defenses of the monastery, and I have no doubt in the world our wishes will be respected. But nominal command must stay with the one who holds that office."

Louis was about to ask who the one in nominal command might be - the obvious question - but before he did, the answer came to him.

Colman mac Breandan.

"Actually, Father," Louis said, "that might be a bigger problem than you think."

Chapter Eleven

I have traveled on the sea-god's steed
a long and turbulent wave-path
Egil's Saga

On the day after Kevin mac Lugaed left Vík-ló, the sun came out and Kjartan Longtooth and his men were gone.

It was first light when Harald brought the news to Thorgrim. The boy, vigilant to a fault, often woke before dawn to patrol around and see how things lay. Thorgrim approved. He used to do the same when he was Harald's age, when rising from his bed was a more effortless proposal.

"Father?" Harald said, soft enough to wake Thorgrim, not loud enough to alarm him. "Father?"

Thorgrim stirred, sat up. The sleeping chamber was awash in the gray dawn, enough that he could see Harald's face without a lamp. "What is it?"

"I was down by the river…" Harald began and Thorgrim could hear the reluctance in his voice. He wanted to tell the boy to just say what he had to say, but he held his tongue.

"*Dragon* was gone from her mooring," Harald continued. "I thought maybe she had dragged it, or broken free and drifted out to sea on the tide. So I went to get Kjartan but he was gone, and his weapons as well. And Gest and the rest of Kjartan's men were gone, too."

Thorgrim flung off the fur that covered him and was on his feet in an instant, the rage that Harald feared already in full flower. "May the gods damn him, that son of a…." Thorgrim shouted and then stopped. He cocked his head and listened. Something was missing, some sound, some undercurrent of noise that had always been there and now was not.

He turned to Harald. "Has it stopped raining?"

"Yes," Harald said, confused, apparently, by Thorgrim's abrupt change of tone.

"Really?" Thorgrim asked. "Does it threaten to rain again?"

"No, father. The sky is clear. Or it seemed clear, anyway, but the sun was not yet up."

And then, as if Odin himself had opened the gates of Asgard to show it off to the world, a beam of sunlight came in through the chinks in the shutter on the eastern wall. Thorgrim stepped toward it, transfixed. It seemed more an unearthly vision than a shaft of light. He moved toward the door, faster with each step, jerked it open and stepped outside.

To the east the sun was rising from the sea, blazing right down the plank road, spewing its brilliance from a point just above the horizon right to Thorgrim's door. Steam was rising from the thatched roofs and the thousand puddles, great and small, scattered around the longphort. Thorgrim closed his eyes and felt the heat of the sun on his face, and suddenly the disappearance of Kjartan and one of the longships and fifty of the warriors from Vík-ló did not seem terribly important at all.

All around Vík-ló men and women staggered out of their homes and looked with wonder at the sky as if they had never seen such a thing as blue overhead. They looked sideways at the great blaze of fire hanging in the east like something they had only heard of in the ancient tales.

And then as their astonishment ebbed, they began to act. Clothing, bedding, furs, all manner of things that had seemed soaked through to the point where they would never be dry again were dragged out of the dark, damp recesses of the buildings and spread out in the sun. Doors were flung open and the kindly spirit of the warm breeze moved through the homes, carrying the damp and chill and despair off in its arms.

Thorgrim saw the sun and the breeze as a gift from the gods, a good omen. He could not recall the last time he had received such a sign that luck was with him, but this surely was one, and it made him happier than he had been for many months. With the coming of the sun that morning Thorgrim could only hope that it would continue, that the gods would favor him for one day at least, because this was the day that his new ship would first taste salt water.

They had been waiting for some relief from the rain. Launching a ship was a serious business, both in terms of the practical considerations of seeing her safe into the water and the spiritual concerns of assuring that she was sent off in a way that was pleasing to the gods, a way that would bring the ship and the men who sailed in her good luck. Thorgrim, indeed all Northmen, considered both to be of equal importance, and neither could be best accomplished in a blinding downpour.

They had been nearly ready to launch the ships when Kevin mac Lugaed and his men had arrived, forcing Thorgrim to postpone it once again. While the Irish were there the day was given over to feasting and further negotiations. It was not a day for blessing ships. And privately Thorgrim did not wish to launch the vessels in the presence of Irishmen and followers of the Christ god. He did not think that would bring them luck.

When the Irish took their leave at last, Thorgrim decided he could wait no longer. If the gods would not stop the deluge, then it was not for him to bide his time in hope that they would change their minds. Rain or no, he would see the ships rolled into the river where they belonged. It was the bold move, and the gods liked bold moves, and now with the gift of a warm and blinding sun they were expressing their approval.

All of Vík-ló came down to the river to see the two new longships swim for the first time. Everyone understood the importance of this moment, with the possible exception of the few Irish wives and slaves. There was an air of excitement, of anticipation, but also a sense of gravity in the gathered crowd. This was more ritual of faith than festival and it had been a long time in coming.

Dragon, Kjartan's ship, now off somewhere beyond the horizon, had been the first of the three ships they had built over the course of the winter. She was smaller than the other two, but not much smaller. She was well-built, a good looking vessel that sat well in the water. Very much the creation of Aghen, the master shipwright, who used nothing more than his eye and his years of experience to oversee her construction, shaping her as she was built.

The next ship was *Blood Hawk*, built for the command of Bersi Jorundarson. She had been given the skald's poetic name for the raven, a nod to Odin and a not so subtle request for his blessings.

The last to be completed, largest of the three, with thirty row ports per side, was Thorgrim's *Sea Hammer*, named thus to be pleasing to Thor, who could give them good weather or ill, depending on his mood. With his former ship burned to the waterline, and with it all the bad luck it carried, and the new fleet so named in honor of the gods, Thorgrim dared to indulge in a meager bit of optimism. The fine weather told him he was not a fool for doing so.

Dragon had been launched a week before in the driving rain. Now, as the sun rose higher in the east, spreading warmth and long shadows over the shipyard and the river bank, *Blood Hawk* and *Sea Hammer* would follow her in.

By the time Thorgrim reached the river, preparations were well underway. *Blood Hawk* had already been eased off the keel blocks and now rested on rollers, a series of logs of similar diameter over which she would be hauled to the water. *Sea Hammer* was being moved onto her own set of rollers, sixty men using levers and blocks and tackle to transfer that great weight. The ship was big and ungainly on land. It was not her element.

Thirty feet from where the men were working *Sea Hammer* off the blocks, a horse and an ox stood tethered to a stake. Their role was not as beasts of burden. It was far more important than that: they would serve as a sacrifice to the gods. Their blood would soak into the fresh wood of the vessels and if the sacrifice was acceptable, then Odin, Thor and Njord could be expected to look kindly on the ships' future voyaging.

Thorgrim watched without comment as his ship was eased down onto the rollers. He watched as lengths of timber were used to shore her up and keep her from tipping to one side or another. He was ready to start bellowing orders if need be, but the need did not arise. The men who crowded around *Sea Hammer* knew their business.

"They're ready to go, Thorgrim," Aghen said, stepping up to Thorgrim's side. The shipwright's tunic was smeared with tar and tallow and had little chips of wood clinging to it. There were chips of wood in his beard as well. He wore just a bit of a smile, but Thorgrim recognized it as the man's most profound expression of happiness.

Thorgrim nodded. The two of them had spent quite a bit of time in one another's' company over the past half a year, enough that they could communicate a great deal while never speaking a word. Such was the case now, and each man knew what the other thought, and that thought was, *Well done. Well done.*

Once *Sea Hammer* was safely eased down onto the rollers, Thorgrim gave the word. The horse and the ox were killed and their blood was let to run into a silver bowl. A great fire was kindled to roast their flesh. Thorgrim stepped aboard *Blood Hawk* first and then *Sea Hammer*, accompanied by Aghen and Bersi, Skidi, Harald and Starri Deathless, whom many of the men at Vík-ló had come to regard as lucky and blessed by the gods.

Bersi held the silver bowl out to Thorgrim and Thorgrim dipped a pine bough into it. He lifted the branch, dripping with the *hlaut*, the blood of the sacrificed animals, and flailed the bough fore and aft, starboard and larboard, sending showers of crimson onto the deck and the strakes, the mast steps, steering oars, stems and sternposts. He chanted prayers to the gods as he did so and the only sound that could be heard were his voice and the swish of the pine bough and the lap of the water in the river, rolling against the banks as if eager to take possession of the ships.

When he was done he shouted an order and a hundred eager hands grabbed on to the sheer strakes of the two ships and heaved them toward the water. He and Harald and Starri remained aboard *Sea Hammer*, keeping their balance with some difficulty as she made her rough, jarring way to the river, and Bersi and some of his men likewise remained aboard *Blood Hawk*.

The two vessels slid into the near-still water at almost the same moment, their bows dipping down as they dropped off the last roller, then surging up again like restless stallions. They settled and floated free on even keels and the men of Vík-ló cheered. They cheered and cheered, the shouts coming like waves from their throats. They cheered for what they had accomplished, they cheered for the end of winter's misery, they cheered for the fine vessels floating tethered to the bank, the water-steeds that would take them to sea, take them a-viking, take them to where they wished to be, which was not the squalid longphort of Vík-ló.

The ships had been launched just as the sun hit its zenith and the tide its fullest state. It was some hours after that, with the sun moving toward the west, that Thorgrim and the lead men of the longphort sat at the table in the great hall, the remains of a meal spread before them. The evening light spilled in through the western windows, lighting the room in a way no fire could.

It had been a long and tiring day, and the fine weather and the successful launch of the two ships and the considerable amount of mead and wine that had been consumed dulled the edge of fury the men felt at Kjartan's betrayal. And, in truth, his leaving was not really a betrayal at all.

He had sworn no oath to Thorgrim, and what cost had been accrued in building *Dragon* he had paid for from his own share of the plunder. His leaving in the night had only felt like a betrayal, and that was enough to make the men furious, for a time. But by the time they gathered at the end of the day to discuss what they would do next, Kjartan and his band had all but dropped from their minds.

Skidi spoke first. He was a blunt man and seemed to have no guile in him, which Thorgrim reckoned a good quality. On the other hand he made little effort to check his speech, saying what was on his mind, never caring what effect his words might have, which was not always so helpful.

"This Irishman, this Kevin, he had a lot to say, as these Irishmen will," Skidi said. "But I am not sure I believe a word of it." Heads nodded at this, all save for Thorgrim's.

"He did have a lot to say," Thorgrim agreed. Kevin had told them of the monastery at Glendalough, one of the finest, and one of the richest in Ireland. It had been plundered before, but not for some time, which meant the wealth would likely have been built up again. The Christ worshipers, Thorgrim had observed, did not care to be without their gold and silver.

This information - the monastery at Glendalough, the potential riches – was something that the Northmen already knew. But Kevin told them more than that, information that was news to them.

He told them that there was a river, or more correctly a series of rivers that would lead them from the sea nearly to Glendalough's walls. Most of the journey could be made in their longships. It might be hard work getting the vessels upstream, but the return, when they were loaded down with plunder, would be simple enough with the lift of the current.

Bersi had raised a concern then. "I've heard of these rivers," he had said. "I've heard from men who have seen them, and they say a longship cannot float on them. I hear they're deep enough for maybe half the distance to Glendalough, and then they're shallow and rocky."

Kevin had nodded as he listened to Harald's translation. "That's right, they're too shallow," Kevin said. "Or, more correctly, they are usually too shallow. You men must have noticed the prodigious rain we've had. A lot of rain, even for this country. Now, with the coming of spring, the rivers are swollen, much deeper than usual, over their banks in many places. I don't say it will be like a mill pond, but from what I understand the rivers are deep enough now for your ships. Now, but not for long."

Kevin described the all but nonexistent defenses at Glendalough, no more than a low stone wall around the monastery. He described the soldiers who were not soldiers at all, save for a handful of them. The rest were local men, farmers and blacksmiths and the like who would take up arms when called upon. He did not have to elaborate. Every man there knew how useless such men were in any sort of real battle.

The man who commanded the defenses of Glendalough, Kevin explained, was a merchant named Colman mac Breandan, who held that office because of his wealth and standing, not because of any particular skill in the military way. There was little Colman could do to stop the advance of even the four ships' crews that the men of Vík-ló could send. With Kevin's own men joining in on the assault there would be no way for Colman or anyone else to prevent the thorough looting of the monastery and the town.

And then came the most tempting bait of all. In three weeks' time Glendalough would play host to the biggest gathering in all that part of Ireland. The Glendalough Fair. Farmers and craftsmen and merchants from all over the south country and from as far away as Frisia and Frankia would descend like flocks of birds to their summer homes. Wealthy men looking to buy, thieves and whores looking to enrich themselves, players and musicians looking for silver, they would all be coming to Glendalough.

The Northmen, Kevin had assured them, would find not just the plunder to be had in the monastery and the town, which was considerable, but all that which the fair would bring. It was not an opportunity to be missed.

"This chance that Kevin brings us," Thorgrim said to the assembled men, "we can all agree it's worth the effort and the risk, if it's everything that Kevin says."

Again heads nodded. "Do you believe him?" Bersi asked.

Thorgrim began to reply, then hesitated a moment as he considered the truth of his response. "Yes, I do," he said at last. "I believe what he says about this fair in Glendalough. I've heard rumors of it from others. I believe the defenses are weak. The monastery is far from the sea, and though they've been raided before they will still think such an attack less likely. Be less prepared. For that matter, the monasteries on the coast are never very well protected."

The others nodded again.

"He betrays his own people," Bersi says. "He comes to join with us in plundering his own people. He might well betray us, too."

"He might," Thorgrim agreed. "It's the way of these people. The Irish plunder one another more than we plunder them. But it's in Kevin's interest to join us, not to betray us. The raid will weaken Glendalough and make him stronger in whatever cow pasture he rules. That's his thinking, anyway. And I'll wager he's right. It's how things are done here."

The men were quiet for a moment, considering all this. Kevin mac Lugaed had come to them with a very tempting opportunity, one they would be fools to pass up. If Kevin was not lying. And they had no certain way of knowing whether he was or not.

"Too much talk!" Skidi said at last, as if voicing Thorgrim's mind. "We sound like a bunch of old women, worrying about what's hiding in the shadows. We all agree there's plunder to be had at this Glendalough. Let us go there and strip the place. We'll cut down anyone who tries to stop us, and if this Kevin betrays us we'll cut him down, too."

At that the men pounded the table in agreement. And so it was decided. They would go to Glendalough.

Chapter Twelve

*In this year, moreover, Norwegian forces came from the
port of Corcach to plunder...but God did not allow them to do that.*
Annals of Ulster

T he world was new-born, like the final day of creation, or so it
felt to Louis de Roumois. The sun — the sun! — had come
blazing over the hills to the east, spreading deep shadows
where it could not reach, and where it could it brought colors that
seemed extraordinary to eyes that had for so long seen nothing but
gray and brown and dull green.

He woke that morning, even before the sun was up, with a dull
sense of anticipation. It took him some moments to recall why he
now felt so optimistic, why he enjoyed this sense of renewal in his
life. And then he remembered. Father Finnian had requested he take
up arms against the invading heathen. Louis felt the joy spread in his
gut like he had taken a deep draught of warm cider. He was smiling
as he stepped from his cell and fell in line with his fellow brethren,
marching off to the dawn prayer of invitiatory with more enthusiasm
than he had displayed in a year of monastic life.

The sun was up by the time those prayers were done and Louis
felt joy building on joy. Finnian drew him aside before he could be
whisked off to do kitchen work or work in the fields or the brewery
or whatever mundane task would have been set for him that day.
Instead they returned to the abbot's house, though this time with the
abbot present, and Finnian explained to the old cleric how Louis'
former skills would be needed for the immediate future.

The abbot listened with less interest than Louis would have
thought a man might have shown with his monastery under threat of
rape and pillage. He was also less free with his wine than Finnian had
been. In fact, he made no offer of refreshment whatsoever. The
whole discussion had the feel of a formality that Finnian was obliged

72

to observe, but it was over soon and Louis and Finnian were on their way.

The bulk of the day was taken up with discussions of logistics; how many men Louis would have at his disposal, where they would encamp, how they would be fed, how much training they might receive before they were made to go blade for blade with the heathens. Louis relished every moment of it. He was desperately eager to shed his monk's robe and don a tunic and mail and feel the weight of a sword on his hip. But he kept that to himself. There would be a time for that, and it would be soon.

One subject that was not raised was Colman mac Breandan and the role he would play in all this, though Louis felt certain it would be, and should. He waited for it, even practiced in his mind what he would say, but Finnian never mentioned the man. And that in turn made Louis suspicious.

How much does he know? Louis wondered. Quite a bit, he guessed. Father Finnian always seemed to have an almost preternatural understanding of circumstances.

Louis de Roumois returned to his cell at an early hour, just as he had every night since arriving at the monastery at Glendalough, but this time with a sense of purpose that he had not felt since the death of his father. He had no reason to think that this represented some permanent change. Once he had routed the heathens, things would most likely return to their same dreary routine. But perhaps not. Perhaps this would be the first step in a journey back to his former life, and that chance was enough to keep the ember of hope glowing.

He fell asleep quickly and slept deep, as he usually did. It was some time later, in the darkest hours of night, that he half-woke to hear what he believed was Failend's voice calling to him as the door of his cell creaked open.

"Brother Louis? Brother Louis?" He thought that was odd because she never addressed him as "Brother," except when she did it in that playful, ironic tone that he found so alluring. But there was nothing ironic in this, just his name, repeated twice, and the sharp sound of something falling.

And then Louis was fully awake and sitting up, alert as if he had been standing watch. His door was open and there was a scuffling outside, a thump of something, someone, hitting the wall, and whoever had called his name was most certainly not Failend.

He was out of bed and across the floor. The moon was full and the light coming in through the open window washed the room in a dull blue glow. Louis flung himself through the door, snatching up the walking stick he kept there and jumping out into the hall beyond.

There were two men, dark shapes in the muted light, one sprawled against the far wall, the other in a half crouch, ready. The one against the wall pushed himself off and charged at the other, swinging something as he did, shouting in outrage. He wore a monk's robe, bulky and loose-fitting.

"Brother Lochlánn?" Louis said, astonished, for he was certain from the sound of the voice that it was indeed young Lochlánn.

The novitiate did not answer, did not break stride as he swung whatever was in his hand at the other man, who jumped back clear of the blow. Lochlánn stumbled and Louis saw the glint off the blade of the dagger in the other man's hand as it caught what little moonlight spilled into the hall. The killer, the would-be killer, took a step toward Lochlánn, a practiced move, swift and sure, knife moving like a snake. Louis stepped up and brought the walking stick down on the man's wrist.

The stranger shouted in pain, called out a single word, but he did not drop the knife. Instead his kicked Lochlánn, sent him reeling again and came at Louis. He came on fast, left arm out, knife held down and ready, but a man with a knife, even a trained man, was no match for Louis de Roumois with a staff.

Louis jabbed at the man, who seemed no more than a dark shape against the whitewashed wall. The man dodged sideways as Louis knew he would and Louis brought the staff around in a sweeping arc that caught the man on the side of the head and sent him staggering.

He was still recovering from the blow when Louis stepped in and drove the butt of the staff into the man's stomach. He heard the breath go out of him. The next blow – Louis could see it as if it had already happened - would put the man down. He shifted the staff so he could swing it like an ax, but before he could move, the door behind the man flew open and the corpulent Brother Fearghus, who occupied that cell, stepped out.

"What, by God, is happening here?" he shouted. More doors opened down the length of the hall.

"Brother, get out of the damned way!" Louis shouted, and Fearghus might have been offended if Louis had not forgotten himself and shouted in Frankish.

"What?" Brother Fearghus asked and then the man with the knife grabbed him by his tonsured hair and his nightshirt and shoved him into Louis.

Fearghus slammed into him and he stumbled back. "Damn you!" Louis shouted, to whom he did not know. He pushed the monk aside and brought the staff up, ready to strike a blow or fend one off, but the man was gone. Louis could see nothing but his vague dark shape fleeing down the hall and the shadowy forms of the other monks peering from their cells.

Louis relaxed. It was over. Pointless to chase after the stranger who had already disappeared into the night. He turned to Lochlánn, who had regained his footing.

"Are you hurt?" he asked.

"No..." Lochlánn said. He sounded a bit stunned and Louis wondered if he had taken a blow to the head.

Another dark shape materialized in front of them. Brother Gilla Patraic, eldest of the monks, the man charged with keeping order in the dormitory.

"What is happening here?" he demanded. Age had not diminished the edge of authority in his voice.

"A robber, it seems," Louis said before anyone else could speak. "Looking for silver or such, I would think. Brother Lochlánn heard him, came out and nearly captured him. Brave, very bravely done."

That sent a murmur through the gathering men. Lochlánn, the focus of this praise, seemed disinclined to dispute Louis' account, as Louis guessed he would be. And so after a little more discussion and speculation as to whether the robber might return (it was decided he would not) and whether men should be posted as watchmen through the night (it was deemed unnecessary) the brothers returned to their cells to get what sleep they could before they were called to invitiatory once again.

"Brother Lochlánn, hold a moment," Louis said in a low voice when the rest had begun to disperse. There was considerably more to this than a simple robbery, that was clear. The fellow with the knife had said one word, just one. Louis had hardly noticed. It was only on thinking about it after the man had fled that he realized the word was "bastard," not a surprising thing to yell in those circumstances. Except he had not said "bastard". He had said "*bâtard.*" He had cursed in Frankish.

Louis looked up and down the hall. They were alone, he and Lochlánn, so he jerked his head toward his cell. Lochlánn hesitated, scowled, and then grudgingly went in. Louis followed him and closed the door.

"What happened? What was that about?" Louis asked. The moonlight shone into the room and he could see Lochlánn quite well. Some people would not sleep in moonlight, sure it would lead to madness. But Louis thought that was nonsense. He had always liked moonlight. Never more than at that moment as it revealed Lochlánn's shrug and his surly expression.

"I don't know," Lochlánn said. "I heard a noise in the hall. I came out and that man was at your door. I thought it was you and I wondered what you were about. I called your name but he turned on me. I picked up a candlestick to fight him."

Louis nodded. The candlesticks, arranged along the hall, were three feet of iron bar with legs splayed at the bottom, formidable weapons. But something in Lochlánn's tale was not right.

"You were asleep? And you heard him?"

"Yes."

"And you took the time to tie the cord around your robe?"

Lochlánn looked down at the cord knotted around his waist. He looked up again, his expression defensive, but he said nothing.

Louis leaned down and grabbed the hem of Lochlánn's robe and pulled it up before Lochlánn could react. Where one might have expected to see bare legs and bare feet, Brother Lochlánn sported leggings and soft leather shoes. Louis could see the embroidered hem of a tunic.

He dropped the edge of the robe and straightened. He looked into Lochlánn's defiant if imperfectly focused eyes. There was a quality about him, and a smell on his breath, that was entirely familiar to Louis.

"You've been drinking," he said. He thought of the carts rolling into Glendalough for the fair, carts filled with all sorts of things normally foreign to the monastic city. Louis smiled.

"And whoring."

"How dare you accuse me of that?" Lochlánn said, but there was little vigor in his denial. Louis waved it away.

"I'm not accusing. I'm observing." It must have required some cunning for Lochlánn to get clear of the monastery, do his business and return unseen. And he would have done so, and no one the wiser, had the killer not come for Louis in the night.

"If you tell the abbot," Lochlánn said, "I'll tell him some of the things they say you are about. See how long you remain after they hear that!"

"Ha!" Louis said. "Nothing I do will get me thrown out of here. Do you think I haven't tried? But no, I won't go to the abbot with tales of your debauchery. In truth, I'm proud of you. More mettle that I would have credited you with. You did well fighting that son of a whore in the hall as well."

"Ah...thank you," Lochlánn said. He did not seem to know if he should be taking this all as a compliment.

"But you went at him too fast, too wild. I understand you were in your cups, but a fellow must be able to fight in any condition."

"Very well..." Lochlánn stammered.

"You can't be angry, I told you that the other day. Make the other fellow angry. Don't fully commit to an attack unless you are certain it will land."

"I see..."

"Look here. Come find me on the morrow when you can sneak away. You seem to have some skill in sneaking around. I'll show you a few things that will much improve your technique."

"Thank you, Brother," Lochlánn said.

They stood there for a moment and Lochlánn began to fidget.

"And I thank you, Brother Lochlánn," Louis said. "Now, good night."

"Oh...yes...good night," Lochlánn said. He turned and hurried from the cell. Louis smiled and crossed the room. He leaned out into the hall, looked left and right. Nothing moving, nothing to be seen. He closed the door.

Odd night, he thought. *And the day will be odder still.*

Chapter Thirteen

All men are heroes at home;
Though you have but two goats and your best room's rope-thatched,
Still it's better than begging.
Hávamál

The ships of Thorgrim's fleet, *Fox* and *Blood Hawk* and *Sea Hammer*, with a couple hundred warriors aboard, were underway two days after the chief men had decided to join with Kevin on the raid on Glendalough. It was another two days after that that they spotted Kjartan's ship, *Dragon*.

They had sailed from Vík-ló and made their way down the coast to the mouth of the River Avoca, which would lead them on their winding course inland to Glendalough, or as close as they could get with their shallow draft vessels. The winds were light and fluky, and though they were able to sail part of the time, most of the voyage was accomplished with oars and grumbling.

They were still three miles from the river mouth when Starri rose from his usual spot aft and climbed up the shrouds to the masthead. He settled himself there, his legs wrapped around the heavy rigging, looking as comfortable as a man standing in a mead hall. He scanned the horizon and Thorgrim waited to hear what he had to say, but he said nothing, so Thorgrim turned his eyes back to the approaching shore.

It was ten minutes after that that Starri called down from aloft.

"Night Wolf!" he said, his voice loud but calm.

"Yes?"

"I see smoke. Not a great deal. A few trails of it."

Thorgrim turned to Agnarr, who was at the tiller. "There's a fishing village at the mouth of the river," Agnarr said. "Just some pathetic little dung hill. Might be cooking fires, or a smith, maybe."

"Very well," Thorgrim said. "We'll know soon enough." He looked astern. The others ships were following in line like carts rolling down a road.

"There," Agnarr said. "There is the mouth of the river."

Thorgrim nodded. He could see it now, the low cut in the coastline. He could see the ragged boundary in the sea where the fresh water and the silt it carried from the land met the cold, salty ocean.

The shoreline grew closer with each steady pull of the oars and the mouth of the river opened like welcoming arms. The northern bank and the village Agnarr had described were still hidden from view. Agnarr pushed the tiller over a bit and *Sea Hammer* swung her bow away from the land.

"Mud banks are shifty here," Agnarr said. "Looks like we're at about a half tide. I'll steer for the center of the river, safer that way."

Thorgrim nodded. "Starri!" he called out and when Starri, still clinging to the masthead, acknowledged the hail Thorgrim said, "Keep a sharp eye out for mud banks and the like. I would just as soon not go aground."

Starri waved to indicate he understood and Thorgrim turned his eyes back to the land. What had earlier appeared to be an unbroken stretch of shoreline was now opening up to reveal the mouth of a wide river with muddy banks north and south and green meadows and bursts of trees rolling away inland.

"You men who are not rowing, get your armor on and take up your shields," Thorgrim ordered. He could still see only part way up the river; whatever might be lurking around the bend was hidden from view. He was not going to be caught with leggings around his ankles.

Fore and aft men shrugged into mail or leather shirts, settled helmets on their heads. Harald, standing near the bow, buckled his sword belt around his mail. From the belt hung Oak Cleaver, the lovely Frankish blade that had been worn by Harald's grandfather, Ornolf the Restless.

Segan, Thorgrim's slave, appeared at his side holding Thorgrim's mail and helmet and Iron-tooth. Segan had spent a good deal of the voyage heaving over the rail, first to windward until he had been shown, none to gently, that leeward was the preferred side for puking. But he was looking much better now as *Sea Hammer* stood into the calm, inshore water.

Thorgrim donned his mail and Segan buckled the belt around him. "Starri," Thorgrim called out, keeping his voice as low as he could, "do you see anything up river? Any ships?"

There was a pause as Starri swept the shore, "Yes, Night Wolf!" he said, then paused again and added, "Perhaps. Perhaps a ship, perhaps a tree…."

They were closing fast now, the oars biting deep into the calm, in-shore water, the motion of the ship settling out until it was nothing but forward momentum. Thorgrim glanced aloft to see that Starri was not daydreaming, but the man seemed to be straining to see what awaited them ashore.

"Night Wolf!" Starri called again. "A ship, to be certain! I can see the masthead. Not moving…anchored or tied up I would think!"

Thorgrim nodded. One ship. If it was indeed only one ship it was no threat to them.

Agnarr steered for the wide center of the river, the place where the keel was least likely to find the mud, and the northern shore seemed to peel back like a hide coming off a fresh kill. Thorgrim could see the mast of the ship now, the light-colored wood of a pine tree, stripped of its bark, shaped and oiled.

"I see no other ships than the one," Starri called down. "She's tied to some sort of dock." He paused, and when he spoke again Thorgrim could hear the edge of excitement in his voice. "Night Wolf!" he called, louder now. "By the gods, it's Kjartan's ship! It's *Dragon*!"

Starri was right. Thorgrim could see that.

Agnarr pushed the tiller over and *Sea Hammer* turned more westerly, lining up with the mouth of the river, and as he did the edge of the village came into view, the first of the thatched huts, a wharf made up of weathered pilings and rough-hewn boards. They were still a hundred or so perches away, but he could see that the ship tied to the wharf was indeed *Dragon*.

There were men aboard the ship, the full complement of her crew, or so it seemed from a distance. Shields were mounted on the river side of the ship. No one seemed to be making ready for a fight.

"Put us alongside *Dragon*," Thorgrim said to Agnarr, and Agnarr nodded and pushed the tiller over just a bit. Thorgrim turned to the men amidships, dressed in mail and bearing weapons and shields.

"We'll go alongside Kjartan's ship," he called. "Stand ready for what might come. We'll greet them with handshakes or crossed swords, whichever they wish." He saw heads nodding, hands refreshing their grips on swords and battle axes.

More houses were visible now, squat and round with conical thatched roofs. They could see a few pigs and goats moving slowly around deserted yards sectioned off with wattle fences. There were no people in the village, no one that Thorgrim could see, but that was hardly a surprise with a longship tied to the wharf. The only odd thing was the animals. Villagers fleeing a raid would have brought their animals if they could. Kjartan must have hit them before they knew he was there.

The tide was flooding and it carried them into the estuary until they had land on either side, the river mouth twenty perches wide. But all eyes were on *Dragon* and Kjartan's men and the village beyond, the wispy column of smoke, the animals wandering in their desultory way. They could see doors and gates hanging open.

"I see where the smoke is coming from!" Starri called out. "A building behind the others. Burned down. Not much left that I can see. A pile of charred wood. Still smoking."

There was a haunted quality to the place, like a graveyard, and it seemed to affect all the men aboard *Sea Hammer*. They were mostly quiet as they watched the village come into view, and when they spoke they spoke in hushed tones.

Agnarr pushed the tiller over. Thorgrim called for the rowers to ease their stroke. He ran his eyes over *Dragon*. He felt the fighting madness creeping up on him. His men forward were ready as well, ready to leap over the sheer strake and come down on Kjartan's men like furies from the sea. But Kjartan's men were seated, or lolling around, not arraying themselves for a fight.

Thorgrim looked astern. Bersi's ship *Blood Hawk* was about one hundred feet behind and following them toward the shore, and behind that *Fox* was also turning in *Sea Hammer*'s wake. He looked back toward the village. With the lift of the current *Sea Hammer* was closing fast with *Dragon*.

"Give a pull and ship your oars," Thorgrim called and the men on the sea chests gave one last stroke and then slid the oars inboard with a practiced ease and laid them fore and aft. With the last bit of way on the ship Agnarr steered straight for *Dragon*'s larboard side, then pushed the tiller hard over to swing the bow away and bring the ships parallel to one another.

"Thorgrim Night Wolf!"

Thorgrim heard the familiar voice over the gap of water between the ships. Kjartan Longtooth, standing on *Dragon*'s afterdeck. He wore mail but no helmet and carried no shield. His sword was still sheathed, and the friendly tone to his words had a false sound to it. Thorgrim said nothing.

"You men!" Kjartan called to the men on *Dragon*'s deck. "Stand ready to throw those lines to our friends. Get fenders over the side, there, get ready to make Thorgrim's ship fast." Men from *Dragon*'s crew stood at their ship's bow and stern with lines in their hands, ready to throw them to the men aboard *Sea Hammer*. Others wrestled heavy fenders made of plaited rope over the side where the two ships would come together.

Thorgrim looked back at Agnarr and nodded. Agnarr pushed the tiller over, bringing *Sea Hammer* easily alongside *Dragon*. She came to a near-stop in the stream and fore and aft the ropes flew the short distance between the ships. A moment later Thorgrim's ship was tied fast to Kjartan's, as *Blood Hawk* came on to raft up to *Sea Hammer*'s larboard side.

Thorgrim ignored the business of tying the ship up, ignored Bersi's approach on the water side. He walked forward, eyes on the village, ignoring Kjartan as well, though Kjartan on *Dragon*'s deck was following him forward. Thorgrim stopped amidships where only the rope fender separated *Sea Hammer* from *Dragon*, and without breaking stride stepped aboard Kjartan's ship.

"Welcome aboard, Thorgrim, welcome aboard!" Kjartan said, speaking a bit quicker than one might naturally speak. "Good to see you again!" His voice dropped to a more conspiratorial tone and he continued. "I regret having to sneak off in the night like I did. Truth is, my men heard of this Glendalough raid and they were frantic to be at it. Never seen a ship's company so eager. I swear by the gods if I had not agreed to go with them, then and there, they would have just taken the ship on their own and no doubt have wrecked it by now. It was not until we reached the river here I convinced them to stop until you and Bersi had a chance to catch up with us."

Thorgrim nodded. Kjartan was lying, of course, and not even trying that hard to sound convincing. *Does he take me for a fool?* Thorgrim wondered. *Or does he think I'm not the worth the effort it would take to convince me?*

It didn't matter. They would get to the truth of the thing in the end.

He ran his eyes over the abandoned hovels on shore. There was nothing moving in the weird, silent village that Thorgrim could see. He turned and looked fore and aft along *Dragon*'s deck. The men of *Dragon* stared at him, a dull look in their eyes. A haunted look.

"What's going on here?" Thorgrim asked, nodding toward the village. "You and your men sacked it?"

"No, no," Kjartan said. "Someone came before us. Half a day before us, I would guess. Tore through it like a pack of wolves."

Thorgrim grunted. He turned toward *Sea Hammer*. His men were lining the side, waiting for word to come aboard *Dragon*. He could see Starri fidgeting. He knew the man was hoping for a fight with Kjartan and his crew, and he would be disappointed. There did not seem to be much fight in them.

"You men," he called to *Sea Hammer*'s company, "come with me." He pushed his way past Kjartan, crossed *Dragon*'s deck and stepped up onto the wharf. Kjartan was at his heels and he heard the rest of his men following behind. He saw *Blood Hawk* settling against *Sea Hammer*'s larboard side and then he turned his back to the river and looked toward the town.

Thorgrim turned to Kjartan. "You found no one in the village?" he asked.

"No one living," Kjartan said. "Plenty of the dead."

Thorgrim crossed the weathered boards of the wharf and stepped onto the trampled dirt of the shore, the rest following. Starri was at his side, along with Harald and Agnarr and Godi and the rest of his house guard. He looked back toward the river. Bersi and a few of his men were crossing *Dragon*'s deck toward the shore, and Skidi's *Fox* was coming alongside *Blood Hawk*. Thorgrim saw Skidi make the jump from his ship to *Blood Hawk*, coming to join the leaders ashore.

"Do you know who did this?" Thorgrim asked Kjartan.

Kjartan shook his head. "A madman. You'll see."

Thorgrim said nothing. A moment later Bersi and Skidi joined them and Thorgrim led them toward the closest house, a miserable little hut of thatch and wattle, the fence gate hanging torn from its leather hinges. As Thorgrim stepped into the yard and he could see that the door, made up of a few rough cut pine boards, was also hanging half torn off. He approached the house but he did not draw Iron-tooth. He already knew what he would find inside.

He stepped through the door and into the dim interior. It smelled of sweat and cooked meat and fish and blood. There was a body lying curled up to the right of the door. Thorgrim stepped closer and he could see it was a man, about his own age he guessed. His eyes were wide, his skin turning dark, his mouth open, a wide patch of dark blood surrounding him like a round carpet. In a darker corner of the hut he could see the white flesh of someone he assumed was the man's wife. She had been stripped naked. Thorgrim did not need a closer look.

He reached out with the toe of his shoe and touched the pool of blood, found it was not a pool at all but a stain where the blood had seeped into the dirt floor. He pushed on the man's shoulder and found his body was stiff and unyielding.

"You got here yesterday?" Thorgrim ask Kjartan. He had seen many bodies in various stages of decomposition, and he had a good idea of how they looked with the passage of time.

"Yes," Kjartan said. "Tied up about midday. Found the village as you see it."

"Come on," Thorgrim said. He led the way outside. The sun was hanging just above the mountains to the west, and dark would be on them soon. He led the men down the village's one hard-packed dirt road. The ruts of wagon wheels and the imprint of human and animal feet were visible where the soft mud had dried in the sun. They found another body fifteen feet up the road, a young man in a filthy shirt, hand clutched to his stomach, his viscera spilled on the ground, a hatchet still clutched in his hand.

The dead were strewn along the road and in the yards and the spaces between the huts. Men and boys, women, girls. Everyone, apparently, whom the raiders had found alive. Thorgrim frowned. Senseless. Such people would fetch a high price in the slave markets in Frisia. Even if there was no desire to transport them so far, it would have been little trouble to sell them in Dubh-linn or to one of the host of Irish kings. Instead they had been slaughtered.

The Northmen were silent as they walked. They found the source of the smoke, a building bigger than the rest, most likely the hall of whoever had played lord over that sorry collection of huts. The thatch had been torn down, the raiders probably looking for anything of worth hidden there.

Whether they had found anything or not it was impossible to tell, but they had set the rest of the building on fire, and now it was no more than a black and smoking ruin. It must have burned all night, and the fire was only now dying for want of fuel. Thorgrim did not doubt there were charred bodies under all that, the men who had fought back and lost or had run inside the hall seeking its illusionary safety. The perimeter of the building would have been ringed with armed men and torches put to the remaining thatch.

"Who sacked this village do you think?" Bersi asked, his eyes on the smoldering wreckage. "Norsemen?"

"Maybe," Thorgrim said, but he didn't think so. He didn't see why Norsemen would bother. What could they hope to find in such a dung heap as this? Hardly worth the effort. No, it was more likely the Irish who did it, one of those petty kings trying to get some advantage over another, trying to teach someone a lesson.

Bersi nodded. Some of the men were using their swords to lift bits of thatch or burned sections of wall, no doubt looking for something of value, but Thorgrim did not think they would find anything.

He turned away from the smoldering hall and led the men farther inland, down the dry mud road past more bodies in various stages of dismemberment. The dogs and pigs had been at some of them.

As the village began to peter out they came at last to the only stone building there, a small church, hardly bigger than Thorgrim's hall at Vík-ló. Like the huts, the church's front door was smashed and hanging on its hinges, iron rather than leather, and it had clearly taken considerable effort to hack in the big oak panels.

Thorgrim mounted the single stone step and pushed past the broken door into the church's interior. The sun had finally dipped below the distant mountains and much of the space was lost in the gloom, but Thorgrim could see it had been thoroughly sacked. The large basins in which the Christ priests held their ritual water had been knocked over and some were smashed. Carvings that had once adorned the altar space had been pulled down and likewise broken up. Pages from the books the priests used were scattered over the floor, the covers ripped away.

Pushed into the near corner of the church lay one of the priests, killed with a spear that had been left jutting from his chest, his face still frozen in a look of shock and horror. Thorgrim stepped past him, walked slowly toward the front of the church. That uneasy feeling that had being coming and going for days now was back, more pronounced than ever.

There was a dead man on the altar. Thorgrim approached slowly and he could hear the soft steps of the men behind him. Another priest. Or so Thorgrim guessed. He had been stripped and beaten and cut until he there was little of him that was not covered in blood. He had been nailed to a balk of timber, arms outstretched, the way the Christ God was always shown.

Thorgrim stopped and looked down at the remains of the man's face. *The Irish did not do this*, he thought. They might have been merciless in sacking one another's villages and ringforts, but they did not tear up holy books and they did not butcher priests. No Irishman would risk the bad luck that such a thing might bring down on their heads.

And that meant it had been done by Northmen, and not long ago. A day, perhaps. Were they moving up and down the coast, or had they gone up the river? How many were they? Were they heading for Glendalough as well, and would they join with Thorgrim's crews or would they fight them?

More game pieces to be moved around, Thorgrim thought. There was another player at the gaming table now. Thorgrim did not know who he might be, but he had a pretty good sense of the sort of man he was.

He turned to Kjartan. "You know nothing of who might have done this?" he asked.

Kjartan shook his head. "No, Night Wolf," he said. "We found this…village of the dead as you see it."

Thorgrim nodded. Two things were clear to him. One was that Kjartan was lying. The other was that Kjartan was afraid.

Chapter Fourteen

Happy is he who wins for himself
fair fame and kindly words
Hávamál

In the pre-dawn darkness, Louis de Roumois woke and joined his fellow brothers at the dawn prayer of invitiatory. When it was over, so too was Louis' vocation to the monastery, at least for as long as he could contrive it to be, which he hoped would be for the rest of his life.

Father Finnian drew him aside as he had the day before, but this time they did not go to the abbot's house. They went instead back to Louis's cell. There Finnian had laid out a tunic and mail and leggings, and a sword and belt, shield and helmet.

"There is not much time," Finnian said. "I have men watching the coast, and they will tell us when the heathens reach the river, but I don't think it will be very long."

When Finnian took his leave Louis stripped off the cord belt and robe, slipped into the leggings, pulled the tunic over his head and the mail over that. They fit tolerably well. They were of good quality. Not the sort of thing he had been accustomed to wearing as a soldier in Frankia, but good enough. And in truth he would have gladly traded in his monk's robe for a leather jerkin and a wooden spear.

He buckled the belt around his waist and adjusted the sword until it hung just right. He sighed. He was a new-made man. He felt the power surging through his veins as if he had taken a deep drink of strong liquor. He felt whole again. Reborn.

There were men to train. There were questions of logistics to which to attend. There was intelligence to gather. But first Louis had other business. Pressing business. He stepped quickly from his cell, down the hall and out the door into the sunlight, foreign and rejuvenating.

"Brother Louis?"

Louis turned. The voice had caught him by surprise, so taken was he with thoughts of the coming confrontation. He turned. Brother Lochlánn was there, though the haughty swagger that generally marked his demeanor was not.

"Brother Louis…you said I should come find you in the morning. You said you would…" His voice trailed off.

Louis sighed. Yes, he had said that. And Lochlánn had been eager enough for the morning's lesson to sneak away from whatever duties he had been assigned, no easy task. The boy would have to return to it soon or suffer for his absence.

"Very well, come with me," Louis said. He led Lochlánn toward the stables, relishing the sound and weight of the mail as he walked, the thump of the sword against his thigh. They stepped out of the bright morning sun into the twilight interior. There were a few stable boys at work, but no one who might question their presence there.

Louis drew his sword, handed it Lochlánn. He picked up a rake and held it as if it were a staff. "Go ahead," he said. "Make your attack."

Lochlánn advanced, but with little confidence. He made a few tentative pokes with the sword which Louis sidestepped with ease.

"No, really, attack me," Louis said. "Make as if to injure me. I'll give you a silver arm band if you draw blood." Louis did not actually possess a silver arm band, but he was fairly certain that would not be an issue.

Lochlánn advanced again, bolder, and Louis deflected the blade with the handle of the rake. Finally Lochlánn made his move, a fast, lunging attack. Louis knocked the blade aside, swung the rake, checking the swing when the handle was an inch from cracking Lochlánn on the side of the head.

"Good," Louis said. "Now, you see how I waited until you had committed to your attack? And how you committed while I was ready for it, and in a good position to parry and riposte?"

They worked through the move again. Louis was patient and Lochlánn was attentive and they went step by step through the attack, the defense, the counter-attack. They drilled again and again, and then Louis took the sword and handed Lochlánn the rake and they went through the scenario once more.

Louis had intended to give Lochlánn fifteen minutes of his time, no more, because he had no more to give. But when the bells tolled for breakfast, Louis realized he had lost track, that he and Lochlánn had been going at it for an hour or more.

He wiped his brow. He and the boy were both sweating profusely. "Go, now, Brother Lochlánn," Louis said. "Your breakfast awaits. If anyone gives you trouble for skipping out on your duties, tell them I had need of your service." In truth Louis did not know if his new-found status gave him the authority to excuse Lochlánn from his work, but it was worth a try.

"Very good, Brother Louis," Lochlánn said. He was smiling. Louis wasn't sure he had ever seen him smile before. "You'll train me some more, won't you? Please?"

"Yes, yes, I promise," Louis said, again not certain that he had the authority to make good on his words. Lochlánn raced off. Louis caught his breath. He considered the task he had been going off to do when Lochlánn had interrupted him.

That will wait no longer, he thought, though he could feel himself hesitating. He was not afraid to do what needed to be done, but he was afraid of the consequences, the possible end of his new status as man-at-arms and the joy it brought him, which he had enjoyed now for less than two days. He sighed, settled the sword on his hip and headed off.

He stepped from the stable and blinked in the morning sun, wiped his eyes and headed for the gate in the vallum and then the gate in the outer wall. Glendalough - not the monastery but the town around it - looked different than it had even the day before. People by the hundreds were flocking to the monastic city. Wagons loaded with goods came creaking up the steep roads to the village in the hills. Peddlers with great bundles on their backs trudged along, leaning on walking sticks for balance. Even garishly painted caravans of players, a thing Louis would never have thought he might see there, came rolling through the streets.

In the fields that surrounded the monastery's stone walls pavilions sprouted like mushrooms, and one by one merchants laid claim to the temporary stalls lashed together in the square. It was as if Glendalough had woken from a deep slumber, was stretching and springing to life.

Incredible, Louis thought, but he spared only a glance for this unprecedented bustle of activity. He walked down a road that ran at an odd angle from the monastic wall, the ground hard-packed underfoot as the mud dried in the morning sun. Soon he was past the small cluster of buildings that made up the town and was making his way through the fields beyond.

A row of tents and pavilions in the distance marked where the *ad hoc* army was making its encampment. This was what the Irish called a *dúnad*, an encampment thrown up by an army on the move. And though they were not moving much now beyond their camp fires and the field on which they were training and the trench that had been dug so they might relieve themselves, that would change soon. Louis would see that it did.

The soldiers called up for duty were arrayed around the field where they carried out drills of some description. They were the *bóaire*, the small-time farmers with a dozen or so cattle, and the *fuidir*, those who were not freemen, not entirely, but tenants of the rí túaithe or one of the Lords of Superior Testimony. Along with rent, taxes, tithing and labor, they owed their superiors a certain amount of military service. And now that debt was due.

Louis walked slowly past the grounds, watching the activity there with more than casual curiosity. Turning the farmers into men-at-arms was his duty now, and if he still held that duty in half an hour's time he would take the task up immediately.

He was not, however, much encouraged by what he saw: a motley band of a hundred or so men, unarmed and outfitted for the farm, not the battlefield. They seemed to be under the direction of a captain wearing mail and waving a sword, and they trained with all the enthusiasm of men who did not want to be where they were, being made to risk their lives for someone they did not like.

At last Louis pulled his eyes away from the spectacle, unable to endure any more of what he was seeing, forcing himself to think on his more pressing business. He looked down the length of makeshift shelters. The largest of them, an oval-shaped pavilion with banners streaming from poles mounted above its roof, was a hundred feet beyond the farthest of the soldiers' tents. Louis set his eyes on it, picked up his pace.

There were no guards at the door flap, which surprised him, but he was grateful for it. He reached the entrance and tossed the canvas aside, burst into the pavilion, one hand on the grip of his sword. A table took up most of the ground within. Its top was scattered with parchments, an ink stand, two tapers with flames dancing at their ends, a few pewter plates with remnants of bread and cheese and roast meat of some sort, a tankard, and behind the desk, Colman mac Breandan, hunched over a document.

Colman looked up as Louis came in. His face showed no expression, and that did not change at all as Louis approached. Colman said nothing. He looked down again and continued to read, as if Louis de Roumois's entrance was a minor irritant, as if Louis was some buzzing insect that had momentarily distracted him.

Louis looked off to the right. Failend was there, seated in a folding chair, a fur across her lap. The light was dim inside the pavilion but there was illumination enough to see the dark bruise on the side of Failend's face. The sight of it swirled up an ugly sediment of emotion; impotent rage, shame, disgust. Louis's first instinct was to call Colman out on her behalf, to ignore his own grievances with the man and to rectify the terrible wrong that had been done Failend, a wrong that was as much his fault as Colman's.

Their eyes met. Failend's face was as blank as Colman's but as he looked into her dark eyes Louis understood that if he fought Colman, he would not be sticking his sword in Colman's gut for her sake, but for his own. Such an act would be as thoughtless and self-serving as was his rutting with her and then leaving her to her husband's rage.

"Brother Louis," Colman drawled. He had a way of coloring those two words with just the right tinge of irony to infuriate Louis de Roumois. Louis shifted his gaze from Failend to Colman, and tried to summon the rage he had felt before the sight of Failend's damaged face had so confused his purpose. Colman was sitting straight in his chair now, as if he had finally finished with important business and could make time for this inconsequential visitor.

"Colman mac Breandan," Louis said, taking a step toward the desk, putting as much menace as he could in the advance, though Colman seemed wholly unimpressed. "It's a cowardly thing to send an assassin in the night. If you want to kill me, be a man and make your attempt face to face."

Colman leaned back and the flicker of a smile moved over his lips, an expression which, if it was intended to drive Louis even closer to complete fury, succeeded beautifully. "An assassin, you say?

An assassin came to kill you? Have you no friends at all in this world?"

Louis took another step forward, placed his hands on the table and leaned in, a move which elicited not a hint of a reaction from Colman. "You know full well an assassin came for me," Louis said. "An assassin you sent."

At that Colman actually chuckled. "If an assassin came for you he did a damned poor job," he said. "You see, Brother Louis, this is why a man like me can never trust inferiors such as...well...yourself. If I wished to kill you, I would have most certainly done so myself, and you would most certainly be dead."

"If you wish to kill me, do it face to face. I come here now to give you that chance."

"If I wished to kill you I would have done it when you were standing limp-cocked and naked in my own home," Colman said. "And perhaps I should have done. But I did not."

Louis glared at Colman and tried to think of something to say, but the logic of Colman's response stripped him of words. Of course, if Colman had wanted him dead, he could have killed him when he found him with Failend. Could have killed him quite easily, and likely suffered no consequences for doing so.

Perhaps you only decided later you wanted me dead, Louis thought, but he still possessed enough sense to see that arguing would only make him look foolish.

Louis straightened and waited for Colman to say something, but Colman, clearly enjoying the moment, allowed Louis to twist in the wind a bit longer.

"Very well," Louis said at last, "you give your word as a gentleman you did not send the killer for me?"

Colman chuckled again. "A gentleman gives his word to another gentleman, not to a cretinous little turd like you," he said. "It is enough for you that I tell you I did not send an assassin. It is, in fact, more than one of my station owes to one of yours."

Louis pressed his lips hard together. In Frankia a man of Colman's station would have been licking the boots of Louis de Roumois and asking for more. But they were not in Frankia. And he was no longer Louis de Roumois, but just Brother Louis now.

Colman let the silence hang a moment more, and then said, "You may go."

And Louis could think of nothing more to say. Once again Colman had humiliated him in every possible way. Even remembering that he had put horns on Colman could not soothe Louis' ego, because Colman did not seem to care.

Louis turned on his heel and headed for the door. He was reaching for the flap when Colman called, "Oh, yes, Brother Louis, come back here. There is business I forgot."

At that, Louis could only shake his head. Colman was summoning him back, telling him "come", as if he were a dog. Colman would not miss even the tiniest opportunity to heap indignity on him. The man was a master. But there was nothing for Louis to do but turn and stand before Colman again like an underling or a slave, and so he did just that.

"It seems," Colman said, "that Father Finnian has decided you should have some position with the men-at-arms. Why, I can't imagine, but Finnian has the abbot's ear, and the abbot has influence with the rí túaithe, so there you are."

"Yes," Louis said. "Father Finnian spoke to me. As did the abbot."

"So I see," Colman said. He waved a hand at Louis. "And I see you are already wearing your soldier outfit. We'll see if it suits you more than a monk's robe. I'm afraid it will be harder to remove when the flames of passion overtake you."

Louis said nothing. He knew better than to try and make a reply.

"Very well," Colman continued. "You saw the 'soldiers' on the field as you came here, I have no doubt. Pray go and see to their training. It's just past their breakfast so I imagine they are not yet too drunk to stand."

For a long moment Louis stood staring at Colman. And then he spoke.

"You have no difficulties with this…arrangement?"

"…With this arrangement, my lord," Colman prompted.

"My lord," Louis added with just the faintest taste of irony, which Colman ignored.

"No, I have no difficulties. Assuming you are worth the victuals you consume. Why don't you go show us if you are?"

Louis stared at him for a moment more. He, Louis de Roumois, the man who had bedded Colman mac Breandan wife, would now supersede Colman as leader of the men-at-arms because Colman was not up to the task. And Colman was not bothered by that? It made Louis very concerned indeed.

And, of course, there was the other thing. Colman said he had not sent the assassin and Louis believed him, which left unanswered the very pressing question of just who had.

Louis turned and left the pavilion.

Chapter Fifteen

You cannot know where false friends
May lurk in wait before you.
Hávamál

There was nothing more to see in the fishing village and nothing at all to plunder, so Thorgrim and his men and Kjartan and the others made their way back down the single rutted road toward the river. The sun was well down behind the mountains now, and the ridges glowed an odd red and orange. The shadows fell deep over that place of the dead and Thorgrim could sense the uneasiness in the ships' crews.

Had they been facing twice their number of living warriors they would have felt no qualms, would have gone enthusiastically into such a fight. But to move past those silent homes and the stiff and blackening corpses in the road, and knowing that the spirits of the dead were not at rest, nothing like rest, was unsettling. And that meant the men would really hate the next orders he had to give.

They reached the ships at last, *Dragon* tied starboard side to the wharf and *Sea Hammer* and *Blood Hawk* tied to her larboard side, and then *Fox.* Bersi and Skidi commanding *Fox* had had the good sense to throw out anchors up-current to relieve the tremendous pressure the four ships were putting on the sorry lash-up to which they were tied.

Good seamanship, Thorgrim thought. It was about as high a compliment as he could give a man.

The ships' crews were more than happy to get back aboard their vessels, and those men left behind to guard the ships were happy to see them. Thorgrim, still standing on the wharf and out of earshot of the men, called Bersi, Kjartan and Skidi Battleax to join him.

"It's too dark for us to move up river tonight," he said, "and we don't know enough of the current here to anchor in the stream, so we will remain tied to the wharf." The others nodded. They were not happy, he knew, but they would not argue because they understood that Thorgrim's decision was right. Thorgrim continued.

"Someone made a bloody mess of this village. Kjartan says he does not know who it was."

All eyes turned to Kjartan who seemed suddenly surprised to be the center of their attention. "That's right," he said, almost stammering. "I don't know who did this."

"Whoever did," Thorgrim said, "I don't think they are a threat to us, I don't think they are still around. But we would be fools to not be vigilant. Each ship will send ten men and we will post guards on the far side of the village in case an enemy thinks to move by night."

Even in the failing light Thorgrim could see the uncertainty on the others' faces. No one looked forward to asking men to step up for that task, to be separated from their fellows and their ship through the dark hours, with some unknown threat in front of them and the village of the dead at their backs.

Thorgrim faced another problem. He did not want to leave the ships because he feared the mischief the men might get into in his absence. He did not trust Kjartan any more now than he had at Vík-ló. Less, in truth. He saw the possibility of betrayal, or that the men's fear of the spirits could overwhelm them.

But he also did not want the men to think he was unwilling to go into that place of the dead. Luckily, he had another means to show he was not afraid of whatever might be out there.

"My son, Harald, will lead the men from *Sea Hammer*," he said, confident that not only would Harald do it, but he would be bitter if not allowed to. "Each of you pick your men, and a trusted man to lead them, and we will see them posted at any possible approach to the village."

Twenty minutes later the sentries were gathered on the wharf, and an hour after that they were positioned in a cordon around the far side of the village, looking out toward the dark countryside beyond. Thorgrim and Bersi went with them to see they were well placed. They returned to the wharf with only the light of the waning moon to guide them. Kjartan was waiting for them.

"Thorgrim, Bersi," he said. He voice had its usual confidence and swagger, but it carried a false note as well.

"Yes, Kjartan?" Thorgrim said. He was curious to see where this would lead.

"My men, as I said, were impetuous. All but forced me to leave Vík-ló when we did. I don't want you, either of you, to think I deserted you, or had any other plans but to join you in this raid." He paused, waiting for Thorgrim or Bersi to acknowledge those words, but neither man gave him the satisfaction, so he went on.

"It was always our intention, my intention, that we would join in this raid on Glendalough. Part of your army, Thorgrim. We would do so now, if that's agreeable."

Thorgrim and Bersi exchanged glances. They had not discussed this. They had not thought they would ever see Kjartan and his ship and men again. There was always an advantage in having more swords and axes if they met any real opposition, even if it did mean sharing the plunder among a greater number of men.

Bersi said nothing. He would leave the decision to Thorgrim, as Thorgrim guessed he would.

"Very well, Kjartan. I'll not ask you to give an oath, but only to give your word that you'll fight with us. And recognize that on this raid, I command."

"Yes, yes, of course. I give my word to that," Kjartan said, a little quickly.

"Very good," Thorgrim said. He shook Kjartan's hand, and Bersi did as well.

In truth, Thorgrim was happy to have Kjartan's men with him to augment his force, but that was not the only reason he agreed to let them join in the raid. He was also curious. Kjartan was a lot of bad things; greedy, dishonest, untrustworthy. But the man was not a coward. Thorgrim had fought in the shield wall with him, and he knew Kjartan was brave enough in the face of even an overwhelming enemy. And yet now he was afraid, and Thorgrim wanted to know why.

The men said their good nights and Thorgrim stepped off the wharf, across *Dragon*'s deck, and onto his ship, which, though just launched days before, was already taking on a familiar and comforting aspect. He found his sleeping place in *Sea Hammer*'s stern and laid down on the furs piled there and felt the black mood come over him like a rising tide.

The black mood. It was a senseless rage that sometimes came on him when the sun went down, and it blotted out all reasonable thought. No one could approach him. When he slept he dreamed of wolves, and sometime the dreams let him see things others could not. Sometimes he woke up in a different place from where he had gone to sleep.

Some people believed he was a shape-shifter, that when the black mood enveloped him he would take on the form of a wolf. But Thorgrim himself did not necessarily think that was true.

In Thorgrim's younger days the black mood came over him almost every night, though he found that the older he grew, the less frequently he was tormented by it. But that night it was back.

For some time he looked up at the stars, the most familiar and unchanging things in all the world, as the anger came over him. Then he shucked off the covers, stood and looked out at the moonlight on the river. He watched as the water stopped its flood, grew slack and then reversed direction, flowing out into the sea and making the ships rafted to the wharf pull and strain on the anchor lines set over the bows.

Finally, as the first hints of dawn appeared over the eastern horizon, he laid down again and let sleep wash over him. He dreamed, but he did not dream of wolves, and it seemed like only moments later that he felt someone shaking him to consciousness.

Thorgrim opened his eyes. Segan was pointing to the men who had built a fire ashore and were cooking an oatmeal porridge for breakfast. Soon after, the sentries came in from their vigil with nothing to speak of, save for a pig that had been killed with a spear-thrust, mistaken for someone sneaking through the brush. There was no talk of eating the creature; they had a pretty good idea of what the pig had been dining on.

With breakfast finished they were underway once more, each ship pulling clear until *Sea Hammer* was able to cast off from *Dragon*'s side and take the lead going up-river. The tide was still on the ebb, and the going was slow as they pulled against the stream. The green banks rolled past. In some places the river moved through wide fields that stretched away into the far distance. In other places thick woods crowded down to the shore so that the longships appeared to be rowing through a steep, green gulley.

Thorgrim watched the water's edge as his ship moved upstream. *Kevin was right about the flood, in any event*, he thought. The river was clearly higher than normal. In some places where it had jumped the banks trees came right up out of the stream like massive reeds, the current boiling around their trunks. In other places the water had completely overwhelmed the river's edge and now lapped the green meadows above.

They pulled for an hour and then Thorgrim ordered the rowers switched out and they continued on. A man was stationed up in the bow keeping a lookout forward, and Starri stayed in his hawk's perch at the mast head, but they sighted nothing of interest or alarm.

An hour or so after noon they passed by another village huddled against the river bank, less impressive even than the first. And like the first, there was a dead quality to the place, nothing moving, no one to be seen. They did not bother to stop.

The sun was once again heading for the edge of the distant mountains when Thorgrim called Agnarr aft.

"This Meeting of the Waters that Kevin spoke of, do you know how far up the river it is?" he asked.

Agnarr shook his head. "I've heard from others that there's no mistaking it, a fork where two rivers meet, but how far from the sea I don't know."

"Very well," Thorgrim said. "We had better tie up for the night. Soon it will be too dark to tell the water from the land."

A quarter mile farther they found a place where the river bank was steep and the water deep enough to bring *Sea Hammer* right against the shore. Thorgrim steered the vessel in and Starri scrambled up the bank, and soon the ship was tied fore and aft, the others astern of her. They spent the night there with sentries once again spread out in the dark, and this time they encountered nothing at all, not even a pig.

The sun rose into a cloudless sky the following morning, heralding another in an unprecedented stretch of fine weather. It made the men nervous. They figured there would be a price to pay for such a gift. The gods were not a beneficent lot.

Chapter Sixteen

A dead man south of me, a dead man to the north,
they were not the darlings of a worthless army.
The Annals of Ulster

Incredible, thought Louis de Roumois. That word had popped into his head many times over the past few days, to the point where he was no longer certain what he was thinking of when it did.

There were any number of possibilities. The weather was one. By the standards of Roumois it was nothing out of the ordinary, but by the standards of Ireland, or at least what Louis had come to think of as the standards of Ireland, it was near miraculous. For the second day the sun was out, the air was warm, the steam had stopped rising off the land and now things were dry, actually dry. Louis could not recall the last time he had felt dry. Even when it was not raining, the damp and the chill were so pervasive that everything felt wet.

The activity swirling around the upcoming Glendalough Fair was no less incredible. He had been at the monastery for more than twelve months and so had been there for the fair the year before, but he could recall none of it. He had been so stunned by his sudden reversal of fortune - from Frankish prince and commander of men to a penniless and orphaned novitiate in the course of a month, exiled to the far end of the earth - that he had been hardly aware of anything going on around him.

That was no longer the case. Now, after a long winter at the monastery, during which nothing seemed to happen, where the days ground on in their tedious routine, now he was very aware of any change in circumstance, and he was astounded by what he saw.

Incredible, too, were the men under his command. They were the most astounding collection of bumblers and half-wits and cripples that he had ever seen, more like a leper colony, he thought, than a force of fighting men.

At that particular moment he was ignoring them. His attention had been drawn to a wagon pulled by two big horses and making its way down Glendalough's main road. It was loaded with something covered by a cloth and, though it was a good quarter mile away, Louis was certain there were at least two women perched on top of whatever it carried. He had a good eye for such things.

Whores? he wondered. That would certainly be a new thing in Glendalough, a welcome thing, he thought. But they would not be the first to arrive. Lochlánn, he was certain, had already found some of their profession during his late night excursion.

The little whore-monger, he thought, but that was no pejorative in Louis' opinion.

Incredible.

He turned his attention away from the wagon and back to the men arrayed before him.

"Take up your spears!" Louis called and the hundred or so men slouching on the field raised their long, iron-tipped shafts and held them at their sides like walking sticks. Spears were the weapons he had chosen for them, spears to be used as pole arms. They would not be thrown. If this bunch threw their spears they would simply miss their enemy while disarming themselves.

In the short time he had for training, Louis knew that pole weapons were the only thing they might master well enough to be more of a danger to an enemy than to themselves. Most of the men, he was happy to see, had received some training in the past, though none as far as he could tell had ever been in an actual battle.

"Spears down!" A hundred spears went from the vertical to the horizontal.

"Step and guard!" Louis called and the men stepped forward and the butt end of their spears swung around, deflecting an imaginary blow. Several men tripped and fell. Several others struck their neighbors. One who was struck cursed and tossed his spear aside and grabbed the offending man by the neck as others rushed in to pull him off.

If you want to hurt the bastard, why did you throw your weapon away? Louis wondered. It was not a hopeful sign that the man's first impulse was to drop his spear, but Louis knew better than to say as much out loud. He did not want to put ideas in the men's heads.

An hour after leaving Colman's pavilion, Louis had taken up the work of training these men. The fellow he had seen drilling them before turned out to be a captain named Aileran, an old campaigner and a man who knew his business. Aileran had been working with the conscripts for days, and he had little enthusiasm left for teaching farmers the ways of the soldier, and so he was more than ready to hand that work over to Louis.

"These sorry bastards are useless enough on a good day," Aileran explained as he gave the men five minutes to fall to the ground and gulp air. "Last night a wine merchant got into their camp, one of these dogs that's come for the fair. Took what silver they had in exchange for the piss he called wine. Enough to get them all stinking drunk. So they're in fine shape today, I can tell you."

Aileran had walked away in disgust. Louis ordered the men to their feet. He did not introduce himself. Men such as these, he knew, would respond to a proper tone of authority, and it would keep them on edge wondering who this new man was, a man who spoke with a Frankish accent, who assumed command and expected to be obeyed.

"And thrust!" The spears came back to their original horizontal position and were driven into the bellies of imaginary heathens. Louis doubted that actual heathens would be killed by such slow and clumsy movements. He had killed many heathens himself and he knew they took more killing than that.

Beyond where the farmers were training in two long lines, about seventy men-at-arms were drilling with sword, shield and ax, the weapons of experienced warriors. It was to this company that Aileran had returned after abandoning Louis to the bóaire and fuidir. These were the real fighting men of Glendalough, the house guards of the various wealthy lords. They had been sent by command of the rí túaithe to serve at the pleasure of Colman mac Breandan, and so, by default, at the pleasure of Louis de Roumois.

Louis allowed himself a few seconds to watch their practice, the smooth interplay of shield and sword as they sparred one on one under Aileran's supervision.

The sight of those men stirred an odd mix of emotions in Louis's breast. They were warriors, his people. It did not matter that they were Irish; they were Christians like him and the bond of fighting men was stronger than that of the land from which they came. He wanted to join them, to train with them and prepare for real fighting. It had been so long since he had donned sword and mail, and while his muscles still remembered the lessons they had learned he did not feel the confidence he once had.

He found it humiliating to be drilling the buffoon farmers when there were real men-at-arms with whom to work. He knew that Father Finnian and the abbot and the rí túaithe expected him to lead these men, all of them. They were looking to him to beat back the heathen invaders. He could not do that if the farmers who made up most of his troops were completely hopeless.

But neither could he lead the men-at-arms if they did not know him and respect him.

Maybe I'll go spar with one of them, put him down in the dirt, Louis thought. That would do wonders to gain their respect.

"Brother Louis?"

Louis turned at the sound of his name. Brother Lochlánn was there but Louis did not recognize him directly. The young man had abandoned his monk's robe and now wore a tunic and mail shirt, a sword belt buckled around his waist.

"Brother Lochlánn..." Louis said, and before he could even ask the obvious question, Lochlánn answered it.

"It was Brother Gilla Patraic," Lochlánn explained. "He said you would need someone to help you. He said I was to do it." His tone was an odd mix of confusion and embarrassment. "To be honest, I think Father Finnian told Brother Gilla Patraic to do it. Brother Gilla Patraic did not seem very happy about it at all."

"That sounds like the way of things," Louis said. Two days earlier Louis would have sent Lochlánn running with a swift kick to the hind quarters, but after all that had happened he was coming to like the boy. And Lochlánn in turn seemed to have abandoned his arrogant, swaggering manner. "Did Brother Gilla Patraic provide you with the mail and weapon?"

"No, he didn't," Lochlánn said. "It's mine...I brought it with me. To the monastery. My father didn't know."

Louis nodded. The boy must come from a family of some means. That would explain the rudimentary weapons training. *Packed off to a monastary against his will,* Louis thought. He was liking the boy more and more.

"Very well," Louis said, "get these men up and back to their drills." He gave a quick jerk of his head toward the waiting men, the spear-bearing farmers who had taken advantage of Louis' distraction to stop and lean on their spears. Some had even collapsed to the ground.

Lochlánn squinted. "What, me? They don't know who I am. Why would they listen to me?"

"They'll listen," Louis said, "because you are wearing mail and a sword, and you will speak to them like you expect to be listened to. Don't hesitate, don't show any want of confidence. Speak like you were the king of all Ireland."

Lochlánn nodded. He considered what he would say and how he would say it. He turned to the soldiers in training. "You men, pray let us get back to our drills!" Not the way Louis would have phrased it, and Lochlánn's voice nearly cracked, but his tone was commanding enough that the men obeyed, though with less snap than Louis would have liked to see.

"Well done, Brother Lochlánn," Louis said in a voice low enough that only they could hear. He turned back to the farmers. "Back and guard! With the butt end, thrust!"

For another twenty minutes Louis ran the men through various drills; thrusting, blocking, forming a defensive line. The practice was aimed as much at training them to hear and obey commands without hesitation as it was to build proficiency with their weapons.

"That's good," Louis shouted when he could bear no more. "Pair off, drill some, one on one. Try not to wound one another this time!" The farmers lowered their spears and slowly organized themselves into pairs, taking their time so that they might get a respite from the training and some relief for their aching heads.

"Brother Louis, have your heard from Father Finnian at all?" Brother Lochlánn asked as they stood side by side watching the new-made soldiers take the first desultory swipes at their partners.

"No, nothing yet," Louis said. Finnian had left the day after asking Louis to take up this duty, off to Líamhain to beg more men-at-arms from Ruarc mac Brain. He had urged Louis to begin training, to not delay. At the same time he asked that Louis keep the threat of the heathens to himself. Finnian did not want to start a panic. Louis suspected that was mostly because he did not want to jeopardize the success of the Glendalough Fair.

"You know...Lochlánn," Louis said. "I wonder if we might leave off the 'Brother' when we address one another. We must act as men-at-arms now, not men of God. Not that the two cannot exist together."

"Of course they can, we are warriors for God," Lochlánn said. "But how shall I address you? Sure, I cannot call you 'Louis', your position is far too much above mine for that."

"A good question," Louis said. The boy was embracing humility and deference to rank faster than Louis would ever have hoped. "I am not sure...I am still new to your language and have not had the chance to learn the words your soldiers use. I'm not sure how I should be addressed."

But in truth Louis *was* sure. He should have been addressed as 'Lord'. His status, his real status, not that of a novitiate at Glendalough, was far above Lochlánn's, far above Finnian's or the abbot's or Colman mac Breandan or even the local rí túaithe. He was the son of a count of a Frankish kingdom and he ranked far above any of the petty pretenders to nobility in that great cow pasture called Ireland.

But he also had sense enough to not insist that his true position be recognized or acknowledged.

"What would be appropriate?" Louis asked. "I am not the leader of these men, you know, Colman mac Breandan is."

"But you are second to him, and beside, Father Finnian says you are to have the real command, and we may thank God for it. What if we called you 'Captain'? Captain Louis de Roumois?"

Louis considered that. It had the right tone; martial, authoritarian, it spoke of rank earned through experience and not simply given because of social standing.

"Very well, you may call me 'Captain Louis de Roumois.'"

Their conversation had been punctuated by the sound of spear shafts cracking against one another and the grunt of men struggling through their drills, but now a shout of outrage drowned that all out. Louis and Lochlánn turned to see one of the farmers on the ground, his right hand clamped over his left arm, blood spilling from between his fingers. The training had stopped as all eyes were on the wounded man.

Without a word, the bleeding man climbed to his feet, snatching up his fallen spear as he did, and before he was fully upright he swung the spear and hit his opposite number on the side of the head. The man went down like his bones were gone and then suddenly everyone was in motion, some swinging at others or clubbing with the butt ends of their spears, some ducking, some trying to break up the fighting men.

Louis and Lochlánn watched the melee. They did not try to interfere. The men-at-arms had also stopped drilling and now stood at a distance taking in the fun.

"There's nothing an Irishman likes more than a good fight," Lochlánn explained. "But they like fighting one another more than they like fighting the heathens."

The two of them watched for a minute more. There seemed to be no order to the brawl, no one faction against another, but rather every man trying to get his licks in. No one had impaled anyone else on a spear point, at least, and Louis took some comfort in that.

Then Louis heard one of the farmers yell, "Lord Colman!" It was not a greeting but a warning to the others. Louis turned. Colman mac Breandan had come up behind him, on horseback no less, and with the soft ground and the chaos on the field Louis had not even heard him.

One by one the fighting men left off the brawl and stood or lay where they were, huffing for breath and looking up at their mounted superior. Colman spoke, the sound of his voice more grating to Louis than the worst screeching of a rusted door hinge. "Very well done, Brother Louis. These are some real fighting men you've trained here."

Failend was behind him, mounted on a horse of her own. In the light of day the bruise on her face was painfully visible, black and purple and red. She wore no expression at all, or nearly none. Only someone who knew her well would have seen the disgust and contempt beneath the immobile mask of her face.

"I'm glad you approve," Louis said, but Colman had not missed his glance toward Failend.

"Are you surprised to see her with me, Brother Louis?" Colman asked. "I dare not let the whore out of my sight. She might hump half of Glendalough in the time it takes me to come out here and see what a failure your efforts are."

"Brother Louis is now addressed as 'Captain', Lord Colman," Lochlánn said helpfully before Louis had a chance to stop him.

"Oh, 'Captain' is it?" Colman said, amused. "Not Lord High Admiral or something more befitting your exalted place?"

"'Captain' will do," Louis said, once again trying and failing to put enough irony into the reply to annoy Colman.

"That is 'will do, my lord,'" Colman corrected. "No doubt in Frankia you too would be called 'Lord' or 'Highness' or some such," he continued. "But of course we are not in Frankia. For some unknown reason you have been exiled from your beloved land and now you are just some sorry little nothing in an Irish monastery. Pray, why is it you can't go back to Frankia?"

Louis glared at Colman, Colman returned the look with one of amusement. Louis wondered how much of his past was known to the man. Father Finnian seemed to know quite a bit. Had he shared it with Colman? Finnian had never struck Louis as a man who told tales.

But he must have told Colman something. Finnian had convinced Colman to give Louis command of the men being rallied to fight the heathens, and he would have had to offer a reason as to why that was a good idea. Louis had reasonably expected Colman to make loud and vocal objections, but so far there was nothing beyond the smirking condescension. Louis found himself at once relieved and suspicious.

"In any event, my lord," Louis said, "it is good to see you have finished with your breakfast at long last. Have you come to train with the men?"

"Train?" Colman said. "Dear God, no. I have come to tell you we have word from the coast, and that word is that the heathens have arrived at the River Avoca."

"Arrived at the river?" Louis asked.

"Some pathetic fishing village was sacked," Colman said. "Most likely by fin gall. Maybe Frankish marauders. All those godless savages from across the sea are one and the same to me."

"And they are coming up river?" Louis asked, his irritation forgotten in the light of this news.

"Yes, that is what heathens do," Colman said. "We would not concern ourselves with them otherwise. I trust your men are ready to march forth and meet them?"

Ready? Louis thought. *Two months of this training and then perhaps they would be near ready.*

"Yes, Lord Colman, they are ready," Louis said.

That claim was demonstrably nonsense and Colman chuckled. "I am pleased to hear it," he said. "We'll begin our march in two hours' time. We can cover five miles by nightfall, I should think."

You can, you fat bastard, you're on a horse, Louis thought. *What of these other poor, half-drunk whores' sons?* But he said nothing. He wanted to get these men moving. He knew that the farther from Glendalough that they checked the heathens' advance the better.

Colman ran his eyes over the sorry looking troops spread out before him. "If we're lucky," he added, "the fin gall will find themselves tripping over the corpses of these miserable creatures. Maybe that will stall them long enough for the real men-at-arms to do their work."

Chapter Seventeen

Do not be the first to kill
nor provoke into fight
the gods who answer in battle.
Gisli Sursson's Saga

The current in the river was not with them, but neither was it running hard against them, and that was something for which to be thankful.

Thorgrim Night Wolf stood at the forward end of *Sea Hammer*'s afterdeck, his eyes moving over the river bank like a hawk on a lift of air watching a field below. He took note of the reeds, half their length buried in the water, but still tall enough to reach up into the air. They stood up right now, whereas the day before they had leaned downstream, as if pointing the way back to the sea and safety. Then, the men at the oars had been fighting the current, the work hard, the progress slow.

It was different now. Thorgrim guessed that some miles behind them, past the village of the dead, the sea tide was on the rise and it was pushing water up the River Avoca, forcing the current to a standstill, river and sea like the shield walls of two armies shoving against one another. Like all good things, it would not last. In another few hours they would be fighting the current again. But for now it was a relief and it was welcome.

"We are some miles up the river now, Thorgrim," Agnarr said, breaking into Thorgrim's thoughts. "We will reach the Meeting of the Waters by nightfall, I would think. Sooner if the current remains as it is a while longer."

"Good," Thorgrim said. He did not care for this nonsense, rowing through the Irish countryside, rarely able to see beyond the banks that hemmed them in. He was eager to get on with their real purpose, the raid on Glendalough. He was anxious to see if Kevin mac Lugaed would be true to his word, or if he had betrayed them already.

The fleet had been underway soon after first light, with the river growing more narrow, the banks closing in on either side with each mile made good. There was something menacing about it. Open water meant safety, room to maneuver, but now the land was inching closer in, as if making a stealthy and silent approach. When they passed through the wooded sections it grew more hemmed in and unsettling still.

Thorgrim's eyes rarely left the banks. He was watching for watchers, looking to see if any were following their progress from shore. He was looking for riders carrying word of the Norsemen's approach off to the minor kings who ruled that part of Ireland, men who commanded real warriors, men who could organize a credible defense if they wished. But he saw nothing.

It was well past the noon hour when Starri, up aloft, spotted the smoke. Not a single, weak tendril this time, but a number of thin columns. They were rising up beyond a stand of trees, a great profusion of green in the distance that blocked the men's sight of all to the northwest.

"Not raiders, I don't think," Starri called down. "Doesn't look like a village burning. Not enough smoke there. It looks like cooking fires to me."

Cooking fires, Thorgrim thought. He had reckoned they must be nearing the Meeting of the Waters; it could not be much farther upstream. Cooking fires meant men, a host of men, and if plans were unfolding as they should, those men would be Kevin's. This was where they had arranged to meet. From here the Irish would advance by land while Thorgrim and his men continued to Glendalough in their ships.

"You men not at the oars," Thorgrim called out. "Make ready for battle. Mail, helmets, weapons." He stepped up onto the after deck and looked back in his ship's wake. *Blood Hawk*'s bow was no more than forty feet astern of *Sea Hammer*. Thorgrim held aloft a sword and helmet until Bersi saw him and waved his acknowledgement and ordered his men to arms as well.

Plans were fine, Thorgrim figured, but readiness was better, because plans rarely played out as intended.

There was a bend in the river a few hundred yards ahead. Thorgrim could see it now, and he could see the smoke that Starri had reported, thin dark lines against the blue sky. A camp, he was certain. He had seen such things often enough.

"Thorgrim!" Starri called down again. "I see another river to the west. It meets this one just as that Irishman described."

"This must be it," Agnarr said. "Meeting of the Waters."

"It would seem to be," Thorgrim agreed. "The other river, the camp." He paused to slip his arms into the mail shirt Segan held up for him, straightened, and let it fall into place. He raised his arms as Segan buckled his sword around him. "Perhaps Kevin has been speaking the truth," he added.

Once he had donned his armor Thorgrim stepped off the afterdeck and walked toward the bow, the man stationed there stepping aside as he saw the lord of Vík-ló approach. Thorgrim rested his hand on the tall stem, the leering head of Thor six feet above him. He looked forward. The river was bending a bit to the north, and as *Sea Hammer* pulled around that bend, more and more of the stretch of water beyond their starboard bow was revealed.

Meeting of the Waters, Thorgrim thought. He could see it now. Off the larboard bow was the mouth of the other river, the one that met the River Avoca at that place to form a sharp angle like three roads intersecting at a single spot. This is where they had agreed to meet up, Kevin mac Lugaed and his men, Thorgrim and his fleet, on that afternoon in Vík-ló with the rain driving down on the thatch of Thorgrim's hall. Meeting of the Waters. Kevin had assured them they would know it when they came to it. And he was right.

Thorgrim looked toward the river that joined the Avoca from the west. He could not recall the name and he didn't really care. That was not the river that would carry them to Glendalough. Thorgrim looked back over the starboard bow, toward the Avonmore, the river up which they would ascend, and he almost jumped in surprise. Here was the one thing he had not expected to see. Longships.

There were five of them, all run bow-first into the mud of the river bank. They were a couple hundred yards upstream and Thorgrim could see they were made fast with ropes running over their bows to the shore. Their masts were still stepped, yards lowered onto gallows, figureheads still in place.

Thorgrim turned and walked aft toward *Sea Hammer*'s stern. "Make ready! There are five longships tied to the shore up ahead," he called as he walked. "We'll know soon enough if they are friends or men looking for a fight."

Harald fell in behind him – there was not room enough with the sea chests in place for two men to walk side by side – and followed him aft. "Are these the men who sacked that village?" he asked.

"I would guess they are, but I can't know," Thorgrim said. He stopped by the helmsman and turned and looked forward over the bow. "Bring the ship in downstream of those others, right there," he said, pointing to a spot next to the closest of the distant longships. The vessels, run up on the bank as they were, looked to Thorgrim like horses staked out on a line.

"Yes, lord," the helmsman said and nudged the tiller aft.

"These Northmen," Harald said, pointing with his chin toward the longships, "what do they want? What brings them here?"

Thorgrim could not help but smile. His son was strong and brave and tireless, but he was not always the most clever, particularly when the tension was rising. Thorgrim hoped age and experience would cure that.

"I don't know, son," Thorgrim said. "I don't know anything more of these men than you do."

Harald nodded, then turned and looked forward in the direction in which Thorgrim and every man not on an oar was looking. The tide had turned, or perhaps they were too far up river now to feel any effect from the sea, but either way they were pulling against the current and their approach to the landing place was slow, deliberate, and closely watched by the men on shore.

Thorgrim could see them as they closed the distance. A crowd of men, too many to guess at numbers. He could see points of color that he imagined were shields on men's arms.

"Night Wolf!" Starri called. He was still at the mast head.

"Yes?"

"I can see tents, a score of tents at least, set just back from the bank. The smoke is coming from there."

Tents. A war camp, Thorgrim thought. Whoever these men were, they were prepared for some serious campaigning, ready to leave their ships if need be and advance overland.

Who are you, you miserable sons of whores? he wondered. *Is Kevin there as well? Or did you kill him and his men?*

The helmsman began to turn *Sea Hammer* to starboard, bringing her in toward the shore. He was doing a good job, playing the current, setting up higher than he normally would and letting the stream push the ship down to where he wanted her to be. Thorgrim did not feel the need to issue orders. Harald left his side and headed forward and with a few other men wrestled out two of the long walrus hide ropes they would use to tie the ship to the shore.

Starri Deathless came down the backstay hand over hand and dropped to the deck beside Thorgrim. They were closing fast with the shore. Thorgrim studied the men lining the river bank, watching them. *Do we go ashore and confront them, or pull for the middle of the river?* This was the moment in which he had to decide, though in truth he knew he had decided already.

"What think you, Starri?" Thorgrim asked.

"Those fellows ashore are gawking like farmers at some festival. They are not making ready to fight," Starri said with undisguised disappointment in his voice.

"I think you're right," Thorgrim said. What men he could see numbered about the same as his. There were a few banners flying on staffs above their heads, but the warriors were not arrayed for battle. If it was a trap, they would walk into it, but they would do so willingly, and they would show no hesitancy or fear.

Off his starboard side Thorgrim saw the other ships turning as well so that they would each come to rest downstream of *Sea Hammer*. Then he saw Godi, standing just forward of the afterdeck.

"Godi, get my banner," he said, and the big man nodded and headed forward to find it. Segan had sewed it up back in Vík-ló, and did so with surprising skill. Thorgrim had never had a banner before but he guessed he should have one now to reflect his new status. Segan had cut up some of Grimarr Giant's old tunics to make the flag, a grey wolf's head on a red swallowtail pennant.

Godi pulled the banner staff from where it was stowed on the larboard side and stepped aft, unfurling the pennant as he walked. He stood just behind Thorgrim holding the red flag aloft as *Sea Hammer*'s bow ran up into the mud and the ship came to a gentle stop. Downstream, the other ships ran up on the shore as well, their oars rising with a neat symmetry and disappearing inboard.

Under Harald's direction the men of *Sea Hammer* ran a gangplank over the bow and out to dry land. Thorgrim, of course, had no qualms about leaping into the mud in which the bow was lodged. He had done it a thousand times. But now there were strangers watching, and they had to see that he was no fisherman or half-starved merchant captain. He was the commander of these vessels, the Lord of Vík-ló, and not a man who muddied his feet going ashore.

Once things were ready Thorgrim stepped forward, the massive Godi walking behind with the banner snapping overhead. Thorgrim stepped onto the gangplank and walked down the sloping wood. Godi stepped on behind him and his great weight made the board sag and nearly toppled Thorgrim over into the mud, but happily he retained his balance.

Thorgrim reached the grassy bank and looked around. There were a hundred or more expressionless Northmen watching him, some with shields, some without, some in mail and some not. The sun was dropping lower in the west and washing the men with orange light that glinted off helmets and the bosses of shields. But no one had a weapon drawn, and that told Thorgrim that he had been right. The men on shore were not preparing for battle. Not yet, in any event.

He ran his eyes along the banners waving above their heads. Boar's heads, eagles, there were none that he recognized. And then he saw one he did. A green banner, a raven with wings spread splayed across it.

The Irishman, Kevin… Thorgrim thought. *Apparently he has found some other allies.*

Without looking, Thorgrim knew that Harald was at his side and he saw Bersi coming over the bow of *Blood Hawk*, and knew Kjartan and Skidi would join him as well. And then the crowd of men parted and Kevin was there, smiling his broad smile, his sharp-cut beard as neat as ever, his hand extended. He took Thorgrim's hand and spoke and Harald said, "Kevin says welcome and they were waiting for us. Won't you come to his tent where we can drink and eat and talk."

As Harald spoke, Thorgrim kept his eyes on Kevin and nodded as he listened. Kevin turned and they walked through the crowd of silent, watching men. Thorgrim followed, and behind him Harald and Godi and then the captains of the other ships.

The camp was laid out in a field several hundred yards wide and ringed by woods that stood like a palisade wall. The trees hid the camp from view of the countryside beyond, and Thorgrim assumed Kevin had put men in the trees looking out for anyone approaching. It was a good position.

The camp itself consisted of a few dozen tents and pavilions as Starri had reported, neatly lined up with cooking fires burning in front of several of them, the flames bright in the fading daylight. Kevin's was the largest tent, a wide, round structure, ten feet tall with scalloped edges where the roof and walls met. Thorgrim always had the impression that Kevin enjoyed his luxuries and that pavilion suggested that he did indeed. Not for the rí túaithe of Cill Mhantáin were the rigors of a military campaign.

Kevin held the flap open and Thorgrim stepped in. There were candles burning. The light was dim but sufficient to see the three men sitting on small benches on the far side of the tent. They were Northmen. The nearest was a big man, nearly as big as Godi. His hair was blond and long and done in two long braids that hung down on either side of his head. There was a wicked scar that ran from the corner of his right eye to the point where it disappeared into his yellow beard. The scowl on his face seemed settled there, the way a cart, if it is never moved, will settle itself into the earth.

The man held Thorgrim's eyes and Thorgrim held his, and neither showed any change of expression or indeed any expression at all. This man would be the leader of the other fleet, Thorgrim guessed. He had learned through long use not to judge someone until he had something on which to base his opinion. But he guessed this big bastard was the one who had brought pointless and bloody death to the pathetic folk at the fishing village, and he was having a hard time not disliking the man on sight.

Kevin was speaking again and Harald said, "Kevin says to sit, all of you, please sit." A servant brought more benches into the pavilion and Thorgrim and his men sat. Harald was at his right side, Bersi on his left, Skidi Oddson next to him. Kjartan, Thorgrim realized, was not there. Strange.

"Kevin says this is Ottar Thorolfson," Harald continued, "and he is called Ottar Bloodax and he commands the men of the longships at the river." Thorgrim nodded, his eyes once again meeting Ottar's.

"It was you who sacked the fishing village at the mouth of the river," Thorgrim said. He spoke in the Norse tongue. He was not asking a question.

"It was," Ottar said. "Better that than let them spread word of our coming."

Either you are a fool or you take me for one, Thorgrim thought. Slaughtering an entire village would not stop word that the Northmen had come from spreading. Just the opposite. But Ottar was making little effort to sound as if he believed it himself. Thorgrim had already guessed why someone would inflict such savagery on that village, and he saw now that he was right. Ottar liked it.

Kevin was the last to sit, and when he did, servants scurried around the now-crowded pavilion handing out cups of wine. When each man had a cup, the man sitting beside Kevin began to speak, and to speak in Norse, though with a decidedly Irish sound to the words.

He has his own man to translate now, Thorgrim thought. *Of course he would.* It was clear Kevin was looking beyond Vík-ló for the chance to grow wealthy off the Northmen.

"My name is Eoin, and I am blessed to be able to speak your Norse tongue," the man said. "Lord Kevin welcomes you and begs I make formal introductions. Lord Ottar, this is Thorgrim Night Wolf, who is Lord of Vík-ló."

"I thought Grimarr Knutson was lord of Vík-ló," Ottar said, his voice like a boar's grunt.

"He was," Thorgrim said. "But he thought I had done him wrong. My son, Harald," he nodded his head toward Harald, "killed him."

Ottar grunted again. That was apparently the extent of his concern for Grimarr Knutson.

Eoin continued. "My lord says we are very fortunate to have two such men as yourselves, with the warriors under your commands. He says if we move quickly on Glendalough, move together, we can gain riches and help my lord extend the reach of his kingdom. And then he looks forward to further cooperation with his friends."

Thorgrim sensed that ugly feeling rising again in his gut and he knew he had been a fool to trust the Irishman. And he knew it was too late now, that he could not pull back and still save face and keep his men together. If he tried, half of them would go off with Ottar. Northmen would follow the bold leader. They would rarely consider whether or not it was wise to do so. It was time to lock shields and advance.

"Tell Kevin," Thorgrim said, his eyes still on Ottar, "that he never said anything to me about joining with Ottar and his men. Tell him I don't care to have plans changed at the last minute." He wondered if Ottar had also been surprised by all this. The look on the man's face suggested that indeed he had.

Kevin made reply and the note in his voice caught Thorgrim's attention and he turned his eyes from Ottar to the Irishman. There was a hesitancy, a nervousness in Kevin that Thorgrim had not seen before. The man was afraid. He was playing some game here and he was losing control.

I knew there was a limit as to how far I could trust you, Thorgrim thought. *Have we reached that limit now?*

Eoin translated Kevin's reply. "My lord did not know that Ottar and his men would be at sea when he spoke with you at Vík-ló."

"That's too bad," Thorgrim said. "Because now we have a problem. Me and my men will not submit to Ottar's authority, and I don't guess he and his men will submit to ours." At that Ottar grunted his agreement. Eoin translated. Thorgrim did not bother to add that neither of them would be willing to submit to Kevin's authority. He did not have to. That was understood by all present.

Before Kevin could reply Ottar drained his cup and tossed it aside. He stood, and in doing so he towered over the others in the pavilion. "I do not care what was said and what was not. I don't care for words at all. I will go up the river and I will plunder this Glendalough and I will take what I wish. The rest of you may follow and you may pick up the scraps me and my men leave behind."

Then Thorgrim stood as well, his hand resting ostentatiously on the hilt of Iron-tooth. He could not recall the last time anyone had been foolish enough to speak to him in that manner, and he could feel the fury rising like a swift incoming tide.

"My men take no one's scraps," he said, his voice low and menacing, his eyes meeting and holding Ottar's. "Let the Irish take scraps. Let Ottar take scraps. Thorgrim Night Wolf's men will be first in all things."

"Night Pup?" Ottar sneered. "A man who would brag that his son fought his fight for him?"

Then Iron-tooth was out and Ottar's sword was out. Kevin shouted something and Eoin stammered a translation. But before either sword was raised there came the sound of men launching a wild and bloody attack on the camp, clear as the call of a wolf on a cold winter night.

Chapter Eighteen

If I were a king who reddens spears,
I would put down my enemies;
I would raise my strongholds;
my wars would be many.
                    Annals of Ulster

Either Colman mac Breandan or Father Finnian had done something clever, and Louis's guess was that it was Father Finnian.

At the mouth of the River Avoca sat a sorry little fishing village. Finnian had kept riders hunkered down there watching for approaching longships. The Northmen had come an hour before dawn, surprising the village. But the watchers were well mounted and had managed to get out ahead of the raiders. They could hear the screams of the villagers as they raced away, bringing word of the enemy to Glendalough.

Other men were stationed at some of the little villages along the Avoca and on the roads that led to Glendalough from various directions. When Kevin mac Lugaed appeared with a force of nearly one hundred men, Finnian and thus Colman knew it. As the five longships that had sacked the village by the sea moved up river, the men at Glendalough were kept informed.

On hearing they would be marching to meet the enemy, Louis gave his poor, exhausted, battered, trainees - including those who had been wounded by their comrades - one hour to rest and then one hour to cook and pack food for two days, and to gather up the most basic of necessities, primarily weapons and what passed for armor. Two hours later the men were pushed into line and marched off, walking in the wake of the house guards who led the way on horseback and left the farmers to march in their dust.

The rest of their *matériel*; the tents and kettles and spits, barrels of ale and barrels of fish and pork, would be left for carters at Glendalough to load on wagons and bring the following morning. Medicine, bandages and splints would be sent as well. If Louis had any say in these matters, and he reckoned he did, there would be men in need of those things by the end of the following day.

One thing that Louis de Roumois had assumed would remain in Glendalough was Colman mac Breandan, but he did not. Even more of a surprise, he brought Failend with him.

"Do you think it's safe, bringing a woman to a fight such as this?" Louis asked as they made ready to leave the monastic city, as he realized it was Colman's intention to bring her. It was not a real question and he did not expect a real answer.

Colman made a snorting sound. "I told you before, if I leave this whore behind she'll have half of Glendalough in her bed. She might be too tired even to hump you when you return. If you return."

Louis clenched his teeth but did not reply. He did not think he was Failend's first lover, but still, because of the part that he had played in her infidelity, he was in no position to express outrage at Colman's ugly words, or take more direct action. At least not yet. He would only be pushed so far, and he could see the limit coming.

And Failend rode with them to meet the Northmen.

They moved south, down out of the higher country, advancing through the remainder of the day and setting up the dúnad in a field just as the sun was touching the mountains to the west.

It was full dark by the time Louis was able to make his way to Colman's pavilion, which, unlike the other tents, had been stowed and brought on the march. For some minutes Colman made Louis stand fidgeting before condescending to address him.

"My riders tell me the heathens have made camp on the north shore of the river," he said. "Just above the Meeting of the Waters. About three miles from here. That traitorous whore's son Kevin mac Lugaed and five longships filled with the sheep-biting Northmen. My men couldn't get close enough to say for certain how many warriors they have. Two hundred or so? Their best guess."

Louis nodded as he listened. He noticed that Colman mac Breandan was not quite so mocking and dismissive as he had been, now that they were miles from Glendalough with a powerful enemy, one that would not be easily stopped, out there in the dark.

"Two hundred men…" Louis repeated, playing with that figure in his head. About the same number as he had under his command, but none of the heathens or Kevin's men would be farmers wielding spears like clumsy oafs. When the men-at-arms whom Father Finnian was off fetching arrived he would have warriors to match the Northmen, but until then he did not.

But he did have some advantages. He had surprise. The Northmen would put sentries around the camp but he doubted they would be sending men out into the countryside. Neither would Kevin mac Lugaed. They would not think it necessary.

"We need to know more of them…how many, exactly, how their camp is defended," Louis said, as much thinking out loud as addressing Colman. "I will go tonight. I'll bring Lochlánn. He's a smart boy, knows the country around here."

Colman looked at him for a long moment, as if trying to decide how much lead to give him. Colman may have agreed to make Louis the *de facto* leader of the troops, but he clearly did not intend to give him free rein.

"Very well," he said at last. "If you're taken I would ask you to have the good sense to die before you reveal our presence."

Louis took his leave, found an inviting patch of grass and lay down to sleep, giving instruction that he was to be woken at the change of the watch. It was less than two hours later that the guard shook him and he sat up, stiff and damp. With a grunt he stood and found Lochlánn among the sleeping men. He nudged the boy with his toe, told him to get up and come along. Lochlánn rose with no words of complaint because he was still too much asleep to speak, and mounted one of the horses for which Louis had sent.

In the weak light of the moon they rode away from camp, the sound of the river tumbling along on their right hand. Finally Lochlánn, recovered enough for words, reined his horse to a stop and said, "We are not far from Cumar an dá Uisce. Meeting of the Waters. Where Colman's riders said the heathen's camp was."

Louis nodded. Time to leave the horses and continue on foot, quiet as they could. They dismounted and tied the horses to saplings just off the road, then continued on along the cool, wet grass. The land began to slope upwards and Lochlánn pointed to the higher ground just visible in the pale light.

"They are camped just beyond there, I'll warrant," he whispered. They walked cautiously to the crest of the hill, keeping low so they would not be framed against the night sky. Once they were in a position to see, they lay down on their stomachs.

The open ground sloped down for about twenty perches and then ended in a stand of trees that looked like a solid thing in the dark. Louis could see nothing of the camp save for a few points of dull orange light where the last embers of the cooking fires were burning themselves out.

"There will be men in those trees," Louis said, his voice as soft as a breath. The Northmen would be fools to not have watchmen ringing the camp, and Louis knew they were no fools. He had no doubt the tree line was filled with men peering out in their direction. "They will see anyone approaching these last few perches," he said. "But we can get as close as this hill and not be seen."

"Yes…" Lochlánn said. He did not sound at all certain.

They left the hill and went back to their horses, then Louis led the way toward the river. They rode as close to the water as they could, then dismounted and pushed through the bracken that grew up from the bank, moving slowly so that the sound of their passing was no more than that of the wind in the trees.

They came at last to the edge of the water, then walked downstream toward the field where the Northmen and Kevin mac Lugaed had made camp. The river's edge was just a narrow strip of land and the two of them moved silently over the soft ground, sometimes wading through water that had come up over the bank, sometimes walking on soft grass or mud, sometimes stepping carefully over the smooth, wet river stones or through the scrubby wood.

Every few feet they came to a halt and listened. They could hear frogs and insects. They could hear the occasional burst of song from the camp and the lapping of the river on the shore. They could hear no sign of alarm.

Fifty feet from the edge of the camp they stopped. Downstream, hauled up on the mud, Louis could see the dim shape of one of the longships, the others presumably hauled up behind it. In his mind he was picturing approaches and the places where sentries might be posted and when the Northmen might be most alert and when they might be most drunk.

He turned to Lochlánn. "I've seen enough," he whispered. "Let's go."

It was several hours later, with the morning sun well up, when the two of them returned to camp and Louis made his way to Colman's pavilion. The sentry at the flap – Colman had sentries now - announced him, but as he had come to expect he was made to stand outside for another ten minutes before he was summoned.

Failend was at the far end of the tent, seated on a stool, looking as if she was trying to get as far from Colman as she could, which was likely the case. She looked up and met Louis's eyes, her expression like a plea for help, then looked away.

Colman was sitting at a small table with a plate of cold roast beef and oat porridge and a cup of ale in front of him. He glanced up, then turned back to the plate. He did not offer Louis a seat, did not even acknowledge him for another minute or so.

"Yes?" Colman said at last.

"I've been to look at the heathens' camp," Louis said. "It's well positioned, but if we strike fast I think we can do some real hurt to them."

Colman grunted and said nothing. Louis stood for another minute, wondering if Colman was expecting more. He was about to offer his thoughts on how an assault might be carried out when Colman spoke.

"How many men do the heathens have?" he asked.

"About two hundred," Louis said. That was the number that Colman's rider had given; Louis actually had no idea, but he did not want to give an answer that might dissuade Colman from agreeing to an attack.

"Two hundred?" Colman said, his eyes a bit wider now. "That is as many as we have, and half of our men are ignorant, clumsy bóaire. Are you that big a fool, or so hungry for glory, that you would attack in such conditions?"

Louis had anticipated this, because it was not a stupid objection. "We will not beat them, and I don't hope too. I want to hit them, fast and hard as we can, then withdraw. Let our farmers get a taste for a fight. Weaken the enemy, put them on their guard, kill as many as we are able. We know their leadership is divided between Kevin and whoever commands the heathens. Perhaps we can get them fighting amongst themselves."

With that Louis shut his mouth. He knew that in his eagerness to be at the enemy he was throwing every argument he could find at Colman, holding nothing in reserve, never a good tactic.

Colman put a piece of cold beef in his mouth and looked at Louis as he chewed, slowly and thoughtfully. He reminded Louis of nothing so much as a cow chewing its cud, but Louis knew Colman's mind was working hard. And Colman, for all his faults, was not stupid. Finally he swallowed, which was apparently the last step in his decision-making.

"Very well," he said. "The abbot and the rí túaithe say you are to have command of the men, so I would not think to interfere. You may not have my house guard. I will need them to protect my lovely bride on our way back to Glendalough while the heathens are amusing themselves tearing your lungs out. You may go now."

It was an odd dismissal, and it left Louis feeling as if he was floating. Colman was not so much giving him leave to act as abandoning him to his own devices with no direction or expectations. Because, of course, Colman expected Louis to lead the men to humiliating defeat.

He stood for a minute outside Colman's tent and watched as the camp came awake, men stoking up cooking fires and fetching buckets of water from the river. He saw Aileran, the captain of the men-at-arms, strapping his sword belt on over his mail.

"Aileran, a word with you!" he called and stepped quickly toward the man, his uncertainty swept away with that one unequivocal action. Louis was all resolve now, and his desire, like lust, to bring the fight to the heathens drove him along. He was happier than he had been at any time since the day of his father's death.

But first he had to do the one thing that was so loathed, and yet so common, in the life of a fighting man. He had to wait.

Chapter Nineteen

If I were a king who reddens spears
My wars would be many;
my words would not be false
Annals of Ulster

They would attack at dusk. That was the plan Louis de Roumois discussed with Aileran. As he spoke, Aileran just nodded, and said nothing. When he was done the Irishman grunted and said, "We'll murder the bastards, we will."

Dusk was a risk, but a tolerable one. With luck the heathens would have spent the day drinking and eating, certain, as night came on, that no enemy was coming. The fading light would make it easier to hide their approach and the sun would be more or less at their backs. The darkness that would come soon after would cover their retreat.

A night attack would have been best, of course, a surprise in the dark hours, but Louis did not think his bumbling farmers were capable of such a thing. The added difficulty of organizing and fighting in the dark was an invitation to disaster.

Ten hours after he made his plans with Aileran, Louis led his men toward the Meeting of the Waters. They took three hours to cover the distance, moving slow and quiet with scouts flung out ahead, and they approached the heathen's camp unseen as far as they could tell. Now he and Lochlánn were once again moving along the bank of the river, seventy men-at-arms and spear-bearing farmers behind them. The rest of the men from Glendalough were secreted behind the rise that he and Lochlánn had climbed in the dark hours of the morning. They were waiting for Louis and his column to get in place.

Louis held up his hand and the men behind him came to a stop and instinctively stepped toward the tree line, even though they were not yet visible from the heathens' camp. Louis could see the longships from where he stood. His view was partially obscured by the trees, but still it seemed to him there were more than the five that Colman's riders had first reported. There seemed to be more like ten ships there. He frowned, but in truth he did not think it mattered.

Louis was not looking to win a victory. He did not plan on losing many men. He wanted to launch an attack, take the heathens by surprise, kill as many as he could, and then go. In a head-on battle, shield wall to shield wall, his men would be cut down in minutes. Less than half of them even had shields.

Bear baiting. That was the only way to stop the heathens' advance. Nip at them, weaken them, make them angry. Bite them and let them bleed.

Louis stared off toward the slow-moving water of the Avoca and listened. He could hear the occasional shout or burst of laughter from the heathen camp, the sound of some heavy thing dropped to the ground. There was a breeze moving through the heavily leafed branches of the trees and that was good as it hid any sound his men might make moving through the brush. The sun was near the edge of the mountains to the west, the shadows growing long. The smell of evening was in the air.

The other half of the army, the men behind the hill under Aileran's command, would attack first. Aileran had wanted to send the spear-men in first, to fling the untrained soldiers at the enemy, send them crashing into their ranks, leading with the wicked points of their spears. Most of the spearmen would die, but they would make the enemy stagger, and then the men-at-arms would come in after, climbing over the spear-men's bodies to get at the warriors arrayed against them.

It was the way that sort of thing was generally done, but Louis had insisted they turn it around. Send the men-at-arms in first, let their courage bolster the farmers behind, who would then advance and do great execution with their iron-tipped spears. And behind the farmers, a few more men-at-arms to see the spear-men advanced when they should, and to cut down any who showed an unacceptable tendency to hesitate.

That was how Louis envisioned it playing out. He was seeing it again in his mind when he heard the battle cry cutting through the cool air, clear as if the man had been twenty feet away. Just one shout, a high, undulating yell, and then silence. Silence that lasted no longer than the time it took startled men to register what was going on and to respond in kind.

Louis felt himself stiffen and sensed those behind him do likewise, heard the soft sound of his men taking a step forward in anticipation. He held up his hand to steady them. From beyond the trees that screened them from the heathens' camp he could hear the shouting build, and with it, running, the clash of weapons snatched from where they had been set down. Panic and surprise were spreading, and he pictured Aileran leading his men-at-arms down the slope of the hill toward the line of trees and the first string of sentries positioned there.

He could hear cries in the ugly language of the Northmen, and in Irish as well, but he could not make out the words. The sentries had done their first duty, which was to alert the camp. Now, with luck, they would do their second, which was to sacrifice themselves to slow the attackers, to die under the men-at-arms' swords until the rest could grab up weapons and get into the fight.

Lochlánn was beside him, sword in hand. His face was white like a corpse in the rain, his eyes wide, the fear in them as sharp as a fresco. But all he said was, "Should we advance now, Captain?"

Louis shook his head. The timing was the thing here. The longer they waited, the more effective their attack would be, but they could not wait until Aileran's men had all been killed. He turned his head and listened. He could hear the shouts of the men, the ring of weapon on weapon, the screams of the wounded, the sounds he knew so well. He felt a thrill run through him, felt himself pulled toward it like a hound on a fox's scent, and he made a conscious effort to remain still.

And then he knew it was time to go. "Let us advance, slow. Keep behind me," Louis said. He stepped off along the riverbank, moving fast but cautiously, pushing the branches aside with the shield in his left hand. He did not want his men to be seen until he was ready for them to be seen.

It was less than a minute before he reached the place where the trees and brush yielded to the wide muddy bank and the open field where the heathens' camp was arrayed. Louis stopped there, right at the juncture of tree line and open ground. It was pandemonium before him, as he had hoped it would be. Men were shouting, running back and forth without direction. They were snatching up weapons and shields and racing off to the sound of the fight. Few wore mail – they had not expected to do battle that evening.

The ground rose gently inland from the river, enough that Louis could not see the actual fight, but there were Northmen and Irish racing in that direction and he knew it was time to take some of the pressure off Aileran and his men.

"Come on, now!" he shouted, drawing his sword and raising it above his head. "With me! Advance!" Louis felt his blood pumping. Excitement like St. Elmo's Fire danced through him as he moved forward, building in speed. The weight of his mail shirt, the jingling, chinking sound it made, the snug fit of his helmet, the delicious feel of sword hilt in hand, it all took him back to that time before the great upheaval in his life, back when he had only to drink and whore with his fellows at night and kill Northmen by day.

"With me! Advance!" he shouted again. He looked left and right. The men-at-arms were with him, just a pace behind, ready to slam into the enemy and cut them down without mercy, because mercy was not a thing the heathens understood or deserved. And Lochlánn was at his side, sword in hand, mouth open in a scream of rage, and Louis knew he would be fine now that the waiting was over and the fighting had begun. He would make a fine warrior, Lochlánn would, if he lived through the next hour.

They reached the edge of the camp where a few score men were still in the process of arming themselves, some taking the time to drop mail shirts over their heads.

"At them! At them! Kill them!" Louis shouted and the others took up the cry as he had ordered them to do. He wanted the enemy to know that they were there. He wanted them to know that now there were killers at their backs. Nothing would spread panic quicker than that.

Louis was the first into the fight. The man before him – Irish, Louis realized, he could tell by the clothes - had time only to lift his sword in defense. It was a weak defense. Louis knocked the sword aside and drove the tip of his blade into the man's stomach, felt that familiar sensation of resistance and then give and then the scream and the wrenching and twisting of the blade as the man collapsed.

By habit Louis pulled the blade free before the man could fall on it, straightened and looked around for the next to take him on. A small man, wiry and red-haired, pale eyes wide, sword and shield in his hand, came charging up. Louis stepped toward him, adjusted the grip on his sword. And then Lochlánn was there, pushing right in front of Louis, swinging wildly at the Irishman.

The Irish warrior took Lochlánn's stroke on his shield. He drew his blade back as Louis stepped up and shoved Lochlánn aside, pushing him clear just as the blade darted forward. Lochlánn stumbled and Louis drove his sword into the red-headed warrior's side, just below his arm. He felt the tip glance off bone and then keep going. The Irishman stopped and the blood erupted from his mouth and Louis pulled the sword free.

Lochlánn was laying on the ground. "Don't get in front of me, don't ever get in front of me!" Louis shouted. Lochlánn, wide eyed, nodded, and Louis figured he was safe enough on the ground, so he turned back to the fight.

The men-at-arms were fully engaged, and more and more of the Northmen were heading toward this second line of fighting. Louis could see Aileran and his men a hundred yards away. They had fought their way through the tree line and were making a bold stand on the edge of the open ground.

Louis's men had cut through the first of the disorganized enemy, but now the Irish warriors, Kevin mac Lugaed's warriors, were forming and gathering and advancing. They were making an organized attack, after a fashion, some with shields, some without, a few wearing mail.

"Men of Glendalough, with me!" Louis shouted. He lifted his sword, looked around. They were with him. He advanced on the Irish line, his men making a blunt dagger-point of warriors with himself at the tip. They were screaming when they hit the enemy, their swords, shields and battle axes in motion. The Irish stood their ground, fought back, met them sword for sword where they could. But there was a great difference between going into a battle prepared and doing so after being taken by surprise, and the stunned Irish fell under the weapons Louis's men wielded.

They fell, but not all, and those who did not stood their ground and closed the gaps in the line and fought with a determination that impressed Louis, enough that he almost regretted the mortal shock he was about to visit on them.

"Spear-men! Advance! Advance!" he shouted and now it was the farmers' turn. Louis knew that fighting brought on a kind of madness in any man but the most cowardly. Once the weapons began to clash fear was set aside, compassion and reason swept away, and each man thought only about driving his weapon into his enemy's guts. He hoped it would be thus with the bóaire, once they had seen the men-at-arms do battle. And it was.

The farmers were screaming as they charged into the fight, spears held level, passing between Louis's men-at-arms and driving into the Irish beyond. The effect was shocking and bloody. Men who a second before had been fighting sword and shield against men-at-arms were skewered by the long iron-tipped ash shafts striking fast and unseen. Men dropped, clutching their guts, others slashed wildly at the spear points. And as the Irish made their flailing defense against this new threat, the men-at-arms kept up their deadly work.

Lochlánn was on his feet again, standing shoulder to shoulder with Louis, working his sword and shield as Louis had taught him. His face was streaked with blood but his movements seemed unimpaired, so Louis figured he was in no bad way.

"At them!" Louis screamed again, making his voice as loud and manic as he could. He did not know if he had screamed in Irish or Frankish but it made no difference. The enemy were on the verge of panic, he could see that, and that last wild banshee scream had pushed them those last few inches. As Louis's men surged ahead the men before them broke and ran, dropping weapons and shields, stumbling over the dead, racing to someplace of safety.

That's it, Louis thought. That was all he wanted to do. They had hurt them, they had shown them that the sacking of Glendalough would be no easy thing, that they faced an enemy of real fighting men. He had planted doubt and recrimination.

Lochlánn was starting to chase after the running men and Louis tried to grab him but he did not have a free hand, so he shouted, "Lochlánn, stop!" and happily Lochlánn heard and stopped.

"Your horn," Louis shouted. "Now!" Lochlánn looked at him for a second with stupid incomprehension. And then the words filtered through the fog of the boy's momentary insanity and he nodded and grabbed the horn he wore hanging around his neck. He put it to his lips and blew, a long, sharp, clear note. It was the only note he could play on the thing, but it was all they needed, a call to retreat that would cut through the battle noise, that he and Aileran's men would hear equally well.

The men-at-arms formed up and stepped back, colliding with the spear-men who were still too dazed from the action to recall what was expected of them.

"You men, let us..." Louis began, turning to face the men behind, and then stopped. Ten paces behind the spear-men stood Failend. Her hair was wild, her face streaked. It might have been dirt or blood. She held a short sword in her hand and it was glistening red. One of the Irish warriors lay at her feet, writhing in death agony, and before Louis could speak Failend lifted the sword and plunged it down into the man's neck.

Mon Dieu... Louis thought and then Lochlánn was prodding him, shouting, "Captain, Captain!"

Louis turned back again. There were more of the enemy heading toward them. He had hoped to break off the fight, to find a minute or two to get his men back to the trees while their foes ran in panicked retreat, but he would not get his wish.

Heathens... Louis thought. These were not Irish but Northmen, and they carried shields and they wore mail. One of them, a great hulking mountain of a man, carried a red swallow-tail banner bearing a grey device of some sort.

"Form a line, form a line!" Louis shouted. "Spear-men to the back!" They had struck the heathens as Louis had planned, they had wounded the bear. Louis had hoped to withdraw as fast as they came.

But now he could see it would not be so simple.

Chapter Twenty

Don't say, "It's been a good day" till sundown
Hávamál

So ready was Thorgrim Night Wolf to drive his sword into Ottar Bloodax's guts that the first sounds of the attack did not even penetrate his blinding red rage. Everyone had leapt to their feet when the weapons came out, but Thorgrim ignored them. His eyes never left Ottar's and Ottar's never left his.

Ottar moved first, darting his blade in, looking for a quick wound, an open belly, a slash to the groin, something that would put Thorgrim down in the first seconds of the fight. But Thorgrim was as quick as Ottar and he swept Iron-tooth from right to left and knocked the blade aside, then stepped toward Ottar to drive his heel down on the man's knee.

The move was well placed. Ottar had extended his leg with the thrust of his sword. The force Thorgrim put behind his heel would have snapped Ottar's knee like a man twisting a leg off a roast chicken. But just as he felt the soft leather of his shoe connecting with Ottar, Harald grabbed one of his shoulders and Skidi grabbed the other and they pulled him away.

Ottar leapt back as he felt Thorgrim's foot strike. Both men bellowed in rage and made to lunge at one another, but Harald and Skidi held Thorgrim fast while Ottar's men grabbed him and held him as well, Otter flailing with his sword and shouting to be let free.

"Father!" Harald was yelling in Thorgrim's ear. "Father! Listen! There are enemies here, the camp is being attacked!" The familiar sound of Harald's voice, the note of urgency, made Thorgrim pause in his struggles. He was breathing hard, but over the sound of his own breath he could hear the swirl of confusion outside the pavilion, the sound of more and more voices taking up the alarm.

The flap of the tent flew open and one of the Irish men-at-arms was there and he shouted something to Kevin. Kevin shouted back, then grabbed his sword and shield and ran from the pavilion.

"Come on," Thorgrim said, Ottar now forgotten. He pushed through the pavilion's flap and out into the evening. Men were running in every direction, but he could see the chief of the action was up by the tree line that separated the field from the rest of the countryside. Whoever was attacking had come from there. They must have come fast, giving the sentries little time to react.

"Harald, go get the others. Bring our men up here!" Thorgrim said and Harald nodded and raced off for the ships. Thorgrim watched the swirling fight three hundred feet away. Between Kevin's lies and Ottar's insults he would just as soon see the lot of them butchered. But he could not suffer an enemy to attack Norsemen, even Ottar's Norsemen, without paying a price for it.

Skidi was at Thorgrim's side and he pointed to the distant skirmish with his drawn sword and said, "Not many of them. They're not wanting in courage, to attack this camp."

"No," Thorgrim agreed. It seemed they had launched this attack against Kevin's men and the crews of nine longships with less than one hundred warriors. Which meant either they were fools or they had some trick planned.

Ottar and his men followed Thorgrim out of Kevin's pavilion. They pushed past Thorgrim, but Ottar stopped mid-stride, half turned and glared at Thorgrim, and Thorgrim returned the evil look. They said nothing, because nothing needed saying out loud. Each man understood that this was not over.

Then Starri Deathless appeared, coming from the ships at the river bank, running ahead of the rest of Thorgrim's men. He was naturally quick, like a long-legged hare, and he was not burdened by mail or shield like the others. He nearly collided with Thorgrim, and Thorgrim pulled his eyes from Ottar as he grabbed Starri's arm.

"Wait for the rest," Thorgrim said. Starri was doing that odd jerky motion with his arms, desperate to get into the fight. Thorgrim looked behind. Harald was running up, and with him was Agnarr and the crew of *Sea Hammer* and the crews of the other ships as well, Bersi's men and Skidi's and Kjartan's.

"Make a line, make a line, we'll advance in a line!" Thorgrim shouted and the men quickly sorted themselves shoulder to shoulder.

The men in Thorgrim's fleet had come ashore prepared for trouble, armed and wearing mail. They had remained together, gathered by the ships, so they were more prepared to plunge into the fight than those who had been enjoying the comforts of camp.

"Follow me!" Thorgrim shouted, holding Iron-tooth above his head. He started forward, toward the place where a huddle of Ottar's men were surrounded by this unknown enemy and were being hacked down, and others in the camp joined the rush toward the melee. The defense was frantic and disorganized. The Irish and Norse had been caught by surprise, and now were interfering with one another as much as they were doing damage to their attackers.

Then a sound, sharp and clear, jerked Thorgrim's attention to his left. It was not a battle sound. It was a musical note. Or, more correctly, something between a scream and a musical note, the sound of a horn blown loudly but with little skill.

Thorgrim turned toward the sound. There were men massed there. Thorgrim had seen them already and thought they were Kevin's men-at-arms shying from the fight. But now he saw they were not shying away; they were locked in combat with men who must have come along the river bank.

"Oh, you clever sons of whores," Thorgrim said. That was why the attacking army had seemed so few. Half of them had come around to hit the camp from behind.

Thorgrim came to a stop. "Hold!" he shouted and heard the ragged sound of men pulling up short. He pointed his sword in the direction of this second fight.

"This way! This way! At them!" he called and charged off in this new direction. Godi was at his side now, shouting in his deep voice, the banner staff in his hands. Thorgrim moved faster, just short of a run. His anger with Kevin, his fury with Ottar, were all burned away in the familiar crucible of battle.

Starri Deathless had shown remarkable restraint, but he could show no more. He raced ahead of the others, ahead of Thorgrim, and Thorgrim knew better than to try to stop him. Starri wore only leggings and soft leather shoes and held a battle ax in each hand. He was screaming as he ran, a high-pitched keening sound, not a sound one would expect this side of the grave.

Norsemen were accustomed to the ways of berserkers, but the Irish clearly were not. The enemy's line had been standing their ground like experienced and disciplined warriors, but Thorgrim could see them start to back away from Starri's headlong, dangerous, manic rush. Starri was five feet from the line when he launched himself off the ground, axes swinging, his body airborne. Thorgrim saw a spear come up from behind the line of men, saw the dark shaft, the iron point, saw Starri come down on the weapon as he plunged into the men-at-arms.

The spear point erupted from Starri's back in a spray of blood and the man holding it died under the stroke of Starri's ax, his head split in two even before Starri fell on top of him.

No, no, Thorgrim thought as he broke into a run. Death was a part of what they did. They brought death, they were merchants of death, and they found death in return. Thorgrim never thought he would much care if any among them other than Harald was killed, himself included. But the sight of Starri impaled on the spear had moved him as he did not think he could be moved. It never occurred to him that Starri Deathless might die.

"Bastards!" Thorgrim roared as he met with the first of the men-at-arms, a young man, just a few years Harald's senior. He wore mail and carried a shield and Thorgrim lashed at him with a stroke that was meant to knock aside any resistance and bite deep into whatever it hit. Mail. Flesh. It was a death stroke, filled with power, and Thorgrim was surprised to find Iron-tooth turned aside by his opponent's deft use of his shield.

Now it was Thorgrim who had to step back and deflect a blow and then another as the young man came at him step for step. Thorgrim lunged, missed, raised his shield to take the man's counter-stroke.

But it could not go on because Thorgrim's men were fresh and nearly double the enemy's numbers. Already they were wrapping themselves around the attackers' flanks, pressing in. The Irish would have to either retreat or die where they stood, and they chose to retreat. Step for step they moved back, their pace increasing as they headed for the wood by the river's edge, fighting as they went. The young man with whom Thorgrim was exchanging blows was calling orders now, his words sounding like Irish to Thorgrim's ears, his accent something else.

Then Thorgrim saw Starri Deathless face down on the ground and he forgot about this enemy in front of him. He took two steps over and knelt by Starri's body, dropping his sword and shield as the fighting moved past him. The spear had snapped as Starri fell on it, but the ugly point jutted out of his back, just below his shoulder blade.

Thorgrim grabbed the hateful thing and jerked it up and it came free of Starri's body, its end jagged and ugly, blood soaked. Fresh blood welled up in its wake, and to Thorgrim's utter astonishment Starri gasped and moaned.

Gently, Thorgrim rolled Starri onto his back. The spear had pierced his right side, just below his shoulder, and it had made a terrible mess going in. The skin was ragged and torn, the blood coated his chest and mixed with the mud into which he had fallen. Thorgrim was accustomed to seeing Starri blood-covered at the end of a fight, but it was not usually his own blood.

He heard footsteps behind him and Harald knelt by his side. "He...he lives?" Harald asked.

"He does," Thorgrim said. They were quiet for a moment and then Thorgrim looked up. "What of the fighting?" he asked. The sound of battle was gone and he had not even been aware of its going.

"They made it to the trees," Harald said. "The Irish who attacked us. They reached the trees and disappeared into the wood and Bersi said not to follow. You were not there, and so I figured Bersi was in command."

Thorgrim nodded. "Yes, that's right. And Bersi did the right thing. In the woods they might have cut you down one man at a time."

Harald nodded. "The other half of the Irish, the ones fighting by the trees, they retreated as well."

"The horn must have been the signal," Thorgrim said. "He's a clever one, whoever is leading those Irish warriors."

At that moment Starri made a groaning noise, soft and weak. His eyes fluttered but remained closed.

"Will he live?" Harald asked. The boy had still not figured out that some things were as much a mystery to his father as they were to himself.

"I don't know," Thorgrim said. He shook his head as he looked at Starri, pale and motionless on the ground. It was so odd to see Starri not moving. Starri was never still, even when sitting quietly.

Had the spear struck just an inch to the left Starri would already be making the journey to Odin's corpse hall. But now his death, if it came, would be long and agonizing and not at all the end he had so often envisioned. And how long would it be before death overtook him? An hour? A few days? Or would he live on as a broken cripple, the worst of all fates?

No, Starri would die in battle. He would live long enough for that. Even if he had to drag himself into the fight, even if Thorgrim had to carry him, which he would, Starri would go down fighting.

Thorgrim picked up one of Starri's battle axes and set it on Starri's stomach and wrapped Starri's hand around the grip. He looked up. More of his men were gathered around, looking silently at their stricken fellow.

"Find a cloak or some such, something we can carry him on," Thorgrim ordered. "We'll bring him back to *Sea Hammer*."

Chapter Twenty-One

A coward believes he will ever live
if he keep him safe from strife
Hávamál

The sun had gone behind the western mountains. The camp was all but lost in the deep shadow, the first stars making their blinking presence known when they lay Starri down near *Sea Hammer*'s stern. Thorgrim had ordered a bed made up for him in the after end of the ship, the place where Thorgrim generally slept. They had piled up furs to make a deep and comfortable pallet and laid him down, moaning and moving his head side to side. There was not much more that they could do.

Most of the men who sailed aboard *Sea Hammer*, who had been seafaring and raiding for more than a few years, had some knowledge of the healing arts. They could set broken bones. They could stitch gashes left by sword or ax. Some could even amputate a limb with a reasonable expectation of success. They could treat the sort of injuries they most often encountered. But they could not do much beyond that.

And Starri's injuries were certainly beyond that, his body pierced clean through. They had washed the wound, washed the blood and dirt from Starri's chest. Bersi suggested that they stitch him closed but Thorgrim rejected that idea. He did not know why. He had an idea that there might be spirits that could get trapped inside Starri if they did that. But he really did not know what to do, so he laid a damp cloth over the wound and left it like that.

Once Starri had fallen asleep or lapsed into unconsciousness, Thorgrim wrapped the wounded man's fingers around the handle of his battle ax and gently lashed them in place with a soft leather thong. He had no notion of when Starri might die, but he could at least be certain he had a weapon in his hand when he did.

"Odin, all-father," Thorgrim said softly, his hand resting on Starri's hand, the one tied to the ax. "If Starri dies now, he dies of wounds he took in honorable battle. Sure there is no difference between that and being killed on the field? If he goes, I beg you will send the Valkyrie to lift him to your corpse hall. It's all he ever wanted."

He stood and looked around and wiped his eyes. He had no idea whether or not Odin paid heed to such a prayer, if the logic of his arguments carried any weight. Of course, he could not tell Odin anything the god did not already know, but he did not imagine such a plea would hurt.

Thorgrim left Starri to rest or die, whichever he would do, and climbed down the gangplank to the shore. He walked a few perches toward the camp, then stopped and looked around. There was little to see in the gathering dark. A few fires had been kindled and in the light of the flames he could see men moving around. The air was filled with the familiar sounds that marked the end of battle: moaning, the occasional cry, raucous laughter from men happy to still be alive, men who were feeling the remnants of the fighting madness and needed some release.

And there was the shrieking of the prisoners. Ottar had managed to find two of the Irish attackers wounded but still alive, and now he was making them pay for their audacity. He had ordered his men to raise tall wooden stakes and he had bound the Irishmen to them and now he was taking his time with the sorry bastards as he vented his fury. The night was filled with their screams and babbled words. Pleading, Thorgrim guessed. He could not understand what was said. There were several men in the camp who could have translated, but Thorgrim doubted that Ottar much cared what they had to say.

Thorgrim was disgusted by the entire affair. At the battle's end, Ottar had been in a blind and senseless rage, racing around the killing place, slashing at the bodies of the few dead the Irish had left behind, screaming like the madman he was. At least a dozen of his men had been killed and Ottar was apparently determined to make those two poor bastards who had lived pay for that loss.

Thorgrim Night Wolf was not shy about killing, he did not slink from brutality, but this was pointless and dishonorable. It was worse than pointless. They might have applied less agonizing treatment to the prisoners and received useful information in return. They might have found out, for instance, who it was who had launched that clever attack, and what they were planning next. If they had let one prisoner go he might have returned to his fellows and told them of what happened to the others and thus put some fear into all of them. Now they would learn nothing, achieve nothing.

Thorgrim shook his head and pushed it from his thoughts. Kevin mac Lugaed and a handful of his men were approaching, and Thorgrim knew there was some hard negotiating on the horizon.

"Harald!" Thorgrim called because he knew Harald was lurking nearby, trying to be inconspicuous. "Go find Bersi and Skidi and Kjartan and tell them to meet me here. The Irish will want to talk. And you come back, too. I don't want Kevin whatever-by-the-gods his name is to be the only one with a man who can speak both languages."

Harald nodded and rushed off. He was still fetching the others when Kevin arrived, Eoin at his side and his house guard trailing behind. Kevin spoke and Eoin translated.

"Kevin says thank you for your good service today. That was the sort of treachery we are bound to encounter. But at least we showed that we can defeat any who would come against us."

Thorgrim turned and spit on the ground. "We defeated no one," he said. "They did just what they came to do. They hurt us and they pulled back before we could hurt them." It always amused him how some men considered clever planning to be treachery when it was their enemies who were being clever.

Eoin translated. Thorgrim could not believe he was telling Kevin something he did not already know, but the man did not look pleased as he replied.

"Kevin says that he understands such an attack should not have happened. And it won't again. But he adds that this shows that there is great wealth to be had at Glendalough, that they would make such effort to stop us."

Thorgrim looked at Eoin and thought, *A poor farmer will use every means he has to protect his one miserable cow, it does not mean the thing is worth a turd.* But he was already tired of talking so he said nothing.

Before the silence could grow more uncomfortable, Harald approached with the others behind. Thorgrim turned to his son. "Tell Kevin that I called for my chief men so we might finish the business that was interrupted. Tell him I don't think Ottar is in much of a talking mood, but that's probably just as well."

Harald rendered the words in Irish. Kevin spoke and Eoin translated. It was like single combat, a battle of translators.

"Kevin says that he apologizes again that he could not alert you to Ottar's presence. He says there will be loot enough for all at the Glendalough Fair, and that Ottar and his men will make it that much easier for us to take and plunder the place. My lord hopes you will not change your mind about joining in with us."

Thorgrim was not much impressed with the assistance that Ottar and his men had rendered thus far, but again he kept his own council. Before he could speak, however, Kjartan stepped closer and said in a low voice, "Night Wolf, might we all have a word? In private?"

There was an odd note in the man's voice, much of the former arrogance stripped away. Thorgrim tried to see his face in the poor light but could see only shadows.

"Certainly," Thorgrim said. He turned to Harald. "Tell Kevin that I must have a word in private with my chief men. Tell him to wait on us a moment." Then Thorgrim, the captains of his fleet, and Harald moved off toward the water, far enough away that Eoin would not pick up their low talk.

"Thorgrim," Kjartan began, "I need not tell you Ottar is a madman. You have seen that well this night." The prisoners had stopped screaming by then, but the sound of their agony was still in every man's ears. "But I have to tell you, he is more mad, and more despised by the gods, than you can imagine."

"You've had dealings with Ottar before?" Thorgrim asked.

"He's my brother," Kjartan said. "We came together from Norway. Three years ago." And then Thorgrim recognized the odd note in Kjartan's voice. It was fear. The same fear Kjartan had shown in the village of the dead. Kjartan must have known then who had butchered all those people.

"What are you saying?" Bersi asked.

Kjartan was silent for a moment, as if summoning the resolve to speak. "I say we cannot trust him. And I don't think we can trust this Irishman, Kevin, even though he never cheated us back in Vík-ló."

Thorgrim could already see how this would play out. They had been tricked into this meeting on the river. Kevin had manipulated them into fighting in the company of another chief who was mad and unpredictable. Already the Irish of Glendalough had shown they would not be easily beaten. Any sensible man would have put back to sea and returned home.

But there were things to consider beyond being sensible. Honor was one. Thorgrim would not admit that Kevin had so easily tricked them. He could not tolerate even the suggestion that he and his men lacked the courage to join with the mad Ottar in a raid up river, or that the strength and cleverness of the Irish might make them shy away.

"So what do you suggest?" Skidi asked Kjartan in his grunting voice. "What is your council?"

Once again Kjartan was silent for a moment before he spoke. "I think the prudent thing to do is to abandon all this, to return to Vík-ló, to look for some other opportunity," he said.

This time it was the others who were silent, considering Kjartan's words. Finally Thorgrim spoke.

"You know we can't do that," he said. A statement.

"Yes, I know," Kjartan said. In the dark Thorgrim could see the others nodding.

"Then it's decided," Thorgrim said. They would press on to Glendalough. They would face head-on whatever fates the gods had in store. They would endeavor to win glory and riches or to die well, and in the end there really was nothing more for which a man who went a-viking could hope.

Chapter Twenty-Two

[T]he Norwegians were defeated, by a miracle of the Lord, and they were slaughtered.

The Annals of Ulster

They retreated into the trees and the Northmen did not follow. Backed farther away, weapons held at the ready, and still the Northmen did not follow. And when at last it was clear the Northmen were not going to follow them into the woods, that they had had enough of fighting, then Louis de Roumois led his men back to where they would meet up with Aileran and the others and make their way back to camp.

A boisterous energy was running through the men. Louis had seen it often enough, particularly at the conclusion of a successful action. He figured it was due to some imbalance of the humors, some trace of fear and excitement and madness still flowing in the blood, looking for a means to dissipate. He had felt it himself in the past and he had enjoyed it, but he did not feel it now.

As he pushed his way to the head of the line of retreating men, he grabbed Failend by the arm and pulled her along. She had moved back into the wood with the rest, had tried to make herself inconspicuous, but she was foremost in Louis's thoughts and he was not likely to forget she was there.

"What in the name of God and all that is holy are you doing here?" he hissed as they walked. "What are you thinking?"

"I was just trying to do my part, to help keep the heathens from sacking Glendalough," she protested, but her voice was as lacking in conviction as her words.

"*Merde*," Louis spat. "Are you mad?"

He glanced over at her as he pushed his way through the brush. Her hair was a mass of brown tangles. The bruise Colman had left was mostly gone but now there was a streak of blood on her face. Her leine was torn and the hem was dark with dirt and blood. She still carried her short sword in her hand, and it, too, had blood drying on the blade. There was a weird look in her eyes, one he had not seen before. She did indeed look insane.

"No, I am not mad," she insisted, despite appearances to the contrary. "Was I supposed to sit there in camp and let my bastard husband glare at me and insult me all day?"

Louis could understand why she would not care to do that, but he was too angry and, he realized, too confused to argue further. They walked on in silence, Louis parting the way through the brush, Failend following, and the rest of the surviving troops, which seemed to Louis to be most of them, making a ragged line behind.

The trees thinned and soon the walking was easier, and then they came out into the open country. The sun had just disappeared behind the mountains, the dark beginning to settle over the river valley, and Louis was happy to be out of the woods.

"This way, Captain," Lochlánn said, pointing with his sword. He had pushed ahead to catch up with Louis, feeling it his duty, apparently, to remain at his captain's side. Louis nodded and turned away from the river, Lochlánn on his right, Failend on his left and the rest behind. A few minutes later they came to the rutted and dusty road down which they had marched from their camp that afternoon. Louis called a halt, and most of the men dropped immediately to the ground, some sitting cross-legged, some lying on their backs.

Soon they could hear men coming down the road, a soft sound, much like the wind in the trees, but accented with the jingling of mail and the occasional thump of a weapon or a shield. Aileran's men. Louis did not think the Northmen would have the will to sally forth from their camp.

"You men, on your feet, form a column," Louis said in a voice just loud enough to be heard. The men stood reluctantly and fell into line on the road. "No, not that way," Louis said. "Do you want to march back toward the heathens? The other direction."

Seventy men turned around, facing in the direction from which they had come many hours before, and behind them Aileran and his men materialized out of the dark. Louis stepped forward and extended a hand. There was still light enough that Louis could see Aileran's face, weary and strained, but his expression brightened as he saw Louis approach. The older man took Louis' hand, squeezed it, then pulled Louis toward him and hugged him around the shoulders. Louis could see the other men-at-arms coming closer, smiling as well, thumping his back in approval.

"Well done, sir, well done," Aileran said, releasing Louis from his grip. Louis stepped back. The others were nodding their agreement. The farmers with the spears might not have appreciated the action to the degree they should, but the men-at-arms understood it had been well planned and had been brought off neatly and well.

Louis nodded. "And you, too. That was a goodly fight. The heathens will not be so bold now, I think. Did you lose many men?"

Aileran shook his head. "Five did not make it out. I pray to God they were killed on the battle field and not left alive. You?"

Louis realized he had not made a count of his men, a gross oversight, but he did not want to admit as much. "We lost only a few. Far fewer than the heathens and Kevin mac Lugaed lost," he said, confident that he was right about that.

"I don't think the heathens will follow this night," Aileran said. "I think they had their fill of us. And I don't think they much fancy wandering around the countryside in the dark."

Louis nodded. "I agree. My men are ready to drop from exhaustion. I propose we march a mile or so up the road and find a place to bed down. Set a guard, sleep on our weapons. March back to camp at first light."

"Yes, that would be best," Aileran said. "Is that a woman?"

The abrupt change of subject caught Louis by surprise. He turned to look in the direction Aileran was looking, though of course he knew perfectly well to whom he referred.

"Yes," Louis said, turning back to the captain of the men-at-arms. "That is Failend, wife of Colman mac Breandan. She followed our column from camp. Had a notion to see a battle, apparently."

Aileran nodded but said nothing more. He turned and ordered his men to fall in behind Louis's, and the line of weary armed men headed off. In the moonlight the road looked like an old scar across the grassy country and it was simple enough to follow. Despite the easy going men stumbled here and there as they walked. Lochlánn's toe caught a small rock and he nearly went down, and Failend kept dropping behind and then taking a few quick steps to catch up again. They had all been pushed to the point of exhaustion and beyond.

Off in the distance, a few hundred feet away, Louis could see where the open country was broken by a stand of trees, a dark towering presence in the night, a good place to which to retreat if an enemy came on them in the dark. He slowed his march and called for a halt, and the column behind him shuffled until they were still.

"We will bed down here for the night," Louis said. "Captain Aileran and I will post guards. The rest of you make your beds here. Keep your weapons handy, sleep in your mail if you have it. Any who have water, share with those who do not." He cursed himself for not anticipating this, for not bringing food. "We move again at first light," he added.

There was no comment, not a word was spoken. The men were too exhausted for that. They stumbled off toward the field and dropped here and there. Some pulled cloaks over themselves; most did not bother. Four minutes after Louis had given the order, the field was strewn with motionless bodies, as if it was his men and not the heathens who had suffered a great loss in battle.

Failend found a spot a bit away from the rest. She sat but she did not lie down. Instead she drew her knees up close to her chest and seemed to stare out into the night.

Aileran appeared out of the dark and he and Louis took a moment to discuss the placement of sentries, then Aileran went off again to see it done. Louis, now bereft of excuses, sighed and shuffled over to Failend and sat beside her.

He had not really spoken to her since Colman had caught them in their act, just a few words when he had the chance. He had managed an apology. She had accepted. She did not seem angry or disgusted with him. Indeed he had the notion that he was more angry and disgusted with himself.

"Have you come to apologize to me again?" she asked. "For humping me and then leaving me to face my husband alone?"

"No," Louis said. "Should I?"

"No," Failend said. "I suppose you've done enough of that. But I always enjoy it."

They were quiet for a moment. Louis watched as the unhappy men chosen to stand the first watch were roused from their sleep and pushed off to their posts. "What were you doing today? At the heathens' camp?" he asked.

"Killing heathens. Like you," Failend said.

"Your husband let you go? Did he know you were following us?" Louis noticed that neither of them cared to speak Coleman's name.

"I told him," Failend said. "I told him I was going to do that, to follow you to the fighting. I don't know if he believed me. And if he did I don't think he would be much grieved to see me dead. It would save him a great deal of trouble."

They were quiet again. Then Louis said, "Aren't you afraid of being killed? Aren't you afraid of your husband, or the heathens?"

For a long time Failend did not answer, as if she was genuinely considering the question. Finally she said, "Yes, I'm afraid of those things. But I'm more afraid of being bored."

That was not at all what Louis had expected, and he did not know how to reply, so he did not. They sat in silence for some time longer and then Louis stood, his muscles protesting the motion. "Good night, Failend," he said, and staggered off to a place at the fringe of the sleeping men and lay down again, flat on his back. He closed his eyes and felt the warm tide of sleep come over him. Then, as it carried him off, he was jostled, just slightly, just enough to pull him back into the waking world. Someone had laid down beside him. Failend. He realized as much in the same instant as he came awake.

"Failend?" he whispered stupidly. He felt her hands under his cloak, just the pressure of them through his mail shirt. He felt them move over his chest and down along his thighs. He heard her make a soft dove-like sound as she nestled her face into his neck.

Louis recognized what she was feeling: that dissipation of energy, the long, slow settling of the passions raised by battle. It was often manifested in a consuming sexual desire. Louis had seen it many times, had felt it himself. For the whores in the taverns along the River Seine there were few nights as lucrative as those when Louis and his mounted warriors had repelled a raid by the Northmen. But he had never seen that particular phenomenon in a woman because he had never seen a woman take part in a battle.

"Failend, this won't do," he said. He rolled onto his side, facing her, and even as he did it he knew he was lost. He could see her face in the moon's light, her smooth white skin, her over-large eyes, the soft brown hair tumbling around her head. His nose was filled with the scent of her; dried sweat, but not like a man's sweat, strong and repulsive, but rather carrying on it the smell of the perfumed oils

Failend used, and under that the scent of a strong, fearless, bold woman.

She reached up with her hand and stroked the side of his face and he leaned down toward her and kissed her. She put her hand on the back of his head and drew him in and he kissed her with growing passion, his exhaustion left in the wake of this stronger need. He left her lips and ran his mouth over her long neck and up behind her ear, breathing in the smell of her skin and hair the way one breathes in the fresh air of an early morning.

He leaned back again, looked into her eyes. They gleamed in the moonlight and he saw the thrill and desire in them. In his head a voice screamed *Don't do this! Don't do this, you damned, damned fool!*

Then he heard his own voice speaking, though he seemed to have no control over the words. "Let's move away from camp, over by the stand of trees," he whispered. Failend gave a small nod, a hint of a smile. Louis de Roumois cursed himself, cursed his weakness and his utter lack of resolve, but still he stood and snatched up his cloak and took Failend's hand and walked her over toward the wood. The guards were arrayed to look in the other direction, toward the heathens' camp, and the rest of the men were in deep sleep. No one saw them move.

Louis spread his cloak down on the grass and Failend laid down on top of it. Louis unbuckled his sword and tossed it aside, then shucked his mail shirt in one smooth, practiced motion and dropped down beside her. Their arms wrapped around one another, their lips pressed hungry together. Failend pulled her brat over her shoulders. They kissed again, their breath coming in short gasps. Louis grabbed the soft, thin linen of Failend's leine and pulled it over her head and Failend struggled with Louis's tunic until he helped her to get it off. They pressed against each other, feeling the delicious sensation of skin pressed on skin and the cool night air blowing over them.

They tried to be quiet and were mostly successful, though once Louis had to clap his hand over Failend's mouth. Still, the distance from the others and the sounds of the night and the dead sleep into which their company had fallen sufficiently covered the gasping, moaning, thrashing noise of their passion. Or so Louis hoped.

When it was over Louis pulled the edge of his cloak over Failend's body and half over his own and fell into a sleep of near perfection. His slumber was marred only by a vague but persistent nagging that prodded at him, even unconscious as he was, until finally, sometime in the deep hours of morning, long before the sky showed even a hint of light, he woke with a start.

He came awake but not fully aware, not entirely certain of where he was. He was naked, and Failend was beside him, and they were outside, which was odd and very dream-like and he was not at all certain he wasn't still sleeping. And then, like a curtain pulled back to reveal a view through a window, Louis recalled everything, and he knew what it was that was nagging at him. He was not on some frolic, some illicit *affair de coeur*, he was in the field. He was campaigning. He could not lie here naked and vulnerable when he expected every man under his command to be instantly ready.

He stood as quietly as he could. Failend moved a bit and made some low muttering sound, but did not wake. He found his leggings and pulled them on and his tunic as well. His mail was lying in a heap where he had dropped it, a dark mound of steel links barely visible in the grass. He stood for a moment staring at it. He did not want to put it on. He had already sacrificed such supreme comfort in order to dress himself. He felt like the mail was too much to bear.

"*Merde*," he said, just a whisper, as he reached for the shirt. It made a soft sound like a shovel in gravel as he lifted it and pulled it over his head. He had told his men to sleep in their mail, and he could not tell them to do a thing he would not do himself. It was the first lesson Ranulf had taught him, and perhaps the most important.

He settled the mail shirt in place and picked up his sword and belt. Before he laid down again he ran his eyes over the field in which his men slept. He could see no one, not the sentries, not even the dark humps that represented sleeping men, but that did not surprise him. The moon had set behind the trees and only the stars were there to cast light on the ground. He thought he saw a figure moving among the men, but he could not be certain.

Coming to wake the next watch, he thought, and with that he eased himself down onto his knees and laid down again next to Failend, his sword at his side. He reminded himself that he would have to move before first light, that he could not be discovered in so compromising a position. That Failend would have to dress herself. But for the moment the warmth of the cloak and her body, even though the mail, the smell of her, was too much to resist. He closed his eyes. He slept.

And then he woke. He did not know why. He did not know how long he had been asleep. He opened his eyes. Failend's face was inches from his. It was still dark, still black night.

He heard a step, soft and stealthy. He pushed himself up on his elbow and the man approaching saw the move and closed the short distance with three quick steps. He put a foot on Louis's chest and pushed him down again. Louis could see the weak light of the stars glinting off the steel of the man's sword. He held the weapon motionless, just for an instant, and then drove it two-handed down at Louis's chest.

Chapter Twenty-Three

Relieve, O King of grey heaven,
the misery you have sent us.
Annals of Ulster

"**B**âtard!" Louis gasped as the sword point plunged down at his chest. He made a sweeping gesture with his right arm, knocking the blade aside, knocking it to his right, away from where Failend lay. He felt the steel scrape against his mail shirt and stab into the soft ground beside him.

The man above him had expected the blade to hit Louis's chest; missing and stabbing the ground threw him off balance. Louis reached up and grabbed the man's sword arm, pulled down and rolled, jerking the killer sideways.

The attacker went down and Louis kept on rolling, coming up on his feet. He snatched his sword from the ground and wrapped his fingers around the hilt and flicked the scabbard off. He heard Failend gasp behind him. The stranger, this apparition of a man, was struggling to stand. Louis lunged and felt the blade deflected by mail. The stranger brought his arm down on Louis's sword and knocked it aside and Louis took a quick step back in case there was a counter attack.

There was none. The man had lost his sword when Louis rolled him over and now he stood in a crouch, a dagger in his hand, a useless weapon against Louis's long blade. The man circled around, working his way to Louis's left, keeping low, the dagger held ready. Louis could hear the sound of voices off in the distance. Their fight had attracted attention, but he knew better than to turn his head and

151

look. Nor did he care to call out, to bring men running and have them discover him and a naked Failend off by themselves.

"Put down the knife and get on your knees and I won't kill you," Louis growled. The man made no move to comply and Louis realized he had spoken in Frankish. He started to reform the words in Irish when the man made a darting move to Louis's right, as if trying to get in around the sword. Louis swung the weapon to block him and quick as a snake the man changed the direction of his attack and darted to the left, not at Louis but at Failend.

"*Bâtard!*" Louis cried again and lunged. He felt the tip of the sword strike but the thrust was not powerful enough to pierce the steel links of the man's shirt. And then, before his dagger could find her, Failend snatched up the attacker's sword and swung it at him in a wide arc. The flat of the blade hit the assassin on the side of the head and sent him staggering.

Failend was on her feet and, to Louis's surprise, she was wearing her leine. She held the man's sword in her hand and brought it back over her shoulder like she was going to chop wood.

"No!" Louis shouted. He brought the flat of his sword down on the man's hand, the sound of the blow loud in the night. The man gasped, the dagger fell. There were footsteps coming closer, one man at least racing toward them. More, perhaps. Louis risked a glance now, saw Aileran materialize out of the dark, sword drawn. He drew the blade back as he ran.

"Aileran!" Louis shouted, "I'm…" but he got no further. Aileran swung his blade in a powerful backhand stroke and caught the assassin in the neck. Louis could see the spray of blood in the moonlight as the man twisted, choked, fell kicking to the ground.

"Damn!" Louis shouted, then shut his mouth tight. He was angry. He wanted the man alive, wanted to learn from him who had sent him and why. He knew tricks that would make men talk. But now the assassin was dead, or would be in another minute. Louis kept his disappointment to himself, however. He did not want to chastise Aileran because the man had thought he was doing right.

When Louis's breath and his anger had returned to something that would allow him to speak he said, "Thank you, Aileran."

Aileran said nothing, just stepped up to the body and squinted down at it. The killer had stopped twitching now and Louis guessed the life had run out of him. "Who is he?" Aileran asked. "Northman?"

"I don't think so," Louis said, trying to summon up the fleeting image he had had of the man, fighting in the dark. He had appeared as little more than a shadow, but Louis did not think he was a Northman.

There were more steps behind, men hurrying through the tall grass. He and Aileran turned. Half a dozen were jogging toward them, swords drawn.

"Captain!" he heard Lochlánn's voice and it was filled with worry. The men slowed as they approached, lowered their weapons, realizing that the fighting was over. "Captain Louis, what in God's name is happening?"

"We were attacked," Louis said, and he saw the eyes darting over toward Failend, who had dropped the sword and managed to get her brat and cloak on over her leine.

Don't explain, don't explain, Louis thought, the best advice he could give himself. And then he promptly ignored it. "For the lady's safety," he said, "I thought it best if she were not to sleep in the midst of all those men. I took personal responsibility for her safety."

"Of course," Aileran said and Louis made himself ignore all the subtle insinuation behind those two words. He nodded to the dead man at their feet.

"Do you know him?" Louis asked.

Aileran knelt beside the corpse, peered close. He grabbed the collar of the man's mail shirt and pulled him to one side so the moonlight would fall on his face. "Not one of my men," Aileran grunted. "No one I know. And not a Northman, like you said."

Louis nodded. "When the sun rises and we can inspect him more closely, maybe we'll know more. Meanwhile we'll let the men get whatever more sleep they can."

With that the others grunted and moved off, but Louis touched Lochlánn's sleeve, a signal to remain behind.

"This fellow," Louis said, nodding toward the dead man. "Is he the one who came for me at the monastery?"

Lochlánn looked down at the corpse. "I don't know, Captain Louis," he said. "They are about the same build, I suppose, but back at the monastery I never had anything like a good look at the man's face."

Louis nodded. He had thought that was the case. "Very well. You go sleep. Maybe we'll learn more in the daylight."

Lochlánn's eyes shifted from Louis to Failend and back. "Do you want me to stay near?" he asked. "In case there is more danger?"

"No, thank you, Lochlánn," Louis said. "I'll be safe enough, I should think."

Lochlánn nodded and left him and Failend alone. Once Lochlánn had disappeared into the dark Louis turned to Failend. "That was well done, hitting that man the way you did. You have skill with a blade."

Failend shrugged. "I pick up a sword, I swing it. Sometimes I hit what I swing at."

"You do better than most of these farmers who play at soldiers," he said. He took Failend's hand and walked with her back toward the sleeping men. He did not think there would be another attack, but they were certainly safer in the midst of the men-at-arms, and he did not care to bed down near a bloody and nearly decapitated corpse. Nor did he care for the rest of the camp to find them off in each other's arms.

Louis spread his cloak on the ground and let Failend lie down, but sleep was no longer a possibility for him. He sat beside her and remained awake through the few hours of darkness left, eyes searching the camp, ears attuned to any sound. But there was nothing to see but the tops of the trees swaying against the stars, nothing to hear save for the tiny night creatures and the snoring of the sleeping men.

At first light Louis stood, joints and muscles aching. He stretched his arms and legs. Aileran was already up and shaking his men awake. He joined Louis, and without a word they headed back across the field to where the dead man lay.

The sun had not yet cleared the mountains to the east. The morning was blue-gray, but light enough that they could see what they needed to see. The dead man was face up, blank eyes staring at the overcast sky. He was drained of blood and his face was the whitest thing around, a sharp contrast to the dark grass on which he lay.

Louis looked at him for a long time and Aileran did as well. Aileran shook his head. "I don't know him," he said.

"Neither do I," Louis said. He picked up the sword from where Failend had tossed it aside. "It looks Irish made," he said.

Aileran glanced at it. "It does," he said. "Chain mail looks Frankish." Louis could see he was right, and those facts told them nothing about who this killer was, or where he was from. Louis lifted the skirt of his mail shirt with his toe. He could see no purse.

"Have some of your men strip him," Louis said. "If they find anything that tells us more about this *bâtard*, bring it to me. Any silver is yours. Give his weapons and mail to the spearman who showed the most courage in yesterday's fight."

Aileran nodded. He and Louis trudged back to there the men were pushing themselves to their feet, stretching and scratching. Louis caught a few smirks thrown in his direction, but eyes were quickly averted when he met them. Salacious gossip moved like a morning breeze through a soldiers' camp.

Three of Aileran's men went to work on the body but found nothing that was of interest to Louis. When they were done they tossed the stiff white corpse into the brush for whatever might wish to make a meal of it.

Louis called Aileran and Lochlánn over to him. "We have nothing for our breakfast so there's no reason for us to tarry," he said. "We'll march directly back to camp and break our fast there."

Five minutes later the band of one hundred and fifty or so armed men were walking – it could not really be called marching – back the way they had come, the column stretching out over two hundred feet of road. Their passing raised a cloud of dust to leeward of them, the road baked dry by the remarkable stretch of good weather. But it would not last. Louis looked up. The dull blue of the early morning sky was already yielding to a milky whiteness as the familiar ceiling of clouds moved in.

They were not alone on the road. Heavily laden wagons rolled along, pulled by slow-moving oxen, slower even than the weary fighting men, and the column would have to swing off the road and march on the trampled grass as they moved past. Sometimes small bands of riders would come up the road and pass Louis's soldiers, casting curious looks in their direction. More traffic in one day than that road would likely to see over the next six months as travelers flowed north and west, following the River Avonmore to the Glendalough Fair.

The morning wore on and the sun rose higher, a pale disk behind a thick blanket of cloud, and there was a watery smell in the air. Rain, soon, Louis could tell. He hoped for his men's sake, and for his own, that they might make it back to the dúnad before the rain began in earnest, and that the tents had indeed been carted down from Glendalough.

Louis de Roumois walked at the head of the column, Aileran on his left side, Failend on his right, Lochlánn a few paces behind as the boy thought was proper. The men behind were quiet, but their spirits were good, Louis could tell. They were proud of their night's work, which they deserved to be. Before, when they had marched from Glendalough, he had been met with curiosity or indifference or resentment as he walked past the ranks, but now they greeted him with grins and nods. This was good. This was how a lethal army was made.

A hundred rods or so beyond where they marched, the road curved off to the left, lost behind a stand of trees, and Louis could see smoke rising from somewhere up ahead. Not a great deal of smoke, but enough to make him curious, and wary, though he was not afraid of a surprise. Aileran had sent scouts out ahead, because neither he nor Louis were foolish enough to go blundering blindly around the country with a powerful enemy near.

Just as Louis began to wonder about the smoke he saw one of the scouts coming back around the screen of trees. He was not running and he did not look terribly excited. That was good. Louis did not order a halt.

"Caravan," the man said when he and the marching column had met. He fell in beside Aileran and addressed them both. "Three wagons. Fancy ones. Women, too. They've made camp by the side of the road."

Aileran nodded. "Making for Glendalough Fair, no doubt," he said. "Players maybe, or merchants, or whores. All three, perhaps."

They came around the bend and Louis saw that the scout had described it correctly, if with less detail than he might have done. Three wagons, heavy ones, fully enclosed and mounted on tall oak, iron-rimmed wheels, their wood sides painted in bright reds and yellows. They were drawn up in a semi-circle in the field beside the road. There were banners flying from staffs near the drivers' boards and at the back ends, and various bits of bunting waving from where ever it could be tied.

In the center of the semi-circle there was a large fire burning and over it a pot. Even from a distance Louis could smell the stew cooking there, and he felt his mouth water and realized how very hungry he was. The smell had reached the men marching behind him and he could hear muttering. He half turned and called for silence, and the men obeyed, though the murmuring faded grudgingly away rather than stopping abruptly.

Sitting in front of the fire was a large man, large in every way, with a massive beard that hung to the middle of his ample belly. Louis might have taken him for a Northmen if he had not been dressed in the Irish manner and wearing no weapons. There were others, half a dozen men that Louis could see and women as well. Louis counted four of them. Young women. Good looking. He heard the murmuring set in again behind him.

"We'll let the men rest for a bit here," Louis said to Aileran. "I'll speak with these fellows." Aileran turned and called the order down the line. The men, however, did not sit immediately but rather continued to shuffle forward, closer to the food, closer to the women, before finding a spot of grass on which to fall.

The big man by the fire watched Louis approach. There was no fear on his face, no anxiety, just a soft look of curiosity.

"Lord, will you join me in my dinner?" the man asked, gesturing with a ladle toward the pot.

"Pray, call me captain, not lord," Louis said. The aroma from the stew pot swirled around him and he wanted desperately to accept the offer of dinner, but instead he asked, "Have you food enough for all my men?"

"No, Captain, I certainly do not," the big man said.

"Then I fear I must decline," Louis said. He was happy to accept the privileges of rank: a bigger tent, a servant, a finer horse. But he would never eat while his men went hungry. The big man shrugged and Louis took a seat on a stool beside him.

"I am Crimthann," the man said. "You've heard of me, I have no doubt, me and my players?"

Louis shook his head.

"What?" Crimthann said, and he appeared to be genuinely surprised. "You look to be a man of the world, and by your accent, sir, I judge you are not from this country. Yet you speak our language tolerably well, so you must have been some time here. How is it you have not heard of Crimthann?"

It was Louis's turn to shrug. "I have been in the monastery at Glendalough these twelve months and more," he offered.

"Ah! That would explain it!" Crimthann said. "Only a hermit could not have heard of us, our fame is so widespread." He glanced over at Louis's men. "It seems maybe your men are hermits as well, or at least have not laid eyes on a woman in a long, long time."

Louis followed Crimthann's gaze. Many of the men, the farmers, were staring at the women with undisguised curiosity, and a good part of desire mixed in. Louis smiled.

"They are what you Irish call bóaire and fuidir. Not proper soldiers. I guess they don't have women such as yours back on whatever pathetic little farms they come from."

Crimthann threw back his massive head and laughed loud. "There are not women such as mine anywhere in the world!" he said. "They perform in such places as I can get away with allowing them to. They help out in other ways."

Louis was curious about those other ways, but this was neither the time nor place to explore that. What he wanted from Crimthann now was information. Traveling men such as merchants and players, Louis knew, heard a great deal about what was happening in the wide world.

"We fought some heathens who were coming up river. Coming for Glendalough," Louis said. "Have you had any word of them?"

Crimthann nodded. "We've heard rumors," he said. "Heard they made a bloody mess of the village Muirbech at the mouth of the River Avoca, and another a few miles in. We came across an Irish fellow, name of Kevin, and he had an army of a hundred men or so, but they were in too much of a hurry to stop for entertainment, even such as we can provide, which is the finest in the land."

"You've heard word of the heathens, but have not seen them?" Louis asked.

"No, we're keeping well away from the river. Because of the heathens."

Louis nodded. "You might do well to keep clear of Glendalough as well," he said.

"What?" Crimthann exclaimed. "And miss the fair? Have you any notion of how much silver will be flowing about the streets?"

"There'll be no silver at all if the heathens make it that far," Louis said.

"Ah, but they won't!" Crimthann said. "I look at you and I see you're a blood-minded one and you'll never suffer a heathen to sack your city!"

Louis smiled. He wished he could share the big man's certainty.

"But just to be safe," Crimthann added, "We'll remain here until we hear of you slaying all the bastards."

"That seems a wise plan," Louis said. He stood and called to his men and they reluctantly stood and fell into line again. A moment later they were on the move, shuffling past the caravan, men straining for a final look at the women who waved and sent them off with smiles not so innocent or demure.

They walked for another weary hour without reaching the dúnad. Louis was beginning to wonder if perhaps Colman had returned to Glendalough, if there was no camp waiting, when Lochlánn said, "Just over the rise ahead, Captain Louis. That's where the camp will be."

Louis nodded and relished the sense of relief. He was exhausted and famished and he could hear the grumbling behind like an undercurrent of noise, like rain on a roof. They crested the hill and Louis hoped above all things to see a spread of tents, or at least a wagon loaded with food. But what he saw first was none of those things.

What he saw first were men. One hundred, one hundred and fifty, perhaps, spread out on the field, tending fires, sharpening weapons, sleeping. There were several wagons, and he could see they were piled with the tents, kettles, barrels of food and ale for the dúnad. It was sight that surprised him, unexpected as it was, and filled him with joy when he realized what he was seeing. Father Finnian had returned, and he had brought with him an army of genuine men-at-arms.

And now the real fighting could begin.

Chapter Twenty-Four

In this year, moreover, many abandoned their Christian baptism and joined the Norwegians, and they plundered Ard Macha, and took out its riches.
The Annals of Ulster

Starri Deathless did not die. For some hours after the sun went down he moaned softly and shifted his head side to side with a slow and deliberate motion. His ax remained lashed in his clenched hand.

Thorgrim sat beside him as the stars overhead made their slow wheel around the sky. Starri grew quiet at last and Thorgrim thought he was gone, but he was only asleep, so Thorgrim slept as well. When he awoke, the sky was a pale overcast and Starri was still alive.

The crews of his four ships were gathered on the shore, building fires, fetching buckets of water, slinging kettles from tripods. Five rods farther up the bank Ottar's crews were doing the same, and inland Kevin's men made ready to break their fast. Three armies, each acting as if the others did not exist.

Thorgrim gently pulled back the furs that covered Starri's chest and then the cloth over his wound. He had to tug where the blood had dried on the bandage, and he did so as gently as he could. Starri moaned and shifted his head, but his eyes did not open.

The wound looked bad, but not as bad as it had the day before. It had closed up some and the bleeding had stopped. Thorgrim had an idea that they could sew it now, that any spirits that might have been there had fled. In any event, the hole left in the spear's wake was closing up on its own. He wished he knew more about treating such things but he had little experience with it. Generally any man so badly injured as Starri was would have been dead already.

Starri Deathless... Thorgrim mused. *You are well named. Maybe you can't be killed.*

He covered the wound again and put the furs back over Starri's chest. Tending to that would have to wait; there were more pressing things now. He stood and picked up his mail shirt and slipped it over his head. He gestured toward Iron-tooth and Segan, who was watching from a few feet away, picked the weapon up and buckled the belt around Thorgrim's waist.

"Harald, Godi, come with me," Thorgrim said and the three of them walked to *Sea Hammer*'s bow and down the plank to the shore. Godi, following Thorgrim's instructions, waiting until Thorgrim and Harald were on dry land before stepping onto the springy board.

Thorgrim ran his eyes over the open ground. The various camps lay spread out before him. From the Irish camp, and walking quickly in his direction, he could see Kevin and the small cadre that seemed to always be in his wake. *They are a shield wall*, Thorgrim thought. *They are like a shield wall blocking my advance.*

"Hold up," Thorgrim said to Godi and Harald and he could not hide the weariness in his voice. They waited until Kevin had reached them and bid them good morning. The Irishman ran his eyes over Thorgrim's mail and the sword at his side. He spoke. Harald translated before Eoin was able to speak.

"Kevin asks, 'where are you going? Is there some problem?'"

"Tell him I am going to kill Ottar Bloodax for his insults," Thorgrim said. "Tell him there is no problem."

Harald translated. Kevin nodded. He did not looked surprised. Then Kevin began to speak, and Thorgrim could hear the calm diplomacy in his voice, even if he could not understand the words. Whatever had been frightening Kevin the day before – and Thorgrim guessed it was Ottar's ferocious unpredictability – Kevin seemed have made peace with it. And that made Thorgrim immediately suspicious.

This time Eoin beat Harald to the translation. "My lord begs you will reconsider. Ottar spoke in haste, and without thinking, as he often does. My lord is certain he regrets his words."

"Your lord is certain Ottar regrets his words?" Thorgrim asked. "Ottar told Kevin this?" He knew perfectly well that Ottar had said no such thing, but he was curious as to how Kevin would answer.

"Ottar did not say those words exactly," Eoin translated. "But he has no wish for a war with your men. He said as much. Such bloodshed would be pointless, especially when there is a fortune to be had at Glendalough if we may all fight as one."

Thorgrim looked off toward Ottar's camp and considered that. He had no doubt that Kevin had told Ottar the exact same thing. But Kevin was not wrong that war between Ottar's men and Thorgrim's would be a bloody and pointless affair, and such a war would surely be the result of Thorgrim's driving a sword into Ottar's guts.

Ottar Bloodax might not understand that in some instances bloodshed could be pointless, but Thorgrim did. He felt his resolve slipping. With age had come reason and thoughtfulness, and he found those things asserting themselves over the heedless passion he had known as a younger man. Once again he did not know which course was the right one. He was not sure if reason was to be celebrated as wisdom or despised as weakness.

"Neither Ottar nor you will have any authority over me or my men," Thorgrim said. "My men will take no orders from any but me."

"Of course, of course," Eoin translated, and Thorgrim could see the relief and pleasure on Kevin's face. There was no relief or pleasure on Thorgrim's face. He felt like a wolf cornered by hounds.

His gut told him to abandon this folly of a raid, that Kevin had played him like a flute and no good would come of it. But he could not abandon it now. No matter how sensible such a course of action would be, it would look like cowardice. His heart told him to kill Ottar, but satisfying as that might be in the moment, he knew that no good would come of that, either.

"Tell Ottar to stay away from me. Tell him that I will suffer no insult from him. I'll kill him if he ever again shows a lack of respect to me or my men."

"Yes, yes," Kevin said. Thorgrim nodded. He wondered what form those words would take when they reached Ottar's ears. *If* they reached Ottar's ears. Which he did not think they would.

Eoin was speaking again. "My lord asks, 'would this be a proper time to talk of our plans for Glendalough?'"

It was. Thorgrim called the captains of his ships together and they sat by the cooking fire and Kevin's men sat as well and they talked. Thorgrim guessed this same scene had played out in Ottar's camp, or would, Kevin and his men serving as the ambassadors between warring tribes, the Irishman bridging the divide between factions of Northmen.

Not much had changed from their first discussion on that rainy day in Vík-ló. Thorgrim and his ships would proceed up-river as far as they could. Kevin and his troops would follow along the shore. Except now Ottar would being going up river as well, and now they knew there would be resistance along the way, a strong and clever enemy dogging them, hitting and running, forcing them to fight their way upstream.

"Kevin says the men who were captured, the ones Ottar killed, they were fuidir, farmers called up for the service they owe their lord," Eoin said. "They are not regular men-at-arms, not real soldiers. My lord does not think it will be any great problem to brush them aside."

Thorgrim nodded. Some may have been fuidir, but not all. The men he had fought were trained soldiers, and they were well led. But he was done with talk. "Very well, then," he said. "Let us move on to Glendalough."

This, apparently, was Ottar's opinion as well. Thorgrim stood and looked up the shoreline toward Ottar's camp and he saw the men there were already loading their gear back aboard their ships. Shields were mounted on the vessels' shield racks and the banners that had earlier been waving at the ends of their long staffs were gone, rolled up and stowed away.

"Ottar is eager to get away from us," Thorgrim said to his men, ignoring Kevin and the other Irishmen. "And I am eager to see he does not. Let us get back to our ships. I am already heartily sick of the land."

Kevin mac Lugaed watched the last of the longships slip off the shore and turn in the stream, its oars like the wings of a swan. He felt varied and contradictory emotions swirling around him.

He loathed those ships, of course, despised the very sight of them, as did most Irishmen. At the same time, he could not help but marvel at their beauty and wonder at the mystery of them. He had a passing knowledge of boats, but the workings of a ship like that, the skills needed to cross an ocean in such a thing, were beyond his comprehension. He envied the Northmen and the mobility that their ships gave them. And he hated them for that and for a hundred other reasons.

"My lord," said Niall mac Olchobar, standing at Kevin's right hand. Niall was Kevin's most trusted advisor, chiefly because he had been loyal to Kevin even when Kevin had been merely one of the Lords of Superior Testimony, and not ruler of all that part of Ireland called Cill Mhantáin.

For Kevin, it had been a bloody road that led him to where he was. He had seen quite a bit of ugly battle, as had any in his position, and he had developed his own personal fighting strategies. They mostly involved always appearing to be in the thick of the fight while actually remaining out of harm's way.

If a leader was wounded, Kevin was the one who would selflessly carry him to safety. If a shield wall was forming up, Kevin remained behind it, ready to strike down any coward who ran, or step in wherever a man fell, though for all his shouting and brandishing weapons he never seemed to find the opportunity. Such little tricks he found did a great deal for both his reputation and his longevity.

So it had been at the great battle at Vík-ló. He watched as Lorcan mac Fáeláin, his former lord, former rí túaithe of Cill Mhantáin, was cut down in the fighting. He had watched Lorcan's chief men, Senchan mac Ronan and Faelan, killed in earlier fights. He had witnessed many others killed as well. Indeed, so many had been killed in those days that when it was over Kevin found to his surprise that he was the most powerful man left standing in Cill Mhantáin.

Kevin mac Lugaed had a nose for opportunity, and following the fighting at Vík-ló the scent was strong indeed. He gathered up a handful of warriors and paid them silver from the various purses he had plundered in the aftermath of the fighting. With those men he spent the next few weeks consolidating power.

The task of establishing his authority was easy enough. The Northmen had killed just about anyone who might object to his doing so, and anyone still alive was quickly cowed by the sight of his growing and well-paid army. By the time Kevin settled himself in Lorcan's former hall in the ringfort at Ráth Naoi, he was the rí túaithe, and there was no one left to challenge him.

"Yes, Niall?" Kevin asked. He was watching the Northmen's ships as they pulled up river, a line of them moving against the stream. He had been right about the height of the water. Their ships would float for another six or seven miles before the river became too shallow for them to continue. And quite a lot could happen in six or seven miles.

"Lord, shall I get the men moving? Shall we prepare for our march?"

Kevin pulled himself from his reverie with a shake of his head. The morning might have been ugly indeed if he had not succeeded in keeping Ottar and Thorgrim apart, telling each what he wanted to hear about the other.

Thorgrim had always been reasonable, surprisingly reasonable for a heathen. Kevin had actually been able to do business with the man, to the benefit of them both. But Ottar was not like that. Ottar was completely insane in the most dangerous way.

Kevin had not quite appreciated the depth of his madness when he had first approached the man in his longphort south of the river mouth. Or perhaps he had appreciated it, and had ignored it, in hopes of making a profitable partnership. He had ignored the corpses of the men – traitors, Ottar had said – tied to stakes outside Ottar's hall. He had ignored the bloody bruises of Ottar's Irish slaves, the squalor in which Ottar and his followers lived.

But he could ignore the signs no longer. Even before Ottar had joined them at the Meeting of the Waters, Kevin received word of what he had done at the village at the river's mouth. And he saw what Ottar had done to those unfortunates taken prisoner after the fighting. He should never have asked Ottar to join in the raid, he understood that now. The best he could do now was to make Ottar Thorgrim's problem, not his.

"Yes, yes, Niall," Kevin said, frowning at his own distraction. "Let's get the men ready to march. I would like to move in an hour's time."

"A full hour, lord?" Niall looked surprised. "The ships will be way ahead of us by then, they'll be lost to sight." Niall had been with Kevin in his discussions with Ottar and Thorgrim. He understood the plan. The Northmen would advance up the river in their ships, the Irish would keep the river banks clear of any resistance. And after the surprise attack of the night before, no one doubted there would be resistance.

"Yes, the ships will be lost to sight," Kevin agreed. "And so the heathens will not see us marching off to the north."

"The north, lord?" Niall's confusion was mounting.

"Yes, the north. Our plans have changed. There's a way through these mountains to the north. We'll take our men that way, make a wide circle around whoever these men are who attacked us. Come at Glendalough from the east."

Niall hesitated but Kevin's expression did not encourage comment. "Very well, lord, I'll see the men ready to march in an hour's time." He turned and headed off, leaving Kevin alone on the river bank.

Once Niall had left him, Kevin allowed a hint of a smile to play across his lips. He was pleased. He knew that he could not control events as if he was ordering slaves here and there. Only a fool or one consumed by hubris could think otherwise. A man was lucky if he could control what he himself did; there was no certain way to make others do as you wished. Once you involved just one other person in your plans then control was lost, and Kevin's plans involved hundreds.

No, he could not control things. He could just put the pieces in place, arrange them as best he could, see what happened, and then take his advantage from that. And so far things were working out better than he could ever have hoped.

Thorgrim and Ottar would never join forces, so they would never be a threat to him. It was far more likely they would kill one another. At the same time, whoever these bastards were who had attacked their camp – and Kevin had to guess it was men-at-arms from Glendalough – they would be far too occupied with the heathens to even noticed Kevin's army taking a long march around to the north and west.

Thorgrim, Ottar, these whores' sons from Glendalough, they could all kill one another here on the shores of the River Avonmore and leave Kevin mac Lugaed in peace to sack the monastic city. The hint of a smile blossomed into a genuine grin.

Chapter Twenty-Five

To the heedful comes seldom harm,
for none can find a more faithful friend
than the wealth of mother wit.
Hávamál

Colman mac Breandan sat at the table in his pavilion. The man
standing on the other side of the table had finished his tale
and now stood waiting for some response. He did not fidget.
He was not the sort to fidget.

It was quiet as Colman thought about what the man had just
said. He could hear the sounds of other men outside, quite a few men
now; the men-at-arms and the bóaire and fuidir come back from the
Meeting of the Waters, and the men-at-arms sent by Ruarc mac Brain
whom Father Finnian had just that morning led into the dúnad. Not
the two hundred Finnian had hoped for, but nearly that number, and
good men, too. Good, well-trained and experienced fighting men.

Slaughtering the heathens would present little problem with such
an army as that assembled. Or so Colman had thought when they had
first marched into camp. Now he was not so certain.

For the past twenty minutes Colman had been listening to the
tale of the fighting at the Meeting of Waters and what had come
after. It made him angry at times, and also relieved, and curious as
well. So much going on in so short a time.

"Nine longships, you said?" Colman asked at last.

"Yes, lord," Aileran said.

Aileran was the only other soul in the pavilion. Failend had been
sent away with Colman's assurance he would deal with her at the
proper time. Louis de Roumois had not even made an appearance.
He was apparently conferring with Father Finnian rather than
begging an audience with his proper superior, and that annoyed

Coleman. He had expected Louis to show up eager to tell his tale, at which point Coleman would have sent him on his way like the miscreant boy he was. But Louis's absence had denied Colman that little pleasure.

"Nine longships…" Colman muttered to himself as he worked out numbers. "Could be as many as four hundred of the sons of whores."

"Yes, lord," Aileran said.

"And the men with that traitorous bastard Kevin? At least a hundred?"

"Yes, lord."

"We are outnumbered," Colman said. It was an observation. There was no panic in his voice or in his heart. But there was concern. If the heathens were to overrun Glendalough he could lose a great deal. Not everything - he had land and holdings and interests spread all over that part of Ireland - but he could lose what he had in the monastic city. And he could lose his sinecure as commander of Glendalough's defenses and the generous income that went with it. He could lose reputation.

"We *are* outnumbered, lord," Aileran agreed, and he sounded even less concerned than Colman. "But the heathens seem determined to stick to the river and that will make it hard for them to attack. I don't think this Kevin mac Lugaed is much of a threat. At Meeting of the Waters we were up against his men, mostly. They did not fight to any great effect. And Louis de Roumois, he's a man who knows his business."

Colman looked up sharp and Aileran made a throat-clearing sound. "Beg pardon, lord. I was just saying…"

"Yes, yes," Colman said, waving his hand as if driving away some annoying insect. Aileran, like all the men in the dúnad, indeed like all of Glendalough was aware of the tension between Colman mac Breandan and the young Frank Louis de Roumois. Most imagined it was due to Louis' being asked to take direct command of the troops. Others guessed at more intimate reasons.

It was clear to Colman that Aileran was trying to downplay Louis's part in the fighting at Meeting of the Waters, his clever planning, his inspired use of untrained men. But Colman could hear the unspoken praise in his telling of the story.

"With the heathens so numerous here," Colman continued, "I'm wondering if we shouldn't go back to Glendalough, make our defenses there."

Aileran, despite his apparent new-found respect for Louis de Roumois, was still Colman's man, the most experienced soldier in Colman's ad hoc army. And Colman was still in command of the defenses of Glendalough, whatever the priest Finnian might think. Before the arrival of Louis de Roumois, Colman had looked to Aileran for support, and he would continue to look to him when the Frank was gone. Which would hopefully be soon.

"Well, lord, I think there's a better way than giving them the ground betwixt here and Glendalough," Aileran said, his words coming slow and thoughtfully. "The heathens, like I said, are keeping to the water, taking their ships upriver as far as they are able, which will be damned far in this flooding. That might give us a better chance."

Colman looked at Aileran and frowned. The words were coming from the man's mouth, but Colman was pretty sure they had originated in Louis de Roumois's head. But what of it? If the Frankish son of a bitch was indeed a good soldier, then Colman could use that to his advantage. Let Louis lead the men to victory. Any such victory, and the reputation and spoils that came with it, were easily enough usurped when all was done.

"Very well, then, we'll do it your way," Colman said. "Now, this assassin, the one who came for the Frankish whore's son?"

"Yes, lord. It was like I told you," Aileran replied.

"Tell me again."

"Well, Captain Louis, he was sleeping off by himself, away from the men…" Aileran said, and Colman thought, *You are a miserably bad liar*, but he let it go.

"And this son of a bitch," Aileran continued, "comes from I don't know where. I heard them fighting and run over."

"You're sure it was the same man? The same Frankish bastard who showed up here a fortnight past?"

"Yes, lord," Aileran said. "I'm sure of it. I had a good look at him at first light. After he was dead, lord."

Son of a bitch, these lying dogs! Colman thought. He could picture the new-minted Frankish coins he had hidden in his home in Glendalough, the few he carried with him in his purse. Given to him as down payment for a job that needed doing, but then this whore's son apparently decided to do the job himself. Or maybe he had been instructed to do it, to save the cost of paying Colman the balance of the fee when the job was done.

If this bastard was going to do it himself, why involve me at all? Colman wondered, but the answer was obvious enough to a man such as him, one used to manipulating others. If the killer failed they would have Colman as a back-up. If he was caught then Colman would have to help him or risk being implicated.

Damned Frankish curs, never to be trusted, Colman thought. He looked up at Aileran again.

"Brother Louis did not have the chance to speak with him?"

"No, lord. They were still going at it, hammer and tongs, when I cut the whore's son down. He never spoke a word that I could hear."

"Good," Colman said. "Good." He looked down at the table once again and turned the various considerations over in his mind. Was that bastard the only one, or were their others? Did it matter? He had been paid for a service, at least in part, and in truth it was a service he would have been happy to perform for free.

"Very well, Captain," Colman said, looking up at Aileran again. "You did good work and I thank you." He picked up the purse that was lying on the table, heard the Frankish silver clinking inside the soft leather bag. "Now, there is more I need of you."

Chapter Twenty-Six

Good is health if one can but keep it,
and to live a life without shame.
Hávamál

The river was growing shallow, but Thorgrim did not notice. He was tending to Starri, still wrapped in his fur nest in *Sea Hammer*'s stern.

They had stitched Starri's wounds closed that morning, working on him while the men at the oars pulled the longship upstream against the current and Agnarr manned the steering board. Harald had offered to do the sewing, thinking himself skilled at that task, but Thorgrim had enough ugly scars on his body, made uglier by Harald's handiwork with needle and thread, that he said he would do it himself.

He worked slowly, drawing the flesh together as best he could. Sometimes Starri flinched when the needle pierced his skin, sometimes he did not. When the wound on his chest was done they rolled him on his side and Thorgrim stitched up his back, and then they laid him flat again. Thorgrim mixed broth with ale and made Starri drink. Starri opened his eyes and looked up at him. There was confusion there, and a faraway look.

"Night Wolf," he said, the words barely a whisper. He said no more, but Thorgrim knew it was a question and he knew the answer Starri was seeking.

"You were wounded, Starri. But you are still among the living."

Starri closed his eyes and nodded his head, just a bit, and then drifted off to sleep again.

"You did that well, father," Harald said. He and Thorgrim were looking down at Starri's seemingly shrunken form. "The stitching. But aren't there herbs or poultices we could apply?"

Thorgrim shook his head. "I don't know how those are made," he said. "Those are the arts that women know. Me, the others here, we can stitch wounds and splint broken limbs. But real healing? That's women's knowledge."

He looked up beyond the confines of the ship, larboard and starboard. The river was still wide here, four or five rods from bank to bank, and Thorgrim could see it was running above its normal confines, the water lapping over grassy fields rather than the pebbly or muddy banks that would normally form the river's edge.

The reeds jutting up from the river bed were bending slightly under the pressure of the moving stream and his men leaned into the oars as they pulled against it. With the water high and the river wide, the current was not so bad here, but he wondered how long they would be able to stem it, and how long it would remain deep enough for their keels to pass over the bottom.

Ottar and his five ships had taken the lead, despite Thorgrim's best efforts to get underway first. That had annoyed him, and he had allowed himself the luxury of indulging his anger. But as he did he had a vision of his children when they were much younger, racing to breakfast after morning chores. He recalled marveling at how silly they were, Harald and Odd fighting each other for the privilege of being first. Their sister would be seated, her breakfast begun, while the boys were rolling on the floor pummeling one another.

When he thought of it that way he no longer gave a goat's turd whether he was first or not. But that was not a sentiment universally shared. As Ottar's ship pulled away from the bank, Harald had said, "Father, if we double the men on the oars we might overtake him, the bastard."

"No," Thorgrim said, his anger burned away like mist. "It does not matter."

They continued up the river all through the morning, and the enemy did not show themselves, and the only threat seemed to be the threat of rain, which grew more pronounced every hour.

As Starri slept, Thorgrim fished out a small piece of whalebone from among the sundry supplies he kept stowed below the afterdeck. All morning he had been trying to recall the correct runes one should use to bring about healing, and he was now reasonably certain he had them right. It was a tricky thing, as the wrong runes could do more harm than good, but Thorgrim had confidence enough in his memory that he sat on the afterdeck, pulled his knife from its sheath and began to carve the geometric shapes into the dull white bone.

It took the better part of a hour, and when he was done Thorgrim placed the whalebone under the furs that covered Starri, then stood and stretched cramped muscles and looked out toward the shore to the north east. The land looked as it had for much of their journey upriver: sometimes it was open country with rolling hills that rose like cresting waves to the higher mountains west, sometimes it was thickly wooded with the oak and maple coming right down to the water's edge. In some places where the river had jumped its banks the trees came right up out of the water.

The countryside was open now, lush spring fields spreading off in the distance, some spurts of brush here and there, sharp rushes that stood out dark green against the duller grass of the fields. Thorgrim looked north and south as far as he could see, and he saw only land. There was not an animal, not a man or a woman in sight.

"Agnarr," he said. "Have you seen anything of Kevin's men?" He himself had been so busy tending to Starri and carving his runes that he had spent little time watching the shore.

Agnarr shook his head. "I don't think I have," he said. "Sometimes we've seen riders in the distance, and wagons. Bound for Glendalough, I would guess. The fair. Sometimes we've seen men walking, but they looked to be peddlers. None of them looked to be Kevin's men-at-arms."

Thorgrim nodded. There were several possibilities. Kevin might be far ahead of the ships, or keeping his men out of sight, keeping his movements hidden from the enemy who had attacked them. That would have been the smart thing. Or Kevin might have met that enemy and been beaten. Or he might have abandoned his new allies entirely. Any of those was equally possible, and since he had no means of discovering the truth of the matter, at least not yet, Thorgrim did not concern himself with wondering.

"I think Ottar is aground," Agnarr said, his voice rising a bit in excitement. Thorgrim turned from watching the shore and looked past *Sea Hammer*'s bow.

Ottar's longship, at the head of his fleet, was four hundred feet or so up river from *Sea Hammer*, and the water around it was churned up into short chop by the shallows. In other places the river tumbled over rocks or swirled in eddies near the banks or flashed dull white in the weak sunlight that came through the overcast.

The crew of Ottar's ship appeared in chaos as if they had been set on by a swarm of bees. The lovely, symmetrical rhythm of the oars had devolved into a flailing mess, with some of the long sweeps still down, some coming up out of the water, some fouling others ahead or astern. Some of Ottar's crew were on their feet, some still sitting. The ship lay motionless in the stream.

Thorgrim could see Ottar himself, right at the stern, waving his arms. He thought he could make out the sound of Ottar's bellowed commands. He strained to make out the words, but could not.

I can just imagine, he thought.

Then order seemed to reassert itself. The oars disappeared into the ship and the men flung themselves over the sides, landing thigh-deep in the water, keeping hands on the sheer strake to stop both them and the ship from being swept away. Then they began to pull.

Foot by foot Ottar's crew hefted the longship upstream. Thorgrim saw lines tossed to the men in the water and they abandoned their hold on the ship's side and tailed onto the lines, heaving away and walking up through the shallow water like teams of oxen. The ship, unburdened by her crew and now lighter by seven or eight hundred pounds, moved easily over the shallow place. A minute later the men aboard the next ship in line were also leaping over the sides.

"Just getting the men over the side lightened Ottar's ship enough for her to pass over the shallows," Agnarr observed. "I didn't think it would."

"Nor did I," Thorgrim admitted.

"I wonder how many more miles we can get upstream before that will no longer work," Agnarr said.

"I don't know," Thorgrim said. "Not many, I'll wager."

He looked down the length of *Sea Hammer*'s deck. His men, those not at the oars facing aft, had also seen Ottar's ship take the ground, and they were already pulling lengths of walrus hide rope out from the storage places under the deck boards and stripping off tunics in preparation for going over the side. Fifteen minutes after that, they too were up to their thighs in water, pushing their way against the current, hauling *Sea Hammer* over the shallow, pebbly bottom of the river.

An hour was spent dragging the nine ships upriver over the shallows before they were able to climb back aboard and take up the oars, driving the vessels north and west. They pulled for another hour and a half before they touched ground again. Ten minutes later they were once more hauling the ships over slick rocks against a racing current.

It was then that the rain set in. The ship right ahead of *Sea Hammer*, the last ship in Ottar's fleet, had just touched the bottom when the first few drops began to fall: fat, noisy drops that left wet spots as big and round as silver coins on the dry wood of *Sea Hammer*'s deck.

"Here it comes," Thorgrim said. He had already prepared an oil cloth to stretch over Starri's sleeping place. Now he unrolled it over the line he had rigged fore and aft and lashed the corners down tight, making a tent of sorts.

He looked up in time to see Harald go over the side. He and most of the others had stripped off their tunics and the skin of their bare backs was white in the muted light of the afternoon. The tow ropes rose from the deck and stretched taught as the crew tailed into them, and *Sea Hammer* was pulled bodily forward. The vessel just ahead, Ottar's ship, shuddered as her keel scraped along the bottom, and Thorgrim could hear the grinding sound of oak on gravel.

He leaned over and looked down through the clear running water. He could see the stones on the river bed, many hues of brown and red and white and black. *Sea Hammer* moved easily over them, not touching at all in her transit.

This may be it, Thorgrim thought, *this may be the last time we will do this so easily.* The next shallow place would likely have less water still, and then they would have to offload gear to get the ships up river. Would it be worth it? Or would it be better to leave the ships and make their way to Glendalough overland? How many men would they have to leave behind as ships' guards? Could they afford to leave that many? These were questions that would need answers soon.

By the time the men had hauled *Sea Hammer* past the shallows and climbed back aboard, the rain was coming down hard, a steady downpour that Thorgrim was certain would become a deluge within the hour. He looked down at Starri. The tent seemed to be effectively channeling the water away from the wounded man, but for the rest there was nothing to be done but to endure the rain. Those who had shed their tunics to go in the river pulled them on again, though the clothes were now as wet as if they had never been taken off.

For the next few hours they rowed through the driving rain. Finally, as the evening gloom settled early on the river, Thorgrim ordered *Sea Hammer* run ashore and the other ships in his fleet followed suit. Ottar, however, showed no sign of stopping. His ships continued up river until they were lost from sight around a distant bend.

"Father," Harald said, his voice a loud whisper, his anxiety clear, "Ottar is getting ahead of us, leaving us behind."

"Let him," Thorgrim said. "I won't play his games. If he wants to take on these Irish without us he's welcome. He and his men will be slaughtered."

They used their sails to make tents large enough for all the crews to huddle under, save for the sorry few who were posted out beyond the river as guards. They had no fires, but the night was not terribly cold and they were not as miserable as they might have been. At first light they made their breakfast on bread and dried fish and then pushed their ships back into the river. The rain, which had let up in the night, set in once more with a willful malice.

They came up with Ottar's fleet two hours later. The river had narrowed considerably, the forest closing in on either side, the banks steep so that it seemed they were pulling into a gully, as if the wide stretch of water was a road though a forest.

Ottar's ships were not in any sort of order and they were not underway. It seemed to Thorgrim like inexplicable confusion, but as they drew closer he could see that three of them at least were anchored in the stream, and the first two were being dragged though yet more shallows.

Harald, having finished his trick at the oars, was standing by Thorgrim's side. "Ottar's aground again, I see," he said.

"Yes," Thorgrim said. "But it's worse this time. See how they've taken much of the weight out of the ship."

Ottar could not get over the shallow river bed, it seemed, just by relieving the ship of the weight of its crew. While gangs of men hauled the vessel up stream, others followed with the yard and sail, barrels and bundles of oars that had been tossed overboard and now floated astern. The crews of the anchored vessels were unloading spars and gear and stores as well.

Agnarr, just aft at the tiller, said, "Ottar's ships draw more water than ours. I noticed that, back at the Meeting of the Waters. They are loaded down with more stores, more gear. I think they were looking at making a long voyage."

Thorgrim nodded. *Sea Hammer* and the other ships in his fleet were lightly provisioned. They had been loaded with the intention of making a quick strike on Glendalough and then returning to Vík-ló. As a result they did not ride deep in the water, not as deep as Ottar's.

They watched for a few moments more as Ottar's men swarmed around the ships, unloading, stretching out tow ropes, hauling the vessels into the shallows. The rain fell in torrents, making it hard to see, filling the long ship inches deep.

"This is madness," Thorgrim said at last. If Ottar wished to see his own men killed, that was fine with Thorgrim, but now the entire raid was threatened. "Agnarr, put our bows right into the shallows, right there." He pointed ahead to a place past where Ottar's men were offloading their ships.

The men of *Sea Hammer* pulled hard against the now-swift current and the longship moved past the anchored vessels. Thorgrim did not miss the angry looks on the faces of Ottar's men as they rowed up the line. Then *Sea Hammer*'s bow ran up on the river bottom with a grinding sound and lurched to a stop so abruptly that Thorgrim had to take a step to keep himself from falling.

Grim faced, angry, he strode down the length of *Sea Hammer*'s deck, aware of his own men watching him now. He reached the bow and vaulted over the sheer strake and down into the water. The river was cold, the surface torn with driving rain, the current strong as Thorgrim waded upstream.

Ottar did not wait for him. Thorgrim was still approaching when he saw Ottar moving in his direction. Ottar walked with an odd gait, leaning slightly back as he struggled to keep from toppling forward in the fast moving water. One hand was held out for balance, the other rested on the hilt of his sword. The water roiled around his knees.

Maybe this will be it, Thorgrim thought. *Maybe we settle it now.* He did not doubt that the fight begun in Kevin's tent, interrupted by the Irish attack, would be resumed eventually. For the sake of this joint venture Thorgrim had tried to postpone it at least until they had finished sacking Glendalough. He had tried to do the sensible thing. But he was done with that now.

"What is the meaning of this, passing my ships by?" Ottar began to bellow as he approached. The rain poured down his face and he wiped it away and spit. His hair, normally as yellow as Harald's, appeared black, soaked as it was, his long braids looked like drowned serpents. "My ships will be first, and you…"

"This is foolish, what you are doing, and you're a fool," Thorgrim said. Ottar stopped, the water rushing around his legs, his mouth hanging partway open. He looked stunned, as if he had been hit on the head with a club. Thorgrim took advantage of the blessed absence of Ottar's voice.

"You lighten your ships to get over these shallows?" Thorgrim asked. "Dumb ass. What happens when you get to the next shallows, will you off-load even more? If the river falls, your ships will be trapped here. Meanwhile you waste time while they make ready for us at Glendalough."

"You bastard, you talk to me like that?" Ottar roared, but Thorgrim was not listening. They were a hundred feet upstream from *Sea Hammer* and here the woods were even closer in on either side, great trees looming over the rushing water like monsters from another realm. And suddenly Thorgrim had a very bad feeling in his gut.

"Hold your mouth, Ottar," Thorgrim said, raising a hand for silence. That only served to further enrage Ottar, who began to roar in anger, a low, ugly sound from his belly. Thorgrim saw the sword coming out of the scabbard.

And then, upstream, near the bow of Ottar's ship, Thorgrim saw one of the men on the tow rope spin around, heard him shout, saw the arrow jutting from his chest. The man stumbled, fell, the water splashing up around his body. Some of the others on the tow rope shouted in surprise, some stood motionless, some dropped the rope.

And then, it seemed, all the demons of Ireland were let loose upon them.

Chapter Twenty-Seven

I am an outlaw to most men;
only arrow-storms await me.

Gisli Sursson's Saga

The dull noise of the rain and the poor light and Ottar's raving made it hard to know what was happening, exactly. Thorgrim turned his head in the direction from which he thought the arrow had come. He could see nothing but the wall of trees, the snarl of bracken, the sheets of water coming down.

And then another arrow came, and another, and half a dozen more. Thorgrim's eyes moved back toward Ottar's ship. Men were staggering, shafts jutting at odd angles from chests, backs, legs. Two more were down, their bodies already caught in the river current. A man kicked and thrashed and tried to regain his footing. The shouting mounted but Ottar had not yet noticed.

Ottar's sword was out and he was coming toward Thorgrim and bellowing something. Thorgrim was not listening.

"Your ship is under attack, you stupid ox! Look!" Thorgrim shouted, pointing. Ottar stopped, scowled, then looked back up river. For a heartbeat he just stood there, motionless. Then he shouted again, a different note this time, and began racing back upstream, lifting his legs high as he ran, a comical effect. Thorgrim could have laughed but he did not because he realized that the Irish had launched a near perfect ambush, and that realization sapped the humor from the thing. They had caught the Northmen unarmed and out of their ships, which were all but helpless in the shallows. All of them, Ottar's men, his men, might be dead in the next hour.

He turned and hurried back to *Sea Hammer*, struggling to keep his footing in the rushing water. Agnarr had ordered an anchor set out and the men were resting on their oars. Now they heard the shouting from upstream, knew something was happening, but they could not tell what.

"To arms! To arms!" Thorgrim called as he came charging up, hefting himself over the ship's side and hurrying aft. He could see the confused looks on the men's faces, but his orders were clear enough, and the men obeyed. Those who owned mail grabbed it up and dropped it over their heads, others grabbed swords, axes, shields from the shield rack.

Thorgrim reached the stern, mounted the afterdeck and only then did he turn and look up river where Ottar's ships were under attack. He could see the arrows ripping through the downpour, finding their marks, easy shots from two or three rods distance. The bowmen were focusing on the lead ship, Ottar's ship, and from what Thorgrim could see they had managed to drop near half the crew.

He turned and looked in the other direction. *Blood Hawk* and *Dragon* had drawn up beside one another and they held their places in the stream with a steady, easy pull of the oars. Thorgrim doubted Bersi or Kjartan could see what was going on upstream, and certainly Skidi Battleax in *Fox*, farther down river, could not. But they had seen the men of *Sea Hammer* getting into their fighting gear and they had followed suit.

Thorgrim waved, pointed to the water on *Sea Hammer*'s larboard side. Bersi waved back, a signal that he understood. A moment later *Blood Hawk* gathered way as Bersi's men drove her forward to run her up onto the shallows beside *Sea Hammer*.

Ottar's ships were four hundred feet up river, midway through transiting the shallows, and all was chaos. Ottar himself was plunging through the shallow water, waving his sword, rallying his men. His men, in turn, had retrieved their weapons from their ships and were leaping into the river, shields on arms, swords and axes in hand. Dead men and lost gear were already swirling down river, past where *Sea Hammer* lay anchored to the shallow bottom. A barrel that one of Ottar's men had been hauling upstream bumped against *Sea Hammer*'s bow and twirled away like a leaf in a mill race. The man floated face-down and motionless, an arrow jutting from his back.

"Come with me!" Thorgrim shouted to his men. He raced amidships, jumped over the side and plunged ahead through the stream. He looked up river to where the fighting was taking place, Ottar making ready to launch his assault on the attackers still hidden in the woods, as around him his men fell wounded or dead under the hail of arrows. Thorgrim thought he could see several arrows embedded in Ottar's shield. The luck that had kept that madman alive so far was working still.

You idiot... Thorgrim thought. Did Ottar really mean to charge right at the woods, up that steep bank, at an enemy he could not see?

The side of Ottar's ship bristled with arrows, the men holding the sheer strake and the tow ropes were being shot down where they stood or were abandoning the ship to join in the attack. And then suddenly there were not enough men left to hold the ship against the current. The rushing water grabbed the vessel's long keel and pulled it from the grip of the few men still holding on, twisted it sideways and sent it sweeping downstream, plunging out of control toward the ships below.

Ottar's men were charging toward their enemy and they did not react at all, as far as Thorgrim could see, as their ship drove itself into the next vessel in the fleet, anchored just downstream. Ottar's ship had turned sideways in the river and its midships hit the bow of the second vessel at nearly a right angle, fouling it, wrenching the second ship's anchor clear of the bottom and sending the two ships, now locked together, down on the third.

"Oh, by the gods!" Thorgrim shouted. He would have been happy enough to let Ottar's ships be driven clear back to the sea, but if they were not stopped then they would strike his own ships and do untold damage.

"Come, follow me!" he called to the men behind him, thoughts of joining the battle pushed aside by this more immediate threat. Thorgrim slipped Iron-tooth back into its scabbard and rushed forward, fighting the fast river current, spitting rain water. He was hampered by his shield and he thought of casting it aside but he still had hope he would need it.

The two ships were turning slowly in the river as they swept down on Thorgrim and his men; with their leering beast figure heads they looked like monsters from a fever dream, and though they were made of wood and iron and tar they were at that moment every bit as dangerous as living sea serpents.

Thorgrim stopped, held up his hand for the others to stop as well, as they watched the two longships drifting down on them. Two of Ottar's other ships were well clear, anchored close to the shore, but the third, anchored farther out, seemed to be right in the path of the drifting vessels.

The ships turned slowly in the current and their momentum built with every yard they gained. Then their motion was checked as the two slammed into the third ship in line and tore it free from its anchor. The impact made the vessels shudder. The sound of crushing wood was audible over the driving rain and the shouting men. Now the three ships were locked together and their momentum was building again as they were swept along.

"Agnarr, Harald!" Thorgrim shouted and the two men came splashing up beside him. "I will take Godi and some men and we'll grab onto the tow rope of whatever ship is upstream, try to stop it. I don't think you will be able to stop the others, just try to shove them to the side so they don't hit *Sea Hammer*. Bersi!"

"Yes, Thorgrim?" Bersi shouted.

"You and Kjartan, get *Blood Hawk* astern of *Dragon*, keep her clear of these ships!"

They had a minute, no more, before the ships would be on top of them. Thorgrim waved his arm and pushed forward, fighting his way through the water, eyes on the ships turning and twisting and bobbing down on them, great malevolent creatures that they seemed to be. They blocked his view of the upper part of the river, but as he charged ahead they turned to reveal Ottar and his men, farther upstream.

The ambushed men were locked in battle with the Irish and seemed unaware that their ships were being swept away, and even if they were, there was nothing they could do about it. Thorgrim could see Ottar, a head taller than any of the others, sword raised, pushing through the water toward the river bank. His men moved forward with him, a line of men, some with shields, most without, some with mail. They had been struggling to pull their ships through the shallows and so had been caught unawares, unarmed and unprepared.

Stupid son of a bitch, Thorgrim thought. He saw Ottar and his men reach the steep, muddy bank, saw they trying to claw their way up, arms hampered by weapons and shields. And then from the dense bracken above them came the Irish with spear-points leading, swords behind, hacking Ottar's men down, ramming iron tips into their chests. Thorgrim could hear the shrieks of agony, the bellows of rage.

Then the ships they had come to stop were on them and Thorgrim had no time for Ottar's stupidity. A tow rope made fast to the upstream-most ship was trailing in the river and Thorgrim guessed that would do as well as any. He plunged ahead, kicking at the water like he could move it out of his way. He could see the rope twisting just under the ruffled surface. Two steps and he was on it, reaching down and snatching it up. The line came up out of the water and he held the one end as the ship at the other end was swept downstream.

"Bear a hand here, bear a hand!" Thorgrim shouted. The line was in his right hand, and he grabbed it with his left as well, but with the shield on his arm he could get only a tentative grip. The strain started coming on and Thorgrim pressed his lips together, tightened his hold and leaned back against the pull.

A man named Armod pushed up beside him and grabbed up the rope as well and Thorgrim felt the pressure ease as Armod took up the strain. Then others were there; Sutare Thorvaldsson and the massive Godi standing like a rune stone, the water breaking around him. The line came straight as a spear shaft and the ship at the far end twisted and turned bow toward them.

We can hold the one, Thorgrim thought. *We cannot hold all three.* If the three ships remained locked together they would pull Thorgrim and the others along with them, or force the men to drop the rope and watch Ottar's ships smash into *Sea Hammer* and take her along in the destruction.

The wayward vessels seemed to pause in their flight. The rope creaked and Armod and the others grunted and cursed with the effort of checking their motion. For a heartbeat they hung there, men and ships, and Thorgrim did not know which force would prevail. Then the two vessels wrenched free from the one they held at the rope's end and continued their mad escape downstream, while the strain on the rope dropped to a fraction of what it had been.

"Thorgrim!" Godi shouted. "There's a tree! We can make fast!" Thorgrim looked over his shoulder, looked in the direction in which Godi pointed. Fifty feet away a big oak rose up out of the river.

"Good!" Thorgrim shouted and together the dozen or so men who were tailing onto the tow rope began walking away with it, making their labored way upstream, hauling Ottar's ship behind like it was some great, reluctant beast they were bringing to the slaughter.

The rain washed down on them but they could not wipe it away, so they blinked and spit and dug their soft shoes into the gravel bed of the river.

Thorgrim wanted desperately to see what was happening downstream with *Sea Hammer*, but hauling on the rope, he could not turn and look. He also wanted desperately to see what was happening upstream with Ottar's attack on the Irish, but now the river bank blocked his view.

And then they were at the oak. The man at the far end of the tow rope reached the tree and took two round turns around the solid trunk and Ottar's ship was fast. Thorgrim let go of the line, spun on his heel to see what was happening with *Sea Hammer* and was nearly knocked over by the force of the stream.

Like a bull baiting, he thought. He had seen that in Hedeby once, a pack of dogs set on an enraged bull that whirled and kicked and thrashed with its horns. The forty or so of his men confronting Ottar's out of control ships reminded him of that. They stood clear as the vessels drifted down on them, then leapt forward, grabbing hold where they could, pushing, leaping clear again as the vessels came plunging down on their own ships.

Harald stood near the bow of the ship furthest downstream. "Push off, push off here!" he shouted and flung his broad shoulder against the vessel's side, its stem and figurehead looming above him. Thorgrim saw the ship move under the pressure from Harald's powerful back and legs, saw it straighten, its stern swinging away from *Sea Hammer* seconds before it would have slammed into her.

Others leapt up and joined Harald and they pushed until the ship was no longer sideways in the river, then they stepped clear and let her drift past *Sea Hammer* and continue on downstream. The second of Ottar's ships followed in her wake as if it was being led on a rope. *Dragon* and *Blood Raven* had been shifted clear and the drifting vessels passed them by no more than a few feet.

Thorgrim watched only long enough to be certain his own ships were safe and then he once again called to his men and they rallied to him. Most had shields now and swords and axes, as ready for battle as they were going to get.

"Ottar's men are being butchered because Ottar's a fool!" he shouted. "We must join in, save the sorry bastards." He spit rainwater and pointed toward the trees right adjacent to where they stood.

"We'll go into the woods there, move along the river bank, take these Irish whore's sons by surprise." He saw men nod. He turned and splashed toward the northern bank of the river

He ran as best he could, a stumbling, exhausting effort through the knee high water, and he spared a glance upstream. Ottar's men were still mostly in the river, fighting an enemy on the shore above. Ottar was still standing, swinging his sword in great arcs while the others fought beside him.

He could see the Irish among the trees. He saw few spears now. The spears had mostly been thrown, Thorgrim guessed, or broken or pulled from spearmen's hands. That meant Irish and Northmen were fighting sword against sword and that meant Ottar's men had a better chance of at least making a good show of it.

Hold them, Thorgrim thought. *Three minutes more...* If Ottar could keep the Irish at it for another three minutes, then he and his men could run right into their flank and do great execution.

Thorgrim reached the river bank, steeper than he had expected, and with some difficulty pulled himself up and into the tree line. He did not wait for the others behind but turned and plunged on through the undergrowth and the saplings and the mature oaks and maples. The leaves above turned the rain aside like thatch and Thorgrim could hear the fighting now. The bracken was wet and the water lashed him as he pushed through, but he could not possibly be any more soaked than he already was.

The afternoon was dark and it was darker still in the woods and hard to see, but Thorgrim sensed someone ahead, someone moving, and he guessed he had reached the end of the Irish line. He drew Iron-tooth and pushed on forward. Another fifteen feet and then he saw him, an Irishman, spear held straight out, looking more as if he was trying to ward off an attack than join in one. There was nothing about the man, save for the spear, that suggested he was anything more than a poor farmer, one of these pathetic creatures called up to do his lord's bloody work, and now he would die for reasons he probably did not even understand.

Thorgrim crashed on through the undergrowth, the noise of his passing hidden by the drum of the rain overhead and the shouting and screaming from the river to his left. He was raising Iron-tooth for a backhand stroke when the spearman finally realized he was there.

The man's head jerked around, his eyes went wide, his mouth opened and he began a feeble thrust of the spear in Thorgrim's direction as Iron-tooth came whistling through the air. The blade caught the man in the throat and the force of the blow sent him sprawling into the undergrowth, a bright gush of blood proceeding him to the ground.

Thorgrim vaulted over his still thrashing body. He could see the next Irishman, the next three men, actually, all bearing spears. They had been looking out toward the river but Thorgrim and his men had managed to make enough noise to catch their attention. Like the man Thorgrim had just killed, they did not look like men-at-arms, and they did not act like it either.

They had not expected an enemy to come charging out of the woods, that was clear, and they seemed to give no thought to fighting. They flung their spears away, turned and scrambled through the woods, Thorgrim on their heels, his men right behind him. Thorgrim could see Harald charging along, knocking saplings aside with his shield. The boy ran like there was something hideous pursuing him, but Harald was the hunter, not the hunted, the worst nightmare of the Irish farmers fleeing before him.

Panic swept up the line of Irish spearmen arrayed along the river's edge. They screamed and cursed and joined the flight, driven by the Norsemen's swords. Through the trees Thorgrim could see glimpses of the river and Ottar's men, some fighting, some doubled over with wounds, some floating motionless. He turned back to the fight at hand.

The Irish spearmen were gone, run off in panic, but there was another line of men ahead, and Thorgrim could see that these were no farmers. Whoever was in command here must have put his most useless warriors on the edges of the fight, his best men in the middle where Ottar was bound to attack. Or perhaps he gave the spearmen leave to pull back when the real fighting began, let the men-at-arms take the brunt of that. These men wore mail and carried shields and did not run at the sight of the Northmen coming from the trees, but rather shifted their positions to meet them head on.

Thorgrim came to a stop. The man before him now was not running in panic but standing his ground, a long sword in his right hand, a shield with a red cross painted on its face in his left. Iron-tooth came down in a wide arc again, but this time the weapon was met with the shield that took the blow and turned it aside. Thorgrim leapt back as the counterstroke came low, under his shield, looking for his calves or knees but finding only air.

Thorgrim stepped in and slammed his shield into the man and made him stagger, then went right in with Iron-tooth, right for the man's unprotected throat. The Irishman was still trying to raise his shield when he died on Thorgrim's sword point. Thorgrim pushed him aside as he fell and leapt for the next man, who was already swinging at Thorgrim with his sword.

*Starri…*Thorgrim thought. They did not have Starri and his manic energy, his unnerving ferocity. With Starri in the fight the enemy knew that something wild and unworldly was in their midst and it put fear into them. But now Starri was fighting a different fight.

The Irish men-at-arms had managed to swing their line away from the river's edge to meet the new threat on their flank, and the two sides, Irish and Northmen, ran into one another like walls of rushing water colliding. Thorgrim saw Harald launch a brutal attack on the man in front of him, his sword and shield moving in a perfect geometric harmony, shield arcing left, sword swinging right. The grace and power of the attack drove the other man back. Godi was beside him, a massive ax in his hand, his attack less subtle but no less effective.

There were two men coming at Thorgrim now, both with sword, shield and mail. They came on shoulder to shoulder, straight at him, but Thorgrim stepped to his right, putting the man on the left beyond sword's reach, and lunged at the man on his right.

The Irishman parried the blade and made a thrust at Thorgrim but Thorgrim took another step to his right, and then another, putting a massive oak between him and the two men, blocking their view of him as if he was trying to hide. He guessed they would circle around, coming at him from either side, which meant the one on the left would reach him first. Thorgrim held his shield with its edge against the trunk of the tree, refreshed his grip on Iron-tooth just as the Irishman leapt into the clear, apparently thinking he would take Thorgrim by surprise.

The Irishman's sword swung around in a wide sweeping blow intended to cut down anything in its path. The blade connected with the iron rim of Thorgrim's shield and bounced off and Thorgrim drove Iron-tooth's point right into a spot below the rim of the man's helmet. He jerked the sword free as the man fell and ran past him, around the tree. It was like a child's game, racing around the trunk, but the second Irishman did not look amused when Thorgrim came up behind him. He had time only to half turn in Thorgrim's direction before Iron-tooth, still wet with Irish blood, cut him down too.

Thorgrim was breathing hard. He paused, looked around. His men were engaged with the men-at-arms now, dozens of private duels. Some he could see, some were lost in the woods. There was more movement to his left, men crashing through bracken. Ottar's men. Thorgrim's attack had forced the Irish to turn away from the river, and that had allowed Ottar's men to scramble up the bank where they could fight their enemy on level ground.

The Irishmen seemed to waver in their attack. Thorgrim could sense them stepping back, fighting now on two sides, no longer certain of where the enemy was. *Push harder, push harder,* he thought. They would break in a moment. They would start to run, and when they did, they could be cut down in flight.

Thorgrim felt an animal howl building in his chest, a wolf howl, a sound that would bring terror to the Irish, that would drive his men on. He leapt forward and swung Iron-tooth at a big Irishman wielding a battle ax, and the move seemed to draw the howl from deep inside him. The sound rang in his ears, rang thought the woods. It took the Irishman by surprise. Thorgrim could see the terror in his face. He dropped the battle ax, turned and fled. Thorgrim lunged at him, fast as a serpent, but he was not able to get a blade on the man.

"Come on! Come on!" Thorgrim shouted and he saw his men pushing ahead, he could see them through the thick woods as they made a line that swept inexorably forward. Then, from some unseen place deep in the trees there came the sharp, clear note of a horn, as if in answer to Thorgrim's call. It was the same note Thorgrim had heard at the Meeting of the Waters and it called the Irishmen to fall back, to get clear, to live and fight again.

"No! Bastards!" Thorgrim shouted. He picked up his pace, knocking his way through the woods with his shield, but there was no enemy in front of him anymore, just saplings, bracken, trees.

"Thor take them!" Thorgrim shouted, but he was gasping for air as much as shouting. It was quiet again, save for the drumming of the rain on the leaves and the rush and tumble of the river nearby.

Harald loomed up in front of him, and Godi and the others. They gathered to him to see what they would do next.

There was more rustling in the woods, a sound like a bear or some large animal moving through the undergrowth. Thorgrim turned and the others turned and they could see men making their way toward them, half hidden in the dark of the woods and the thick brush. Then Ottar stepped clear of the trees. His shield was in splinters, and he seemed to realize it just at that moment, and he tossed it aside. His sword was covered with blood, too much for the rain coming through the leaves overhead to wash away. His arm and his beard and the ends of his braids were likewise bloody.

No one moved. Ottar and Thorgrim looked at one another. Thorgrim had no idea what might come out of Ottar's mouth.

Ottar frowned. He squinted at Thorgrim as if he, too, had no idea what would come out of his mouth. Then he turned and spit on the ground. "Finally showed up, did you?" he said, then turned and disappeared back into the woods.

Chapter Twenty-Eight

Let a man never stir on his road a step
without his weapons of war;
for unsure is the knowing when need shall arise
of a spear on the way without.
Hávamál

Harald Broadarm sat on *Sea Hammer*'s afterdeck and gently tilted a cup of broth and ale into Starri's mouth. It was not the sort of task he would generally welcome. Tending the wounded, he understood, was as much a part of campaigning as caring for one's weapons. But he was never very comfortable doing that work, and he feared that being the youngest man there the others would tend to pawn the job off on him. Just the thought of that made him resentful.

But this was different. This was Starri, whom Harald liked very much. Most of the men liked Starri, or they ignored him, or, Harald suspected, they feared him. Harald's own feelings were different than the others, more complex, though he would not have thought of them in that way. Starri was part of Thorgrim's inner circle, part of his father's household, and that alone made Harald's relationship with him different. He and Starri had fought side by side many times. They had suffered much together, and had shared triumphs and wealth. Harald liked Starri Deathless. And he envied him.

He envied Starri's absolute fearlessness. He understood, of course, that Starri was fearless mostly because he was insane, but still he could not help but wish that he, too, could plunge into battle with no concern at all for injury or death. His father seemed fearless as well, but with Thorgrim it was a different sort of fearlessness. He took battle seriously. He wore mail and a helmet, carried a shield. He did not court death as Starri did.

Harald had no lack of courage, and he would have killed any man who suggested he did, or he would have died trying. But he was not without fear. There was an image that had fixed itself in his head, an image of a battle ax striking him right where his neck and shoulder met and splitting him near in two. For some reason that idea frightened him terribly, and he could never shake it in the moments before battle. It was his secret shame.

He doubted that Starri felt any such fears.

"What's happening?" Starri asked. His eyes were open, his voice was soft, though now there was a hint of strength in it. He had been unconscious, either asleep or passed out, almost the whole time since his wounding. The sounds of the battle had roused him, and he had been awake on and off since then, though still too weak to stand or do much of anything.

"They are getting the last of Ottar's ships up the river," Harald said, looking past *Sea Hammer*'s high sternpost. Downstream of where they lay at anchor Ottar's fleet was just getting over the shallow water where yesterday the Irish had ambushed them. Most of the ships' stores and gear had been taken off to make the vessels ride high enough to float. Ottar's men, those still alive and not too badly wounded to work, were loading those things back on board the vessels that had made the transit.

Harald shook his head. *Idiots*, he thought.

Starri was silent for a moment and then asked, "Don't they fear they'll be trapped above the shallows? Doesn't Thorgrim fear that?"

"Father doesn't worry about our ships being trapped," Harald explained, "and Ottar is too stupid to worry about his." He looked down at Starri and could see that further explanation was needed.

"We're not carrying a lot of provisions. Our ships are light enough to pass over the shallows once the crews go over the side," Harald continued. "Ottar's ships must be unloaded to make it. They must take out the stores and the yards and oars and all manner of things. Even if the level of the water drops, we should be all right. But Ottar could have real trouble."

Starri nodded. Harald gave him another sip of the broth and ale. A minute passed before Starri spoke again.

"Ottar's company is much diminished?" he asked.

"It is," Harald said. He had told Starri all this before, soon after the end of the battle, when Starri had been eager to hear the tale.

Starri had become so inflamed by the story that he had tried to rise from his bed, even though the fighting was over. It was only with considerable effort that they were able to persuade him to remain supine.

"Ottar lost forty men at least," Harald said. "That's forty dead. Another fifteen wounded, I would guess. It was a slaughterhouse. Father says whoever was commanding the Irish really knew his business, set as perfect a trap as could be set, and we walked right into it."

The Norsemen had spent the hours following the battle setting things to rights. The wounded were looked after, the dead gathered up and buried. That part did not take very long. Ottar had lost around forty men; at least that was the number that filtered into Thorgrim's camp. But most of the bodies had been swept away downstream. Some had been found but most were not. It was not a comforting thought to the shipmates of the dead men. A warrior likes to think he will be sent off to the next world in the proper way, and not have his flesh devoured by ravens and vultures.

When those few burials were done, Ottar had loaded men aboard two of his remaining ships and gone in search of the vessels that had drifted off and were now lost from sight down river. Thorgrim decided then to move his own ships over the shallows, and the men from Vík-ló spent an hour or so hauling the vessels against the current. By the time Ottar returned with his wayward ships in tow Thorgrim's fleet was safely at anchor upstream of the low, churning water.

When Ottar saw Thorgrim's ships were now ahead of his own he flew into a rage, just as Thorgrim and all the rest knew he would. This, Harald suspected, was the real reason his father had ordered the ships hauled up river, even after saying it was a bad idea. He was baiting Ottar, and doing so for the sheer pleasure of it.

Ottar's ship ground onto the downstream end of the shallows and Ottar jumped over the bow. He stormed through the knee deep water, which slowed his progress enough to make his approach seem much less threatening than he intended. Thorgrim and his men were aboard their ships, anchored in eight feet of water and resting under the sails spread like tents against the still falling rain. Heads turned in Ottar's direction, but no one moved or spoke or even acknowledged his coming toward them. Thorgrim kept his back turned to the man.

When Ottar reached the end of the shallow stretch he stopped and bellowed Thorgrim's name. Thorgrim continued to ignore him and Ottar bellowed again. This time Thorgrim stood and moved slowly to the afterdeck. He rested a hand on the tall sternpost and looked across the thirty feet of water that separated him from Ottar, water too deep for Ottar to cross.

"You get ahead of my ships, Thorgrim Night Pup?" Ottar roared.

"Yes, I did," Thorgrim answered simply.

"You will not get ahead of me!" Ottar said, louder now, more enraged. "You will not!"

Thorgrim looked around in mock confusion. "But I already have, Ottar," he said. "And if you don't hold your tongue I'll get underway now and leave you for the Irish to finish off."

There had been a change, a big change, in the hours following the fight. When they had first met at the Meeting of the Waters, Ottar's men had outnumbered Thorgrim's. That was not the case now. Ottar had lost nearly a full ship's crew. Now his strength was at best equal to Thorgrim's.

But that was only part of it. Ottar was the sort of leader that men followed because he was stronger and more violent and more pitiless than anyone else. Warriors joined him because they feared him and they figured others would fear him more. They figured his mindless brutality would lead them to plunder. But the Irish had made Ottar look like a fool, and his men understood, even if Ottar did not, that it was Thorgrim who had saved them and saved their ships.

"You bastard!" Ottar shouted. "Ravens will pick out your eyeballs!"

"They might," Thorgrim agreed. "But it is not you who will feed me to them." With that he turned and ducked under the sail and left Ottar standing in the rain. Ottar continued to shout for a few more minutes, but no one was listening, and that made him seem an even bigger fool, so he turned and headed back downstream. It was not until the next morning that Ottar and his men began the laborious work of once again hauling their ships against the current.

"Here's something I don't understand," Starri said, then closed his eyes as if the effort of speaking was getting to be too much.

"What of Kevin? Was he not supposed to be moving his men along the river bank? To stop the Irish waylaying us as they did?"

"We don't know where he is," Harald said. "We know he's not here, but we don't know where he's gone. Beaten by these other Irish, run off, we don't know."

He looked down at Starri for a reaction, but Starri seemed to be asleep. He waited for a moment more and, when he was certain Starri had drifted off, he stood and stretched and considered what he would do next.

Oak Cleaver, he thought. His sword, the beautiful Frankish blade, once his grandfather Ornolf's, which now he carried. The edge had taken some damage in the fighting and it needed tending, and the blade could use some oil against the miserable wet weather. But when he looked forward he could see his father heading aft and the look on Thorgrim's face, a look Harald knew well, suggested that Thorgrim had his own ideas of what Harald would be doing next.

Thorgrim stepped up by Harald's side and looked down at Starri. The rain had tapered off to a mist, which was a great relief, though most likely a temporary one.

"How is he?" Thorgrim asked.

"Better, I think," Harald said. "He had some broth. He spoke, wanted to know what was happening with the raid. With you and Ottar."

Thorgrim gave a half smile. "Well, if you figure that out I'd be grateful if you could tell me as well," he said. He looked over the starboard side at the riverbank, three rods away. Somewhere, lost from view, Thorgrim's scouts kept watch for another ambush. It was the prudent thing to do, though no one thought the Irish would be so imprudent as to strike again in the same place.

"Once Ottar is ready to get underway he'll try to get past us again, get upstream," Thorgrim said. "I don't want that to happen. For a number of reasons. So we will get underway now and get well ahead of him."

Harald nodded. He, too, wanted to stay ahead of Ottar, mostly as a matter of pride. But he could guess at his father's other reasons.

With each mile they dragged the ships upstream, each dead man they buried or arrow they pulled from a ship's side, the raid on Glendalough seemed to take on greater and greater importance. No longer a raid but a quest. All the men seemed to feel it. Thorgrim feared Ottar would somehow manage to ruin any chance of a successful attack, or make some dumb mistake that would get them all killed. And Harald guessed his father wanted to twist the knife of humiliation in Ottar's guts.

"Kevin is gone," Thorgrim continued. "Where, I don't know, but he's not here. So I need you to take some men, twenty or so, and follow us along the river bank. I need you to keep an eye out for another ambush, like Kevin should have done."

Harald felt the excitement rise, the pleasure of anticipation. Thorgrim was offering him a command of his own, an important task and a leader's role, a chance to show off skill and boldness.

"You and your men are scouts, you understand?" Thorgrim said, apparently sensing the excess of eagerness in Harald's face. "You are not to fight an army with twenty men. You're just to warn us if they're lying in wait before we blunder into them."

"Yes, father," Harald said.

Thorgrim looked him in the eyes and said nothing for some time. "I mean it," he said at last. "Scouts. You are not to fight."

"Unless it's just a few of the Irish, right?" Harald said. "A patrol, or just a few men-at-arms? We should kill them before they can reveal our presence, shouldn't we?"

Thorgrim let out a breath. "Yes, in that case you may fight. But try to take prisoners. They're more of a help than dead men. I'm trusting you to use your judgement. Use it well. If you want to see what stupidity will get you, just look to Ottar."

Harald nodded, but the words had barely registered. In his mind he was already leading his men stealthily along the river bank, and going sword against sword with the Irish son of a bitch who had launched the brutal, bloody attack of the day before.

Chapter Twenty-Nine

*[T]he Irish suffer evils not only from the Norwegians,
but they also suffer many evils from themselves.*
Annals of Ulster

Failend felt like she was floating, like she was moving through a dream world. A dream world like no dream she had ever experienced before; a dream filled with terror and discomfort, with hope and exhilaration, with exhaustion and lust and amazement. A dream that seemed to encompass every kind of feeling she could have imagined, whipping her like a gale of wind and rain.

She had killed a man. At least she was fairly certain she had. By the river, during the fighting at the Meeting of the Waters. He had come stumbling through the line of Irish warriors and she had been there and she had struck him down. But he was still alive so she plunged her sword into his neck.

At least that was how she remembered it. It was all a swirl in her head, and hard to recall exactly what had taken place. She was not even certain how she felt about it. Astonishment, confusion. Not remorse. There was no remorse. She wondered if that should concern her. But of course he was just a heathen.

When the fighting was done they had left the killing field, marched back along the river bank and then through the trees to the road. The men were very excited, very animated. They had fought well. That was Failend's impression of the battle. It was based on the men's reaction, since she was in no state of mind to draw any conclusions on her own. They had done well. And now they were excited.

Making love to Louis de Roumois, the attack by the assassin, Aileran killing the man after she, Failend, had knocked him on the head, it was all part of this extended dream. She could still see the spray of blood from the killer's neck as he went down. She felt like her whole life was a wagon rolling down hill, building speed, and now it was moving as fast as it could move. It was nearly out of control, threatening to come apart.

Back at the dúnad she had returned to her husband's pavilion, bracing herself to face his fury. And he had been furious, so much so that he sent her away, told her to return later. "I will see to you then," he had said, and said no more. He did not look at her.

And she had not returned. She knew there was only a beating at her husband's hands waiting for her, and she did not feel the need to endure it.

She waited for the chance to speak to Louis alone. "Aileran will tell my husband he found us together," she told him.

"No he won't," Louis said. "Aileran and me, we're soldiers. There is a bond between fighting men."

Failend shook her head. "Aileran's my husband's man. He has been for many years now. He owes more to my husband than he owes to anyone."

"I think you're wrong," Louis said. "But even if you're right, and Aileran tells him, it will not be some new revelation to your husband. He cannot hate me more."

Failend let it go. It was pointless. Louis de Roumois was one of the most extraordinary men she had ever known, but he was still a man, and there were things he would not understand. He was not stupid and he was not naïve. But when it came to his fellow soldiers, he viewed loyalty the way a dog views loyalty: simple, complete and unwavering. In some things Louis did not grasp nuance.

After the successful fight at Meeting of the Waters, Failend had thought they would march back to Glendalough. She was certain Colman would wish to do so. He would want to enter the city in triumph. But they did not.

Instead, they remained in the dúnad because Louis was not done with the Northmen. There was a place on the river where he guessed the heathens would have to drag their ships over the shallow water, and he convinced Colman to let him set a trap there. Colman agreed. All this Failend heard from Louis. She did not see her husband, and though she waited for him to order her dragged to his pavilion so that he might punish her for her many sins, he did not.

What he did, to her surprise, was ignore her and she continued to float through her dream world.

Louis de Roumois gave up complaining about her marching with the army. He told her she was not a child, if she wished to do this thing, and Colman said nothing about it, than he would not stop her. She guessed Louis did not want to leave her behind at the dúnad with Colman while he marched off to fight the enemy. She suspected that he actually liked her company in the field.

He found her a mail shirt, one that had been made for a young man. It was tight across the chest but otherwise fit her well. He found her a helmet, though it needed rags stuffed in its sides to keep it in place. He showed her how to hold her sword, taught her the basics of thrust and parry, ordered an embarrassed Lochlánn to work with her.

Two days in the dúnad and then in the predawn dark, Louis and Aileran roused the men and got them under arms and marched them off toward the river. Failend walked at the head of the column at Louis's side. She felt the weight of the mail on her shoulders and the pull of the sword and dagger on the belt around her waist and the incongruous soft brushing feel of the leine around her legs.

The sun came up and the light revealed a misty grey morning, and with the lifting of the night came a lifting of the dream feeling that had enveloped her like the fog. She was marching off to a fight, but this was not a new thing to her. She had marched with the men to the Meeting of the Waters and back again. The mail, the sword, she had grown used to them over the past few days. She felt like she was waking up, like the wagon, rolling down hill, had reached a flat place and the momentum was coming off it, and it was slowing down.

This was not a dream anymore. She was awake in a new place, a wonderful place. This was the place she had been looking for ever since she had gone from girl to woman. She was not bored.

They came to the edge of the wood line that bordered the river and Louis called for the men to halt and rest, and he and Aileran and Lochlánn headed into the trees. Failend came with them because she wanted to, and it seemed that people had stopped trying to tell her what to do, which she reckoned a good thing. They paused when the river was in sight through the trees, then crept up to where they could see. There were no ships, only the woods and the churning water running over the shallow bottom.

They went back to where the rest of the men, nearly two hundred in all, waited in the tall grass.

"The archers will be first at the river bank," Louis told the men. "They'll shoot down as many of the heathens as they can. Then you men with spears, you'll be right at the water's edge. When the heathens attack, the archers will drop back. The heathens will have to fight their way up a steep bank and you will be there to kill them when they do."

Failend could see anxious looks flashing back and forth among the bóaire and the fuidir. At the Meeting of the Waters there had been no archers, because the archers were among the men Father Finnian had brought. In that fight, Louis had sent the men-at-arms in first, the farmers behind them. It was an arrangement that the bóaire and the fuidir had liked, and it worked well. But now they were being ordered to take the first assault.

"Kill two of them, that's all I ask," Louis continued. "Use your spears. Kill them as they come. Kill two and then you can drop back and let the heathens run right into the men-at-arms."

With this the bóaire and the fuidir nodded. Two men. They could stand fast for the time it took to kill two men. That seemed like a thing they could do.

Later, before the fighting had started, Failend asked Louis if he thought the spear-wielding farmers would really stand long enough to kill two heathens each.

Louis shrugged. "Some will," he said. "Some will run at the first sight of a heathen. But some will stand and keep killing. It's the way of men in battle. No man ever knows what he'll do, and no commander either, until they are in the middle of it. But if I had told them to hold their ground and fight to the end, if they saw no hope of escape, then I can guarantee they would run like rabbits."

Louis and Aileran led the men down to the water's edge and positioned them as Louis had described. They stood ready and waited. The rain set in and they waited, the cold drops working their way down through the leaves and soaking them through. And then the heathens came, just as Louis had said they would.

In silence the Irish stood ready, tense and fearful, unable to see from their cover of bracken and trees what was going on down river.

Only Louis and Aileran saw, approaching the river bank on their knees like supplicants to the altar, parting the brush, peering out like frightened creatures. But Failend knew they were not frightened because they were not the ones being hunted.

Ten minutes later, in a voice that was little more than a breath, Louis told her that the heathens were unloading their ships to lighten them enough to drag over the shallows. It seemed to Failend there was little need for such quiet. The rain was loud and the great beastly heathens were louder still, calling to one another in their coarse gibberish.

Failend knew that the heathens were not frightened either, because they did not know how close death hovered above them.

It was almost an hour after they first appeared downstream that the Northmen discovered the proximity of death. The fighting, when it started, played out almost exactly as Louis had envisioned. The spearmen did their work, and when the heathens finally managed to get among them, Failend stood with Louis, her sword in hand. She even managed to slash at some of the bastards as they came at her, though Louis or Lochlánn seemed always there to take the brunt of the attack.

This fighting was not like the Meeting of the Waters. Then, her head had been whirling, she had hardly been aware of what was going on. It was different now. She could see. She could think.

And because of that she understood what it meant when more of the heathens appeared out of the trees to their left, when the men-at-arms were forced to swing away from the river bank and meet this new threat. In the end the Northmen had driven the Irish off. But they had not won the day. Far from it.

Louis and Aileran led the men, somber and weary, back to the dúnad. Some of the wounded walked with arms flung over the shoulders of comrades on either side, a few were carried in makeshift litters. Failend stumbled along. She felt exhausted like she had never felt before. And she felt strong in a way she had never felt before.

Once again she did not return to her husband's pavilion. The great surge of power that the fighting had brought on had not dissipated. What she wanted, and wanted desperately, was to be with Louis, to go to his tent, to run her hands over him and feel his strong arms on her naked flesh. She shivered as she thought about it. But even the reborn Failend retained some sense of discretion, so she avoided Louis, found a tent that had been owned by one of the men killed at the Meeting of the Waters, and made her camp there.

The next day mounted patrols were sent out along the river to keep an eye on the heathens, but the rest of the men remained in the dúnad. Louis and Aileran and some of the lead men among the warriors Finnian had brought met in Colman's pavilion, where they discussed how next to unleash their fury on the Northmen. Or so Failend imagined. On a few occasions she could hear raised voices from within the oiled cloth walls. She kept her distance.

With Louis occupied in planning the campaign and Lochlánn off leading one of the patrols, there was little for Failend to do and no one with whom she wished to speak, so soon after the sun went down and the gray day melted into black night she crawled into her tent to sleep. Under the dead man's blankets she slept soundly and dreamed wild dreams. It was still dark when someone shook her awake.

She gasped and sat up quick, and her hand fell on the grip of her sword, but she could see nothing. Then she heard Louis's voice, soft, just a few feet away.

"Failend?" he said, and now she could see his outline against the darker land beyond. She wondered why he had not just slipped into her tent and lay down beside her.

"Yes?"

"We're going out to scout the heathens. Do you wish to come?"

She was quiet, trying to make sense of this in her sleep-numbed brain. "Yes," she said again and picked up her sword and slipped out of the tent.

Somewhere above, the moon was casting its light behind the thick overcast of clouds and blunting the edge of the dark. Failend could see Louis now, or at least the dark shadow of him, and a larger figure behind whom she recognized as Aileran.

"What's happening?" she asked, realizing she had said "yes" before she really had any notion of what was going on.

"Aileran had word from one of his men," Louis said in a low voice, "that the heathens have sent a small band along the river. Said they were camped not more than a mile or so from here. We were going to take a look. Fight them if we can."

Failend looked from Louis to Aileran, who stood just five feet away. She could see other men now, a dozen or so under arms. A small war party.

"And you want me to go?" Failed asked.

"Certainly," Louis said, and she could hear the pleasure in his voice. "You seem to delight in this sort of thing."

Failend nodded though she knew no one could see her. The gesture was more for herself. "Captain Aileran," she said, turning in his direction, "you don't mind?"

"No, ma'am," Aileran said, his voice like a grunt.

"It was Aileran suggested it," Louis said.

Failend nodded again. She was awake now, her senses sharp like a rabbit on the verge of bolting. There was something wrong here. She was certain of it, Louis's blindness aside. Aileran might tolerate her presence, but he would not encourage it.

She knew she should decline the offer. It was the smart thing to do. But she could not leave Louis to whatever waited down the road. And, in truth, she was curious, and curiosity seemed to outweigh fear these days.

"Very well," Failend said. "I thank you, Captain Aileran. I'm delighted to come." There was nothing else she could say. She pulled her mail shirt over her head, strapped her belt around her waist and made certain sword and dagger were hanging properly, then headed off at Louis's side into the predawn dark.

Their horses were gathered just beyond the camp and the patrol mounted in silence. The road was barely visible in the feeble light, but they found it and headed east, down river, over ground that would have been quite familiar to Failend if she could have seen it. They did not speak. Only the soft thump of the horses' hooves and the jingle of mail disturbed the quiet, and even that made so little noise that the insects in the grass and the frogs off toward the water did not pause in their songs as they passed.

Failend was soon lost in the steady, wordless ride through the night world and she had no sense of the passage of time. An hour, she thought. They had been riding about an hour and the dawn still showed no sign of arriving when Aileran said, softly, barely a whisper, "Here. Hold up here."

The sound of riding men stopped and the night became more quiet still, weirdly quiet. "Just over that rise," Aileran said. He pointed to a small hill just south of the road, barely visible against the sky.

Failend frowned. *How could he know that's the right hill?* she wondered. *I can hardly see the damned thing…* But not for the first time she assumed Aileran, as an experienced man-at-arms, had ways of knowing things that she did not understand.

"Let us go have a look," Louis said in the same breathy whisper. "Failend, with us."

They dismounted and Aileran turned to the men-at-arms behind, who were also sliding off their horses. "You come with us to the base of the hill, then wait there," he said. "Do not move. We'll shout for you if we need you. If we do, there'll be no more need for quiet."

The men made soft murmurs of understanding. Aileran turned and headed toward the rise, more a grassy mound than a hill, Failend and Louis at his heels, the rest following behind. At the bottom of the rise the men-at-arms stopped and the three continued moving up on their own. They crouched as they climbed and kept low as they reached the top.

There was nothing to see beyond the crest, no smoldering campfires, no sleeping men sprawled about, no guards half awake. Nothing but field, stretching away, and beyond it the dark shapes of trees by the river.

"Got the wrong hill, maybe?" Aileran said, his voice even softer than the rustle of the swaying tree branches. He looked back at Louis and Failend, then waved his hand and led them down the far side of the slope, putting the high ground between them and the dozen men-at-arms.

The land began to level out as they reached the bottom of the hill and once again Aileran signaled for them to stop. They paused and listened, but could hear only the night sounds. Failend felt jumpy, like little bolts of lightning were shooting through her. She was perfectly silent, but in her mind bells tolled a danger warning.

"There," Aileran said. He pointed out into the dark but Failend could see nothing, and Louis apparently could see nothing, either. He took a step past Aileran and then another step as he peered out across the open ground.

Then Aileran shouldered Failend aside. She saw his arm move. The blade of his knife reflected the dull light of the sky and the sight of it made her furious, instantly and completely furious. Furious at Aileran's treachery, at Louis's stupidity, and furious mostly because Aileran considered her so little a threat, such an afterthought, that he just pushed her out of the way so he could get on with the important business of killing Louis.

Aileran cocked his arm for a powerful straight thrust that would plunge the knife right into Louis's back. The blade was darting forward when Failend stepped up and brought her arm down hard on his wrist, striking with her mail-clad forearm, knocking Aileran's hand and knife aside.

Louis turned and said something in a harsh whisper but Aileran's attention was on Failend now. She could not make out his face but she could see his arm coming up, knife still held in his grip, as he turned toward her. Her left hand shot out and grabbed his wrist. She knew she did not have anything like the strength to hold him, but she needed only to slow him down for a second, no more.

Aileran made a grunting noise and shook off Failend's grip but by then her dagger was out of its sheath and swinging around at Aileran's chest. She had time enough to wonder if the needle-sharp point would punch through his mail, and then the blade hit and did not pause as it parted the tiny metal rings and plunged into his chest.

A gurgling noise came from Aileran's throat, and he staggered and Failend could see his hands flailing at the knife jutting from him. She let go of the grip and let Aileran stumble back, one step, two steps, and then he dropped to the ground, still kicking feebly as the life drained quickly and silently away.

"Failend! By God..." Louis gasped, still with sense enough to speak soft.

"He was trying to kill you. And then me," she said, fairly certain that the second part was correct. She pointed to Aileran's knife on the ground.

"Kill...why?"

"Why do you think, you dumb ass?" she hissed. She looked up at the hill, half expecting to see the silhouette of the dozen men-at-arms who had accompanied them coming over the rise, but she saw nothing. She forced herself to breathe normally and listened. Nothing.

"Those men," she said, nodding toward the hill, "are with Aileran. Even if they're not part of this, they'll take us back to Colman and it will be no better than if Aileran killed us here. Worse."

Louis seemed to be nodding. "So...?"

"So we have to run. There." She pointed to the trees at the far end of the field. "Get clear of these men, hide, and then figure what to do."

Louis was nodding again. Failend stepped over toward Aileran, who was now motionless on the ground. She could just make out the handle of her dagger sticking up from his chest. She took a grip and pulled, and with some effort drew the weapon free. She was wiping it clean on the tail of Aileran's tunic when she noticed the purse hanging from his belt. With no thought as to why, she cut the purse strings with the dagger, sheathed the weapon and tucked the soft leather bag into her belt.

"Let's be off," she whispered. She turned her back on Aileran, on the hill that concealed them from the view of the men-at-arms. She and Louis de Roumois moved quickly through the tall grass to the dark trees by the water's edge.

Chapter Thirty

At every door-way,
ere one enters,
one should spy round.
Hávamál

They had no small boats, so Thorgrim ordered *Sea Hammer* rowed up to the north bank of the river, her bow driven into the mud and Harald and his twenty man scouting party set ashore. They were wearing mail and helmets and carried swords or axes or spears. Their shields hung from straps on their backs. The weapons were for defense, if needed. Their job was not to fight, as Thorgrim had told Harald, and then told him again and then one more time to be certain he understood.

"Stay out of sight as best you can," Thorgrim said. He was standing at *Sea Hammer*'s bow. Harald and his men were already ashore. "A scout is most effective if he is not seen. Stay close to the river, close enough to give us warning if need be, but you don't need to stay in sight of it. Wherever you can best see what's happening."

"Yes, father," Harald said. Thorgrim had told him this already and Harald struggled to keep the impatience from his voice. "I'll meet up with you when you have anchored for the night," he continued, repeating his father's instructions before his father had the chance.

"Very good. Good luck," Thorgrim said. He said it in an off-hand way, without any note of sentimentality, which Harald appreciated. Then Thorgrim turned and walked back to *Sea Hammer*'s afterdeck, giving orders to the rowers to back water as he passed.

Harald watched the ship pull away from the bank, then he turned his back on the river. "Let's go," he said and he pushed past his small army and took the lead, working his way up the steep bank, digging his toes into the ground to keep from slipping.

He reached the top of the river bank and stepped into the trees. From downstream where the shallows began, forest and brush crowded the shoreline and followed the river bank as far as he could see. For all he knew the dense woods ran clear up to Glendalough, but he doubted it. He paused for a moment and assumed the posture of someone waiting for others to catch up, but he took that moment to stop and think.

We can't stay in the woods, he realized. *We can hardly move through here.* In order to prevent another ambush he had to stay ahead of his father's ships, and they would certainly move faster over the water than he and his men could move through the overgrown forest.

Have to move away from the river, he thought next. With any luck the woods did not extend very far inland from the shore. If that was the case, they could move quickly over the ground and still keep an eye on the river bank. If that was not the case he did not know what he would do.

"Very well, follow me," he said, once the last of his men were up the bank. He spoke softly which seemed only proper. He pushed on through the trees, through the undergrowth that whipped at him and grabbed at his mail and leggings. He heard the others following behind.

He and Thorgrim had picked the men, mostly older hands, men who had been with them since Dubh-linn, and in a few cases since they had first come over to Ireland with Ornolf aboard his ship *Red Dragon*. Harald had expected his father to insist that one of the more prominent men among the crew, Agnarr or Godi or even Bersi, perhaps, also join the patrol. Someone to keep an eye on Harald as Harald ostensibly lead the twenty. But Thorgrim had done no such thing. That surprised Harald. And it made him happy. And nervous.

He could see now that the woods were thinning, a hopeful sign, and after another thirty feet of fighting through the bracken the forest tapered off to saplings and then to a field of waist-high grass. Harald held up his hand and the men behind him stopped. He crouched low and moved out ahead, parting the grass as he went, eyes moving left and right, ears sharp for any sound. A partridge burst into flight five feet in front of him, a chaos of beating wings and squawking bird. Harald jumped, gasped, and his hand was on the hilt of his sword before his mind had even registered what had startled him.

The noise of the wingbeats faded and Harald remained motionless, listening. He heard nothing, no sound of men alerted to their presence by the startled bird, nothing but the breeze and the river some ways behind them. He waited a minute more, then waved for the others to follow.

They found a road another two rods away, beaten and well-traveled, a road that was now a wide band of dark brown mud after the days of rain. The tracks were still visible: wagon ruts and the footprints of many men who had passed that way. The footprints of the small army that had ambushed them by the river, Harald guessed. One of his men found a broken and discarded spear shaft, the iron point bent at the tip.

"This is good," Harald said, meaning the road. "Ulf, Vemund," he called to two of his men and they stepped forward. Ulf and Vemund were young men, only a few years older than Harald, if that. They were tall and fair; Vemund's long hair blonde to the point of being nearly white. And they were also swift of foot and athletic, one of the reasons Harald had chosen them.

"You'll go ahead of us," Harald said. "Stick to the tree line. Be cautious, keep hidden as you move. If you see anyone, anything, one of you come back and report. The other keep watch."

Ulf and Vemund nodded. They knew what was expected. They were to make certain that the patrol didn't blunder into some enemy coming down the road, or anyone else who might betray their presence. They turned and hurried up the road at a jog.

Harald beckoned to two others. "You two, you take up the rear. Follow a couple hundred paces behind us, make sure no one is coming from that way. The rest of you, with me."

They moved out, Harald leading them off the road and back toward the trees where they could find cover quickly if they had need of it. The tall grass parted in front of them as they walked, a short column of armed men moving through the wet morning, woods to the left, open country to the right. Somewhere up ahead Ulf and Vemund were outpacing them, moving swiftly along the path of the river, alert like deer in an open meadow. Or so Harald hoped.

The going was easier than Harald had thought it would be, the ground open and forgiving, and soon they were several miles from the point where Thorgrim had set them ashore.

Can't lose the river, Harald thought, one of a dozen worries and considerations that crowded his mind and made him forget how pleased he was to be in sole command of this patrol. He had to move fast, but he also had to stay close to the water, because that was where an enemy might be lying in ambush. It would also prevent him from getting lost and wandering hopelessly around the countryside. But the woods to the left obscured his view of the water, and he could only hope that the road they were following was not trending away from the river banks.

They walked on, and to Harald's relief the tree line soon yielded to open ground, and the river came into view once again. It was not more than a dozen rods to the south, a gray, rippling water course running through a dark green, rolling countryside.

There were no ships to be seen, but Harald had not thought there would be. When they first set out Harald had caught the occasional glimpse of the longships as they made their way up river, but soon he and his men had outpaced the fleet. They were still well ahead of them, apparently, which was good. That was where they were supposed to be.

Olaf Thordarson, one the few left who had sailed with them from Vik, knelt beside him and they looked out over the low, rolling hills. "Do you see anything of Vemund or Ulf?" Olaf asked.

"No," Harald said. "But I wouldn't expect to, if they're doing what they should."

Olaf grunted. "Look beyond that hill," he said and pointed to a place half a mile away, a hill that rose up from the river's edge and obscured the ground beyond it. The road tended away from the river there, going north around the hill rather than cresting it.

"Looks like smoke to me," Olaf said once Harald was looking in the right direction. Harald nodded. It did look like smoke, a thin trail of smoke rising up over the edge of the hill, dissipating into the low-hanging mist.

Harald frowned. "I wonder where Vemund and Ulf have got off to," he said. Smoke must mean men, and men would mean something that should have been reported back. He felt a little tremor of fear. Not fear for his physical safety, or that of his men.

That would not even occur to him. It was fear of failing in the eyes of his father. That, above all things, frightened him.

"Let's go," he said, louder than he had spoken before. He stood and led the way forward, downhill through the tall grass. There was no cover here, no way to hide the column, so they moved at a near jog over the open ground, chainmail making its soft shushing sound. They did not run. Harald knew better than to tire men out needlessly when the possibility of a fight was always present.

They reached the bottom of the sloping ground and began climbing the hill that Ulf had pointed out. The smoke was more clearly visible now, the fire that was its source apparently growing in strength. Harald slowed as they reached the crest of the hill, crouched lower and signaled to the others to do the same. He moved forward slowly, eyes searching the country beyond.

Harald stopped. He turned to the others. "Get down," he said and the sixteen men at his back went down on one knee. Harald bent lower still and moved slowly toward the top of the hill. He went down on both knees and then hands and knees as he climbed the last few feet to where he could see beyond the hill's crest. Then he laid on his stomach, hoping he could not be seen against the gray sky, and looked.

The river bent away to the left, and once again there were trees lining the bank, a few hundred yards of thick wood before it gave way again to open land. A tolerable place for another ambush.

To the right the road wound around the hill and tended back in the direction of the water, passing just fifty yards or so in front of where Harald lay. But it was the source of the smoke that had his attention now. It was a cooking fire, a fairly substantial one with a big iron pot hanging from a tripod above it. There was a big man tending the fire. He and his fire were ringed by three of the oddest wagons Harald had ever seen. They were tall with wide oak wheels and high wooden sides painted yellow and red that managed to look cheerful even on that gloomy day. Flags and bunting were mounted at various places, the wet cloth moving just a bit in the breeze.

Harald remained motionless, watching. The wagons were no more than a hundred yards away. He could see another man rummaging through a trunk beside the middle wagon and someone else – he was fairly certain it was a woman – climbing into the wagon nearest him.

Just as he was considering what his next move might be, Harald saw a door open at the back of the wagon to the left and a man step out from the dark interior. He wore a blue tunic and yellow leggings. There was something gray slung over his shoulder which to Harald's practiced eye looked like a mail shirt. His nearly white hair stood out sharply in the gray light.

"Vemund, you stupid bastard," Harald muttered to himself. Now he knew what he would do next. Give Vemund a good thrashing and send him packing back to the fleet, then drag Ulf off whatever whore he was currently riding and do the same to him.

He stood and turned and signaled for the others to follow. He could feel his anger mount and he hurried down the far side of the hill toward the caravan and his wayward scout.

You put the whole rutting thing in danger, you and your limp cock, he thought as he hurried along. He saw Vemund look up at their approach, saw him drop the sword and belt in his hand and struggle to get the mail shirt over his head, and that made Harald even madder still.

What Harald did not see was the line of Irish horsemen in the trees. He and his men were still fifty yards from the caravan when the riders came bursting out into the open. One moment it was quiet, save for the muted sound of voices from the wagons, and then the air was filled with men shouting, urging their mounts forward, the pounding of hooves in the soft dirt, the shouts of surprise from Harald's men as they turned to face this new threat.

"Bastards!" Harald shouted, and with that one word he meant to encompass them all: Vemund, Ulf, Ottar, Kevin, the Irish, all of those who were making his life a misery. His father had trusted him with this crucial task and now the whole thing was falling apart like a rotten log. It made Harald furious. He would not allow this to happen.

"You men with spears, up front!" he shouted and the six of his men who carried spears stepped forward to take the brunt of the horsemen's attack. "Shield wall, make a shield wall!"

There were no more than ten mounted warriors, a scouting party like his own. They had probably spotted Vemund and Ulf as the idiots followed their cocks to the wagons. They would have guessed there would be more Northmen coming behind, so rather than attack the two they had set their trap and waited.

The mounted men were closing fast, coming on at a gallop, swords drawn, spears down. It was a bold move; Harald's band outnumbered them, but the Irish likely hoped the men on foot would scatter before the thundering horses and be cut down as they ran.

Harald pulled Oak Cleaver from his scabbard, ready for the horsemen, ready to kill any of his own men who ran, but he did not think that would be necessary.

"Steady, wait for them," Harald said. It took extraordinary courage and considerable experience in battle to stand firm in the face of such a charge. These men had both those things and they would hold their ground and brace for the horsemen to ride down on them. But Harald would not.

With a shout he pushed forward, past the line of his men, came to a stop ten yards ahead of them. He was still shouting, Oak Cleaver dancing in front of him, the blade threatening his attackers and challenging them. He could see looks of surprise on the rider's faces one hundred feet away. He saw one horseman swerve and nearly collide with the man beside him.

But they recovered fast because clearly they, too, were trained and experienced men. The rider in the center of the charging rank was fifty feet away as he lined himself up with Harald, spear held low, the wicked iron tip steady and pointing right at Harald's guts. The man would expect Harald to jump to his left, to try and get out of the path of horse and weapon. Harald knew it. It was the natural thing to do.

Forty feet. The horse's teeth were bared, its feet throwing up big clods of dirt behind. The pounding of the hooves was the only thing Harald could hear. He took a tentative step to his left like a man ready to break in fear. He took another.

Twenty feet and the spear point was coming at him like an arrow shot from a bow. The warrior on the horse was shouting. Harald crouched slightly than pushed off hard, not moving to his left but leaping to his right, leaping right across the path of the charging beast.

The horse lashed out at Harald with snapping teeth, missing by a foot, no more, as Harald crossed the animal's path. He could see the shock on the rider's face as he whipped his head around to see where Harald had gone. The Irishman pulled the reins over hard and tried to swing his spear across the horse's neck as Harald drove Oak

Cleaver right up into the rider's side, felt the point pierce mail, pierce flesh, hit bone and drive in farther.

The rider's shout turned to a scream and the horse rushed past and Oak Cleaver was pulled free from the man's side, but the blade had done all the damage it needed to do. Harald raced back to the line his men had made, but there was no line now. The Irish had hit his band with all the power their horses and weapons could deliver. Two of his men were down, but three of the horses were rider-less and one was wounded, bucking and rearing as its rider tried to remain in the saddle.

"At them! At them!" Harald shouted but his men had already recovered from the shock of the Irish assault and were fighting back. Olaf Thordarson grabbed hold of a rider's spear as the man rode past and used it to pull the rider down from his horse. The Irishman still had his feet in the stirrups, struggling for control of his weapon, when Olaf finished him with his battle ax.

To Harald's right a man whirled his horse around, turning the animal in a full circle, assessing the fight. Harald leapt at him, leading with Oak Cleaver, but the rider saw him coming and batted the blade away, coming back with a counterstroke that forced Harald to leap aside.

"Back!" the mounted man shouted, "Back, back!" There were only five men still mounted but they reacted without hesitation, driving spurs into their horses' flanks, jerking reins sideways as their mounts once again gathered speed, charging back toward the tree line, back the way they had come.

"Stop them! Stop them!" Harald shouted, but it was a pointless gesture. In three paces the horses were beyond the reach of Harald's men. Harald chased after the riders and several of his men did likewise, but they covered no more than twenty feet before they pulled to a stop.

Harald leaned forward and gasped, sucking in lung-fulls of air. He could feel the sweat standing out on his brow and running down his sides under his tunic and mail. Then he straightened and turned back toward his men and the bloody results of that short, hard fight.

"Are any alive?" Harald asked. "Any of the Irish still alive?" His men glanced down at the Irish warriors strewn on the ground, the one still hanging from his stirrups. Olaf turned one of them over with his foot. Heads were shaking.

"No," one of Harald's men answered at last. "None still alive."

Idiot, idiot, Harald chastised himself. He turned and looked toward the river. The last of the riders was just disappearing around the edge of the woods that ran along the bank. They would report on Harald's presence to whoever had sent them. And there was not even a prisoner left alive to tell Harald who that was, or how many men he commanded, or where the rest of his army was.

He turned back to his men. He had to make a decision, and fast, because he knew that there was nothing more fatal to command than indecisiveness. Once the Irish scouts returned to their camp a larger force would no doubt be sent out to hunt them down. The only reasonable thing to do was to go back the way they had come and meet up with his father's fleet. Explain what had happened, admit the mistakes he had made.

And even as Harald thought those things he knew he would do nothing of the kind. He would find another way. He would return to *Sea Hammer* either successful or dead. And then his eyes moved beyond his men to the three wagons sitting just fifty yards away.

Chapter Thirty-One

[O]ft doth a man ill counsel get
when 'tis born in another's breast.
Hávamál

Thy spent one more day working the longships up the River Avonmore toward Glendalough. One more day during which Thorgrim Night Wolf and Ottar Bloodax pointedly ignored one another. But neither of those things could last.

They were running out of water, or at least water deep enough to float their vessels. The shorelines to larboard and starboard continued to close in on them, the river only three or four rods wide, and the current ran stronger with each labored mile they made upstream. It was two days after the ambush, and they had kept to the oars for most of that morning, pulling hard and making little headway against the rushing water.

"This won't do," Agnarr said to Thorgrim. They were on the afterdeck, Agnarr at the tiller, Thorgrim scanning the banks. Their thoughts were on the men forward, leaning into the oars, sweat running down red faces as they pulled.

Thorgrim had been looking out for Harald and his men, trying to catch some glimpse of them on the river bank. He did not expect he would. In truth he would have been angry if he had, because that would mean Harald was not concealing himself well and was not far enough up river to properly scout out an ambush.

But there was no sign of Harald and his scouting party and Thorgrim hoped they were doing a proper job. The rest of the men were paying a price for having them probing ahead, fighting the current with twenty less men to row than *Sea Hammer* would normally have carried.

"You're right. This won't do," Thorgrim said. "We'll run her up on the bank, there." He pointed to a stretch of low, gravely riverbank off the starboard bow. "This is as far as we get."

"Are we near to Glendalough?" Starri Deathless asked. He was sitting up now, though still in his nest of furs, still barely able to stand. There was more power in his voice, however, more strength in his movements, limited though they still were. His flesh was not as pallid as it had been just the day before.

"I don't know," Thorgrim admitted. "None of us has been this far up river. It was Kevin who was supposed to lead us to Glendalough."

Starri nodded. "Kevin," he said. "What will you do with Kevin?"

"I'll kill him," Thorgrim said. He did not need to think about it because he already had, in some detail. "If I can catch him I will kill him. I will do it slowly if I'm able. I'll see that his death is without honor, so that I never have to meet him again in the corpse hall."

Starri gave a weak smile. "Kevin follows the Christ god. They don't expect to go to the corpse hall," he said. "I don't think they want to."

Thorgrim nodded. He had forgotten that. "Where do these people think they will go when the gods take them?" he asked.

"I don't know," Starri said.

Before Thorgrim could reply, *Sea Hammer*'s bow ran onto the sand and gravel shore and he had to put theological concerns aside. The Avonmore ran through mostly open country there, which Thorgrim reckoned unfortunate. He would have preferred trees to hide the longships' presence. Trees were few, however, though there were some at the top of the river bank to which they made their bowlines fast.

He looked down river toward the rest of his fleet, and Ottar's ships beyond. Bersi's men were rowing hard, pulling *Blood Hawk* stroke by painful stroke upriver as Thorgrim's crew had done *Sea Hammer*. Now they pulled her toward the river bank and beached her beside Thorgrim's ship. As they tied her off Bersi Jorundarson made his way forward and dropped into the river by her bow.

Thorgrim walked forward and jumped down from *Sea Hammer*'s bow into ankle deep water. Farther downstream *Dragon* and *Fox*, still under oars, drove their bows into the shallow river's edge and their men went over the sides with ropes in hand to make them fast ashore.

Ottar's ships were following a dozen rods behind his.

What will you do, Ottar, you bastard? Thorgrim wondered. *Pass me once again?*

Five minutes later he had an answer, as Ottar's ship turned to starboard and ran its bow into the river bank some ways down river from *Fox*, and his other ships did the same. This was as far up the Avonmore as any of them were going to go by water.

Bersi came dripping out of the river and joined Thorgrim, and Kjartan and Skidi Oddson came walking up from where their ships were tied, and the four men stood in a circle. "We'll get the ships no closer than this," Thorgrim said. "We'll cover the rest of the way to Glendalough on foot. I don't know how far that is."

The others nodded and looked around, as if there was something that might indicate how far off the monastery lay. Thorgrim looked up at the sun.

"Too late to continue today, and the men are done in from rowing and towing the ships," Thorgrim said. "And it's not as if we have a hope of surprising the Irish. We'll make a fire on the shore here, give the men a decent supper."

Heads nodded again.

"We'll send men out to find a prisoner, someone who can tell us how far we are from the monastery," Thorgrim continued. "Also…." He paused, not wishing to say what he had to say, "we'll have to speak with Ottar and his men. Kevin was our go-between, but he seems to have run off so now we have no choice. We'll need the crews of all the ships if we have any hope of raiding Glendalough. Even then it's in doubt. These Irish aren't fools and they aren't cowards, and there are a lot of them."

Heads nodded. There was quite a bit going unsaid because there was no need to say it. No one trusted Ottar and no one wished to fight by his side, but the only other choice was to abandon the enterprise, and having come so far that was not really a choice at all.

"We need to meet with Ottar and his lead men," Thorgrim said. "We'll meet on the shore, half way between his ships and ours. Kjartan, will you go to him and tell him?"

Kjartan gave a half smile. "I will, but you'll get no answer back," he said. "He'll kill me on sight. And if he fails, his men will."

Thorgrim frowned and he could see the uncertain looks on the others' faces. "He'll kill you?" Thorgrim asked. "You said he's your brother."

"He is," Kjartan said. "But that makes no difference to him. I swore an oath to serve him. Back at the village, at the mouth of the river. And then I saw what he had done there. I always knew he was a madman but I…I don't know what I thought."

There was a note in Kjartan's voice that Thorgrim had never heard before. Regret. Fear. Kjartan continued.

"I knew the gods would not favor a man who butchered for no reason, and I did not want to be cursed by his bad luck. So I abandoned him first chance I had. Joined you. I did not think we would see him again."

"But we've been in his company for a week or more," Skidi said. "Why has he not killed you yet? Or tried to?"

"He's not seen me," Kjartan said. Thorgrim nodded as he thought back to the few times that he and his lead men had met with Ottar. Kjartan had indeed made himself scarce. He had always kept *Dragon* well away from Ottar's fleet.

"Ottar must not see much," Thorgrim said.

"Only what he wants to see," Kjartan said.

In the end Bersi was sent to speak with Ottar. When he came back he reported that Ottar had cursed and spit and raged and then at last agreed to meet once the men had had their supper. That was fine with Thorgrim. The later the better. There was much he still needed to learn, much he needed to do. He called Godi and Agnarr, his most trusted men now that Harald was away.

"I need you two to take a few men, whoever you wish, and go out beyond where our lookouts are posted," he told them. "Try to grab some traveler, someone on the road. Bring them back here where I can question them. We need to know where Glendalough is, how far." How he was going to question an Irishman without Harald there he did not know, but he hoped signs and the few words he had picked up of the Irish language would suffice.

Perhaps he would make Segan translate. Thorgrim was fairly certain the Irish thrall knew more of the Norsemen's tongue than he let on.

Godi and Agnarr chose three others and they clambered over the high bank of the river and were gone. Thorgrim fetched two bowls of the strew that was cooking in a big iron pot over the fire and brought them back to *Sea Hammer* where he gave one to Starri and ate the other himself. The gray afternoon faded into night as Thorgrim waited for his men to return, hoping they would be back before he had to meet with Ottar.

To pass the time he sharpened his dagger, a thing he had not done in some time. Starri was the one who usually sharpened weapons. It calmed him, and his skill at the task was clearly a gift from the gods. It was a skill too great to be otherwise.

When the blade was as sharp as Thorgrim could make it, he slipped it into its sheath and stood. He thought Starri was asleep, so it surprised him when he spoke.

"It will take me hours to undo the damage you have done to that knife's edge," Starri said. He spoke softly and did not open his eyes.

"I know," Thorgrim said. "That's why I did it. So you would not be bored."

Starri made a little grunting sound, and Thorgrim was about to say more when his attention was drawn to the river bank. Something was happening. It was nearly full dark by then, the fire bright and casting its illumination around the gravel shore. In the light of the flames he could see the unmistakable bulk of Godi coming down the banking, and with him Agnarr and another man. Their prisoner, he hoped.

Thorgrim moved to the bow and hopped down to the beach, and as he approached the fire he realized the man with Godi was Vemund, one of the men who had gone with Harald. He felt a sudden foreboding, a flash of dread, but he could see Vemund's face and he did not look like a man who had come to report a tragedy.

"Vemund," Thorgrim greeted him and took his hand.

"We found him on the road, lord, a mile or so away," Godi said. "He was looking for us."

"Harald sent you?" Thorgrim asked, careful to keep any note of concern from his voice.

"He did, Lord Thorgrim," Vemund said. "He is well and his men are well. Mostly. We were surprised by horsemen, lord, Irish horsemen. Harald led the men in the fight against them. He fought like a bear, lord, killed more than I can count. Harald was at the forefront. He inspired the others."

"Hmmm," Thorgrim said. Vemund was pouring on the praise for Harald like a child pouring honey on porridge. *What did you do, that you so want to get in my good graces?* he wondered. *And Harald's?*

"We lost three men, lord, not Harald's fault at all, but the Irish…."

"Good. It sounds like you behaved well, you all behaved well. Some of the horsemen escaped?" Thorgrim asked, and his clipped tone suggested that simple, unadorned facts would be preferred.

"Yes, lord," Vemund said.

"And they sent no more men to hunt you down?"

"Not while I was still with them, lord," Vemund said. "We continued on along the river, lord, for another hour or so and saw no other Irish. Harald sent me back to find you. Tell you what we learned."

Thorgrim nodded. There was a crowd gathered now.

"We met travelers, lord, going to the Glendalough Fair," Vemund continued. "They knew something of the town."

Thorgrim folded his arms and listened as Vemund relayed the tale. He told what they had learned of the defenses of Glendalough, the house warriors who had gathered there, the crowds assembled for the fair. The monastery was no more than four miles away by land, Vemund said, and the road by the river lead straight to it. A road crowded with travelers and flowing with plunder.

"Good, Vemund, you did well," Thorgrim said at last and the relief on the man's face was evident. "Get something to eat, and then you must return to Harald with word from me."

Vemund nodded and someone handed him a bowl of stew and a wooden spoon. Thorgrim stared into the fire. It was nearly time to meet with Ottar and his men, but that was fine. He knew now what he needed to know. He knew where Glendalough was. He knew how far away it was and how to get there and how big the monastery was and how poorly fortified the town.

And most important of all, he knew more than Ottar did.

Chapter Thirty-Two

*In this year, moreover, many abandoned their
Christian baptism and joined the Norwegians...*
                                        The Annals of Ulster

It was late afternoon before Louis de Roumois and Failend dared emerge from the thick wood into which they had fled.

They had run across the open ground, Failend's hands still sticky with Aileran's blood, his body left behind in the dark. As they ran they tried to listen for Aileran's men in pursuit, but in the quiet they could hear nothing above their own breathing and the thump of their footfalls and the jingling of their mail.

The tall grass yielded to bracken and saplings and soon they were in among the taller trees, and there they stopped. They said nothing, just stood and breathed hard with mouths open. They could hear the river rolling along somewhere beyond that place.

For a few minutes they remained as they were, and soon their breath was back to normal, and the quiet of the night settled down on them. Failend knew there was only one thing to do; plunge deeper into the woods, maybe make their way to the river and see if there was a place they could cross to the other side. Anything that would put distance between them and Aileran's men.

She knew it, but for the moment she felt frozen in place, and so, apparently, did Louis. Instead of pushing on they turned and looked back the way they had come, but the open ground was hidden from view by the woods. They stepped back through the trees and brush, moving carefully, making little noise, and when they came to the edge of the tree line proper they went down on a knee and stared out into the night.

There was nothing. No sound, nothing moving.

"Aileran had told his men to wait," Louis said softly. "Said he'd call for them if they were needed."

"They won't wait forever," Failend said. "They'll find him and they'll look for us. We're murderers now, in their eyes."

It was hard to gauge how long they remained there, kneeling, watching. It seemed quite a long time. Failend was about to suggest they leave off and go deeper into the woods when they heard something, some sound. Far off but not so terribly far off. Something being dropped, or a voice, maybe. A bird or an animal?

And then a voice, clear as steel hitting steel. "Captain?"

Failend tensed and she felt Louis tense. It was one of Aileran's men, and he was still at the far side of the field. He was trying to speak loud and whisper, all at once.

They waited. The voice came again. "Captain Aileran?" Quiet. And then the voice again, loud and surprised, "Oh, by God!"

"We must go," Louis said, just as Failend opened her mouth to say the same. They stood and turned and made their way into the wood. They could see nothing, the dark night made darker by the close-set trees. Failend felt Louis's hand reaching for hers and she took it. It made the going even more awkward, holding hands as they fought their way through the woods, but at least this way they would not be separated.

Failend had no idea of the direction they were running, or if they were even moving in a straight line. It was entirely possible, she realized, that they might be going in a great loop and would emerge from the woods right at the feet of Aileran's men-at-arms, come looking for them.

"Louis," she said in a harsh whisper, but even as the word was leaving her mouth she could see the trees were thinning and then they found themselves on a steep bank looking down at the Avonmore which roiled and curled below them. Failend could see the bank on the far side and the rippled surface of the water, and she realized that the dawn was coming, that the first light of morning was spreading out behind the thick clouds overhead.

They stood still and silent for a moment, listening to the soft sounds of the river and the occasional call of a bird. They listened for the sound of pursuit, armed men crashing through the wood, but they heard nothing.

"They'll come for us," Failend said. "When its light enough, they'll come searching. Our trail will not be hard to find."

Louis nodded. The path they had made running through the tall grass and then crashing through the woods would be simple enough for any hunter to follow. "We should cross the river," he said.

Failend looked down at the water. It was moving fast but did not look terribly deep. "Yes, we should," she agreed.

They made their way carefully down the steep bank and into the river that lapped up against the grass. The water was cold, much colder than Failend had expected, and the force when it hit her ankles nearly took her feet out from under her. She stumbled, held her arms out, steadied herself, then followed Louis out into the stream.

They reached the middle of the river and the water came only up to Louis's waist, though it was much higher on Failend's shorter frame. Her feet were unsteady on the slick rocks, and it occurred to her that, given the current and her mail shirt, if she fell she would never be able to stand again on her own.

Louis offered his arm and she clung to it as they worked their way through the deepest part of the water. Soon they came out on the other side, the river dropping to thigh level, then ankle depth and then they stood dripping in the cool air of the morning. That side of the river was also lined by wood, and they climbed up the bank and into the trees, plunging in until they reached a place where they were well concealed. Then, as if of one mind, they stopped and knelt and peered back across the river.

In just the time it had taken them to cross the Avonmore the morning had grown considerably more light. Where before they could see only the dark shape of the woods, now they could see the trees and the brush and the river bank, all browns and grays and dull greens in the dawn.

They waited.

"We should keep moving," Louis said.

"Yes, we should," Failend agreed. But neither of them moved, and Failend knew it was because neither of them could endure the idea of an unknown enemy at their backs. If someone was coming for them, they had to know.

They waited in silence and Failend's mind ran over the events of the past...hour? Two hours? Certainly no more than that. Incredible.

Her whole life, which had been rolling away in one unanticipated direction, was now flung off in another.

She had killed Aileran. There was no question about that, no ambiguity like there was over the Northman at the Meeting of the Waters. She had driven a dagger right into Aileran's chest. Right into his heart, she imagined. She looked down at her hands. Crossing the river had washed them clean of Aileran's blood and she was glad of that.

My soul will never be washed clean of this, she thought, but in truth she was not entirely sure how she felt about what she had done. She poked at her feelings of guilt, probing to see how deep and painful they ran.

Not very, she realized. Aileran was going to kill Louis. No doubt he would have killed her, too. Her dear husband, using the cover of battle to eliminate two problems at once.

At least he thought enough of me to want my lover murdered, she thought.

Then Louis reached over and grabbed her arm and she was startled out of her reverie. She looked over at him and he pointed across the river. There was movement in the brush, and as they watched, a man, one of Aileran's men, stepped out of the woods and stood on the far bank. He looked up and down the river, turned and looked back the way he had come.

Failend realized she was holding her breath. She opened her mouth and let air waft into her lungs, but otherwise she did not move. The man on the far bank was still looking around. He looked across the water, looked right at the spot where she and Louis were concealed, and it seemed impossible to Failend that he could not see them. But there was no change in his posture, no indication that he saw anything but trees and brush.

He stared in their direction for a moment more, then turned and disappeared into the woods.

Failend let out her breath and heard Louis do the same. They looked at one another and they smiled in their relief. It was a natural reaction but an odd, incongruous one as well.

They remained where they were, motionless, listening, watching. How long they stayed there Failend did not know, but it seemed a very long time. The sun was well up, it was full daylight, though muted and soft under the overcast, when Louis finally spoke.

"They've given up, I think. Gone back to the dúnad. They will have to tell Colman they failed to kill us."

Failend nodded, thought, *Aileran's corpse will tell him that, I suspect.*

For a minute more they remained where they were, then Louis stood up and Failend did as well, her muscles stiff and protesting. She felt her stomach growl, and would have been happy for something the eat. She reminded herself that she had just killed a man a few hours earlier, but she had to admit that seemed to have little effect on her appetite.

Breakfast, however, was not going to happen anytime soon.

Louis looked around. "We should put some more distance between us and your husband's army," he said.

"You can probably stop calling him my husband now," Failend said.

Louis nodded. "Anyway, we should move. That way." He pointed inland, away from the river, but Failend shook her head.

"There's nothing there, just open country," she said. "Maybe some bands of outlaws. We should cross the river again, see if there are travelers on the road who can help us."

She remembered then that she had taken Aileran's purse. She looked down and saw the little bag was still wedged in her belt and she pulled it free.

"This is our entire fortune right here," she said, "unless you happened to have brought your own purse." She tugged the end open and dumped the contents into her open palm. There was not much. A wedge of silver cut from a larger coin, a simple gold ring, and three other silver coins, intact, identical and new-looking.

Louis looked down at the little hoard, then leaned in and looked closer. "Merde…" he said, but in a thoughtful tone. He reached down and picked up one of the three coins, held it up between thumb and forefinger and scrutinized it in the weak light.

"Bâtard…" he mumbled.

"What is it?" Failend asked.

"See here," Louis said. He lowered the coin and pointed to the profile of a man stamped on the side and the blocky letters that encircled him.

"Not a great likeness," Louis said. "I would not have known who it was, if it was not written there."

"I don't know letters," Failend said.

"It says 'Eberhard I'," Louis said. "My brother, count of Roumois. Minting his own coins now, apparently."

Failend shook her head. "Your brother's coin? How does Aileran come to have such a thing?"

"He must have got it from your...from Colman," Louis said. "My brother must think I'm still a threat. The man who tried to kill me back at my cell, he said just one word. Bâtard. I remember now. He was Frankish. He must have been sent by my brother. He must have paid Colman with my brother's coins to have me killed. And Colman paid Aileran out of that."

Failend nodded. *So, Colman didn't care that I was humping someone,* she thought. *At least not enough to have my lover killed. Or have me killed. It's all about some stupid dung heap in Frankia.* This realization did not make her happy.

"Come along, let's go," she said, her tone more snappish than she intended. She pushed her way back through the woods, then back down the river bank, and began crossing to the other side. She did not ask Louis's opinion of her actions, and Louis said nothing, just followed behind.

They came out on the other side of the river and then made their way up the bank and back into the woods. They moved cautiously; both were nearly certain that Aileran's men had returned to the dúnad by then, but not so certain that they dared show themselves in the open. So they worked their way through the wood to where it yielded to the open ground. They found a patch of thick brush and hunkered down there. Each took a turn looking out while the other slept.

It was sometime in the late morning as Failend was keeping watch that she heard the riders approaching. She turned her ear in the direction of the sound. Horses, to be certain. Not too many of them, but more than one. She nudged Louis and he sat up. His hair was tousled and there was a confused look on his face.

"Riders," Failend said in a low voice, wondering as she did why she did not speak out loud. No rational reason not to, but it just seemed like a bad idea.

Louis cocked his head, listened. He nodded. He got to his knees and the two of them looked out toward the road, a quarter mile away. As they did the riders appeared from the north. There were ten of them, men-at-arms, with spears and shields. They rode at a slow trot but there was no urgency about them.

"Scouts," Louis said.

"Looking for us?" Failend asked.

"I'm sure they are," Louis said. "And for the heathens too, I would imagine."

They watched as the riders moved past. If any of the men-at-arms even looked in their direction, they could not tell. Soon after, Louis took over and Failend laid down and gave herself over to a fitful sleep. She woke to Louis shaking her softly.

"Listen," Louis said. Failend listened. Birds. Branches moving in the breeze. Insects. And something else, far off. Sharp sounds, like little things breaking.

"It's a fight of some sort. A mile away. Maybe more," Louis said. They listened but could hear very little, and they could not say for certain what it was they were hearing. Twenty minutes later the riders were back, going the other way. They were riding fast now, and there were fewer of them.

"Whoever they were looking for, they found the heathens, I'll warrant," Louis said.

They continued to wait, continued to watch. They had agreed to remain there until dark, but Failend's stomach no longer cared for that plan, and it was becoming more vocal. She was thirsty as well.

"See here," Louis said, pointing toward the road, pointing in the direction from which they had heard the fighting. There was something moving a long way off, a wagon of some sort. They watched as it made its slow approach, drawn by a team of four oxen, and soon realized there was a second wagon behind it, pulled by a similar team. A few minutes later they saw a third.

"Ha!" Louis said. "I know this fellow! A player and his company. His name is… Crimthann! Yes, that's it."

"Will he help us?" Failend asked.

"I think so," Louis said. "He seemed a decent sort. He'll feed us, at least, though we may have to give him Aileran's hoard in exchange."

"Then let us go," Failend said and she stood for the first time in hours. "He's welcome to cut my throat as long as he gives me a decent meal first."

They stepped from the brush and into the tall grass. They made their way toward the road, heading for a spot where they would meet up with the wagons and their promise of food and drink and, if luck was with them, safety as well.

Chapter Thirty-Three

I pray a prayer to God
that neither death nor danger may come to me...
may [I] not die by point or edge.
The Annals of Ulster

The monastic city of Glendalough sat cupped in a valley surrounded by the high country of Cill Mhantáin. The stone cathedral and the other buildings on the monastery grounds and the vellum and the village clinging to its periphery were all clustered at the base of those steep slopes, where the mountains rolled off in every direction like great ocean swells frozen in place. They were not jagged, forbidding mountains, but rather soft and rounded and tree covered, and when the weather was fine and warm in the summer months they seemed to invite travelers to wend their way through the narrow gaps and meadows between them.

In such a meadow, a few miles to the east of Glendalough, a haphazard camp was spread out over the lush spring grass. Not just a camp but a dúnad, the camp of an army in the field, an army on the march. But they were not marching that day. They were not fighting. They were not doing much of anything. They were just waiting.

They were waiting by order of Kevin mac Lugaed, who commanded the forces there. And Kevin's chief worry at the moment was that his dinner would be ruined by his steward, who was an indifferent cook. The cook back at the ringfort at Ráth Naoi was considerably better, but she was old and would not have tolerated the rigors of campaigning, even though Kevin's campaigns tended to be no more rigorous than a hunting party.

Happily, Kevin's steward had performed better than he normally did, and the roast was served just as Kevin liked it, and the spring vegetables had not been reduced to a viscous mess. Kevin sighed with satisfaction as he pushed the empty plates away and leaned back. And then he heard a voice from beyond the door of his pavilion calling to him and he thought, *Dear God, can I not have a moment's peace?*

"Come!" he shouted. The flap covering the door was lifted and Niall mac Olchobar stepped in. He wore mail and a sword, as was fitting a man-at-arms in the field, though Kevin himself wore only a tunic and leggings and several gold chains around his neck.

"Yes, Niall, what is it?" Kevin asked in a weary tone.

"There's someone to see you, lord," Niall said. "Ah…a priest, lord."

There was hesitation in Niall's voice, as well there might be. "A priest?" Kevin said, frowning. "Did the watchmen bring him in?"

"No, lord," Niall said. "He just appeared in camp."

"Where did he come from?"

"Ah…I'm not certain, lord."

Kevin frowned deeper. He might be an indifferent soldier at best, but he was no fool, and he knew better than to let himself to be caught unawares. There were watchmen surrounding the dúnad, men-at-arms positioned in hidden places looking out in every direction with orders to stop anyone – anyone – who approached the camp. And yet somehow, with the sun well up and no rain or fog, this priest had managed to come unseen into the dúnad.

Kevin stood and stepped past Niall, out of the dim tent and into the watery light of a late morning sun filtered through heavy clouds. The priest was there, just beyond the line of stakes to which the tent ropes were secured, but before acknowledging him Kevin ran his eyes over the dúnad and the countryside beyond, a thing he always did on leaving his pavilion.

There was little activity in the camp. The hundred or so men-at-arms under his command were busy at various tasks; cooking, tending to weapons, sleeping, practicing with sword and shield. They did those things to fill the time as they waited for Kevin to gauge the moment when they should strike. And to decide who they should strike.

Beyond the camp there were the mountains, mountains rolling off to the distance, and the gray sky above. To the west of the dúnad were a pair of rounded hills that in Kevin's mind looked so much like a woman's breasts that he found it titillating to look at them. And he knew that if the hand of God were to suddenly brush them away he would be able to see Glendalough just a few miles distant.

Niall had followed Kevin out of the pavilion, and now he stepped up beside him and gesturing said, "This here's the priest, lord."

Before Kevin could say anything the priest took a step toward him and said, "Kevin mac Lugaed?"

Kevin looked the man over. The priest wore the standard dress of his tribe, a black robe with a cowl falling down his back, a gnarled hickory walking stick in hand. He was smiling, but it was an odd sort of smile. A knowing smile, sympathetic and yet determined.

Here looking for a bloody tithing, I'll warrant, Kevin thought, then said, "Yes, I am Kevin mac Lugaed. And you are?"

"Father Finnian," the priest said. "It's a pleasure to meet you. One hears much of Kevin mac Lugaed, but you were not so easy to find."

Dear Lord, he's starting in with the arse kissing already, Kevin thought. *I don't imagine this one will go away for anything less than a gold chalice.*

"Welcome to my camp, Father," Kevin said. He wanted to ask the priest how he had managed to elude all of the watchmen, but somehow he knew he would get no satisfactory answer. Instead, he asked, "May I help you, poor man that I am?"

"Yes," Finnian said. "You may help me. And I may help you."

Kevin nodded. He waited for more but nothing more came. Finally Kevin broke the silence.

"So, we may help each other," he said. "And how is that?" He was fairly certain he knew the answer already. It would involve salvation in exchange for silver, he suspected.

"You have done well for yourself this past year, Kevin mac Lugaed," Finnian said.

"God has been good to me, Father," Kevin said.

"He has," Finnian agreed. "Last year you were but a Lord of Superior Testimony. Now you are rí túaithe of Cill Mhantáin. And a wealthy man."

Here we go, Kevin thought. "As I said, God has been good to me," he said. "And I have shown my gratitude to God."

"Have you indeed?" Father Finnian said. "How? By conspiring with the heathens to sack Glendalough?"

Finnian's words hit Kevin like a punch to the back of the head: shocking, painful and unexpected.

"Heathens....sacking Glendalough?" he sputtered as he searched for a reply. And then his balance returned, and he realized that he did not need a reply because this Finnian was just a simple priest, and by the look of him and his mud-splattered robe not a particularly important one. Kevin took a step in his direction, a menacing step, with Niall beside him. He expected Finnian to back away, which he did not. But no matter.

"How dare you suggest..." Niall began but Kevin could see that this conversation might be one best kept private.

"Niall," Kevin interrupted. "Pray, leave us."

Niall looked at Kevin, looked at Finnian and then back at Kevin. He did not want to leave, that was clear, but he bowed and said, "Yes, lord." He shot an ugly look at Finnian and then marched off, because there was nothing else he could do.

Kevin turned back to Finnian. "I will not tolerate your accusations or your insolence, *Father*," he said, low and threatening. "Do not presume to come into my camp and impugn my character thus."

"Do you know why you have remained rí túaithe of Cill Mhantáin?" Finnian asked, as if he had not even heard Kevin's words.

"Yes. Because God wishes it," Kevin said.

That answer brought a flicker of a smile to Finnian's lips. "Well, yes, that is the chief reason," he admitted. "But it is also because Ruarc mac Brain allows it. Lord Ruarc could, in fact, crush you at any moment like the loathsome insect you are."

Kevin heard the words, but for a moment the insult was too shocking to register. No one had dared speak to him that way in a long time, and Finnian spoke the words in the same calm, matter-of-fact voice he had been using all along.

Then he realized what Finnian had said, and once again he felt the surprise blow to the back of the head. He felt a flash of rage and he was on the verge of shouting, but he stopped himself. He stood straighter, drew in a deep breath. He was not the sort to let others get the better of him, verbally or otherwise. He would not let some sorry, powerless priest lead him around like an ox with a ring through its nose.

"I have not had the honor of meeting Ruarc mac Brain," Kevin said. "I know he's a powerful man. A fair man. He has that reputation. I do not think he is much interested in me."

"You're right, Lord Kevin," Finnian said. "He cares no more for you than he does for the dung that clings to his boots. But yonder, in Glendalough," Finnian nodded toward the breast-like hills to the west, "wait nearly two hundred of his men. They are there at my behest to try and stop the heathens from sacking the monastery. The heathens, I should say, that you encouraged to come here."

Kevin frowned, but that was all the anger he allowed himself to display. "That's absurd…" he began but Father Finnian stopped him with a wave of his hand.

"Understand, lord, that I make it my business to know what's going on in these lands about," Finnian explained like a patient tutor. "It's the abbot's wish that I do and so I see that wish fulfilled. So I know what you've done, and I suspect now you are waiting for the heathens to kill one another and to kill those who would defend Glendalough and then you'll sweep in and pick up what remains."

"That is ridiculous," Kevin said but even he heard the lack of conviction in his voice. He could no longer muster the proper outrage because, of course, the priest was exactly right. That was exactly what he was doing.

"It's true that Ruarc mac Brain does not care a whit about you," Finnian continued. "But if his men-at-arms die at the hands of the heathens, or worse, at the hands of your men, then he will care very much. And he has many, many more men than you do. I think you know that."

I should just kill this bastard, Kevin thought. *Take him into my tent and kill him. Then I can do as I wish, and Ruarc mac Brain none the wiser.*

Kevin pressed his lips hard together and looked in Finnian's eyes and gathered his resolve. And Finnian met his gaze, his brown eyes deep and patient and thoughtful. He looked as if he knew what Kevin was thinking and was not in the least concerned about it.

They stood like that for a moment, and Kevin felt his resolve draining away like water from a broken cup.

"What is it you would have me do?" he asked, the question coming out like a sigh.

"The heathens will attack soon. Today. March there now, quickly. Join the men defending Glendalough, the local men and

Ruarc mac Brain's, and we will surely drive the heathens back to the sea. Then you can appear to be a hero, and no one the wiser."

Kevin nodded. He did not move.

"Look for a man named Louis de Roumois who has command of the men there," Finnian continued. "He will tell you where to make a stand."

Kevin nodded again. Still he did not move.

"Now would be an excellent time," Father Finnian prompted.

Kevin nodded again. "Niall!" he shouted. "Get the men ready to march! Steward, my mail and sword!"

He looked at Father Finnian. The priest had just taken every plan that Kevin had laid over the past half a year and turned it all on its head. And still the man's expression had not changed, not even in the slightest.

Chapter Thirty-Four

*[T]ogether they attacked the Norwegians fiercely and actively
and pugnaciously, and there was hard and vigorous fighting
between them on both sides.*
                                                The Annals of Ulster

The Glendalough Fair had begun. The muddy streets and the
town square were jammed with people, the booths full, the
vendors shouting, the players taking the stage. Jugglers and
fire-eaters and sundry performers and thieves were at work in every
open place. Men, women, high-born, low-born, priests, monks,
tradesmen, farmers, they were moving like flotsam in the tide. The
sky was overcast but the day was warm and dry. There was a
boisterous, joyful celebratory quality, notable in a town that had spent
the past five months hunched against the winter's rain and cold.

It made Lochlánn profoundly uneasy.

He had always liked the fair. He had come twice as a child, and
after his father had exiled him to the monastery he had looked on its
annual arrival as a happy disruption to the tedium of monastic life.
Not just happy, but vital. He was sure he would have gone mad if he
had not had that one yearly debauchery to look forward to. He had
become remarkably adept at slipping away to partake of the pleasures
of the fair without being discovered by Brother Gilla Patraic or any
of the other monks who kept such close and disapproving watch
over things.

But this year was different in ways he could never have seen
coming. Good ways. He thought of that as he rode slowly through
the crowded square, the half dozen men under his command riding
behind him.

His circumstances had changed, and he had changed too. Here
was proof: one of his fellow monks, loitering by a pie stand, had

looked right at him as he rode by and did not recognize him at all. That was not terribly surprising. Lochlánn was wearing mail and a helmet and a sword on his belt, a shield hanging from a loop on his saddle. No one at Glendalough had ever seen him attired thus. This was the new Lochlánn, the resurrected Lochlánn.

He had been in the saddle since dawn, and his thighs burned and his buttocks felt like they had when he had been paddled as a child. He had been an experienced horseman once, but years at the monastery had softened those parts that needed to be tough if one was to spend hours on horseback. But he forgot the discomfort as he rode through the Glendalough Fair.

A man named Senach rode beside him. He was a young man, just a few years older than Lochlánn. Senach was one of the men-at-arms who had fought with them at the Meeting of the Waters, and though Lochlánn was somewhat intimidated by Senach's training and his status as a professional soldier, he liked the man. And Senach, in turn, seemed respectful and in no way resentful of Lochlánn's position.

"They don't know of the heathens, do they?" Lochlánn said as they waited for a herd of swine to cross their path. "The folks here, they don't seem much worried that they might be butchered on the morrow."

"There have been rumors, I think," Senach said. "They have to know that something's afoot, what with the men-at-arms that've gathered here and the bóaire and the fuidir called up. Even these ignorant bastards have to have guessed there's some sort of threat."

Lochlánn nodded. That was pretty much how he figured it. These people had seen the men-at-arms, they had heard the rumors, maybe even seen the wounded from the Meeting of the Waters who had been sent to the monastery to mend. But the fair was something they had been anticipating for many months, and there was money to be made. The soldiers had marched off and no heathens had been seen, and Lochlánn imagined that was enough for these folks to dismiss any threat of raiders from the sea.

But Lochlánn knew, and Senach knew, how real and immediate the threat really was. There were two or three hundred of the murderous bastards just a few miles downriver, and despite the hurt done to them, they were still coming.

"God help us all if the heathens get here, get among these people," Lochlánn said.

Senach grunted. "It'll be like cattle scared by lightning," he said. "Be a damned stampede."

They reined their horses over and walked them through the crowded square and then down one of the beaten roads that led out of the village, east and then south along the Avonmore. It was time to return to camp, time to rejoin the army.

Lochlánn had spent that morning and early afternoon leading a patrol. They had ridden along the northern shores of the two long lakes that filled the mountain valleys just west of the monastic city. The day before, Colman had ordered him to take command of the horsemen, to ride out at first light. Lochlánn had been flattered by the trust placed in him, but he did not care to take orders from Colman, and he did not want to leave Louis de Roumois.

Louis, however, had told him he should go. It was good experience, and it would elevate Lochlánn in the eyes of the men, even if it was Colman who had sent him out. So Lochlánn had picked his six riders and, as the first hints of light had appeared, they rode off to the west.

They found nothing of interest. No heathens, no enemy lying in wait, which was what Lochlánn had expected. The heathens, if they came, would come from the east, up the river that he and Louis had been making run red with the Northmen's blood. But it was important to defend against surprise of any kind. It was possible that some of the bastards had worked their way around to the west. So Louis was sent to make sure they had not.

That job done, and after a slight detour to take in the fair, Lochlánn led his men back toward the dúnad, several miles east of Glendalough. It was from there that they had been staging their attacks on the heathens, hoping to drive them off before they came within sight of the monastic city. If there was no panic in the streets of Glendalough it was because of how well they had succeeded with that defense.

They had ridden less than half a mile when they came upon a company of the bóaire. The men were sitting by the side of the road, tearing chunks off a loaf of bread and handing it around. Their long spears stood like sentries beside them, butt ends pushed into the soft ground. Lochlánn was surprised to see them there. He had expected to find the dúnad where he had left it, and the men in camp there.

Lochlánn reined his horses to a stop beside them. The bóaire looked up as they did but they did not move or react in any other way.

"Why are you men here?" Lochlánn asked. "Why are you not in the dúnad?"

This question seemed to confuse the men, and for a moment no one answered.

"Ain't no dúnad," one of them said at last. "Packed it up this morning, marching us all back this way."

"On whose orders?" Lochlánn asked. "Captain Louis?"

This was met with shrugs. "We just got word to move," the man said, "one of them men-at-arms give the order. All the army was coming back this way. The rest is down the road just a little way, I would suspect."

Lochlánn nodded. These men did as they were told and did not ask questions, and he could see he would get no useful information from them. He spurred his horse forward, and the stab of pain in his backside reminded him of how much he wished to be out of the saddle.

They crested a rise and just as the spearman had said, there was the rest of the army spread out before them, somewhere around three hundred men, most of them sitting or lying in the grass on the side of the road.

What are you doing here? Lochlánn thought. It had always been Louis's intention to yield no ground to the heathens, to fight them as far from Glendalough as he could. But now the army had fallen back nearly to the monastery's doorstep. He wondered what had happened to make Louis so alter his plans.

He must have some plan in mind, Lochlánn thought as he led his men down the short hill to where the men-at-arms were gathered. He reined his horse to a stop once more and swiveled around in the saddle.

"You may dismount if you wish," he said, which apparently they all did, as each man swung his legs over his saddle and dropped gratefully to the ground. Lochlánn did the same, gritting his teeth in pain as his feet took the weight. He stood straight and tried very hard to look like a man perfectly at ease.

"Thank you for this morning's work," he said to the others. "Pray, return to the company of your fellows." The men nodded and led their horses off. Lochlánn waited until they were gone before he tried walking himself. With a few tentative steps he reached a spot where half a dozen men-at-arms lay stretched out on the grass.

"Have any of you men see Captain Louis de Roumois?" he asked.

Glances were exchanged, Lochlánn could not help but notice, and then one of the men said, "Ain't seen him. Don't think he's here."

"Where is he?" Lochlánn asked.

The man shrugged and some of his fellows shrugged as well. "Don't know. Heard rumors," another said.

"What rumors?" Lochlánn demanded, worry building on top of exasperation.

"Don't know," the first man said.

Lochlánn let out a breath. He could recognize a pointless effort when he saw one. He walked on, trying to make his gate as normal as possible, the weary horse trailing behind. A little ways off he saw a cluster of banners on poles, and beneath them a handful of men engaged in discussion. One of them was Colman mac Breandan, and he recognized a few of the others as the captains of some of the house guards. He did not see Louis de Roumois, but that did not mean he was not there.

The horse was hearing the siren song of the spring grass so Lochlánn let it go and walked stiffly across the field to where the men stood in conference. He bowed his head as he approached and said, "My lord Colman."

"Lochlánn," Colman said. "Back? Any sign of the heathens?"

"No, lord," Lochlánn said. He looked around the assembled company. Louis was not there. "The country to the west seems clear of them."

"Very well," Colman said. "Then we can assume they are all together to the east, and will attack from there." This last was not directed to Lochlánn. Indeed, Colman seemed to have already forgotten Lochlánn's existence.

"My lord…" Lochlánn said and Colman turned back to him and fixed him with a stare that could not be called friendly.

"Yes?" Colman asked.

"Well…lord…I was…" Lochlánn stammered. There were several things he wished to ask, but none of them were really any of his business, and he did not expect an amiable reply.

"You are wondering where your particular friend Louis the Frank is?" Colman supplied.

"Well…yes, in fact," Lochlánn said.

"Run off," Colman spat. "Showed us the man he really is. He killed my captain, Aileran. Murdered him and ran off with my bitch wife. I don't know if he took her by force or if she went with him willingly, but either way they're gone. Off with the heathens, I would suspect."

Lochlánn said nothing, because he could think of nothing to say in answer to such a suggestion. It could not be true, he was certain of that. So something else must have happened. What that was Lochlánn could not guess, and he was so shocked by Colman's words that he could not put his thoughts in order.

"But why have you brought the army here?" Lochlánn managed to ask. "Why do we not fight the heathens to the east? Why let them get this close to Glendalough?"

This question brought a murmur from the other men, a low sound, more a series of grunts than actual words. Lochlánn could not tell if it was a sound of disapproval that he should ask such a thing or if they were wondering the same thing themselves.

"It is no business of yours, boy," Colman said, "but I'll say this…we were exposed, flapping around like wash on a line where that damned Frank had us. No support. Here we have all of Glendalough behind us. We have some place to fall back on."

He paused as if waiting for an argument, not just from Lochlánn but from any of the men there. There was more throat clearing, but still no actual words.

"There," Colman said, now directing himself to Lochlánn. "That's far more explanation than you warrant. Now go and find some way to make yourself useful." He turned away, the discussion done.

Lochlánn staggered off. He gave no thought to where he was going, he just walked, the pain in his legs serving as a counterpoint to the turmoil in his mind.

"Louis de Roumois did not murder Aileran and he did not run off," Lochlánn said. He spoke the words out loud, but softly, to himself, as if trying them out to see how real they felt. And they felt real enough. It was inconceivable to him that Louis could have done such a thing.

Or, mostly inconceivable. There certainly seemed to be odd forces at work in Louis's life. Hadn't that man come to kill him, back at the monastery? That was what had started all this, as far as Lochlánn's trading his robe for a mail shirt. And the assassin had come again in the field, after the fighting at the Meeting of the Waters. And then Louis had been with Failend, or so it seemed. The rumor in the army was that they had been rutting, which seemed a reasonable assumption.

"Louis did not do these things!" Lochlánn said again, forcing more conviction into his voice this time. And even as he did, he understood that there were greater worries than the possibility of Louis de Roumois's betrayal.

He looked off to the west. The sun was dropping low and the light was leaving the sky, but the darkness was spreading over Lochlánn even faster than that. Whatever sort of man Louis was, the fact remained that he had been responsible for the victories they had won over the heathens. It was Louis who had held the murderous hoard at bay and stopped them from laying waste to Glendalough thus far. And now he was gone.

And on the morrow, the heathens would come.

Chapter Thirty-Five

Bearer of golden rings,
My hopes of life were meagre…
                    Gisli Sursson's Saga

There was a light mist falling, but the ground was firm underfoot, not churned to mud. The road was just a quarter mile from the river, right where the scouts had said it would be. Thorgrim could see it for himself now as he made his way through thigh-high grass. There seemed to be nothing standing in the raiders' way, human or otherwise. A short march to Glendalough and the riches to be had there.

Simple. But Thorgrim knew it would not be simple at all, because such things never were.

From the river banks the meadowland ran inland with only an occasional stand of trees to interrupt its inviting expanse. Less than a mile distant the fields melded into the steep, rounded mountains that rose up in every quarter and as far off as the eye could see.

Not that the eye could see much just then. The sun was less than an hour above the horizon. The day promised to be more overcast than the day before, and the threat of rain that had been hanging over them like a curse seemed even more likely to become a tangible thing.

"Look at that whore's son, just look, lord," Godi said. He was walking beside Thorgrim across the field and nodding his massive head toward Ottar and his men. They were in a ragged line to the left, Ottar at their head, a man bearing his banner walking beside. Ottar was a big man with a long stride, but Thorgrim could see he was walking faster than his normal gait, making his men work to keep up, in an effort to be first to the road and thus take the lead from Thorgrim's forces.

Thorgrim shook his head in disgust. "Stupid bastard," he said.

With the men who had been left behind to guard the ships and the others who had been killed or wounded, the army of Northmen that advanced on Glendalough numbered no more than two hundred and fifty. That was a decent force, and they were all good, experienced fighting men, but Thorgrim did not think the Irish would have fewer men than that, and they would likely have many more. And the Irish were well led. He had seen that already.

The only way to fight them and have a hope of victory was to fight together, all the Norsemen attacking as one. It was something Ottar certainly understood, but seemed determined to ignore.

"Should we move faster? Keep up with him?" Godi asked. He was carrying Thorgrim's banner, the grey wolf's head on a red pennant, and the two of them were walking at the head of Thorgrim's men.

"No," Thorgrim said. He would not play that game. "Let them go first, let them get a mile ahead if they want. They can meet the enemy alone. After they've done what hurt they can to the Irish we'll use their bodies as a rampart."

Ottar reached the road first, as was his intention, his warriors streaming behind, and they fell into a loose column three or four men wide.

Thorgrim looked past Ottar's crews and as far to the west as he could see before his view was obscured by the hills and the mist. He wondered what was happening out there. Even before they left the river he had sent out his scouts and Ottar had sent out his, but as of yet no word had come back. And Harald was out there, somewhere. Somewhere ahead of them. At least that was where he was supposed to be. Thorgrim feared that the longships might have passed Harald's patrol, that Harald and his men were actually somewhere behind them, farther down river.

We'll find out soon enough, he thought.

The road rose and fell over the smaller hills but it tended up, always up, rising into the mountains and the monastery that was supposed to be in a valley somewhere ahead. Thorgrim's men made a column in Ottar's wake and they moved on. The mist grew thicker and blew past in cloudy veils until one could no longer say if it was mist or rain.

They tramped on for half a mile or so before Thorgrim became aware of something happening, some ripple of change in Ottar's men up ahead. Vali, who had been walking on the far edge of the column, came jogging up to the head and fell in beside Thorgrim.

"One of the scouts is back, I think, one of Ottar's men," he said.

"Good," Thorgrim said. Now, he hoped, they would learn something of the enemy. But after ten minutes had passed he understood that he would not learn it from Ottar. Whatever news Ottar's man had brought, Ottar was not sending it down the line to Thorgrim.

That stupid ox, that great stupid whore's son bastard, Thorgrim thought, though he knew he was a fool to think Ottar would share any news. He cursed himself and he cursed Ottar and he cursed Kevin and he cursed Glendalough.

An image of his hall at Vík-ló flashed before him, comforting and familiar. He felt a longing to be there, and it surprised him. Odd. It was the same longing he used to feel when he thought of his farm in East Agder.

Have I been so long from my home that I'm forgetting it? he wondered. *Are the gods telling me I will never return to Norway?*

Or was Vík-ló his home now? He could not deny his desire to be there just then, to be done with this ill-conceived raid and to be feasting and drinking with his fellows in the big hall built by Grimarr Knutson.

And then his thoughts were interrupted by Godi who said, "Here, lord."

Thorgrim looked up. Armod Thorkilson was one of the scouts Thorgrim had sent out and now he was returning at a near run. He drew up beside Thorgrim and fell in step with him.

"The enemy, they're just ahead, lord," he reported. "A mile or so, not more."

"Why am I just hearing of this now?" Thorgrim snapped. "Ottar's scout was back ten minutes past."

"Yes, lord," Armod said. "We were together. He run off as soon as we saw the enemy, but I stayed so I could see how many they were, lord. How they were positioned."

Thorgrim nodded, embarrassed that he let his ill humor goad him into chastising a man who did not deserve it. "You did well, Armod," he said. "What did you see?"

"They look to be something more than three hundred men, lord," Armod said. "Men-at-arms with shields. And spearmen. There are mounted warriors as well, on the flanks. They are drawn up on a line at the top of a short rise. Not a great hill, but a hill, anyway."

Thorgrim nodded. "Drawn up in a shield wall?"

"Not as I saw them, lord. But near enough."

"Good," Thorgrim said, though he was not actually sure what he meant by that. Several things. Good observations on Armod's part. Good that they knew how the enemy was arrayed. But mostly good that they would meet the enemy very soon, kill him, be done with all this.

Vik-ló... Thorgrim thought. And they walked on.

They were going uphill again and the mist was most certainly a light rain and Armod, who was walking just a few paces behind Thorgrim now, said, "Right over this hill, lord, and then the road dips down and on the next hill, that's where I saw the Irishmen's line."

Even as Armod was talking, Ottar's warriors up ahead were leaving the road and spreading out along the top of the hill, turning their marching column into a line of men, shoulder to shoulder. They were forming a shield wall, or what would be a shield wall when the order was passed.

Thorgrim turned and walked backward and he waved his arm in the air.

"The Irish are just beyond this hill and they are ready for us. Make a line, make a line, there!" He pointed off toward what would be the right wing of the Norsemen's assault and his men jogged off to form a line that would link with Ottar's, a line of shields and swords and axes and spears that they hoped would sweep the Irish before them.

As his men formed themselves, driven to hurry by Bersi and Kjartan and Skidi Battleax, Thorgrim stepped to the top of the hill and looked out over the quarter mile that now separated him from the Irish defenders.

It was just as Armod had described. A line of men snaked across the rise opposite them, nearly at the crest of the hill. They held shields that would have looked bright and cheery in the sunlight but which on that misty day looked muted and dull. Thorgrim could see helmets, and spears like reeds jutting from a river. Three hundred men.

No. More than three hundred, certainly.

Armod had been right about the horsemen as well. There were about thirty on the left flank and thirty on the right. The biggest danger to a shield wall was that an enemy could get around the ends and get behind it. With nothing to which they could anchor those ends, such as a river or a marsh, the Irish were looking to their mounted warriors to keep the Norsemen from turning the flanks. And if the horsemen were brave and knew their business they would be able to do so. Worse, they would be able to attack their enemy's flanks, or get behind the Norsemen's shield wall.

Well, there's nothing for it, Thorgrim thought. Right at them, bold and reckless. He had seen that win the day, many times. Show the enemy that you are more insane than they are, and less afraid to die.

I am not afraid to die, Thorgrim thought. It was an observation, no more. And it was not fearlessness. Fearlessness was something else. This was more akin to weariness, and a barely formed notion that he was ready for his reward at Valhalla. He was not like Starri, who longed for the corpse hall. Thorgrim simply no longer cared if he was in Midgard, the world of men, or Asgard, the place of the gods. He did not care if he lived or died, as long has he died in honorable battle. And that made him a very dangerous enemy.

He looked to his left. Ottar and his captains were getting their line formed up, just as his own captains were doing. Thorgrim knew he should speak with the man. He let out a breath. Charging the Irish shield wall seemed a much more inviting prospect than summoning the patience to deal with Ottar. But he was resigned to do everything in his power to make this raid a profitable one. He owed that to the men who followed him.

He walked down the line, past his own warriors and past Ottar's. "Ottar!" he called as he approached.

Ottar turned, his long braids swinging like loose ropes in the wind. "You!" he said. "Do not get in the way of my men. Do not let any of the dogs who follow you get in the way of my men."

Thorgrim stopped ten feet away and looked at Ottar. He had hoped against all reason to have some meaningful discussion about the coming fight. But he could see that would not happen, so instead he replied, "Ottar, when this is over we will fight and I will kill you. But for now, see that your men form a shield wall with mine and we will go at the Irish line yonder. See none of your men run away. I'll personally kill any who do. And see you do not run away yourself."

He turned as Ottar was opening his mouth and walked back toward his men as Ottar began to shout. "Night Pup! I'll kill you now! Get back here, you whore's son!" But Thorgrim kept on walking because he knew Ottar would not act against him now, not with Glendalough lying at their feet. He would not start a private war when there was another, more lucrative one waiting for him. Nor would his men tolerate his doing so. Even Ottar could only push his men so far.

Godi and Agnarr were standing at the head of *Sea Hammer*'s men, who in turn were at the center of the line of men from Vík-ló.

"You had a profitable talk with Ottar, I trust?" Agnarr said.

Thorgrim made a grunting sound. "I have had more profitable talks with the swine on my farm," he said. "We can only hope that he and his men will hold the left wing, and that we can drive these Irish back quick. If this is not a fast victory then I think it will not be a victory at all."

The Irish on the hill were starting the beat their shields with their swords and shout what Thorgrim had to guess were taunts and insults. And suddenly Thorgrim felt alone and exposed. Godi and Agnarr were there, and they were good men, men he loved and trusted. But Harald was not there. And Starri was not there. It did not seem right at all to be looking at a shield wall without them on hand. It did not seem like a good omen. Not a good omen at all.

Then he heard Ottar roar like some great beast of legend and Thorgrim looked to his left. The big man stepped back into the line of his warriors and called an order. Their shields came together, each one overlapping the one beside it. The shield wall was formed.

Thorgrim turned to Godi and Agnarr. "Let's go," he said and they, too, stepped back and took their place in the line, shields up, weapons ready, and Bersi and Kjartan and Skidi Battleax stepped into the line as well.

Ottar was already moving forward, giving no thought at all to what Thorgrim's men were doing, and Thorgrim had no choice but to call for his men to advance with Ottar's. Otherwise the shield wall would have been broken, which was the second greatest danger to men fighting in that array.

The line moved faster as it headed down the hill. The Irish stopped their banging and locked their shields together, but the jeering continued, pointless as it was. The Norsemen reached the bottom of the low hill and began up the slope of the next, some men walking on the road but most spread over the fields to either side. Thorgrim's eyes were everywhere: on his men, on the Irish shield wall, on the horsemen on the flanks.

Particularly on the horsemen. They were keeping put for the moment, waiting to see if the enemy would try and turn the flanks of the Irish line. But if - actually when - they charged into the battle they could send the Northmen into panicked flight and cut them down as they ran. That was another thing that Thorgrim had seen before.

The Irish line was one hundred yards away and they were closing the distance fast. Thorgrim could see now that it stretched out beyond his own line at either end. The Northmen would not have had men enough to turn the Irish flanks even if they had hoped to. The Irish could bend the ends of their own line around and strike his men and Ottar's from two directions. And there were the horsemen as well.

"This will be a hard fight," he said to Agnarr.

"It will," Agnarr agreed.

They were close enough now that Thorgrim could make out the faces of the men who stood in opposition to them: warriors with swords and axes like those of the Northmen, and behind them, the spearmen who had been so deadly during the ambush at the river. And behind all of them were some of the commanders on horseback, waiting, watching the enemy come on.

Then one of those mounted leaders shouted something and the shout echoed down the line and the Irish did something that Thorgrim did not expect at all. The men-at-arms in the shield wall stepped aside, making space between them, and the spearmen stepped up through the line, spears held down, faces grim.

"What by Odin are they doing?" he heard Godi ask, but it was clear enough to Thorgrim. They wanted the Northmen to hit the line of spears first. They wanted the spearmen with their long pole arms to drive the points through the line of Norse shields and take down as many of the enemy as they could, to make holes in the shield wall which the men-at-arms would then hit with full force and drive through.

Fifty yards away. It was not a bad plan, not at all, but there were only a hundred or so spearmen against a shield wall two hundred and fifty strong. Thorgrim could see that the men with the spears were not men-at-arms. They wore leather, not mail, and they had no shields because shields would have hindered them in the job they had to do. They looked scared.

"Yell!" Thorgrim shouted. "All of you, make a noise, make a noise!" Thorgrim led the way, sending up a terrifying howl from deep in his guts, sending it up to the gods and raising his sword as his speed built. Godi made a great noise as well, and all up and down the line the men shouted and shrieked and howled and cursed, and Ottar's men did the same. It was a sound from the underworld, and it drove the Northmen on to greater and greater speed, their pace becoming a fast walk and then a jog as they rolled on uphill.

The spearmen took a step back. Thorgrim could see mouths open, eyes wide in panic. It took men who were trained and experienced and well-motivated to stand fast in the face of such an onslaught, and these men were none of those things.

"Kill them! Kill them!" Thorgrim shouted, holding Iron-tooth high as he charged on. The sound of five hundred feet building to a run made a base note under the higher, louder keening of the manic Northmen. The Irishmen with the spears took another step back, and another.

Then the two lines hit, Northmen and spearmen. A man stood directly in Thorgrim's path, an older man with a milky eye and an unshaved face and a look like he was fighting down panic and losing. His good eye met Thorgrim's and he lunged forward with his spear, the black dagger tip coming right at Thorgrim's face.

Brave bastard, Thorgrim thought. With some training he might have made a good warrior. But that was never going to happen. Thorgrim caught the spear with Iron-tooth and turned it up, out of line, and without breaking stride took another step and brought the blade down on the spearman's leather-clad head.

The look of surprise remained frozen on the Irishman's face as he died and Thorgrim wrenched the sword free, felt his foot step on the man's corpse as he pushed past.

That was enough for the Irish spearmen. If they managed to kill any of the Northmen, Thorgrim did not see it, but as the screaming shield wall rolled over them they reacted as he knew they would. They panicked.

All along the line he saw spears tossed aside and spearmen turning and fleeing the five yards back to the protection of the shield wall. But now the Irish men-at-arms could not let them through, because doing so would have meant making gaps in the wall just as the enemy was on them. So they held their shields together and the panicked spearmen pulled and clawed at them, desperate to get through, desperate to not be caught between the two shield walls.

But it was too late for them. The armies came together like ships colliding, crushing the men between them. Thorgrim saw one of the Irish men-at-arms do the most sensible thing; he brought his ax down on the spearman's head and killed him before the man could pull the shield wall apart. But the panicked men had done their damage. In their desperate attempt to get to safety they had staggered the Irish shield wall, thrown it into disarray just as the Northmen slammed into it with all the momentum they could muster.

Thorgrim's whole world closed down. Seconds before his thoughts had covered the entire length of the Northmen's line, but now he was concerned only for what was happening within a sword's length of himself, because that was all he could see and it was all the area over which he had any control.

His shield came hard against that of the Irishman in front of him, and Thorgrim's forward momentum was stopped, but the force made the Irishman stagger. Thorgrim drove Iron-tooth forward, right through the gap over the two shields in front of him, but the warrior there – a young man, but hard looking, no fear on his face – twisted sideways and the blade missed by inches.

Something hit the bottom of Thorgrim's shield, a sword blow, low, looking for his guts or his thighs. He brought his shield down, felt it hit the blade, and then went over the top with Iron-tooth. This time he caught his opponent, drove the tip of his sword into the man's shoulder and felt it bite.

The man jerked back, tried to bring his sword up, and would have died on Iron-tooth's point if the man to his right had not driven his own sword at Thorgrim and forced him to fend off the blade.

The Norsemen were jammed together, shoulder to shoulder, and pressed against the Irish in front of them and it was hard to move, hard to work a blade. At least it was for Thorgrim Night Wolf, or any other man of average height. Godi, at his side, rising like one of the nearby mountains above the line of fighting men, had no such problems. His choice of weapon was a battle ax, a perfect choice for a man who could loom above the others and strike down like he was chopping kindling.

He did that now. With a roar he brought the ax down on the shield wall in front of him. The blade hit the rim of a shield with a ringing sound and kept on going, breaking the iron, splitting the wood. Thorgrim saw the look of surprise on the Irishman's face, but the man beside him, the man who had gone for Thorgrim's legs, did not hesitate. He turned his shield toward Godi and drove his blade at Godi's chest and might have killed him if Thorgrim had not moved quicker still.

Iron-tooth struck like a snake, straight at the man's throat, driving in right below the strap of his helmet and never pausing as it passed on through. Thorgrim pulled the sword back in a shower of blood and the man went down and a hole opened in the shield wall.

"Forward!" Thorgrim shouted but the men around him recognized the opportunity even before he spoke, and they pushed hard, shields leading, weapons lashing out as they forced the Irish back.

Thorgrim looked up and down the line. It was hard to see what was happening, but he had a sense that the Irish defense was crumbling, that their shield wall was coming apart. The panicked spearmen had begun that process, and now the ferocity of the Northmen's attack was driving it on.

"Keep your shields together!" Thorgrim shouted. He did not want his own shield wall to crumble, did not want this to turn into three hundred individual fights. He wanted to get the Irish running, and butcher them as they did and then move on to Glendalough.

Their own shields were still overlapping as they pushed through the Irish shield wall and hacked left and right at the enemy. There were no reinforcements that Thorgrim could see, no men in reserve to fill the holes as they appeared. The commander of the Irish line had cast his lot, had put all his men into the shield wall. But of course the Northmen had as well.

A man stood in front of Thorgrim now, an ax in one hand, shield in the other, and a look of unadulterated fury on his face. He hacked down with the ax and Thorgrim caught it with his shield and the blade buried itself in the wooden boards. Thorgrim twisted the shield, hoping to jerk the ax from the man's hand, while the man jerked the ax in the other direction, hoping to pull Thorgrim off balance.

For an instant they stood motionless, opposing forces balanced one against the other. Then the Irishman let go of the ax handle. Thorgrim staggered and his opponent came at him with a short sword he had snatched from his belt.

The blade darted in at Thorgrim's throat but before it reached its mark Godi's ax came down on the man's arm, snapping it and cutting it half off. Thorgrim saw the man's mouth open wide in a scream of pain and surprise and outrage and then Godi's ax came down again and the scream was cut short.

And the Irish shield wall was indeed crumbling. There was no doubt now. Thorgrim could see men falling back, men dying under Norse blades. He could see the line bending where Skidi Battleax was leading his men in a frantic push.

"Forward! Forward!" Thorgrim shouted. "At them!" He put his weight against his shield, shoving hard against the man who stood opposing him. And then he stumbled. One second there was resistance, the next second there was none as the man gave up, dropped his shield, turned and ran.

Thorgrim straightened fast, sword and shield up, ready for a renewed attack, but none came. All along the line the Irish were turning and running, up and over the crest of the hill at their backs and the Norsemen were on their heels.

"Men of Vík-ló!" Thorgrim shouted. "Hold your line! Hold your line!" The Irish had devolved into panicked confusion but he could not let his own men do the same. That would mean pissing away any advantage they had gained, giving the Irish the chance to fight on. He had to keep them together, keep them organized, attack the remnants of the Irish line and take them apart.

He looked left and right. Some of Ottar's men were chasing after the Irish, but his own men were resisting the urge, strong though it was.

"Men of Vík-ló! Forward!" Thorgrim shouted and the crews of his four ships rolled forward, ready to hit the Irish again, to finish that part of the day's work and move on to Glendalough.

And then the mounted warriors struck.

Chapter Thirty-Six

I fed his corpse to the blood-hawk,
My sword's edge swung and cut...
                    Gisli Sursson's Saga

The riders came from the right and Thorgrim cursed himself because he had forgotten they were there, which was what the horsemen no doubt wanted. They had stayed out of the fight, standing ready to hold the flanks against an attack, or to swoop in if the shield wall broke. And that was what they were doing now.

Thorgrim heard the shouts at the far end of his line and turned to see the mounted warriors, two hundred feet away, charging down on his men, swords rising and falling, horses snapping ugly yellow teeth and lashing out with their hooves. He saw a man fall, arms and legs kicking as the horse reared and came down on his chest. He saw a horseman chop down with his sword and saw the weapon come up again streaming blood.

"By the gods!" Thorgrim shouted. "Come with me!" His words were aimed at any of his men within earshot, but in particular Agnarr and Godi, and he ran off confident that they were with him. He ran toward the end of the line, where the horsemen were wheeling and hacking and prompting their mounts to kick and bite.

"Make a wall! Make a wall!" he shouted as he ran, closing the distance. The mounted warriors had timed this well. If the Northmen had had the chance to form up in opposition they could have stood firm against this attack. But the horsemen had hit fast and hard and the panic was spreading.

Thorgrim stopped. His men were not listening. "Godi, Agnarr, to me!" he shouted and the two stepped up on either side. If he could not get his men to form a shield wall then he would form one himself, even if it was only three men wide.

"Forward!" Thorgrim shouted and the three of them stepped off. The nearest horseman was twenty paces away, going sword and shield with one of Bersi's men. The rider did not see Thorgrim coming until Thorgrim was nearly within sword striking distance. Then the man looked up, saw the three shield-bearers charging him. He spurred his horse forward, right at Thorgrim's short wall, Bersi's man forgotten. Ride right through them, that was his intention, scatter the three men and hack them down. But as he came on Thorgrim and Agnarr and Godi all lifted their shields together, swinging them up at the horse's mouth and its wicked teeth.

Thorgrim felt the boss of his shield hit the horse and saw the horse rise up on hind legs, rearing in surprise. He felt a hoof strike his shield with power enough to drive it back into his chest, but he held his ground. The rider was hanging on, desperate to keep from being thrown. Godi's ax came down and struck the man just under the left arm. The rider screamed, and in the process of pulling the ax free, Godi jerked him from the saddle. The horse spun in place and charged off, now panicked and rider-less.

Movement to the right and Thorgrim saw a few more Northmen come running forward, shields held ready, and they stood fast as another of the mounted Irish men-at-arms came down on them. They worked together, the men of Vík-ló, holding off the attack from horse and rider, striking out as the man wheeled and struck at them.

More men were racing to join this new fight, coming with shields up and blades ready. There were only about twenty or so mounted warriors still engaged at that end of the line. They had taken the Northmen's flanks by surprise, hit them hard, but now the Northmen were sorting themselves out and soon they would form a real defense, effective and deadly.

One of the riders yelled something; it meant nothing to Thorgrim but clearly it meant something to the other riders because they all jerked their reins over and wheeled their horses and charged off down the far side of the hill. They were not fleeing; they were falling back. They had done what they needed to do. They had thrown the Norsemen's line into temporary confusion and given the Irish men-at-arms a chance to put some distance between them and their attackers, give them a moment to reform their line before their retreat turned into an bloody rout.

Thorgrim lowered his shield and rested the tip of Iron-tooth on the ground and watched them ride away. He turned to see what was happening on the other parts of the field. The horsemen on the right flank of the Irish line had hit Ottar's men just as those on the left had hit his, but they too were riding off, having inflicting what hurt they could.

He walked up the remainder of the slope. Bodies were strewn over the ground, some Northmen but mostly Irish, and of those they were mostly the poor spearmen who had been thrust out in front of the shield wall. Some were wounded and crawling pathetically away, some moaning and waving arms, but most were still.

At the crest of the hill he stopped and looked down the far side. The Irish line had retreated a few hundred yards, but now they were forming up again, remaking their shield wall. The mounted warriors had saved them from complete destruction, and now they were ready to take up the fight again.

Thorgrim looked past their lines. In the distance, less than a mile away, was Glendalough.

Glendalough....

He realized that after all this time, all the struggles to get to this place, Glendalough had taken on some mythic quality, like Asgard or Valhalla.

Glendalough.

It did not look much like a mythic place in real life, seen through the light rain that was falling, under the leaden skies. He could see the church, an impressive stone affair with a short, square tower rising up at one end, and a steep roof that had to be forty feet high at the peak. There was a scattering of buildings around it, and farther away from the church, which seemed to form the center of everything there, were more squat, thatched buildings, a few roads crisscrossing between them, a few buildings bigger than the rest.

The homes of the local jarls, Thorgrim guessed. There would likely be hoards found buried in those houses, if they had time enough to search for them.

Beyond the cluster of buildings he could see a lake that wound its way into a sharp, narrow valley far off, and just behind the town a steep, humped mountain rose up. It was beautiful country, he had to admit as much. Almost mythical.

Thorgrim wiped the rain from his eyes and blinked. The monastery and the village did look prosperous, by Irish standards, and he guessed there was wealth enough to be had there. But first they had to get though the army of Irishmen which was reforming in front of them.

"You men, get in line, get in line, we must hit those Irish bastards before they can get themselves straightened out!" he shouted, and Bersi and Kjartan and Skidi took up the cry, and quickly the men of Vík-ló were hurrying back into some sort of formation.

We must link with Ottar, Thorgrim thought. He turned toward the left wing of their line and saw he was too late. Ottar was already charging down the hill, his sword held high. He looked like some sort of mad beast. Behind him his men were running as well, shouting, banging swords on shields, a great disordered mob flinging itself across the eighth of a mile that separated them from the Irish.

Stupid bastard, Thorgrim thought again, and realized how often those words came to mind when considering Ottar Bloodax. He looked over at the Irish. They were still broken and disorganized but they would not be for long. He could see captains pushing men into line, the milling men-at-arms quickly becoming a shield wall once again. If Ottar could hit them before they managed to restore discipline he would break them once and for all. If not, his wild attack would be suicidal.

This will be a close thing, Thorgrim though, but he did not think Ottar would be that lucky. They had driven the Irish line back once, but those men were not farmers, they were men-at-arms, and they would not be so easily pushed again.

"Let's go!" Thorgrim shouted, holding Iron-tooth high and heading down the hill, making for the Irishmen at the far side of the field. Their line was not perfect, but it would do, and they could not wait any longer and let Ottar's men be butchered. He did not particularly care if Ottar and his men lived or died, but if they were slaughtered now then there would be no possibility of taking Glendalough, and that Thorgrim cared about very much.

He heard his men cheer as they rolled forward, heard them howl and scream and bang their weapons in a din that would loosen the bowels of all but the hardest men. Ottar and his crews had halved the distance to the enemy, but already the Irish were falling into place, locking shields in a solid wall of multicolored circles, and behind the shields, conical helmets, shirts of mail, leather jerkins, swords and axes poised.

Once more Thorgrim wiped the rain from his eyes and spit out the water he had managed to get in his mouth. The ground was soft under foot, the light rain growing harder, as was his breath as he pushed to cover the distance. He was not running. He was moving at a pace somewhat short of a jog. He did not want his men winded and heaving as they came to grips with the Irish, though he wondered if perhaps he was thinking more of himself.

From his left he heard the renewed clash of weapons as the quickest of Ottar's warriors reached the Irish line. Ottar was first among them; Thorgrim could see his massive head and shoulders rising above the others as he whirled his battle ax at the enemy. He saw Ottar tear a hole in the Irish shield wall with his weapon, but before he could step in more men were there to fill it.

Ottar, however, was all but alone, with most of his men just catching up. Rather that delivering a massive, shocking blow to the line, they were coming at it in ones and twos and Thorgrim could see they were being cut down as they came. And then the mounted warriors were there, sweeping around the far end of the Irish line and charging into Ottar's flanks. He heard the screams of agony, the bellows of outrage and surprise. He saw men dying under the horsemen's long swords.

Stupid, stupid, he thought, but that was all the thought he could give to Ottar, because he and his men had almost reached the right side of the Irish shield wall. Once again they would fight shield to shield in that packed killing ground, and if they could break the Irish again then there was a good chance they would be broken for good, and the way to Glendalough cleared.

Thorgrim paused and Godi paused and they let the line of men behind catch up and envelope them. They took their place with the others and pushed on. Thorgrim was breathing hard and he realized that his shoulder ached, and he guessed that he had taken a blow there but had not realized it until then. He did not think he was bleeding. He could not feel that familiar sensation of warm blood running down inside his tunic.

It all had an unreal quality to it – the men at his side, the men before him, the shield in his left hand, Iron-tooth in his right. Hadn't they just been through this? Hadn't they just driven a shield wall back? Was this the way the gods would curse him, make him stand in the shield wall, in the rain, over and over again, with never the feasting at the corpse hall after?

One last look to his left. He could not see much of Ottar's men. There were too many others crowded into that small stretch of Irish meadow, but from what he could see, and what he could hear, Ottar and the others were not having a good time of it.

And then they reached the Irish men-at-arms, shields hitting shields with their dull sound like axes cutting into tree trunks. The Irishmen's line staggered and bowed under the impact of the men from Vík-ló but it did not break, and once again Thorgrim's world closed down to that spot of land, Godi on one side, Agnarr on the other, an enemy in his front. He was shouting, bellowing, working shield and sword in that tight place. His arm was tiring. His face was bleeding. He could feel the warm blood running down his cheek, though he could not recall the thrust that had cut him.

His foot slipped but he recovered in time to stop an ax blow with the edge of his shield. The grass under foot was being trampled into mud and that made the footing precarious. And still the enemy stood and wielded their weapons, and the shields pushed against each other, and the blows came slower, and they came with less force but still they came.

This cannot go on, Thorgrim thought. They could not stand there and flail at each other until one army or both collapsed to the ground in exhaustion. Something had to give way.

And then it did. Godi brought his ax down hard on the man to Thorgrim's right, not for the first time, but now the man's shield, already damaged, shattered under the blow. The Irishman looked at the broken wood boards with the sort of dumb amazement that comes from being exhausted beyond words, and then Thorgrim darted Iron-tooth forward and drove the point through the man's shoulder.

The Irishman made a choking sound, part fury, part agony. He twisted and fell and he left a hole in the shield wall. It was just the chance for which Thorgrim longed. He stepped forward, into the gap, ready to beat it wider, to break the Irish line.

And then he stopped. Beyond the gap in the line he saw something he had not seen before, and he knew it was the end of the Northmen's hopes.

More men. Fresh men, armed men, shields ready. They were not more than a hundred yards away. They were marching fast toward the battle ground. At their head flew a banner, what looked to be a raven on a green field.

Kevin mac Lugaed had come to join the fight, and Thorgrim did not think he was coming to fight on the Norsemen's side.

Chapter Thirty-Seven

Best have a son though he be late born
and before him the father be dead:
seldom are stones on the wayside raised
save by kinsmen to kinsmen.
Hávamál

Harald Broadarm was right on the verge of killing the player, Crimthann, or at least hitting him hard enough to shut him up, when he saw the two men-at-arms coming toward them.

The two of them, Harald and Crimthann, had been riding together on the seat of the wagon for a few hours by then, the wagon which provided the perfect solution to Harald's dilemma. Having fought the Irish patrol, and allowed some to escape, Harald knew he had managed to alert the rest of the Irish army to their presence. He knew he could not continue toward Glendalough on foot. He was sure that other riders would be sent to hunt them down.

But neither could he go back to his father and admit defeat. It was then that he realized the gods had provided him with another way; they had brought him an answer to his plight, hauled it right up to him behind great teams of oxen.

Crimthann had been tending the fire that was burning in a ring in the center of the half-circle of wagons when the Irish had burst from the woods and attacked Harald's men. When the fighting was over, and Harald's attention turned once again to those fantastical vehicles, the man was still there. He must have seen the entire fight – it had taken place not one hundred yards from him – but he seemed to have not moved a bit, or reacted in any way.

The fighting done, Harald gathered his men. He ordered that those who were too wounded to walk be carried, likewise the one man who had been killed. The dead Irishmen were stripped of anything worth having and their bodies tossed in the tall grass. There was no time for anything more fancy.

"Come with me," Harald said and he led his band across the road and over toward the man and his cooking fire. Oak Cleaver was still in his hand and the other men carried weapons unsheathed as well. None of them had any idea what to expect.

Of all the possibilities, Crimthann's greeting was perhaps the most unexpected.

"Quite a show you put on!" he roared as Harald and his men approached. "I make it my business to offer the finest performances in all of Ireland, but I don't know if I could do better. Come, come, sit, eat!" He waved a massive arm at the various benches and logs that made a circle around the fire pit.

And so after setting the wounded and dead carefully down, Harald sat and the others sat, and they ate, and Crimthann went on and on about the quality of the shows he staged and the places his players had been and the people, great and common, for whom they had performed. And all the time Harald ate and considered what to do with this man and his fellow players.

Besides Crimthann there were six other men that Harald could see, and three women. He took note as he shoveled stew into his mouth and Crimthann talked. He could kill them all, but he did not much care for killing men who had done him no harm or posed no threat. And he would be hard pressed to kill a woman. Quite the opposite, his tendency was to be protective to a fault.

But he could not let them go, either. Harald was looking to the wagons as a movable hunting blind and he could not have the players roaming the territory telling the Irish men-at-arms what had happened. And so that left but one choice.

"Thank you for the meal, Crimthann," Harald said, putting his bowl down and wiping his mouth with the back of his hand. "You say you are bound for Glendalough?"

It took the better part of two hours to round up the oxen and harness them to the wagons and stow away all the gear and get the caravan rolling. Harald had the impression the players had been at that one spot for some time. He wondered if they had been earning their keep servicing travelers the way they had done Vemund and Ulf. Those two Harald had given the unpleasant task of heading out across country to find the fleet and report to Thorgrim what they had learned of the enemy and Glendalough.

It was late afternoon when they were finally underway. Crimthann drove the lead wagon with Harald beside him to see there was no mischief. Crimthann's men drove the other wagons, since they were used to it, each with one of Harald's men beside him. The rest of the Northmen stayed hidden inside with Crimthann's players. They were under strict orders to not harm the Irishmen, or distract themselves with the women.

Crimthann seemed not to care much that his wagons had been commandeered. He had hardly stopped talking since Harald first approached him. Harald found the man interesting at first, and amusing. He learned a great deal that was useful about Glendalough and the fair and the country around there. It took Crimthann about an hour to tell Harald everything he wished to know. But then he just kept on talking.

At first, Harald had hinted that Crimthann might consider being quiet for a spell. Then he'd suggested it. Finally he told the man outright to shut up, but none of it did any good. Harald did not kill men who were no threat to him, but Crimthann was becoming a genuine threat to his sanity.

I'll give him ten more minutes, Harald thought, *and if he does not shut up by then I'll beat him with a rock.*

"Now, up north, in the lands of the Uí Néill," Crimthann was saying when Harald saw the two coming at them from across the field. It was late afternoon and they had seen no other travelers on the road, not even the Irish patrol Harald was sure would be looking for them.

"Hold a moment, Crimthann," Harald said and the big man stopped in mid-sentence and looked where Harald was looking. Two men, or maybe a man and a boy, as one was considerably smaller than the other, were walking toward them. They wore mail shirts and swords at their sides and carried helmets. There was nothing threatening in their manner. Indeed, they looked as if they expected to be welcome.

"Stop the wagon," Harald said and Crimthann pulled the reins and the team of oxen slowed to a stop. There was always the chance that this might be a trap, so Harald knocked on the wooden wall of the wagon at his back and said in a loud whisper, "Be ready, there,

Olaf Thordarson." Then he turned to Crimthann and said, "I will speak to these people. Not a word from you." Crimthann nodded.

Harald had shed his mail and helmet and sword so that he might pass for one of the players, but he still had his dagger on his belt and he had made certain Crimthann was well aware of it. Now he and Crimthann waited as the two approached, and Harald marveled at the unaccustomed silence.

The taller of the men-at-arms approaching was young, Harald could see, in his early twenties and well made, with dark hair to his shoulders. He looked unconcerned as he crossed the field. He raised his arm and called, "Crimthann! My good fellow! We meet once more!"

Crimthann said nothing, because of course Harald had ordered him to silence.

He picks this moment to finally do as I say? Harald thought and gave Crimthann a subtle kick, which Crimthann correctly interpreted.

"Good day!" Crimthann roared with his usual volume and enthusiasm. "I know you...wait...do not tell me...Louis!"

"Yes, that's right," the young man said. He and his companion had reached the wagon and were standing by the seat, looking up at Harald and Crimthann. Harald searched their faces for some sign of alarm or suspicion, but he saw none.

But he did see something else that surprised him, though he kept it to himself. The second one, the smaller one, was a woman. She was dressed in mail and wore a sword, but she was most certainly a woman, and an attractive one at that. Among his people, the Norsemen, it was not unheard of for a woman to wear battle gear and even to join in the fighting on occasion. Not common, but not unheard of, and so Harald was not particularly shocked to see a woman in mail and carrying a weapon, though he had never known of an Irishwoman dressing in that manner.

"We were with a patrol," this man, Louis, was explaining to Crimthann, "and we became separated. Our horses were spooked and ran off. So now we're stuck and we are very happy to see you, my friend."

"And I am happy to see you!" Crimthann said and then said no more because he did not know what Harald would allow him to say.

Harald ran his eyes over the two. Their mail seemed of good quality, and the fact that they had mail at all, and that they had been with one of the patrols, told him that they were not just common foot soldiers, nor farmers called up to defend Glendalough from the wrath of the Northmen. They were people of consequence, and as such might be useful and valuable.

You were so distracted you let your horses get away? What were you doing? Harald wondered, though he had some ideas.

"We are going to Glendalough," Harald said. "Would you like to ride with us?"

Louis looked over at him for the first time. "Thank you. I don't think we've met. My name is Louis," he said and Harald heard the first notes of suspicion. "And who might you be, friend?"

Harald thought about giving himself an Irish name, but he knew his accent would put the lie to that, so he said, "My name is Harald. Harald of Hedeby. Finest juggler in that land, or any. That's why I came to join Crimthann, whose fame is well known there."

"I see," Louis said, and Harald was afraid that he did indeed see, more than Harald wanted him to see. Harald stood and stepped down on the wagon's tongue and then hopped to the ground, landing right in front of the woman.

"Please, ride with us," he said, gesturing to the back of the wagon. He could not let them go now, not if they suspected something. "You don't know comfort until you've been in Crimthann's caravan," he added, but Louis and the woman took a step back.

"That's kind of you," Louis said and Harald noticed that his was not an Irish accent either, "but our men will be nearby and we must wait for them."

Harald nodded. *He won't leave the girl,* he thought. *I just need to get the girl...*

"At least come in for some food and ale," Harald said and the man smiled, nodded, then took another step back and pulled his sword, the move so quick Harald could not form a conscious thought in the time it took him to get the weapon clear.

But Harald did not need to think in order to act, and even as the blade was leaving the scabbard he stepped forward and seized the man's arm with his left hand while his right snatched the dagger from his belt. He heard Crimthann roaring something behind him and the knife came around at Louis's throat, but Louis was as fast as Harald, and he knocked Harald's arm aside with his mail-clad arm and jabbed at Harald's face with his fist.

He connected, hitting Harald right on the side of his head, but it was a weak blow and had little effect. Indeed, even a hard blow to Harald's head generally had little effect. Harald brought the knife back up, intending only to press it to the man's throat in order to make him more cooperative, but now the woman was on him, grabbing his arm and with one hand and slashing at his face with the other.

Harald tightened his grip on Louis's sword arm and tried to fend the woman off, but she was snarling and clawing like a wildcat. Harald could only thank the gods that in the excitement of the moment she had not thought to draw her sword. Then he was aware of movement behind him and around him and he thought maybe Crimthann was coming to aid his friends, but instead he saw Olaf Thordarson and some of his own men running up on either side. They pulled Louis and the woman away, pinned their arms, held knives to their throats.

"Don't hurt them," Harald said, speaking his native tongue for the first time in some hours. It was a language which Louis and the woman seemed not to understand since they did not look at all relieved to hear Harald give that order.

The two were stripped of their weapons and brought around to the back of the wagon and pushed up the steps and into the dark, lantern-lit interior. There were more of Harald's men there and some of Crimthann's, including one of the women.

"Tie them up?" Olaf asked, nodding to the two prisoners.

Harald turned to Louis. "Must I have my men tie you up," he asked, "or will you give me your word you will not fight them?"

Louis looked around at Harald's men and Harald could guess what he was thinking. They were warriors, and well-armed, and he had nothing but his bare hands. "We give our word we will not fight," Louis said, probably not a hard decision.

Harald climbed out of the wagon and back up to the seat. Crimthann snapped the reins and the oxen moved again in their lumbering way, the three wagons rolling slowly on toward Glendalough. Harald scanned the road and the trees as they passed, looking for some sign of the Irish, or of his father's men or ships. He feared that with all the delays he had endured he had fallen behind the fleet, that rather than scouting ahead he was playing catch-up and did not even know it.

Soon it grew too dark to continue on, so Harald ordered Crimthann to pull the wagon off the road and the other two wagons followed behind. They made camp there, Crimthann's men cooking supper under the watchful eyes of Harald's. As that was going on, Harald climbed into the back of the wagon where guards stood over Louis and the woman.

"You are well?" Harald asked, sitting on a bench opposite them. The benches were strewn with furs and the soft light of the lantern fell on the bright-painted interior and washed it in a warm glow, giving a sensual feeling to the space.

"Well enough," the man said. There was no fear in his voice, no anger or bitterness. Nothing, really, that Harald could hear, though of course they were both speaking a language which was not their native tongue.

"You are part of this heathen army?" the woman asked, and she did not sound nearly as calm as the man.

Harald frowned. "'Heathen?'" he asked. "I do not know that word."

"Heathen," the woman said. "One of these strangers who does not believe in God."

Harald shook his head. "I believe in God," he said. "I believe in many gods."

"You do not believe in the true god."

This was all getting confusing. Harald had some notion of what the Christ followers believed, but he never understood it entirely. He thought they only believed in one god, though he had heard others speak of three gods, and he was never quite sure what they really believed.

"You are one of these fin gall who have come to plunder Glendalough?" the woman said and that clarified things. Harald smiled in understanding.

"Yes!" he said. "Yes, that's right. And who are you?"

"I am Failend, wife of Colman mac Breandan, who commands all the soldiers at Glendalough," the woman said. "This is Louis. He is a Frank. He is my servant and my body guard. My husband will pay a great deal to have me back."

Harald nodded. She may have been telling the truth about her name, and perhaps about her husband, but this Louis most certainly was not her servant, or anyone's. "Your husband will pay a great deal?" Harald asked. "You mean, more than I could get for you in the slave markets of Frisia?"

"Yes," Failend said. "Much more."

Harald nodded again. *Will he pay after he learns what you and this Louis have been up to?* he wondered, but he did not ask. He had no intention of selling her, of course, but it would not hurt to let her think he did. Then he thought of Starri Deathless.

"Do you have any skill in the healing arts? Do you know the treatment of battle wounds?"

Failend looked surprised by the question. There was a flicker of uncertainty and then she said, "Yes. Yes, I do. Very much."

"You know what herbs to use to heal wounds? How to make poultices and such? What charms are most powerful?"

"Yes," Failend said again, and Harald could hear more conviction in her voice now. "In Glendalough I have a great reputation for being a healer."

Harald looked into her eyes, brown and wide. Her hair, which had been tied in a queue, was now tumbling around her shoulders. She was very beautiful. He wondered how much of what she had said was true. Maybe half, he reckoned.

"I'm glad to hear that," he said. "I may have need of your skills. Now, my men will bring you food and then you may sleep here."

He stood up and suddenly felt very tired. "There will be a guards outside the door, so you need not worry for your safety," he added, though they all understood that the guards were not for Louis and Failend's benefit. "Tomorrow we will reach Glendalough."

Harald woke early the next morning, eager to be on the road. The fear still nagged at him that he had fallen behind Thorgrim and the fleet. He roused the others and stood by with mounting impatience as Crimthann stoked up the cooking fire and prepared breakfast. That finished, the men and women of the caravan packed the camp away, rounded up the oxen which had been set to graze and yoked them to the wagons. The sun was well up, and a light mist falling, by the time Harald was able to climb up onto the seat and order the wagons underway.

"How far to Glendalough?" Harald asked.

Crimthann shrugged. "A few miles, no more," he said.

A few miles... But Harald was not sure he wanted to go to Glendalough. If he did, he would likely find himself right in the middle of the Irish army gathered to defend the place. That would be a bad thing. But how close to get? And where were the ships and men? The "heathens", as Failend called them?

He wondered briefly if his father ever felt such indecision, if Thorgrim ever agonized over which route to take. He did not think so. He knew his father was only a man, and men encountered such troubles as these, but he could not imagine Thorgrim Night Wolf waxing uncertain on matters of how to lead his men.

The morning wore on and the mist grew into light rain, and Harald's anxiety mounted with each laborious turn of the wagon's wheels, each ponderous step of the four oxen that pulled the heavy rig. There were signs on the road that men had walked that way, a lot of men, but whether it was an army or crowds of travelers bound for the Glendalough Fair he could not tell. Even Crimthann seemed to sense his mood and managed to avoid talking, mostly.

The Irishman had been silent for going on twenty-five minutes when he spoke again. "Up over this rise yonder, and we should be able to see Glendalough," he said.

Harald nodded and pressed his lips together. It was time to make a decision – press on or turn around. He could put it off no longer. And then he heard a noise, faint but clear, and markedly familiar.

"Stop the wagon," Harald said. Crimthann pulled the oxen to a stop. He opened his mouth to speak, but Harald held up a hand and Crimthann shut his mouth again. Harald cocked his head in the direction of the unseen town. He could hear shouting, soft as a distant brook, but shouting to be certain. He could hear the faintest of pinging sounds that he guessed was the ring of steel on steel.

"Battle," Harald said. "They're fighting! Go! Go!"

Crimthann looked at him, confused.

"Go!" Harald shouted. "Get your damned oxen moving!" Crimthann nodded and snapped the reins and once again the oxen moved on at their agonizing, deliberate pace. The road ran up a low, rounded hill that obscured from sight whatever was beyond it. Harald wanted to leap from the seat and run up the hill, but until he knew where the Irish warriors were, he knew he and his men had to stick to their role as part of Crimthann's caravan of players.

Then the oxen crested the hill and pulled the wagon up over the top and Harald saw more fields beyond, another hill a few hundred paces off, and dozens of bodies strewn over the open ground. He sucked in his breath in surprise. The sounds of the fighting were louder. The battle had started on the hill in front of him and moved beyond the next rise. That was the killing field now.

"Faster!" he shouted and Crimthann snapped the reins, but the effect on the oxen was negligible. Harald thought about abandoning the wagon, he and his men taking to foot.

Not yet, not yet, he thought, though he was not sure why. He turned in the seat and slid the little wooden shutter back and looked through the window. He could see his men and Louis and Failend and Crimthann's people and they all looked as if they wanted very much to know what was happening.

"Fighting up ahead, Olaf!" Harald shouted through the opening. "Get ready."

"I'm ready," Olaf assured him and the others nodded. Then Harald thought of something.

"Hand me that spear, pass it up," he said and Olaf grabbed a spear that was leaning beside him and handed it butt-end first to Harald, and Harald pulled it through the narrow window. He turned in the seat and reached out with the point and gave the aftermost oxen, starboard side, a jab in the rump.

The oxen bellowed and Crimthann bellowed and Harald poked again. The animal moved faster now, trying to escape this torment. Harald reached over and jabbed the oxen on the larboard side and it, too, picked up the pace, building to a run. The wagon rocked violently and shuddered over the uneven road as it gained speed, moving downhill, the aftermost oxen running harder and forcing those in the front to do likewise. They were bellowing louder now and Crimthann was still shouting and Harald jabbed the brown and white rumps again.

The caravan thundered down the slope and then up the other, the oxen's feet pounding the soft ground. They crested the second hill and there, spread out before them, was Glendalough; the church, the scattering of monastic buildings and houses and workshops, less than a mile away. But Harald could spare it only a cursory look, because closer still he saw two lines of men, pressed close, weapons rising and falling. Shield walls. A battle full underway. And before he could even figure what exactly was happening, who was who, one side broke and turned and began to run, put to flight by the overwhelming numbers of the other side.

Harald held on to keep from being thrown from the seat as the wagon careened forward, barely in control, if at all. He watched the men run right across the wagon's path, a few hundred paces ahead, no more. He did not know what had happened, but he did know one thing: the men who were running were not Irish, they were Norsemen, his people. And the Irish men-at-arms and mounted warriors were coming behind to kill them as they ran.

Chapter Thirty-Eight

Nevertheless the Norwegians were defeated,
by a miracle of the Lord, and they were slaughtered.
The Annals of Ulster

This is an end to it, Thorgrim Night Wolf thought. *This is an end to it.*

Kevin mac Lugaed's men were pushing hard to get into the fight, all but running, and when they joined the rest, the Irish would outnumber the Northmen two to one at least. And Kevin's men were fresh, not exhausted and bloodied like Thorgrim's men and Ottar's

He wondered if Ottar still lived, but he could not look because he was fighting in the shield wall, and if he turned his head ,he would be struck down. He could feel his strength going, but he could also feel the men in front of him weakening. His blows were slow and awkward, as were those of the men on either side of him.

Time to end this, he thought, and shouted "Godi!"

The call seemed to stir Godi, who was tiring as well. Like a giant awakened he roared and the great battle ax came down. The blade met a shield held high to stop the blow, shattered it and barely paused as it hacked into the shield bearer's chest.

Thorgrim saw the Irishman's eyes go wide and he lunged, not at Godi's man, who was already dead, but at the man beside him who was now exposed with the destruction of his partner's shield. Iron-tooth found flesh and slashed on through and the man fell and a gap opened in the shield wall.

Once again Thorgrim leapt forward, slashing at the man to his left as Godi came in on his right and Agnarr battered the Irishman in front of him. It was a gap, an opening, an opportunity. And it was too late.

The raven banner was fifteen paces away and coming on fast, the men beneath it shouting and banging shields. Most of the Irishmen in the shield wall, Thorgrim realized, had not seen them coming, did not know help was at their backs. But now they knew, and in these reinforcements they saw their own salvation rushing across the rain-soaked field with weapons drawn. And the Norsemen saw death swooping down on them.

"Back!" Thorgrim shouted. "Back!" He stepped back and Godi did likewise, and then Thorgrim stepped back once more. It was a hard thing to do, nearly impossible, to back a shield wall away. Retreat was never the idea. A shield wall was about standing firm and battering the enemy until one side or the other broke and ran, or died where they stood.

"Back! Back! Men of Vík-ló, back!" Thorgrim shouted. His men had drilled in this, they had practiced moving back while maintaining the integrity of the shield wall. But not too often, because retiring from the field was not something Thorgrim had envisioned doing very often. But now they obeyed. They stepped back, and back again. They held their shield wall intact and they fought and they backed away.

And then it all collapsed around them.

It started when Kevin's men reached the Irishman's line. They were shrieking their hideous Celt war cries as they came charging up, leading with their shields, bright-painted and pristine, not gouged, battered and broken like those of the men who had been fighting for so long. They joined the line and rolled forward, and the weary Irish men-at-arms found renewed strength in this reinforcement. Together they charged at the Norsemen's line, a frontal assault, a wild, heedless push that drove the Northmen back and shredded their formation like a torn sail in a gale of wind.

And just as things were falling apart for Thorgrim's men, the mounted warriors hit them on the flanks. It was timed perfectly. The Norsemen were staggering under the ferocity of the Irish attack on their front when the riders charged in among them again, slashing with their swords, breaking up any ordered defense with their horses' flailing hooves.

The attack on Glendalough was done. Thorgrim's hopes of holding the line as they backed away were done. The Northmen turned and fled, the most instinctive reaction, and the very worst.

The Irish howled their victory call and pressed on after them, hacking down any who stumbled and fell behind, killing the wounded as they overtook them. And all the while the horsemen chewed on the flanks and slashed and killed and sent the panicked men running into the others and tangling them in their flight.

It was as bad a rout as Thorgrim had ever seen, and he knew it would only get worse. He called to the men as he jogged back, trying to bring some order to their flight, trying to establish some kind of defense to cover their retreat, and knowing all the while that it was pointless. His mind flailed for some way to prevent the complete destruction of his men and Ottar's.

Where do we go? he thought.

He pictured the terrain surrounding them. If there was some defensible place where they could make a stand, if they could reach their ships, they might yet live. But there was no place they could hope to defend, and they would never make it to the ships, running in panicked flight as they were. The best he could hope for was to rally the men at the top of one of those small hills and fight until the Irish killed them all. At least they would die good deaths.

And then he saw movement to his right and he turned in time to see the oddest of sights. A wagon, a large caravan, really, crested the hill over which the road ran. It was a massive, bright-painted thing drawn by four oxen which seemed to be terrified and well beyond control. The vehicle shook and swayed and looked as if it might come apart, and the animals bellowed and tossed their heads and thundered on.

There were two men on the seat mounted on the face of the wagon. One was a huge fellow who held the reins, though Thorgrim doubted they were doing much good. And beside him, unmistakable with his bright yellow hair and squat and powerful form, was Harald Thorgrimson. Harald Broadarm.

The wagon raced downhill and Thorgrim saw Harald grab the reins from the big man's hands. He pulled them hard to one side and the oxen turned in their flight, just a bit. Then suddenly there was another wagon coming over the hill, charging along in the same frantic way, also pulled by a team of beasts that charged ahead in wide-eyed, mouth-foaming panic. And then a third.

Thorgrim could do nothing but watch. The Irish were still in full pursuit, racing after the fleeing Northmen, but now Thorgrim could see what Harald intended to do. He would drive his wagon right into the Irish flanks. And none of the Irish seemed yet to have noticed.

And then they did. The Irish were no more than fifty paces away when Thorgrim saw heads turn toward the onrushing wagons and arms point and he heard men shout their warning. The line wavered and broke as the men-at-arms realized they might be trampled and crushed. Some scattered, some pressed on, and then Harald's wagon plowed into the end of the line and kept on going. Thorgrim could see men driven under the hooves of the crazed oxen, men tossed in the air, others running back, running forward, running to the sides as they tried to escape.

The lead wagon was slowing as it drove through the fighting men, but then the second wagon hit the lines, careening past Harald's, breaking down any semblance of order the Irish had maintained. It slewed sideways, came up on two wheels, hung there for a second, then toppled on its side. Then the third one hit.

Thorgrim looked back over his shoulder. The Norsemen had stopped running. They had turned to watch, transfixed by the sight of the wagons tearing through their enemy like a scythe through dry stalks. The Irish were stunned and they seemed unsure as to what had happened. Men were still running in every direction. Other were standing fixed to one spot, stunned, and some were shouting, waving arms, and trying to reform their lines.

"At them!" Thorgrim shouted. "At them!" He held Iron-tooth aloft and began jogging toward the Irish men-at-arms. It was madness. He and his men were exhausted, beaten, they were on the verge of being slaughtered, and now he was leading them forward again in another headlong assault.

"At them!" He looked over his shoulder. His men were following. They began to cheer.

Harald, incredibly, had maintained his seat through all that wild ride. Forty feet ahead Thorgrim saw him leap down to the ground. He ran around to the back of the wagon and pulled a door open. Thorgrim heard him shout something, what, he could not tell, but suddenly Harald's men came bursting out through the open door, while doors of the other two wagons were flung open and more men appeared. They shouted like madmen and brandished weapons and charged for the nearest of the men-at-arms.

There were not many of them, fewer than twenty, but their appearance was a complete surprise to the Irish at a moment when they had already had surprise piled on surprise.

"At them!" Thorgrim shouted again and he could hear the sound of the men behind him building in volume. They were thirty feet from what was left of the Irish line. He could see confused men, frightened men, stunned men looking blankly on as their enemies came at them one more time.

And then it was the Irish who were done. The shock of being struck by the wagons, of Harald's men coming out fighting, of the rest of the Norsemen charging at them with a renewed frenzy, broke the last of their resolve. Some men turned and ran, and then more ran, and soon the entire army, all those men who moments before had been tasting victory in their mouths turned and raced back the way they had come.

Thorgrim could see mounted men who he took to be the leaders of the men-at-arms shouting for their warriors to make a stand, to turn and fight. But it was pointless in the same way that Thorgrim's attempts to do the same twenty minutes before had been pointless. The leaders could see that as well, and they could see they would soon be alone on the field, so they reined their horses around and charged off to join the flight.

The Northmen reached the spot where the wagons had come to a rest, two of them toppled over now, and they drew to a halt. No one told them to stop, they just did. They stood there, looking as stunned as the Irish had been, heaving for breath and watching their enemies, who a moment before had be coming to cut them down, now showing them their heels.

A strange quiet spread over the field, a profound quiet after the noise of nearly six hundred men locked in battle. Thorgrim turned and there was Harald lumbering up, a big grin and a smear of blood on his face.

Thorgrim shook his head. He did not know what to say, so he stepped up to his boy and he embraced him and Harald returned the embrace, but awkwardly and uncertain. Then Agnarr was there, and Bersi and Kjartan and Skidi and they were able to find words of praise and thanks, and Harald grinned and clearly found the whole thing terribly embarrassing.

"They've run off," Bersi said, nodding toward the Irish, "but they are not beaten. And they are not done."

In that he was right. Thorgrim could see as much. They all could. The Irish had run pell mell for several hundred yards until the effort and the realization that the Northmen were not following had brought them to a stop. Now they were forming a line of sorts at a place roughly between the Norsemen's line and the town of Glendalough.

"They won't attack again," Thorgrim said. "Not today." He looked up at the sun. There were hours of daylight left, though it felt much later. Still, he was sure the Irish were done for that day. He knew that his own men were as well.

"No, they won't attack today," Skidi agreed. "But like Bersi says, they're not done. They'll hold that ground where they stand. Get themselves sorted out. They'll fight again on the morrow."

Thorgrim nodded. The Irish would most certainly fight on. Why wouldn't they? They were fighting for their own land, and they still outnumbered their enemy two or three to one. The question, therefore, was whether the Northmen would also stay and fight, or retreat to their ships and just sail away. They would keep their lives if they did the latter, but would have nothing else to show for their efforts.

And that was not a question that Thorgrim alone could answer.

"Let us get our men back, back to the top of that hill there." He pointed to the rise where the first shield walls had met at the commencement of the fighting. "Let's get those wagons of Harald's up there, we can make a wall of sorts. Then we'll figure out what the gods would have us do next."

The men were silent and grateful to be done fighting as they trudged back toward the hill in their rear. Those who could find the strength helped tip the wagons back on their wheels and untangle the oxen, four of which were dead, and then drive the ponderous vehicles back up the hill. Once at the crest the wagons were arranged in a line across the road. It was not much of a defense, but it was something at least.

Ottar still lived. He was limping and he wore a wide and blood-soaked bandage on his left arm and his mail shirt hung in tatters, so much that Thorgrim wondered why he bothered keeping it on at all, but he was still alive. He was silent as they made their way back to the hill, happy now to let his men simply follow what Thorgrim's were doing. But soon Thorgrim could hear his raving and shouting again. Still, Ottar kept his distance, and as long as he did that Thorgrim was happy to let him rave and shout.

The wagons were plundered for food and ale. There was not much to be had, but there were not as many of the Northmen left, and they found provisions enough to at least stave off hunger, if not sate it.

The men ate where they sat, or lay flat on the wet grass, ignoring the light rain that fell, or tended their wounds or their fellows' wounds. Thorgrim called his captains together. He called Harald as well. Harald had earned his place at the council.

They found stools and benches in the wagons and made a circle a ways off from the men. "There are two paths we can take," Thorgrim said once they had settled. "We can stay and fight tomorrow, or we can go back to the ships and sail away and forget Glendalough. I don't see what other choices there are. Tell me what you think."

The others considered the question, but Thorgrim guessed they had already considered it, and so they did not have to think on it long.

"The gods have favored us," Skidi said, breaking the silence with his grunting voice. "Harald saved us, sure, and I will be grateful all my life for that." He nodded toward Harald and Harald smiled uncomfortably. "But sure the gods put those wagons in Harald's path and drove the oxen as they did."

The others were nodding as they listened. Thorgrim had a good idea of where this was going, and he imagined the others did as well.

"The gods always favor the bold ones," Skidi continued. "It would be madness to stay and fight, and that's exactly why the gods might look with favor on us if we do. And it'll surprise the Irish so much they'll likely shit their pants."

Thorgrim looked at each man, each man's face, but these were men who kept their own council and he could read nothing there. But he knew what their answer would be.

"What say you all?" Thorgrim asked.

"I say fight," Kjartan said.

"Fight," Skidi said.

"I would rather fight," said Bersi, "but before we say yes or no we need to hear from Ottar. If he will stand with us, then we should fight. But if he is determined to leave then we have no hope, no matter how bold we might be. There would be no dishonor to us if we're forced to leave because Ottar won't fight."

Again the others nodded. "Then I will go and speak with Ottar," Thorgrim said.

"I don't think you'll have to," Skidi said and he nodded to a place beyond their circle. Thorgrim looked over to see Ottar limping toward them, his face fixed in its usual scowl, the ends of his yellow braids dark and stiff with dried blood.

He stepped up and looked around, and his eyes lit on Kjartan. His scowl deepened and his eyebrows came together and his hand moved to the hilt of his sword, but so slowly and so painfully that there seemed little menace in the gesture.

"Kjartan, you bastard, you pile of shit, why am I not surprised to see you here?" Ottar growled, but his voice, like the motion of his arm, seemed to lack the strength of a genuine threat. "You've been hiding from me all this time, you little cowardly puke."

"I've been hiding from no one," Kjartan said, making no move to ready himself for an attack. "You've been too blind to see me."

Ottar stared at Kjartan for a few seconds more but said nothing else. Instead he turned to Thorgrim. "Well, Night Wolf? Will you stand and fight or run like a frightened puppy?"

"We were just wondering the same of you," Thorgrim said, "Though I didn't see much fighting from your men today. You cowardly whore's sons ran around like chickens with a dog loose in the yard."

"You are also a pile of shit," Ottar said. "*We* were the dogs today, you were the chickens. You and those rutting Irish. But we mean to fight and we mean to wring every bit of silver and gold out of that filthy monastery and share every woman there amongst us. Make these swine pay and pay dear for what they did today. Will you stand with us?"

Thorgrim looked at the big man, towering over him. He had several gashes across his face and forehead, some quite deep. The blood made weird patterns where it had been channeled by the old, twisted scar across his cheek. His stance was defiant, his words as offensive as ever, but the spirit was lacking, the fire was burning down.

Ottar, of course, had the same problem Thorgrim did. Neither man could hope to win if they remained but the other did not.

"Yes, we will stay and fight these bastards, just as we planned from the start," Thorgrim said.

"Good," Ottar said. "Once it is dark one of us should take his men and move around that way." He pointed toward the north. "At first light we can fall on the Irish from two sides. They won't expect us to divide our men that way."

Thorgrim looked off in the direction Ottar was pointing and he saw what the man had in mind. If they managed to get in place unseen then they could attack the Irish in the front and on their left flank at the same time. Ottar was right. The Irish would not expect that. It was not a bad plan.

But it also seemed too clever by half for Ottar. Why was he suggesting it, Thorgrim wondered, and why the sudden interest in cooperating?

"I can see your mind work, Night Pup," Ottar said. "You wonder what trick I'm playing. The answer is none. I care only about killing these bastard Irish and taking their silver and having their women. I leave it to you to decide who will go north and who will remain here. You see? No tricks. I let you decide."

Thorgrim stood. Ottar still towered over him, but standing made things a bit more even. "Very well," he said. "Me and my men will go north. We'll stay out of sight. At first light you attack, and once the Irish make ready to fight you in their front we will attack their flank."

Ottar nodded. He looked around at the others. He said nothing. Then he turned and limped back to his own men.

"He cannot be trusted," Kjartan said, speaking the words like a simple statement of fact.

"Probably not," Thorgrim agreed. "But he and his men will start the fight, and once it is begun they'll have no choice but win or die. If they do not start the fight at all then there will be no dishonor to us if we withdraw. Like Bersi said. The dishonor will be Ottar's, not ours."

Thorgrim spoke those words with a certainty he did not necessarily feel. *We go into battle outnumbered three to one, with men we cannot trust to fight and no place to go if we are beaten*, he thought.

Still, he was sure he had been in worse situations, even if he could not at that moment recall when.

Chapter Thirty-Nine

The first prey was taken by the heathens...
and they carried off many prisoners,
and killed many and led away very many captive.
Annals of Ulster

Like the others inside that fur-strewn wagon, Louis de Roumois was wondering what the hell was going on outside.

They were moving fast, that was clear. The oxen seemed have galloped away with the wagon, running faster than he would have thought such ponderous beasts capable of running. The wagon was tipping and thumping and groaning with the strain. It seemed impossible that it had not yet turned on its side. What Louis did not know was whether any of this was happening for a reason, or if it was all beyond human control.

He looked around at the men and women seated near him. Crimthann's people were terrified, holding on tight to anything substantial they could grab. The heathens were not nearly so frightened, but they seemed not to know any more than Louis did about what was going on.

The wagon took a sickening tilt to one side and Louis was certain the wheels had come off the ground and that they were going over. He put an arm around Failend and held her close, hoping to provide some cushion if they were flung across the interior. But, incredibly, the wagon came down on all four wheels again with a jarring crash that tossed two of Crimthann's men to the floor. The wagon staggered on for a minute more, then came to a stop so fast that Louis and Failend were flung forward, tumbling into the one called Olaf.

Louis could hear screaming and shouting outside the wagon and then the back door was flung open and Harald was there, yelling at

his men in their native tongue. Louis could not understand the words, but the men leapt to their feet and snatched up weapons and tumbled for the door, and Louis guessed it was a call to arms.

And that meant there was a battle taking place. Through the door Louis could see the other two wagons, both of which had managed to turn on their sides. Harald's men were climbing out of those as well, while around the wagons Louis could see men-at-arms – Irish men-at-arms – standing in a dazed confusion or running or lying wounded or dead on the ground.

"Come on!" he said to Failend. He stood and pulled her to her feet and pulled her to the door in the back of the wagon. He stopped and peered out. The Irish were running back toward Glendalough, and from the other direction a line of screaming Northmen were racing toward them. It was madness, chaos, and it was their only chance of escape.

Louis hopped down to the ground and helped Failend down after him. "We have to run!" he shouted.

"Where?" Failed asked.

And that was the question. *Where?* Not toward the Northmen, clearly. But they could not go to the Irish either. Word would have gone out that they had murdered Aileran. They would probably both be hanged as soon as they were discovered. Certainly Colman would insist on it, before they could start talking.

"Glendalough," Failend said.

"What?" Louis asked.

"Glendalough!" Failend said. "We'll go to Glendalough!"

Louis shook his head. "Glendalough? Are you mad?"

"No, see here. All the soldiers will be in the field. There will be no one there, at least no one who will know us. My husband has a hoard buried in the house. Let's dig it up. We'll need silver if we are ever to escape."

Louis looked over at the town, dull gray and brown and green in the mist. *Glendalough.* It was brilliant. Failend was right. Anyone who might cause trouble for them would be in the field, not in the city. The town would be in chaos, and it was easy to disappear into chaos. Perfect.

"Let's go!" Louis said. The Northmen were closing fast and the Irish were running for the high ground distant and the two of them

were alone by the wagons, save for the wounded and the dead. "This way!"

They ran in the direction that the Irish were running, just two more men-at-arms fleeing the Northmen. But as they did they angled their course off toward the town, leaving both sides behind. They hoped no one would notice them.

*Must keep ahead of the damned heathens...*Louis thought and he picked up his pace. He took three long strides before he remembered that Failend's legs, which he loved so dearly, were much shorter than his. She would not be able to run so fast. He turned and saw she had already fallen behind, and he slowed so she could catch up.

"Louis!" she gasping as she stumbled toward him. She pointed off to the right and Louis turned to look. Most of the heathens had stopped once they reached the wagons but Harald's men had gone chasing after the fleeing Irish. They were coming back now, and two of them had spotted him and Failend and they were coming toward them, swords drawn.

"Behind me, get behind me!" Louis shouted and he hoped to God she would obey. He and Lochlánn had trained her with a sword, but just a bit, and he knew that a little knowledge could lead to a lot of trouble if one over-estimated one's skills. But Failend did not argue. She drew her sword but stepped aside, putting Louis between herself and the heathens. Louis drew his sword as well.

The two men were slowing to a walk, making their approach with some caution, splitting up so that they could come at Louis from two directions. Louis did not recognize them. They must have been in one of the other wagons. Judging by the way they moved and held their weapons they did not seem to think Louis and Failend would be much trouble, their cautious approach notwithstanding.

We have no time for this, Louis thought. He would have to eliminate this threat, and do it quickly.

Both men were still just beyond the reach of Louis's sword when Louis turned hard on the one to his left, lunging straight and true. The man leapt back, and as he did, the one on Louis's right moved in fast, leading with his sword. It was what Louis knew he would do.

Louis spun back, caught the incoming blade with a wide, sweeping motion, knocked it aside, stepped in and kicked the man hard in the stomach. The man doubled over. Louis brought his knee up and connected with the man's face. Through his leggings Louis

felt the man's nose break as he was flung back. Louis whirled to meet the first Northman just as the man's long sword came swinging around in a wide arc aimed at Louis's head.

Louis ducked and the blade made a whirring sound as it passed inches above him. Louis slashed at the man's legs and he felt his sword bite. The Northman shouted and fell forward, blood welling from the rent in his leggings.

"Come on!" Louis called and he and Failend began running again. The two heathens on the ground would stay on the ground for some time, but if any of the others had seen that fight they would come swarming like bees.

Louis glanced behind to be sure Failend was keeping up with him, but he did not dare slow enough to see what the enemy – heathens or Irish – were doing. He crested a low hill and could see Glendalough spread out below, the velum and the outer wall, the big church, the low, crude buildings. He could see Colman's house. He could see hundreds of people jamming the streets and swarming over the square. It was every inch the chaos he thought it would be.

"Louis!" Failend gasped. Louis stopped and turned. Failend was doubled over, heaving for breath. He stepped over to her.

"Are you hurt? Wounded?" he asked.

She shook her head. She was breathing too hard to speak. Louis let her gulp air and looked back the way they had come. The heathens had gone no farther than the overturned wagons. The Irish were several hundred yards away, and between them there was nothing but green grass and patches of mud and a smattering of dead and wounded.

"The fighting is done. For today," Louis said.

Failend had straightened by then, though her mouth still hung open. "How do you know?" she asked, and those were all the words she seemed able to speak.

"They're done," Louis said. "There's no fight left in those men, on either side. I can see as much. They must have been fighting some time before that heathen driving the wagon crashed into them."

Failend nodded. "What will they do?" she asked. Her voice was returning.

"The Irish, I think, will get their men in the best position they can and make ready to fight tomorrow. It's what I would do, if I was still in command," Louis said, surprised by the involuntary bitterness in his voice. "We'll see if it's what your hus...what Colman does."

"The heathens will stay and fight again?"

"I don't know," Louis said. "If I had my guess, I would say they are discussing that right now. Or at least they will be soon."

For a few moments they stood watching the armies in the distance. No one seemed to be looking back at them, two lone figures hundreds of yards away on a battlefield strewn with men, living and dead.

"Let us go," Failend said. She nodded toward Glendalough at the bottom of the long slope on which they stood. They turned and headed downhill through wet, knee-high grass.

Even from a distance they could see that the muddy streets were scenes of madness, much like Louis imagined Judgement Day would be. The heathens were coming and everyone in Glendalough, the hundreds who lived there and the hundreds more who had come for the Glendalough Fair, were frantic to get away. The grass yielded to trampled earth as they came closer to the town. Louis and Failend walked on, and finally the trampled earth became a street that ran between the close-packed wattle and thatch buildings to the town square.

Carts creaked and groaned their way through the crowds, men with their families trailing behind led horses or donkeys laden with as much as they could bear. Peddlers and merchants hefted their wares on their backs like pack animals and stumbled along. All were moving as directly away from the distant armies as they could. They did not seem to care where they were going, only that they were leaving the town and the warring men behind.

Louis and Failend pushed their way through the crowd, weaving and twisting past the squat ugly buildings they knew so well, low wattle and thatch constructions that served as homes and workshops: the potter, the woodworker, the blacksmith. The door to the latter building hung open and Louis looked in as he passed. The tools were gone, and the bellows and even a stool that he knew usually stood in the corner. Only the anvil remained, and Louis imagined the smith was loath to leave it behind, but had little choice.

They pressed on. People were shouting, children were crying, beasts were whinnying and lowing and snorting. Two men were

rolling in the mud and beating one another with their fists, but no one paid them any attention.

"Madness," Failend said. They came out of the far end of the street and into the square. Most of the stalls which had been so laboriously constructed over the past weeks were empty, the merchants who had taken them having packed their goods and fled. Some had collapsed, their frames and thatch trampled in the mud. Panicked livestock, sheep and goats and pigs, raced through the crowd, lending another level of chaos to the scene.

Louis and Failend cut across the square, across the flow of traffic, which made the going harder, but finally they reached the fence that delineated the border between Colman's home – Failend's home – and the square. Here Failend stopped. She turned to Louis and put a hand on his chest.

"Wait here," she said.

Louis shook his head. "Why?"

"Someone must look out, in case the soldiers come," she said. "Besides..." She faltered a bit, then continued. "This is my house. If I'm caught taking my husband's silver they cannot call me a thief. Or it will be harder, anyway. But they could hang you."

Louis frowned. He did not like this, not at all. But what she said made sense. They had discussed Colman's hoard as they walked toward the town. Possession of that wealth would mean freedom, escape. It meant purchasing horses and passage to Frankia, it meant lodging, and bribing anyone who needed bribing in order for them to make their way to safety. The silver and gold and jewels hidden in the big house meant life, and without it they would soon be hunted down like wolves and killed,.

"Very well," he said. "I'll stay outside and keep watch. Don't be long."

"I won't," Failend said. "I'll try not to be. Colman sometimes moves his hoard. If it's not buried where I think it is it might take me some time to find it. So don't worry if I'm not right out. I'll come for you or call out if I need your help."

She reached up and kissed him. Then she turned and walked through the gate and up to the big house, so grand by the standards of the Irish, the site of such heights of pleasure for Louis de Roumois, and such depths of despair.

*   *   *

Failend slowed as she approached the door, that familiar door. It occurred to her that it might be barred from the inside, but she doubted it. Cautiously she lifted the wooden latch and felt no resistance. She lifted further, careful to make no noise, and when she felt the door was free she pushed it open just wide enough for her to squeeze through.

She stood in the twilight interior and listened. She could still hear the sounds of panic in the streets, but muffled now by the thick wattle and daub-built walls of the house. She heard the scurrying of mice somewhere up above, in the thatch, perhaps. She heard nothing else.

Because Colman was a wealthy man he had windows fitted in the house, two of them, with glass, high up. They let the dull light of the rainy, misty late afternoon fall around the big room, leaving the interior of the house washed in greys and blacks. Failend could see the raised floors against either wall with their piles of furs, and the hearth and the pot hanging over it, the table and chairs, yet another mark of wealth. It was all so familiar, her everyday life for the past four years. She knew she would not miss it at all. None of it.

She moved across the room to where a tapestry hung down the wall, a lovely piece of work with colors that leapt out when the sunshine fell on it. She stepped behind the cloth and let it drape naturally over her slim frame so that in the dim light there would be almost no chance that anyone would see she was there.

There was no need for her to search out Colman's hoard. She knew exactly where it was buried. In the four years they had been married he had never moved it, only dug it up on occasion to add more silver. She could see that the rushes and the dirt that covered it were undisturbed, so it must still be there.

She told Louis she had to look for it because she needed time. How much, she did not know. Maybe more time than she would get. It was a gamble, but it might well pay off, and that meant it was worth fifteen or twenty minutes at least.

She stood motionless. The only sound that was not muffled and distant was that of her breathing. She had no way to judge the amount of time that passed. It seemed she had been there a long time. But she knew that, waiting as she was, she could expect the minutes to crawl by at a maddeningly slow pace.

Louis will come looking for me if I am too long in waiting, she thought. More minutes slipped by, and then she heard a sound from deep in the house. Not mice this time, but a person, certainly, coming in through the kitchen door that opened onto the alley behind. Sneaking in, hoping to remain unseen.

Welcome home, Failend thought.

Still she did not move. She heard the footsteps, soft on the hard earth floor and rustling through the rushes scattered there. She heard them stop as the newcomer paused and looked around and then, apparently satisfied, continued on.

Three or four more steps and then more rustling as a layer of rushes was brushed away, and then the faint scrape of metal on dirt. A knife, Failend guessed. She stepped silently from behind the tapestry. Twenty feet away, kneeling with his back to her, digging in the dirt, was Colman mac Breandan.

His shoulders rose and fell as he worked, clearing the earth away from what Failend knew was a small silver chest packed full with a few jewels, a few bits of gold, and a considerable amount of silver. Broaches, arm rings, finger rings, hack silver, coins, Colman had amassed an impressive hoard. Nor was this his only hoard, but Failend doubted they would have the opportunity to relieve him of the others, hidden in other halls and sundry shops and mills that Colman owned in that part of Ireland.

Go on, you son of a whore, dig it up for me, she thought.

Then Colman stopped digging. He slipped the knife back in its sheath and reached down into the hole he had made. He hefted the box out and as he twisted to set it aside he finally caught a glimpse of Failend standing behind him. He gasped, stood and turned, his hand reaching for the hilt of the sword that still hung from his belt.

And then he realized who it was and his hand dropped to his side again and his body seemed to relax.

"You should have drawn your sword," Failend said, taking a step toward him. "It would have been the first time it was out all day."

"Ha!" Colman said. "So, the little slut-at-arms has come home. Is the Frank here? I had hoped to hang the two of you side by side. You've already been pronounced guilty of Aileran's murder, you know. But I'll hang you one at a time if I must."

Failend took another step toward him. "I don't know where Louis is," she said. "This is not his business, it's mine."

"What? Have you come to beg for your life? No, wait…" Colman said, and Failend saw the understanding spread across his face. "You came to steal my hoard, you little bitch!"

"I did," Failend admitted and with that she pulled her sword from the scabbard and held it low and in front of her. "And I waited for you. Because I knew you would choose your silver over your men, if you thought there was even a chance the heathens might sack this town."

Colman smiled. "You make this all so damned easy!" he said. "You come here, dressed like that, armed, intent on stealing my hoard. There's no need for me to go to the trouble of hanging you. I'll just kill you here and now."

He was still smiling as he once again reached for his sword. He grabbed the hilt and had the weapon halfway out of the scabbard when Failend darted forward and drove the point of her sword into his hand. She saw it sink deep and she guessed it had gone clean through. Colman shrieked, not a particularly manly sound, jerked his hand away and held it up to his face. Blood was flowing like a red stream from the deep wound.

"You bitch!" he cried. "Damn you, you damned slut!"

"Don't call me a slut," Failend said. "I am done with you calling me that."

Colman moved his eyes from his ruined hand to Failend, his expression a mix of rage, confusion and, for the first time, fear.

"You…" was all he said. He held his arm up for her to see. The blood ran down his forearm and dripped on the floor, but Failend did not miss his left hand reaching around for his knife. She darted forward again, sinking her sword point into his left shoulder and leaping clear as he swung at her.

"Ah, damn you, damn you!" Colman shouted. His teeth were clenched and his arms were hanging useless at his sides. He was breathing hard, and Failend could see him summon the will to remain calm.

"Very well," he said. "Take the hoard. Take it and go."

"I will," Failend said, but she did not move. They were silent, staring at one another.

"This was not about you, you know," Colman said. "Aileran, the Frank, all that. It was a different matter. It was not about you."

"I know," Failend said. "And that's what makes me angry enough to kill you."

She watched Colman's face, his eyes. He was not a fool. He knew now that he would not talk his way out of this. His right hand whipped out at Failend and she felt the spray of blood across her face and then he was coming at her. She raised her sword.

In truth she did not know if she could kill Colman, but he spared her that decision. He charged forward as her blade came up. She moved her arm, no more than an inch or so, and the point tore into his throat.

Colman's eyes went wide and he made an ugly gurgling sound. Failend slashed sideways, freeing the blade in a spray of blood. She stepped aside quick as Colman pitched forward onto the floor. He fell with a soft thud that Failend felt through her shoes. Colman's legs were jerking, but she wiped the blade of her sword on his leggings and slipped it back into her scabbard. She went over to the hole Colman had dug and hefted the silver box, making a grunting sound as she did. The hoard was heavier than she had expected.

She tucked the box under her arm and stepped back over to where Colman lay. He was still making soft noises, though it was not entirely clear to her that he was still alive. She put her foot on his shoulder and rolled him on his back. He flopped over with no resistance. His throat was a ruined mess, the torn flesh lost in the great wash of blood. His eyes were open. She leaned down, looking for some sign of life, but she could see none.

"Goodbye, husband," she said. She crossed the room and opened the door, stepped out into the mist and the panicked madness in the streets. She closed the door behind her.

Chapter Forty

Cattle die and kinsmen die,
thyself too soon must die,
but one thing never, I say, will die, --
fair fame of one who has earned.
Hávamál

T he battered remnants of Thorgrim's army remained at their wagon barricades until nightfall. They prayed or slept or gamed or tended to weapons or injuries. Then, after the sun went down and darkness had spread like a cloak over a dead man's body, they waited some more.

Thorgrim called Bersi and Kjartan and Skidi together. Harald was not there. He was leading a small scouting party out toward the Irish lines. The plan that Thorgrim and Ottar had devised called for Thorgrim's men to work their way unseen into a new, advantageous position, and Thorgrim had to be sure the Irish would not try to do the same thing.

"The fires your men have burning, keep them burning low, but be certain they're visible to the Irish," Thorgrim said to his captains. "We'll leave the most badly wounded men behind to tend them. In the very deep hours of the night we'll move to the north and find a spot where we'll be hidden from the Irish until we're ready to spring on them. That will be once Ottar begins his attack."

The others nodded and made sounds to acknowledge their understanding which grated on Thorgrim's nerves. The black mood was taking hold of him, he recognized the signs. He was growing irritable and snappish and soon he would start lashing out at anyone who spoke to him, unreasonable as that might be. It was time for him to leave the company of men.

Thorgrim went off by himself and sat and stared out at the dark and the few points of light that he could see, a dozen or so fires out by the Irishmen's camp and others in the town of Glendalough. Cooking fires, people making ready to put the torch to the buildings there? Thorgrim did not know and did not care. The hours slipped by.

Harald returned and found Thorgrim sitting alone. "Father, the Irish have not moved at all," he said. "They don't seem to have anything in mind but to make a stand where they are."

Thorgrim grunted his reply. Harald recognized the black mood, he had seen it all his life, so he said no more, just nodded and slipped away. Starri Deathless was the only person who had ever been able to remain in Thorgrim's company when this darkness was on him, and now Starri was gone, back aboard *Sea Hammer*, alive or dead Thorgrim did not know.

Thorgrim's mind was still in the present world when Bersi and Harald came looking for him hours later. They approached cautiously, hesitantly, which only made Thorgrim more angry still, but he held his tongue.

"Father, it's near the midnight hour, I would guess," Harald said. Thorgrim grunted. He had been waiting for this time, the darkest part of the night, when the vigilance in the Irish camp would be at its lowest. His and Ottar's plan of attack would work only if they had surprise with them. Indeed, surprise was the only possible advantage they might have over the Irish who so outnumbered them.

"Come on," Thorgrim grunted. He stood and headed off into the dark. He did not ask if the men were ready to follow because he knew Harald would not be so foolish as to come for him if they were not. As if in silent answer he heard the soft sound of nearly one hundred men, all that remained of his ships' crews, following behind in the dark.

Thorgrim knew the country well, having studied it during the hours when there was light enough to see. He had even climbed up on top of one of the wagons to get a better look at the way the land rose and fell. Now he moved with confidence, and he led his column along a low stretch of ground behind a hill that shielded them from the Irish lines and the enemy scouts who most certainly must have been out there watching.

They walked for twenty minutes or so, and then Thorgrim held up his hand for the men to stop. He heard behind him the barely audible bumping and rustling of men coming to a halt. He climbed up the hill to his left. It was a dark night, and though the rain had stopped, the sky was still blanketed with clouds, and no moon or starlight made its way through.

At the top of the hill he lay down flat and looked to the distance. He could still see the lights of the Irish camp as he had earlier, but they seemed more bunched together now. Before, he had been looking at the Irish defenses straight on. Now he was looking down their flank.

Perfect, he thought.

He made his way back down the hill. He understood he would have to speak to the others and he loathed the thought, but he knew there was nothing for it. "We stop here," he said to Harald and Bersi. "Let the men sleep in their line. Lookouts on the hill top. Everyone up before first light."

"Yes, father," Harald said and Thorgrim turned away, satisfied that things would be done as he wished. It was one of the advantages of having a young man in charge whom one had trained from birth.

Thorgrim walked off into the dark, up the hill once more, sitting down on the wet grass near the crest. The lights of the Irish camp were ahead of him, and to his left, farther off, were the campfires they had left burning by the wagons. Those were tended by the men too wounded to fight, in hope that the Irish would believe all his men were still at that place.

He closed his eyes. He could feel conscious thought swirling away like the last moments of wakefulness before sleep. He felt the primal rage, the animal impulses deep inside him swirling around, rising up, sweeping him off, and he let himself go.

Nothing good ever came from the black mood, at least nothing of which Thorgrim was aware. But sometimes it allowed him see things, it carried him beyond the place where he was and let him see what his enemies were doing, where they were strong or where they were weak and vulnerable. The wolf dreams, as he called them, were rarely wrong.

The wolf dreams came to him that night, vivid and torturous. He saw himself running with a pack. They were being pursued through a thick wood, but he had a sense that there should have been more of them, that his pack was not the size it was supposed to be, not even close.

And as they ran he sensed the pack thinning even more until soon there was just him and a few with him, and their pursuers were closing in. Closing in. He could hear their snarling in the night, he could see their wicked eyes. He turned and snapped but there was nothing into which he could sink his teeth. He twisted and bit and charged and could find nothing. There was nothing around him. It had all been taken away.

It was a dream of despair, of hopelessness, of rage that had no outlet. He was howling and biting and lashing out and there was nothing around him but darkness.

And then he was awake. It was still nighttime, the sky and the land still black as pine tar. The fires in the Irish camp were little more than a series of dull orange points in the distance. Thorgrim could hear snoring behind him, and the sound of a few men moving carefully.

He thought of the wolf dream. *What was that?* he wondered. He had seen nothing that might be of help. He had learned nothing.

There was more movement behind him, voices speaking very soft, no more than a whisper. He had no sense for how much time had passed, but he guessed it was time to rise and to get in position. They would make ready for that moment when Ottar led his men against the shield wall, and then he and his men would hit the Irish on their flank, and if all went well they would crush them between the two armies.

Three hours from now we might be sacking Glendalough, Thorgrim thought and immediately regretting thinking it. The gods did not care for that sort of hubris. He clutched the Thor's hammer amulet he wore around his neck. There was a cross hanging there as well, a gift from an Irishwoman, a Christ follower, as they all were. The Christ worshipers might be happy with only one God, but Thorgrim was happy for the help of any.

There will not be a damned thing left in Glendalough worth taking, he thought next. They had pissed away any chance of surprise like yesterday's ale. The people would have already carried off anything that was of any value, and much that was not.

He stood in a crouch and walked down below the crest of the hill, then stood to his full height and stretched. With the passing of the wolf dream came the passing of the black mood and he felt more himself now, more ready to face what was to come. Including his death, which was more likely than not.

"Father?" He heard Harald's voice behind him in the dark. He turned and could just make out his son's shape as Harald came up the hill. He could hear the hesitancy in the boy's voice. Harald would not know what sort of reception he might get.

"Yes, Harald?" Thorgrim said, knowing those two words, spoken in a reasonable tone of voice, would tell Harald all he needed to know about his father's state of mind.

"We've got the men up and in order," Harald said. Thorgrim could sense, more than see, his son's presence at his side. "First light should be soon. I think."

"Good," Thorgrim said but he could still hear hesitancy in the words. "Is there something else?"

"Ah, yes..." Harald said. "It's...Kjartan. And his men. They're gone."

Thorgrim was silent for a moment, trying to make sense of this. "Gone?"

"They were on the far left end of our line. Everything seemed fine. I thought they were with us, ready to fight. But now they are gone."

"They didn't just wander off?"

"I've been out over the ground, back toward the wagons. They're not there. Maybe they went back to join Ottar?"

"Maybe," Thorgrim said. But only if Kjartan had been lying about the bad blood between him and his brother. He remembered that Ottar had not reacted with his usual violence on seeing Kjartan yesterday. He had done nothing more than curse at him. But what would it mean if Kjartan and Ottar were not really feuding? Why the ruse?

Thorgrim had a bad feeling about all of this.

"If he's gone, he's gone, run off like cowards, the lot of them," Thorgrim said. "Men like that would be of no use in a fight anyway." He took a step toward Harald, put a hand on his shoulder. "Let's go join the men," he said. "This is our lucky day. Today we'll either enjoy the riches of Glendalough or the glory of Odin's corpse hall."

They made their way back down the hill and found their men standing and shaking the stiffness out of their limbs and rubbing their arms to get the blood moving. It was not a cold night but the damp had a way of working into the bones, and the men moved in place to drive the chill out like an evil spirit. Thorgrim found Bersi and Skidi.

"So, Kjartan's run off I hear," Thorgrim said.

"Yes, the bastard, the pile of shit," Skidi spat. "At least if we die today we'll not have to see his miserable, cowardly hide in Valhalla." This was met with a grunting agreement.

"The more plunder for us, " Thorgrim said. "No man here will be unhappy about sharing their portion." He looked off to the east and thought he could detect a lightening in the darkness there. "Dawn will be soon. Let's us go to the top of the hill and watch for Ottar's attack. Then we'll give the Irish bastards the surprise we have prepared for them."

He led them up the hill. They approached the crest on hands and knees, and then laid down on their bellies and stared out into the blackness and remained silent as they watched. Birds were singing their morning song somewhere out in the tall grass, and from a great distance they could hear a cock crowing, its harsh voice carrying a far in the still air.

They remained in that position for some time and then Thorgrim saw that the day was most certainly getting lighter, the thick blackness, now fading into something gray. He could see the men on either side of him, and a vague suggestion of the hills around them and the mountains off in the distance.

"Another ten minutes," Skidi breathed, "and it'll be light enough to see Ottar." That was part of the plan. The Irish could not know Thorgrim's men were there, and the best way to stop them from knowing was to give them something else to look at. And so Ottar would have his men in a shield wall on the crest of the hill where the barricade of wagons had been made. Nothing would catch and hold a warrior's eye so well as a shield wall.

The sun continued to rise behind the heavy layer of cloud and the land around them was slowly revealed, gray and wet. The hills seemed to take shape as if the gods were raising them up from the earth. Glendalough, far off, was still lost in deep shadow, but the higher places began to show themselves in the grudging daylight.

They could see the Irish now. They were formed up in a shield wall, ready for the Northmen's attack. They would not to be caught unprepared.

Thorgrim and his captains turned their heads as one and looked back to the hill from which they had come. The wagons were visible now, but they seemed to obstruct the view of the field beyond.

"Do you see Ottar's men?" Thorgrim asked.

"No," Skidi said. "The wagons might be in the way."

They waited. The daylight spread across the valley and fell on more and more of the open ground and the mountains in the distance and the town and monastery of Glendalough. And finally the far hill, the wagons, the road, the fields, all were plainly visible in the morning light.

And Ottar's men were gone.

Chapter Forty-One

Do not be the first to kill,
nor provoke into fight
the gods who answer in battle.
Gisli Sursson's Saga

"Down, down, everyone down off the hill," Thorgrim said, his voice just above a whisper. "Agnarr, you stay, keep a watch." He crawled backward from where he and Bersi and Skidi were lying on the crest of the rise. It was light enough now that he could tell his men apart as they stood waiting to throw themselves into the desperate fight.

Thorgrim looked up at the sky. He could not speak because he did not know what to say. He had to think. Think.

He turned to Bersi and Skidi. "Ottar has abandoned us. It looks as if Kjartan has gone with him, the blackheart bastard."

"They must have returned to the ships," Bersi said.

"Yes," Thorgrim agreed.

"They'll sail off," Skidi said. "And that whore's son shit Ottar might burn our ships first." Thorgrim could hear a touch of panic, not something he had ever heard in Skidi's voice before.

Thorgrim nodded. It was exactly what he was thinking. Ottar would burn their ships, or divide his men among the nine vessels and take them all. He would do it to get his revenge on Thorgrim, and to make certain Thorgrim and his men were left behind so that the Irish would be occupied in hunting them while Ottar and his men escaped down river.

"We must get back to the ships," Thorgrim said. There would be no talk of taking the monastery now. They would be lucky to get away with their lives. Very lucky.

'*Three hours from now we might be sacking Glendalough*', Thorgrim recalled his thinking. *Idiot.*

"Thorgrim!" Agnarr called down, just loud enough to be heard. "The horsemen are mounting."

"Very well," Thorgrim said. He looked to the east, as far as he could see, and considered the terrain he had studied. They were hidden in a low place, but there was higher ground all around them. No matter which direction they moved they would soon find themselves on an exposed hilltop, in full view of the Irish men-at-arms.

But they could not remain where they were, either. The horsemen would soon be sweeping the area. They would find the Northmen even if they did not yet know they were there.

He looked back over the way they had come. They could keep out of sight behind the hill until they reached the high place where the wagons were positioned. Then they would have no choice but expose themselves as they made their way over the hill and back to the ships. It would be an all-out retreat or a running fight, but there was nothing else they could do.

"Skidi, you take the lead," Thorgrim said. "You know the way. Move quickly, but once you're up on the top of the hill by the wagons, where the Irish can see you, then you run like Hel herself is on your heels. Get around behind the wagons, maybe they'll hide you. Lead the men into the woods as soon as you can. Bersi, keep the men together and keep them moving, don't let them get spread out. Harald and I will be at the end of the column."

They nodded, moved off. Thorgrim called Agnarr down from the hill.

"The horsemen were mounting," Agnarr said, "but they did not seem to be in any great hurry. They were still just standing around."

"They don't know we're here," Thorgrim said. "They think we've all gone back to the ships. They're probably arguing about whether to follow, and they're taking their time about it. As these Irish will. So, that will buy us a few minutes, anyway."

The men were in a loose column now, two or three abreast. Those who had straps had slung their shields over their backs, the other carried their shields on their arms. All had their swords sheathed. They would not be fighting and they knew it. They would be running for their lives.

Skidi, at the head of the column, began to walk, surprisingly quick for so squat and broad a man. The line of warriors followed behind, moving faster as they spread out. Finally the last man stepped off and behind him Thorgrim and Harald.

"The Irish will see us when we go over the hill," Harald said, speaking low. "What will we do?" He had not been elsewhere when Thorgrim gave his instructions to Skidi.

"We run," Thorgrim said. "What more can we do?"

What more? Harald, trusting soul, had probably thought Thorgrim had a plan, but Thorgrim was all out of plans. One betrayal after another, one run of bad luck following another, one traitorous whore's son after another had stripped him of plans, ideas, nearly stripped him of hope.

Run like a bastard, try to reach the ships, pray to Thor and Njord that the ships were still there and still intact, and then try to reach the sea. That was the plan. It was the best he had just then, and he had no time to come up with better.

The column was moving at a slow jog, just about right, Thorgrim thought. Move fast but save strength for the real foot race to come. They hurried back over the ground they had covered in the dark hours of the night. They made little noise. Thorgrim was certain they could not be heard as far away as the Irish lines.

All right... Thorgrim thought, *all right...* They had not yet been seen.

Not so far now...

They covered the last hundred yards quickly and then Thorgrim could see Skidi and the men at the head of the column leaving the low ground and climbing the hill to where the wagons stood in their defensive barrier. He saw them reach the left-most wagon and race around it and it hid them from sight, mostly. And in their wake, strung out more than Thorgrim would have liked, a hundred or so more men, all pushing hard for the same destination. The river. The ships. The sea.

Perhaps a third of his men had disappeared behind the wagon when he finally heard the cry of alarm from the Irish lines.

Not too rutting vigilant, are you? he thought, but the Irish had all the advantages now and they did not have to be all that vigilant.

"Go, go, go!" Thorgrim shouted. No need for quiet anymore. No real need to tell the men to move faster, either. They had heard the cries from the Irish lines and they were running up the hill, racing for…what? There was no protection to be had until they reached the ships, and with the Irish coming to ride them down, the ships and the river were far, far away.

Thorgrim and Harald started up the hill, racing after the men. Some of those ahead were throwing their shields away so they would be better able to run, a very bad idea.

Idiots!

The shields might make it harder to run, but if the horsemen caught them on open ground they would be the only thing standing between them and a spear in the neck or a hoof kick to the head. And Thorgrim could not imagine they would make it to the ships without a fight.

"Keep your shields, you stupid bastards, keep your shields!" Thorgrim shouted as loud as he could, but that was not too loud because his breath was short. Harald took up the cry. He seemed to have no trouble either breathing or yelling.

Up the slope, and when they were half way to the wagons, Thorgrim stopped and turned toward the Irish line, and he did not love what he saw. The mounted men were spurring toward them now. He could hear voices shouting: warnings, encouragements, orders, he could not tell. It didn't matter. He and his men had been seen, and soon, five minutes if they were lucky, they would be fighting on foot, on open ground, against mounted warriors, the most dangerous of circumstances.

Thorgrim watched long enough to get a rough count. Forty or fifty, he thought. Forty or fifty mounted warriors against his hundred or so on foot. The riders were spreading out as they gained speed, whipping their horses on.

"If they attack like that, like some undisciplined mob," Thorgrim said to Harald, "if they think they can just ride us down, that will be good for us. If our men can make a shield wall and stand fast."

He turned and hurried on, now a dozen paces behind the end of the column. He and Harald pushed up the hill and around the wagon. Thorgrim saw the smoldering remains of the campfires. He wondered what had become of the wounded men he had left to tend them. Gone back to the ships, he hoped.

The dark and rutted road stretched out ahead, and the open ground beyond that. Skidi was leading them away from the road and toward the nearest wood that lined the river. If they could get among the trees then the horsemen would not be able to ride them down. The Irish men-at-arms would probably not be able to fight on horseback at all, and Thorgrim did not think they would try to fight on foot. They were outnumbered, and it was only the horses that gave them an advantage.

If we get among the trees... he thought. He looked back over his shoulder, but the wagons obstructed his view of the riders. It would be a close thing, either way.

His mouth was open, his breathing harder as he and Harald ran across the field in the wake of the men. He understood the impulse that the others had to throw their shields away. Thorgrim's shield was on his back and it thumped as he ran and he wanted very much to toss the clumsy thing aside, but he did not. Harald, he was certain, was slowing his pace so the old man could keep up, and it annoyed Thorgrim extremely. He might even have said something if he had the breath to speak.

Skidi and those at the head of the line were still a couple of hundred paces from the edge of the woods when the first of the riders came pounding around the wagons in their rear. Thorgrim heard them, the sound of their horses, their shouts to one another, and he turned to see them coming on at a full gallop.

End of the race, Thorgrim thought. They would not reach the woods before the riders reached them. They had to turn and fight. He opened his mouth and managed to shout, "The riders are on us! Form a square! Shield wall! Form a square!"

He yelled as hard as he was able. It was a poor effort. He gasped as he yelled, but once again Harald was there to lend him his young, powerful lungs.

"The horsemen are on us!" Harald shouted, still running at Thorgrim's side. "Make a square! Shields up, make a square!"

They saw Skidi at the head of the column stop, turn, and start waving his arms as he drove the men back toward Thorgrim, back to where they could all gather and form a defense. Bersi was pushing men into a short shield wall, and then another at a right angle to that, as the entire line was turned into a square. Thorgrim hoped they would sort themselves out in time. He hoped that not too many had thrown their shields away.

He and Harald reached the cluster of men last of all. Thorgrim could hear the sounds of the hoof beats, loud and close behind him, could feel the tremor of the galloping horses in his legs. The men in the square stepped aside and made a gap in the shield wall. Harald and Thorgrim stepped in, turned, locked their shields with those on either side.

The Northmen had made a fort, a small, square fort, walls made of flesh and bone, shields on four side. If they could stand fast as the riders came down on them they might yet live. What they needed were spears to reach out and drive into the horses and riders as they tried to break the walls. But they had no spears, only swords. Swords were not at all ideal for that work, they were too short, but they would have to do.

"Stand ready!" Thorgrim shouted. The horsemen were a hundred paces behind and closing fast, but they were apparently confident of an easy victory and were not bothering to get in any sort of order. They were just rushing in, swords and spears held high, screaming their war cries. They thundered down on the Northmen, no doubt hoping the raiders would break and run and then they could be easily hacked down as they fled.

"Stand fast!" Thorgrim shouted. "You'll live if you stand fast! Brace yourselves, keep your shields together!"

And then the horsemen were on them, their huge beasts wheeling and turning at the last second, shying from hitting the seemingly immobile line of shields and men. The horses snapped and kicked and the riders flailed with swords, but the shield wall did not break and the horses did not drive the men into panicked flight.

It was the Northmen's chance to strike back now. Blades darted out from behind the shields, well-honed points found the riders' legs and guts and the horses' necks and rumps. Riders screamed and slashed at their attackers and horses reared up in pain and surprise. Thorgrim saw a man tumble to the ground. He rolled and tried to free his weapon and Olaf Thordarson stepped forward and drove a sword clean through his mail, then stepped back into the shield wall before any of the other horsemen could react.

"Hold your ground and kill the bastards!" Thorgrim shouted and he drove Iron-tooth at the rider who wheeled his horse in front of him. The rider parried the blade, brought his own sword back over his head, meaning to bring it down like an ax, but Thorgrim was too quick for him. He took a half step ahead of the shield wall, thrust forward and up.

The point hit the man just below his raised arm and sunk inches deep. Thorgrim pulled it back fast and regained his place in the line. The rider dropped his sword, clutched his wound, hunched over sideways as his horse turned and ran off, away from that wall of death.

The riders were yelling to one another and then one by one they jerked their reins over hard and galloped off. Not far off, only fifty paces or so, far enough to be free of the Northmen's swords as they reconsidered their tactics. And Thorgrim saw opportunity.

"Run for the woods!" he shouted, pointing with his sword. "Keep together, the horsemen will be back at us in a second, but run for the woods!"

The men understood. They turned all together as if they were doing some elaborate dance and began running toward the distant wood, racing off in the direction Skidi had been leading them before the riders came. They stayed close, they did not spread out, because every man knew as Thorgrim did that the riders would be on them again before they reached safety. And when the riders were back, only the shield wall would save them. But every foot closer to the woods was a foot closer to escape.

The mounted warriors, of course, knew this as well, and so Thorgrim did not take his eyes from them for long. No more than a minute after Thorgrim's men had begun their dash over the open ground he saw them divide into three groups and charge back toward them. The riders drew apart as they closed the distance, the center group of horsemen, twenty or so, driving straight for the Northmen as those to left and right began to spread out.

"Make your square! Make your square!" Thorgrim shouted. That was all the ground they would get for now. Time to fight off another assault.

The Norsemen had stayed close and it only took seconds to reform their square, shields held at chest height and locked together.

"They'll hit us on three sides!" Thorgrim shouted. "Don't let them break us! If we break we're all dead men!"

Of course, even if they did not break they were all dead men, most likely. Every man knew it. But they stood straight and they dug their back feet into the soft ground and they refreshed the grip on their swords and they waited.

They did not wait long. The horsemen to the left and right swung far out from the close packed Northmen, then swerved their mounts and charged for opposite sides of the square, giving themselves a hundred paces or more to build momentum as the pounded down on the shield-bearers. The center rank of horsemen did not swerve. They came straight on, swords raised, horses hooves tearing up the turf and sending clods of grass and dirt flying back in their track.

"Stand fast!" Thorgrim shouted, letting his voice build into a battle cry. And then the horsemen were on them.

In his years of seafaring, Thorgrim had often enough endured massive boarding seas, great combers of dark water rising up, curling overhead, and slamming down on him and his crew and his ship like the hand of an angry god. And that was what the impact of the mounted riders was like.

The Irishmen had spurred their animals to a frenzy and this time most did not shy and swerve from the wall, and because Thorgrim and his men had no spears they could not even reach the horses or riders until they were all but on top of them. The cumulative weight of fifty horses and fifty riders slammed into the square from three sides at nearly the same instant. Like a boarding sea. Like the hand of an angry god.

Thorgrim saw the animal in front of him rear and kick. He ducked to his left, felt the horse's right hoof hit his shield and drive him back. The horse lashed with its left foot and it hit the man beside him – it was Vemund – right in the forehead. The blow sent Vemund reeling back, shield and sword flying from his hand. Then the horse came down on all four feet and Thorgrim saw the rider spur it in the flanks and the animal charged on, right into the middle of the square.

Or what had been a square. It looked to Thorgrim like a ship that had gone up on the rocks in heavy surf, torn to smaller and smaller bits as it was hammered again and again.

The rider who had downed Vemund spun his horse and, seeing Thorgrim, bounded forward, sword up. Thorgrim moved by instinct and the memory drilled into his arms and legs. He let the rider's sword begin its descent, stepped aside as the blade passed within inches of his chest. He had time enough to see the surprise on the man's face as he lunged, Iron-tooth piercing his mail and driving into his stomach. Thorgrim pulled the blade free and looked for the next rider because that man was done.

There were still fragments of shield wall, groups of men standing together and warding off the swarming horsemen, but they could not last. The horses and the swords coming down from above would drive them apart and they would be killed piecemeal.

Agnarr was beside him now, to his left, and Godi to his right. He could see Harald ten feet away, swinging Oak Cleaver in wide arcs that cut down anything that came within reach of the blade.

"Thorgrim!" Agnarr shouted and Thorgrim looked over fast as one of the mounted warriors spurred toward him. The rider had a spear, held low, and he was driving for Thorgrim's chest. Agnarr leapt forward and grabbed the shaft of the spear and twisted it up. The Irishman grunted and his horse turned under him.

Agnarr pulled harder and Thorgrim tried to get at the mounted man, but the horse was there, blocking him, its teeth snapping. The Irishman pulled his foot from the stirrup and kicked Agnarr in the head and Agnarr grunted, let go of the spear, stumbled back.

The horse turned, further blocking Thorgrim's way. He saw the spear draw back and then dart forward. He saw it hit Agnarr's chest, and the mail shirt Agnarr wore did not slow it in the least. It buried itself in Agnarr's body, right up to the shaft. Agnarr's eyes went wide and blood poured from his mouth.

The spearman pulled the weapon free and spun his horse away from Thorgrim and charged off before Thorgrim could avenge Agnarr or even think of doing so. He looked from the mounted man to Agnarr, who had sunk to his knees. His eyes were looking right ahead, blood was running down his beard, but his sword was still tight in his grip. Then he pitched forward, face down on the Irish sod.

Thorgrim spun around, Iron-tooth in front, looking for a man he could kill. He saw one of the mounted men-at-arms going sword to ax with Vali and he raced over. The rider did not even see him coming as he drove his sword into the small of the man's back. The man arched, screamed, fell, as Thorgrim pulled the point free.

"Make for the woods!" Thorgrim shouted, putting all he had into his voice so that he might be heard above the melee. He had wanted to avoid a wild rush, one in which the riders could cut them down, but there was nothing else they could do now. Some at least would make it. But he would not. He would not even try.

Godi was with him again, and he saw Harald hurrying over. "The woods! Get to the woods!" Thorgrim shouted again, pointing with Iron-tooth, wondering if they did not understand. He saw Harald's eyes go wide, his mouth open. He caught the shadow of a movement behind him and he spun around. One of the mounted men was charging down on him and it seemed all he could see was the massive head of the horse, the yellow teeth, the foam spewing from his mouth.

With two steps Godi was between him and the horse, his huge ax swinging like he was felling a tree. His blade struck the rider in the chest and flung him backwards, the ax head buried in his breastbone. The horse reared as the rider fell back, the reins still tight in his hand. It seemed to happen slowly, like moving underwater. Thorgrim saw the wicked hoof coming up in front of him and he moved to the side, or thought of moving to the side, as the hoof struck him on the head.

And then everything was black.

And then it was not.

He opened his eyes and he was not certain where he was or how long he had been asleep. It seemed like a very long time, but he could still see men's legs and horses legs and he could hear the clash of weapons and the yelling of fighting men and screams of wounded men and wounded horses.

I'm on the ground, he thought. He was lying on his side, on the ground. But he could make sense of nothing else that was going on.

He felt hands on his arms and he was being lifted from the ground and he tried to guess whether or not his legs would hold him. He waited to be set on his feet, but instead he felt himself lifted and draped over a shoulder and he thought he could see Godi's legging and he thought he could see Harald nearby, and then once more everything went black.

Chapter Forty-Two

[S]ix will not manage to swap
bloody blows of the battle-god's
shield piercer with me.
Egil's Saga

W hen Thorgrim opened his eyes again he saw only brush and ferns and the trunks of trees around him. He did not move - he was not sure he could move - save for his eyes. He listened. He could hear the sound of running water like a river. He could hear soft rustling noises, like men were nearby and making just the smallest of movements. He could hear a breeze blowing the tops of the trees. Nothing more.

Then he heard a louder rustling and Harald's voice saying, "Father?"

At that he turned his head and suddenly Harald's face was there, blood-smeared and anxious. "Father?" he said again. "Can you speak?"

Thorgrim thought about that and realized he could speak and he could do a damned sight more than that. "Yes, yes, I'm fine. Help me to sit up," he snarled.

"Are you sure..." Harald began but Thorgrim gave him a look that suggested further argument would be unwise, so he put his hands under Thorgrim's shoulders and lifted as Thorgrim pushed himself up.

Godi was there, on the other side. "Get me to my feet," Thorgrim said but Godi shook his head.

"We'll lean you against this tree a bit, let the blood flow some," the big man said and Thorgrim gave him the same look he had given Harald, but found it did not have the same effect on Godi. Godi and Harald pulled him back a few feet and eased him against the trunk of

309

some massive tree. Thorgrim felt his head swirling and he closed his eyes and waited until it settled out.

He opened his eyes again. Harald had gone back to doing what he had apparently been doing a moment before, which was wrapping a torn cloth around an ugly cut on his forearm. Half of Godi's face was a wash of blood, but Thorgrim guessed it was from a scalp wound which looked far more dramatic than it was. Olaf Thordarson was there, as was Ulf and a few others. Ten, by Thorgrim's count. They all had wounds of some description.

"Where are the others?" Thorgrim asked. He saw Harald and Godi exchange glances and he knew the answer.

"They didn't make it," Harald said.

Thorgrim nodded. He remembered Agnarr, with the spear in his chest, Vemund felled by a horse's hoof. All the others he had seen fall. He himself should have been left to die, but he would not chastise his son or Godi for that mistake.

"The Irish?" Thorgrim asked.

"They bought our men's lives dearly," Harald assured him.

"We made a slaughter of them," Godi said. "Killed near half, I would think. But they were still too much for us. You called for everyone to run for the woods and we fought our way here. Hard fighting. This is all that made it." He indicated the handful of men sitting or leaning on trees around that dim-lit patch of wood.

"They didn't even try to hunt us down," Harald said. "We reached the woods, ran in deep as we could. We could see them riding along the tree line but they never even tried to flush us out." He was looking for some bright spot in that disastrous morning, Thorgrim could see that. It was what men did.

For some time they remained where they were, silent, vigilant. Those who had been dressing wounds finished their work and sat with blood-soaked hands and clothing and faces and stared off into the dark places in the woods.

Finally Thorgrim was certain he had strength enough to stand. He leaned forward and pushed himself off. He heard the start of a protest in Harald's throat but it died there. He stood and felt the blood rush to his head and his legs and for a moment it was all he could do to keep himself from toppling over, but he resisted the urge to steady himself on the tree.

Having set that example he said, "Are you men able to move on? Any too wounded to walk? We must see what's become of our ships."

One by one the men stood, a few resting hands on their fellow's shoulders as they regained their balance. Thorgrim gave them a minute to find the strength in their legs. He looked from man to man. None of them looked good, but they did look as if they could make it the mile or so back to where *Sea Hammer* lay tied to the bank. Or had the morning before, at any rate.

Thorgrim pushed his way through the woods. He planned at first to keep to the trees as they made their way down the river, but ten feet of fighting through the brush convinced him that it was pointless to try. He worked his way back toward the edge of the woods. When he was able to see the open ground, he paused and held up his hand for the others to do the same.

He scanned all the country he was able to see and he saw nothing moving save for a few hawks circling high above. He stepped out and advanced cautiously through the tall grass. Nothing. He turned to the others.

"Come on," he said. It seemed the Irish had greater concerns than hunting down a pitiful band of survivors.

They walked along the edge of the trees, sticking to the open ground when they could, but kept close to cover in case they heard the sound of horses in the distance. They did once, the sound dull but distinct even with the soft wind blowing. They ducked back into the trees and watched as a patrol of a dozen mounted men passed down the road. They moved slowly and Thorgrim could see them scanning the surrounding country as they rode by.

"Guess they're not done with us after all," Godi said in a soft voice. Once the sound of the horses was lost in the distance they started out again, their ears more alert than ever for any indication that the riders were returning, but they did not hear or see them again.

They came at last to the place where they had left the river the day before. The grass was still flattened where two hundred and fifty warriors, strong and eager, had passed on their confident way to Glendalough. Now the ten who returned walked back over that same beaten grass and up the slope to the river bank.

The river itself remained hidden, but Thorgrim could see a single mast rising in the distance, which meant one ship at least was still there. He was one hundred paces away when he knew for certain it was *Sea Hammer* with her distinctive weather vane at the masthead. He felt a trace of hope, the first he had allowed himself in more time than he could recall.

He climbed up on the bank. From there he had a view of the river and the shoreline, two hundred feet in either direction, and his hope died a quick and silent death. *Sea Hammer* was there, her bow resting in the mud, but she was filled with water from her afterdeck all the way to the mast step. She must have been stove in someplace aft, filled and settled to the bottom. If her bow had not been run ashore she would have been entirely submerged.

There were dead men everywhere. Thorgrim could see bodies floating in the shallow water of the river's edge. He could see men flung aside on the gravely beach where they had made their last camp on the voyage up river. He could see men in the grassy bank where they had crawled in the final agonizing moments before their deaths.

These were the guards who Thorgrim had left behind, men who probably did not think they would have to defend the ships against fellow Northmen. It was likely that they had not even drawn their weapons when Ottar and Kjartan and their men arrived and began butchering them.

Ottar's ships were gone, and so were *Fox* and *Blood Hawk* and of course Kjartan's *Dragon*. Thorgrim pressed his lips together and let the anger and the fury and the raw hate, hate such as he had never felt before, fill him until it overflowed. He realized that his hands were trembling. He gripped the hilt of Iron-tooth and made his way down the steep bank.

At the edge of the river he ran his eyes over *Sea Hammer*. She seemed to be in tolerable shape, aside from the fact that she was filled with water. If the hole that had sunk her was not too large there was a chance they could get her floating again, if the Irish gave them time enough. But he did not think they would.

He spared only a second for his ship, because, love her as he might, there were men who had died protecting her and they needed to be looked to. It was even possible that some were yet alive. He had half expected to see Starri's corpse splayed out on *Sea Hammer*'s deck or floating in the water that filled her hull, but he was nowhere that Thorgrim could see.

He turned and walked slowly down the river bank, the rest of his men following behind. The dead were strewn around. Some were Ottar's men but mostly they were his own guard. He saw the faces of men he knew well, men with whom he had fought side by side and suffered through the long winter at Vík-ló. Men with whom he had felled trees and built ships and gone to sea. Now their skin was bluish gray and the eyes that were still open stared unseeing at the horror around them, and their mouths gaped in frozen screams.

You are in the corpse hall now, brothers, Thorgrim thought, and he was sure that was true, though he could see more than a few had died with their swords still in their scabbards, cut down by men they thought were their friends.

Then he heard a sound, a groan, off in the grass to his left, and he felt a flush of dread, like he was hearing a call from the grave. But then he realized it was a wounded man making a feeble cry. He hurried over, his men still following behind.

The gravel beach melded into the grassy bank and Thorgrim walked in the direction of the sound. There was someone lying in the grass, a man, flat out, face hidden from view. Thorgrim stepped closer, looked down at the figure.

Kjartan.

"You bastard," Thorgrim said, his voice flat and even. Kjartan's hand was on his stomach and Thorgrim could see the gleam of intestine under his palm. His mail and leggings were torn and soaked with blood. It was a wound that would be fatal, but not quick. Thorgrim had seen this sort of thing before. It might take Kjartan many agonizing days to die.

But Thorgrim would not give him that chance. He wanted to see Kjartan die and he did not have time to wait. And more important still, he would not let Kjartan die of a wound had in honorable battle. Much as he would love to see Kjartan suffer through his final days in Midgard, he would be happier to think of him suffering until the end times in Hel's icy realm.

He pulled Iron-tooth from its sheath. Kjartan's sword lay five feet away, half hidden in the grass. Kjartan would die now and he would die with no weapon in his hand, a coward's death, and the Valkyrie would spit on his corpse.

Then Kjartan opened his eyes and he looked into Thorgrim's. He opened his mouth, closed it, opened it again. "I tried, Night Wolf," he said, and his voice was stronger than Thorgrim expected. "I tried."

"Yes, you tried," Thorgrim said. "And now you die."

Then Thorgrim heard another voice, and it called, "Night Wolf…" A strangled voice, and again Thorgrim felt a flush of dread at this sound from the grave. He turned and saw Starri Deathless pulling himself to his feet. His tunic was torn and bloody, and his face and hair and scraggly beard were matted with blood. He looked as if he might fall over, but he didn't, and Harald and Olaf rushed over to hold him up. They grabbed his arms and took his weight and for a second Starri just closed his eyes and let his head loll.

Then he opened his eyes again and looked up. "Yes, Night Wolf, I still live," Starri said in a voice much weaker than Kjartan's. But Thorgrim was relieved to hear it, and to hear Starri's assurance that he was still alive, because from the look of the man Thorgrim was not entirely sure to which world he now belonged.

Starri took a step closer and Harald and Olaf moved with him. "Kjartan and his men, they did not abandon you. They did not come to steal the ships. They came to stop Ottar," Starri said.

Thorgrim frowned. He looked down at Kjartan, who was trying to sit up. Kjartan clenched his teeth and a shudder went through him. Then Godi stepped around Thorgrim and helped him, putting a massive hand on Kjartan's back for support.

"Last night," Kjartan said, "I guessed what Ottar would do. Not before that. Forgive me, Night Wolf, I told him. Back at the mouth of the river, when I thought I might join with him, I told him about Vík-ló and the wealth you had left there. The longphort, how it was all but deserted, only women and old men…"

And Thorgrim understood what the man was saying. *Vík-ló.* Ottar had abandoned them to their deaths so he could take the ships and sail to Vík-ló, now undefended, claim it all for himself. Thorgrim did not know what to think; he could not even tell what he was feeling. Rage, fear, a need for vengeance. It flailed him like a lash, over and over. He thought he might vomit.

"I took my men and tried to stop him," Kjartan said. "I was too great a coward to tell you what I'd done. I thought if I could stop him it would set things to right."

Thorgrim looked over at Starri. "He tells the truth, Thorgrim," Starri said. "He and his men, they fought Ottar. I fought with them. Ottar slaughtered them all." Starri gave a weak smile. "But he did not kill me, because I am Starri Deathless."

Thorgrim nodded. *Maybe Starri really cannot be killed*, he thought.

Then Starri spoke again. "Kjartan cut a hole in *Sea Hammer's* bottom," he said. "Sunk her where she sits. That's the only reason Ottar did not take her when he took the others. That's the reason Ottar did not give Kjartan a quick death."

Thorgrim looked down at Kjartan. He did not know what to do.

"Godi, help me stand," Kjartan said. Godi reached his hands under Kjartan's shoulders and lifted him as if he was a child and stood him on his feet. Kjartan sucked in his breath and pressed his hand tight against his side and closed his eyes. When the surge of pain had passed he opened his eyes again and pointed to his sword.

"Godi, my sword. Please." Godi leaned down and picked up the weapon and Kjartan took it by the grip. He turned to Thorgrim.

"Night Wolf, for what I have done I owe you my life. You owe me nothing. But still I'll ask this of you. We fought once, and we did not finish that fight. Let us finish it now."

Thorgrim looked into the man's eyes. Kjartan was all but pleading with him. He did not want to spend his last days dying in agony, and he did not want to die with such dishonor to his name. Thorgrim slipped Iron-tooth from his scabbard.

Kjartan gave a weak smile and lifted his sword to waist height, which was as far as he could lift it. Thorgrim extended Iron-tooth in a pantomime of a lunge and Kjartan parried it with a feeble gesture. Thorgrim drew Iron-tooth back, bringing the blade up over his left shoulder for a powerful back-hand stroke. Kjartan was still smiling, just a bit, and he did not flinch at all as Thorgrim swung the blade and took his head clean off at the shoulders.

Epilogue

There is much sorrow everywhere;
there is a great misfortune among the Irish.
Red wine has been spilled down the valley.

Annals of Ulster

When the Irish men-at-arms returned from riding down the Northmen, from the indescribably butchery of smashing the square and cutting down the fleeing men, Lochlánn did something he had not done in some time. He prayed.

Certainly he had prayed many times during the years he had been at the monastery. Many times a day, in fact. But it was not something he did by choice, and he was grudging and sullen about it. But now it was different. This was real prayer because he meant it. He was genuinely looking for divine guidance.

The past days had been more dreamlike than any in Lochlánn's life. More nightmare-like. A great shapeless mass of fear and horror, anger, excitement, a drive to kill, terror at the thought of being killed. He could hardly recall now what had happened. They had struck the Northmen, been driven back, drove the Northmen back. He could not put the events into any sort of order in his mind.

At one point a wagon, one of the wagons he and Louis and the men had passed on the road from the Meeting of the Waters, had come crashing into their lines. That had changed the momentum of the battle in an instant, and taken victory from their hands. That much he remembered.

He wondered if he would be better at recalling what happened on the battlefield once he had gained more experience with such things.

I must ask Louis about that, he thought. And then he remembered. And it was like a knife in the gut.

He had been up more than half the night after that first day's fighting, tortured by his fears of the coming battle. He had been afraid before — Louis had assured him that only lunatics did not fear combat — but this was different. Because this time he would not have Louis de Roumois beside him. This time he would be going into battle with his world turned upside down, with his friend, the man he admired most in the world, nowhere to be found. And not just gone, but having run off after being revealed as a murderer, a fornicator, a thief.

He still did not see how that was possible. But he was starting to wonder what other explanation there could be, and as his uncertainty grew, his former love for Louis de Roumois began turning to anger and rage, smoldering and threatening to ignite.

They fought the heathens without the leadership of the young Frank, and despite Colman's blunder in sending the spearmen out ahead of the shield wall, they had beaten them. Most of the raiders had been killed, a handful escaped. None of the patrols had seen any sign of them. The fighting was over and Lochlánn prayed.

He felt better when he was done, like finishing a bath or stepping into the sunshine after a swim in a cold, fresh stream. But he still had no answers to the many, many questions that the past few days had raised.

No one else, however, seemed very curious about those things. He heard the occasional vague question as to where Colman might be, or hushed, bitter discussions of Louis or Failend, but that was pretty much it. With the fighting done, the men-at-arms seemed content to remain where they were, while the bóaire and the fuidir were quickly melting away, returning to their farms.

Lochlánn stood on the hill where the army was camped and looked down toward Glendalough a mile away at the bottom of the slope. He could see from there that the streets, which had been packed tight with people just two days before, were now deserted. He could see the monastery and the buildings around it. He looked for Colman's big house and could just see its high-peaked roof rising up above its neighbors.

He stared at the roofline. *I wonder...* he thought. Colman was gone, and knowing something of Louis's history with Colman, and guessing even more, Lochlánn had to think there was some connection between his disappearance and Louis's. And the next thing he knew he was walking down the long hill toward the cluster of sorry buildings that made up Glendalough.

It took him half an hour to reach the muddy streets. Evidence of the people's quick exodus was everywhere; household goods of all description lay trampled in the dirt where they had fallen from whatever they had been piled onto, the merchants' stalls were stripped bare and half falling down, doors to homes and shops, hastily abandoned, were left hanging open and thumping in the breeze.

Lochlánn walked slowly through the familiar streets as if he was walking through a graveyard or across the field of a recent battle. It was the most haunting thing he had ever experienced.

Then from the monastery a bell began to peal, calling the monks to sext, the midday prayer. The sound made Lochlánn jump and suck in his breath, but he recovered fast. There was something solid and comforting in the sound. The people of Glendalough might have run in terror, but the people of God behind the velum had remained, and life went on as it always had.

Lochlánn made the sign of the cross and continued on. He came at last to the big home of Colman mac Breandan. He paused at the gate and looked across the yard at the house. Nothing seemed out of place, and there was no sign that anyone was there. He opened the gate and approached the door. He moved cautiously, though he was not sure why.

He stopped in front of the door, grabbed the latch and tried it. It lifted with little resistance so he swung the door open. "Lord Colman?" he called, loud but not overly loud. "Failend?"

He swung the door wider and stepped inside. It was dimly lit from two windows high above, and Lochlánn could just make out the shapes of a table and chair, the loft above, a cooking pot over the hearth, and Colman's body lying sprawled out on the floor.

Lochlánn rushed across the room to Colman's side. His first thought was to help the man, but before he even reached Colman's side he could see there was a great pool of blood dried on the rushes and soaked into the dirt floor, and Colman's face was black with death. The man was gone and had been for some time. A day at least. There was nothing that Lochlánn could do to help him physically, and as he was not yet a priest, there was nothing he could do in that capacity, either.

He took the last few steps slowly, scrutinizing the corpse at his feet and the things surrounding it. Colman's throat had been slashed.

His sword was out of its scabbard and lying a few feet away, so he had not been surprised by his killer, or at least had had time enough to draw his weapon. There was a small hole in the floor by Colman's feet. Lochlánn looked down at it and could see the impression of something square that had been buried there.

A small chest? Lochlánn wondered. *Colman's hoard? Was this just a robbery?* He heard a noise behind him, and he turned fast and his hand fell on the hilt of his sword. There was a man standing in the door, but in the dim light Lochlánn could not make out who it was. And then the man spoke.

"Brother Lochlánn?"

Lochlánn felt himself relax. His hand came away from the sword. "Father Finnian?"

Finnian took a step into the room. There was another man with him, a young man, just a few years Lochlánn's senior it looked like, and dressed in the same black robe as the priest. Finnian's eyes moved down to Colman's body, lying at Lochlánn's feet.

"I found him this way!" Lochlánn protested, suddenly realizing how this must look. "He was dead, has been dead, some time."

Finnian held up his hand. "I know, my son, I know. I can see he's been dead a while. And I know you've been with the men-at-arms all this time. But tell me why you're here?"

Lochlánn's eyes darted over to the other man and back to Finnian, and Finnian caught the gesture. "This is Brother Segan," Finnian said. "He is a dear friend of mine, a very brave young man. Very bright. He can speak the heathens' tongue, and many others. He's lived with the heathens at Vík-ló this past year and he has kept me informed as to their plans. It's fair to say that they would be sacking Glendalough now if not for him."

Lochlánn nodded to the young man and Segan nodded back. "I don't know why I'm here, Father," Lochlánn said. "I guess I was looking for Colman. Or Louis. Or the truth of what happened. I want to know if Louis really…. I don't know."

"The truth," Finnian said. "That's a thing we would all like to know, very much."

"Do you know?" Lochlánn asked. "Do you know what happened? With Louis and Failend and Aileran? I am hard-pressed to believe Louis murdered Aileran in cold blood. But still…"

"As am I," Finnian interrupted. "But I don't know the truth of what happened any more than you." As with most things that Finnian said, it sounded as if there was a great deal more, just below the surface, which the priest might or might not reveal. Most likely not. "That's why I came looking for you," he added.

"Are the heathens gone?" Lochlánn asked next. "Have they sailed away, those that still lived?"

"I only know what I've heard," Finnian said. "From the travelers and others I speak with. What I hear is that most are gone, but one ship remains, and a handful of the heathens. And they should be stamped out."

"Are men being sent to do that? Mounted men would be best. They could move fast, catch the heathens ashore."

Finnian nodded. "That would be best, but the thing of it is, with Louis gone and Colman and Aileran gone, there's no one who will give the order."

"No one," Lochlánn agreed. "They sit around the camp like it's Christmas day."

"So you should go," Finnian said. "Are there a score of men who would ride with you, if you ask? You would need no more than that."

Lochlánn considered the question. "Yes, there are," he said.

"Then go," Finnian said.

Lochlánn shook his head. "I am no one," he said. "I am the least experienced man there."

"But it must be you. This is why. If Louis and Failend are hoping to escape, they will most likely follow the river to the sea and try to find a ship to Frankia. Anyone who goes after the heathens is likely to come across them as well. If any of the other men-at-arms catch them, they will hang them on the spot."

"And maybe that's what they deserve," Lochlánn said.

"Perhaps," Finnian said. "Perhaps not. That's what we must find out. So if you catch them, you will bring them back here. And we can find the truth of this thing."

"I'll try to bring them back. If I find them," Lochlánn said, but he doubted very much that he would. And in truth he was not certain how he would react if he did. But he told Finnian he would do his best, and he bid him farewell and headed back up the hill to the camp. He was halfway there before it occurred to him to wonder how Finnian knew to look for him at Colman's house.

Thorgrim Night Wolf wanted to bury his dead. He wanted to lay them out in proper graves with their weapons at their sides, the way a warrior should go to his reward. But he felt a greater obligation to the living than the dead, and he did not think he had much time, so he trusted that the Valkyrie were doing his men the honor that he could not, and turned his attention to the ship.

He climbed over the bow and walked aft, wading into the cold river water that filled the after end of the hull. The water was clear and no more than a few feet deep, so he could see the submerged vessel well enough.

It was back aft, just forward of the afterdeck, that he saw the hole Kjartan had chopped through the hull. It was not terribly big, maybe a foot in diameter, though he had cut through three strakes, which would make repairs more difficult. But for now they should be able to apply some sort of patch, bail the ship out and be off down the river.

"Night Wolf!" Starri said, and he spoke in a hushed voice that told Thorgrim with absolute certainty that something was not right.

"What?"

"Someone's coming. From that direction." Starri was standing on the shore, leaning on the side of the ship ten feet away, and pointing up river. Thorgrim turned and looked, but he could see only the water and the trees for about a hundred paces before the river bent around to the north and hid the rest from view.

He looked at Starri. Apparently the battering he had taken and the many wounds he had suffered and the blood he had spilled had not damaged his extraordinary hearing.

"How many?" Thorgrim asked.

"I'm not sure. Not many. They're on foot."

Thorgrim turned to Harald who was also on the shore. "Get the men hidden, get ready. Don't show yourselves until I do. These may be men-at-arms searching us out."

Harald nodded and hurried off, calling to the men in a low voice to hide themselves. Their best hope, Thorgrim knew, was that these newcomers were indifferent to the Northmen's presence. Otherwise they would be enemies. They would not be friends. He and his men had no friends there.

Thorgrim hopped over the side of the ship and hid himself behind her, the river water up to his knees, and Starri stood beside him. They waited, and the afternoon was utterly silent, save for the water and the breeze and the occasional bird. And then he heard the sound of feet making small splashing sounds as they walked through the water. They came closer, then stopped.

It was silent again and then Thorgrim heard a man speaking. He spoke Irish and Thorgrim did not understand the words. Then another spoke, and Thorgrim was certain that one was a woman.

Thorgrim moved slowly out into the river, down *Sea Hammer*'s length and stopped just short of her stern. He heard the strangers take a few steps closer and then he moved around the end of his ship and pulled Iron-tooth from its scabbard as he did.

Two people. A man and a woman, both dressed in mail, which caught Thorgrim by surprise. The man's left hand held the end of a sack which was draped over his shoulder. The woman gasped at Thorgrim's sudden appearance, but the man drew his sword with a speed and ease that spoke of training and experience. He did not let go of the sack.

"Who are you?" Thorgrim asked, but the man just shook his head to indicate that he did not understand. Thorgrim had not expected he would.

"Harald!" Thorgrim called. "Come here. Bring the others." He heard Harald come out of hiding and the sound of other men coming out of the grass and the splash of their feet hitting the water. The woman also wore a sword and she pulled it now, a bit late, Thorgrim thought. The man took a step back, half shielding the woman as Thorgrim's men approached from three sides. His eyes moved from man to man and he looked ready for a fight, but he did not look afraid, and Thorgrim gave him credit for that.

Harald came splashing out to where they stood, and Thorgrim was about to tell him to ask these two who they were when he saw Harald smile wide.

"Look!" Harald said. "It's the healer woman!" He turned to the two in the river and spoke to them in Irish. Thorgrim saw a moment of uncertainty on their faces, and then the dawn of recognition.

"Who are they?" Thorgrim asked. "How do you know them?"

"They were my prisoners. In the wagons, the wagons I took from Crimthann," Harald said. "I don't recall the man's name. The woman is Failend, and she said the man is her bodyguard. She said she's a very skilled healer. We could have use of her. Starri could. And many of the men are wounded."

"Very well," Thorgrim said. "Tell them to give up their swords and they will not be harmed."

Harald spoke to them. They spoke back and Harald replied, a negotiation of some sort, but Thorgrim trusted Harald to do the right thing. He saw the Irishman's eyes moving from weapon to weapon, man to man. He could guess the man's thoughts as if he were speaking them out loud. *Can I kill them before they kill me? Will they kill the woman, or take her? Are our chances better if I give up my sword, or would we be better off if we died fighting?*

Then the man made a choice. It was the choice Thorgrim hoped he would make. The only reasonable choice. He reversed his sword and handed it hilt first to Harald. Then the woman did the same.

"Tell them to come to the shore," Thorgrim said. "Tell them they will not be harmed if the woman looks to our wounded." He considered ordering the man to hand over the sack, but he decided against it. Plenty of time for that later.

Harald opened his mouth to speak, but Starri spoke first. "Thorgrim," he said. "More coming. Riders. They're getting closer."

Riders… That certainly could mean but one thing. Mounted warriors scouring the countryside, and if they were alert enough to find the trampled grass leading from the road to the river bank then they would find the ship and they would find the Northmen whom they sought.

"Let's go," Thorgrim said. "Down the river. Stay close to the bank. Take those two." He gestured toward their new prisoners. "Don't let them get away."

The men turned and began splashing downstream. Godi stepped behind the man and the woman and gave them a little push, and Harald said something, his tone soft yet urgent, and they began moving too, with less reluctance than Thorgrim might have expected.

They must know that riders mean Irish men-at-arms, Thorgrim thought, *and that could well mean rescue for them. And yet they hurry as fast as we do.*

They stayed close to the bank where the water was shallow, and soon even Thorgrim could hear the sound of the horses. It grew louder with each second and then it stopped, which meant the riders had reached the river bank. Soon they would be swarming over *Sea Hammer.*

"Into the trees, everyone into the trees!" Thorgrim hissed. They had almost reached the bend in the river which would have hidden them from the Irish men-at-arms, but not quite. They splashed ashore and pushed their way through the bracken and in among the trees, the forest cool and damp and dark, and they were hidden from view. It was no great difficulty to hide them all. They were only ten men and two prisoners. Ten men, all that was left of the crews of four longships.

Thorgrim was bringing up the end of the column and he came last into the woods, but rather then push on he stopped and turned, crouching to make himself invisible, and looked back upstream, back toward his ship and his dead.

The Irish were coming over the bank and spreading out along the shore. They wore mail and had weapons drawn. There were only twenty or so, but they would have been enough to kill all of Thorgrim's men, exhausted and wounded as they were.

For a few minutes the Irish moved cautiously along the river bank, ready for a surprise attack if it came, but soon they realized there would be no attack, that this was a camp of the dead, and there was no Northman there who could hold a sword any longer. Thorgrim saw weapons go back into scabbards. He saw the Irishmen cutting purses off Norse belts.

Then he saw a few men climb aboard *Sea Hammer* and that, to him, was the most intolerable of all, as if they had profaned a temple, as if they had put one of their crosses on an alter to Thor. They were on his ship, his sacred ship. They were violating his beloved vessel.

It's gone, he thought. *It's all gone now.* Not so long ago he had been Lord of Vík-ló. He had wealth and commanded four long ships and three hundred men. And now he had nothing. Nothing.

He had been betrayed. He had been led to this place and, because he was a fool and blind and wretchedly stupid, he had allowed it to happen. He had let nearly three hundred fine men die. He had been stripped of everything. He was no better than a slave.

Thorgrim clenched his teeth and pressed his lips together. He knew he might scream, or he might sob, or he might fling himself at the bastards who were defiling his ship, and he did not want to do any of it. He wanted Thor to strike him dead as he crouched like a thief in the woods.

The Irishmen who had been aboard the ship climbed back down to the riverbank. The one who was in command gave an order. Thorgrim could hear it clearly, even with the distance that separated them. Harald and Starri were crouching next to him now, and Thorgrim was about to ask Harald what the man had said when he saw one of the Irishmen crouch down and lay something on the gravel, then fish some small, dark thing from a pocket. He began moving his arm in short, quick jerks, the unmistakable motion of striking steel on flint.

Bastards, Thorgrim thought. *They're burning my ship! They are burning my ship and I can do nothing but watch. And when they're done they'll hunt us down and kill us all.*

The man with the fire-steel made a few more strokes, then leaned over and blew softly on the tinder. Thorgrim could see a little trail of smoke rising from the beach.

No, he thought. *I am not ready to die. I cannot die like this.* He had lived through many years and many things, good and bad, joy and sorrow, but he could not let it end there. He could not die until he had brought vengeance down on the heads of those who had done this to him. He could not leave Midgard until he had taken back what was his and made those who would steal it pay for their crimes. He would not leave that world until he had shown the gods he was worthy of the next.

He heard shuffling on his other side and turned his head to see the two they had captured, the man and the woman, inching up to where they could see. He heard the man whisper something, a single word, and to Thorgrim it sounded like a name, one of those odd Irish names. He turned to Harald.

"Ask this one if he knows the man who commands those soldiers," Thorgrim said. Harald leaned over and asked in a harsh whisper. The man hesitated before replying, and Thorgrim knew the truth even before he spoke.

"Yes," Harald said. "He knows him. He did not say how, or how well."

Thorgrim nodded. It didn't matter. He reached out and grabbed the sack the man still carried over his shoulder, Thorgrim moving so fast that he had the sack in his hand before the man could react. It was heavy, heavier even than Thorgrim had thought it would be. He could see the sharp edges of something square, like a box, and he had no doubt as to what it contained.

"Tell him," Thorgrim said to Harald, nodding his head toward the prisoner, "to go tell those soldiers there are sixty warriors coming up the river bank. He's to tell them to run before they're taken. If he does that and returns, he gets his hoard back and the woman is unharmed. If he fails, or betrays us, the woman will die before we do."

Harald nodded and rendered the words into the Irish tongue. Thorgrim could see the anger on the man's face, and the uncertainty. It might not be so easy to convince the soldiers to flee from an unseen enemy.

He looks clever enough, Thorgrim though. *He'll manage.*

And then the young man stood, grim-faced, and pushed his way through the trees to the river, because he had no choice. Thorgrim watched him splashing upstream. He saw the reaction of the soldiers as they saw him coming. They turned and stared as he approached. They drew their weapons.

The young man stopped fifteen feet short of the leader, his hands held up and spread apart in a gesture of supplication. Words flew between them. Thorgrim looked at Harald for translation but Harald only shook his head.

Thorgrim looked back up river. The soldiers seemed to be spreading out, trying to encircle the young man, and the young man in turn was gesturing toward the bend downstream.

"Harald, Godi, anyone who can walk, with me," Thorgrim said. "Draw your weapons."

He stood and pulled Iron-tooth free and stepped from the woods into the river. He heard the others following behind him. They might not be sixty, but they were Northmen and they were warriors and they were armed, and they would show the Irish soldiers the truth of the man's words.

And that they did. As Thorgrim led the way up river, stepping with determination as if he was looking for a battle, he saw Irishmen pointing in their direction, saw them backing away from *Sea Hammer*, stepping back from the river's edge. He heard a sharp order and the Irish soldiers turned and made their way toward the river bank and their mounts, picketed out of sight. They were not retreating in panic. But they were retreating.

Thorgrim continued his advance, but slowly, giving the Irish time to ride away. When at last he heard the sounds of hooves pounding off, he called to the others and they came limping out of the woods, the girl in their company. They made their way back to *Sea Hammer*. The tinder that the man had laid on the gravel was still smoldering.

Thorgrim stopped a few feet from the young Irishman. "Harald, tell this one he did well."

Harald translated. The man nodded. He did not smile. There was a troubled look on his face, something different from the one he had worn earlier. Thorgrim wondered if there had been more to his encounter with the soldiers than was immediately apparent.

Thorgrim swung the heavy sack off his shoulder and handed it to the man, who took it with a look of surprise. He spoke and Harald translated.

"He says the Irish are gone, but they will be back, and they will come with many more men."

Thorgrim nodded. He wondered why this fellow was telling him this. Did he not want to see the Northmen defeated? Did he not want to be rescued?

"He's right," Thorgrim said, addressing his crew, his army, his ten exhausted and wounded men. "We have an hour, perhaps. No more. Probably less. We need to stop up that hole that Kjartan cut in *Sea Hammer*. We can stuff some of these dead men's tunics in it, that will do for now. Bail her out and get her down river, far enough to be safe while we make her seaworthy."

The others nodded.

"Then what will we do?" Harald asked.

"Then we're going to hunt down the bastards who put us in this place and we'll make them pay," Thorgrim said. "We will make them pay."

He turned and led the way across the beach and over the sheer strake of his ship, his beloved ship, staggered and wounded like the rest of them. He stepped aft, into the shallow water that lapped over the deck, and his men followed behind. There was much they needed to do.

Would you like a heads-up about new titles in The Norsemen Saga, as well as preview sample chapters and other good stuff cheap (actually free)?

Visit our web site to sign up for e-mail alerts:

www.jameslnelson.com

Other books in *The Norsemen Saga*:

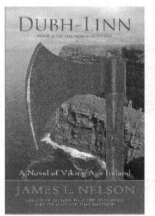

Fin Gall: Book I   *Dubh-linn: Book II*   *Lord of Vík-ló: Book III*

Glossary

adze – a tool much like an ax but with the blade set at a right angle to the handle.

Ægir – Norse god of the sea. In Norse mythology he was also the host of great feasts for the gods.

Asgard - the dwelling place of the Norse gods and goddesses, essentially the Norse heaven.

athwartships – at a right angle to the centerline of a vessel.

beitass - a wooden pole, or spar, secured to the side of a ship on the after end and leading forward to which the corner, or clew, of a sail could be secured.

berserker - a Viking warrior able to work himself up into a frenzy of blood-lust before a battle. The berserkers, near psychopathic killers in battle, were the fiercest of the Viking soldiers. The word berserker comes from the Norse for "bear shirt" and is the origin of the modern English "berserk".

boss - the round, iron centerpiece of a wooden shield. The boss formed an iron cup protruding from the front of the shield, providing a hollow in the back across which ran the hand grip.

bothach – Gaelic term for poor tenant farmers, serfs

brace - line used for hauling a **yard** side to side on a horizontal plane. Used to adjust the angle of the sail to the wind.

brat – a rectangular cloth worn in various configurations as an outer garment over a *leine*.

bride-price - money paid by the family of the groom to the family of the bride.

byrdingr - A smaller ocean-going cargo vessel used by the Norsemen for trade and transportation. Generally about 40 feet in length, the byrdingr was a smaller version of the more well-known *knarr*.

clench nail – a type of nail that, after being driven through a board, has a type of washer called a rove placed over the end and is then bent over to secure it in place.

curach - a boat, unique to Ireland, made of a wood frame covered in hide. They ranged in size, the largest propelled by sail and capable of carrying several tons. The most common sea-going craft of mediaeval Ireland. **Curach** was the Gaelic word for boat which later became the word curragh.

derbfine – In Irish law, a family of four generations, including a man, his sons, grandsons and great grandsons.

dragon ship - the largest of the Viking warships, upwards of 160 feet long and able to carry as many as 300 men. Dragon ships were the flagships of the fleet, the ships of kings.

dubh gall - Gaelic term for Vikings of Danish descent. It means Black Strangers, a reference to the mail armor they wore, made dark by the oil used to preserve it. *See fin gall.*

ell – a unit of length, a little more than a yard.

eyrir – Scandinavian unit of measurement, approximately an ounce.

félag – a fellowship of men who owed each other a mutual obligation, such as multiple owners of a ship, or a band or warriors who had sworn allegiance to one another.

fin gall - Gaelic term for Vikings of Norwegian descent. It means White Strangers. *See dubh gall.*

Freya - Norse goddess of beauty and love, she was also associated with warriors, as many of the Norse deity were. Freya often led the **Valkyrie** to the battlefield.

halyard - a line by which a sail or a yard is raised.

gallows – tall, T-shaped posts on the ship's centerline, forward of the mast, on which the oars and yard were stored when not in use.

gunnel – the upper edge of a ship's side.

Hel - in Norse mythology, the daughter of Loki and the ruler of the underworld where those who are not raised up to Valhalla are sent to suffer. The same name, Hel, is given to the realm over which she rules, the Norse hell.

hird - an elite corps of Viking warriors hired and maintained by a king or powerful **jarl**. Unlike most Viking warrior groups, which would assemble and disperse at will, the hird was retained as a semi-permanent force which formed the core of a Viking army.

hirdsman - a warrior who is a member of the **hird**.

jarl - title given to a man of high rank. A jarl might be an independent ruler or subordinate to a king. Jarl is the origin of the English word *earl*.

knarr - a Norse merchant vessel. Smaller, wider and more sturdy than the longship, knarrs were the workhorse of Norse trade, carrying cargo and settlers where ever the Norsemen traveled.

league – a distance of three miles.

leech – either one of the two vertical edges of a square sail.

leine – a long, loose-fitting smock worn by men and women under other clothing. Similar to the shift of a later period.

levies - conscripted soldiers of 9th century warfare.

Loki - Norse god of fire and free spirits. Loki was mischievous and his tricks caused great trouble for the gods, for which he was punished.

luff – the shivering of a sail when its edge is pointed into the wind and the wind strikes it on both sides

longphort - literally, a ship fortress. A small, fortified port to protect shipping and serve as a center of commerce and a launching off point for raiding.

Odin - foremost of the Norse gods. Odin was the god of wisdom and war, protector of both chieftains and poets.

oénach –a major fair, often held on a feast day in an area bordered by two territories.

perch - a unit of measure equal to 16½ feet. The same as a rod.

Ragnarok - the mythical final battle when most humans and gods would be killed by the forces of evil and the earth destroyed, only to rise again, purified.

rod – a unit of measure equal to 16½ feet. The same as a perch.

ringfort - common Irish homestead, consisting of houses protected by circular earthwork and palisade walls.

rí túaithe – Gaelic term for a minor king, who would owe allegiance to a high king.

rí ruirech – Gaelic term for a supreme or provincial king, to whom the **rí túaithe** owe allegiance.

sheer strake – the uppermost plank, or strake, of a boat or ship's hull. On a Viking ship the sheer strake would form the upper edge of the ship's hull.

shieldwall - a defensive wall formed by soldiers standing in line with shields overlapping.

shroud – a heavy rope stretching from the top of the mast to the ship's side that prevents the mast from falling sideways.

skald - a Viking-era poet, generally one attached to a royal court. The skalds wrote a very stylized type of verse particular to the medieval Scandinavians. Poetry was an important part of Viking culture and the ability to write it a highly-regarded skill.

sling - the center portion of the **yard**.

spar – generic term used for any of the masts or yards that are part of a ship's rig.

strake – one of the wooden planks that make up the hull of a ship. The construction technique, used by the Norsemen, in which one strake overlaps the one below it is called *lapstrake construction*.

swine array - a Viking battle formation consisting of a wedge-shaped arrangement of men used to attack a shield wall or other defensive position.

tánaise ríg – Gaelic term for heir apparent, the man assumed to be next in line for a kingship.

thing - a communal assembly.

Thor - Norse god of storms and wind, but also the protector of humans and the other gods. Thor's chosen weapon was a hammer. Hammer amulets were popular with Norsemen in the same way that crosses are popular with Christians.

thrall - Norse term for a slave. Origin of the English word "enthrall".

thwart - a rower's seat in a boat. From the old Norse term meaning "across".

Ulfberht – a particular make of sword crafted in the Germanic countries and inscribed with the name Ulfberht or some variant. Though it is not clear who Ulfberht was, the swords that bore his name were of the highest quality and much prized.

Valhalla - a great hall in **Asgard** where slain warriors would go to feast, drink and fight until the coming of **Ragnarok**.

Valkyrie - female spirits of Norse mythology who gathered the spirits of the dead from the battle field and escorted them to **Valhalla**. They were the Choosers of the Slain, and though later romantically portrayed as Odin's warrior handmaidens, they were originally viewed more demonically, as spirits who devoured the corpses of the dead.

vantnale – a wooden lever attached to the lower end of a shroud and used to make the shroud fast and to tension it.

varonn – spring time. Literally "spring work" in Old Norse.

Vik - An area of Norway south of modern-day Oslo. The name is possibly the origin of the term *Viking*.

wattle and daub - common medieval technique for building walls. Small sticks were woven through larger uprights to form the wattle, and the structure was plastered with mud or plaster, the daub.

weather – closest to the direction from which the wind is blowing, when used to indicate the position of something relative to the wind.

wergild - the fine imposed for taking a man's life. The amount of the wergild was dependent on the victim's social standing.

yard - a long, tapered timber from which a sail was suspended. When a Viking ship was not under sail, the yard was turned lengthwise and lowered to near the deck with the sail lashed to it.

Acknowledgements

My warmest thanks to Nicky Grene for his insights into the country around Glendalough and for the great kindness he has always shown me and my family on our visits to Ireland. Thanks also to my sister, Stephanie, for her on-going support in general and for the wealth of Glendalough books, pamphlets, postcards, tour guides and maps she sent me. Thanks to David Mullaly for his help with this book and earlier volumes in this series, and for leading me into temptation with regard to buying Viking antiquities. Thanks again to David Bellows for his help. On-going thanks are due to Steve Cromwell for the look he has developed for these books. The fact is, people do judge books by their covers and Steve has been instrumental in helping build the popularity of this series. Thanks again to Alistair Corbett for the great, moody background photo. Thanks to all my great readers who help spread the word about this series and to my family for all their support.

And to my beloved Lisa....

Made in the USA
Middletown, DE
12 April 2016